Walled

Mercy

What people are saying about . . . Walled Mercy!

"Author Faye Spieker skillfully presents a tale of suspense birthed from the fires of deep loss and madness. The intriguing plot introduces characters that will capture your heart. This is suspense that will stir your soul and renew your faith. Highly recommended."

~ Nancy Mehl
Defenders of Justice Series
Nancymehl.com

"What a riveting tale. Faye Spieker's portrayal of a delusional psychopath gave me the creeps. I was on the edge of my seat. Transfixed to the exciting end."

~ Mary Davis award winning author

"I liked how the non-believers' opinions were given the same amount of respect as the believers. And the depiction of the hypocritical church goers juxtaposed to Ray's honest faith in action."

~ Thom Phelps, author and artist.

"Faye Spieker, has a great imagination and a way with words, but I was astounded at the tale she told in Walled Mercy! This is one of those 'read at the stoplight' books for me and I'm excited for everyone to read it! Hold on to your seats!!"

~ Patty Ralston, avid suspense reader.

Walled
Mercy

A story by

Faye Spieker

Published in USA
ISBN-13:978-1503337695

Dedication

This book is dedicated to my wonderful family, husband Jon Spieker, sons Adam, and Todd. My extraordinary daughter-in-law Erin and grandson Foster. Thank you for the ideas, encouragement, and prayers.

Thank You!

To Donita K. Paul and her wonderful writer's group that have helped me in immeasurable ways to bring this book to life.

Jill Case Brown

Mary Davis

Jim Hart

Heidi Likins

Carol Reinsma

Special thanks to John Matsko, a former police officer, who helped with law enforcement details.

"I can't stand your religious meetings.
I'm fed up with your conferences and conventions.
I want nothing to do with your religion projects,
    your pretentious slogans and goals.
I'm sick of your fund-raising schemes,
    your public relations and image making.
I've had all I can take of your noisy ego-music.
When was the last time you sang to me?
    Do you know what I want?
    I want justice—oceans of it.
    I want fairness—rivers of it.
That's what I want. That's all I want."

Amos 5:21-24 The Message

Chapter 1

"Run!" Elam cried. "Where? Where do I run?"

Charging through the park, the old man splashed into a shallow puddle. Mud splattered onto his legs. He stopped by a bronze statue of a soldier on a horse to give his pants a frantic rubbing.

"The poison has come. The acid burns," he said to no one.

Words whispered in the air. "Hurry! Climb on my back."

Frozen in a half-standing position, the old man now stared at the ground.

Listening.

Again, the voice. "Elam. Come now, sit here. Safe from the attacking ground. For only God is good."

In a head-swimming twirl, he felt himself lift and he sat on the horse's back, behind the army officer that held his sword angled into the sky.

"How did I get up here? Magic?" His mind made the question, but he spoke the words aloud.

The horse's backside dappled in brown spots. Could these be handprints of mud? This idea traveled through his mind but kept going. The reasonable thought vanished, and he said, "No, not magic. God. He has saved me from the evil that prevails in this world."

The quivering of the horse's muscles thrummed against his legs as the animal sidestepped and pranced in place. The bronze soldier strained to keep his long saber in the air.

The horse spoke again. "We must hide. Evil swallows up the good. We must protect our souls from the filth."

Elam spoke to the horse. "If only God is good then what does evil eat?"

The horse whinnied, "The world will die soon. We must not die with the world."

"Jesus saves," said the old man.

"Jesus saves you from this world. We must hide."

Elam struggled to keep from slipping off the back of the stallion. The soldier shouted a command. "Shoot those flying demons that lay white drops of poison on my steed." For a spit of time, in only a splash of real thought, Elam saw the pigeons as they really were.

"Jesus saves the world!" Elam shouted. "If we hide, how will they know?"

The words crashed through his befuddled mind like pinballs smacking.

"If we *hide*, how will they know?" He slipped down off the metal horse and began to weep.

***

Ava pulled in a lungful of air, bent her head back, and shrieked into the treetops, "Mo-mm-eeeee!"

With an impatient swipe, she pushed a tear-soaked strand of hair out of her face. She sat cross-legged in the middle of a patch of bright green ferns. Balling her shaking hand into a fist, she rubbed wet eyes. Ava trembling, dragged in huge gasps to get enough air into her body.

Will Mommy look for me?

She couldn't be sure. Always afraid, she never knew who or when to trust.

Her second-grade teacher, Mrs. McAlister, said she'd like to scoop Ava up and take her home.

Ava wished that, too.

Great-grandma, her Grammie, had said she looked like a delicate porcelain doll. Ava didn't know what kind of doll that was, but it sounded very beautiful and fragile. She knew fragile meant easy to break, weak, and probably scared, too.

Maybe I'm invisible.

She let loose with another heart-stopping cry. She had walked into the forest, hoping for some peace from the shouting.

Only wanting to get away for a while, and now she couldn't find her way back.

Again, she sent out a terrified wail and listened to her own panicked cry as it cut through the pines. She froze at the sound of heavy footfalls coming from beyond the aspen trees.

***

Okay, where is my wife? She is going to be late, again!

James tossed a sleeping bag into the back of the SUV's and slammed the lid down in irritation. He had taken the day off specifically to help watch the kids while his wife got ready for her trip. Bad enough having to keep two toddler boys corralled for the entire weekend, now she'd disappeared.

He looked up at Pikes Peak. The view of the mountain usually helped calm his frustration.

That's the best thing about living in Colorado Springs.

He hated letting Nikki drive his Explorer, but of their two vehicles, this one was the safest for a road trip.

James glanced down at the crumpled back bumper as he remembered the most recent time Nikki drove it. He grit his teeth. Nikki, late for picking up the kids at Grandma's, had backed out of the garage in a panic. How could she have forgotten that her own car sat in the driveway?

Both cars suffered a serious crunching. Though he hadn't seen it happen, the thought of it made him cringe.

He turned back at the house. His younger boy Jonah, almost two, peered at him through the screen door. Clutching a half-eaten cookie in one hand, Jonah traced a finger along the textured wires and flashed a drooling grin as he leaned his forehead into the mesh.

"Daddy!" he called as he lifted the cookie into the air and waggled it.

James gave a soft sigh and waved back. "I see you, Jonah."

The next moment the toddler's older brother, just turned three, walked past him and lifted the cookie out of the boy's hand. The wailing that ensued exploded out the screen door. James's shoulders collapsed, his head bobbing forward in complete surrender to the exhausting morning.

5

Nikki powerwalked up to the house, wearing gym shorts with a grey Broncos sweatshirt. Her blonde hair was pulled back in a ponytail that bounced in rhythm as her arms pumped up and down. He knew she'd been determined to lose the last bit of pregnancy fat, but for the life of him he couldn't see any. She pounded out the last few steps up the drive.

He began his mantra before she reached him. "Nicole Mae! What are you doing? Where have you been? You're going to be late. Please tell me you're completely packed." The rush of questions that spilled out made her pull back and stop short.

She bent over to catch her breath. He could see the thin mountain air still gave her problems on the up hills. Then she smiled at him with the calm expression of one used to soothing outbursts of worried panic. To James, it seemed condescending.

"Will you calm down? I'm all ready to go. I wanted to get a little bit of a walk in before I left."

"You're going to a mountain retreat, for Pete's sake. You can walk when you get there." He raked his fingers through his short cropped hair. "I put your sleeping bag in the car. Where's your suitcase?"

"Upstairs. What's Jonah howling about?"

"Conner snitched a cookie from him. I'll take care of it. You shower and get ready." He took three steps toward the house.

"I have plenty of time." She wiped her face with the edge of her shirt.

James turned around and walked backwards. "If you don't leave soon you're going to hit Denver traffic."

"I'm not going through Denver."

He stopped dead. "What?"

"The retreat isn't at the church campground."

"Do you know how to get there? Can you follow someone?" Again, a panic crept into his voice.

"Yes, don't worry. I'll figure it out ... somehow."

"You have the address, just put it in your phone."

"Um..."

"You do have your phone?"

"Well, I think. It's in your car. Somewhere. The last time I had it was yesterday. I went to get groceries for you to use while I'm gone."

"Call it."

"I did. The battery is dead."

James stared unblinking at her *I'm sorry* expression.

He opened his mouth, but Nikki spoke first. "Don't worry. I'm sure it's in there under the seat or beneath the stuff in the back."

At the mention of the junk that Nikki insisted on keeping stashed in the back, James's head began to throb. "We don't have time to look for the phone now. Get the charger cable. Pack that, and when you can find your mobile, then charge it." He rubbed his forehead then gritted his teeth as he spoke. "Don't forget to call me when you do."

"I will, if there's coverage at the camp. I've never been there before."

He groaned. "I'll get your mom's old GPS. It'll have to do." He walked off in irritated determination as he grumbled out his last words, "That's one more thing *I* have to do."

***

"Shut up, you stupid kid." A tall man with a stubbled beard stepped out of the bushes and glared at Ava. His eyes were bloodshot and puffy. A whiff of bad smell drifted across the ferns.

Ava wrinkled up her nose.

He grabbed her arm near the shoulder. "Where do you get off running away like that?" He yanked her up to her feet, almost toppling himself when the action threw him off balance. "Your mama made me search the entire camp area for you. She thought for sure you'd got swept up in a creek."

Mommy *did* care. But Ava wished she had come herself instead of sending Ben. He took her hand, and the two walked in silence, trudging uphill over ground covered with tall grass, weeds, rocks, and fallen logs.

"Found her!" Ben announced as he neared the campsite. Smoky flames crackled in the hollowed-out fire pit beside the pop-up tent trailer. Ben must have started the blaze even though,

7

according to him, this was not *his* job. His blowup this morning began the screaming that had driven her into the woods. Ava, always stunned at how fast anger jumped to scary loud, ran off hoping they wouldn't notice her.

"Ava Christine Martin, where have you been? I thought you'd been taken." Her mother often spoke this worry with fearful concern. Ava knew it by heart. "Someone could have spirited you away to ... who knows where?"

But the next sentence held the harshness she'd also become used to. "Why do you do this to me? You do it on purpose, don't you?" The angry woman pushed her hand up to her own nose and sniffed, an unconscious habit that in recent years had become a part of her personality. "Get in the tent trailer," she snapped.

Ava said nothing.

"Leave her alone. Is there no mercy for a child that was lost?" Grammie half stood out of her lawn chair under the awning before her leg muscles gave way and she plopped back down.

Ava didn't understand the word "mercy." But the way Grammie said the word she knew this was something to wish for. A desperate need for some of that "mercy" welled up in her heart.

She opened the entrance to the well-used camper, climbed the two steps, and pulled herself up and inside. She tried to turn quickly to close the door before her mother yelled again. Too late.

"Shut the door! You're letting the bugs in."

Ava yanked on the handle, heard the click, and caught a glimpse of herself reflected in its window. She'd tried to pull her hair back with a barrette this morning, but the clasp now hung off center. Strands of sweaty hair clung to her forehead, her eyes red and swollen.

With robotic motions, she walked to the back of the trailer, threw one leg up onto the raised bed, and rolled her tired body onto the cushion, not bothering to take off her shoes. She made a move to put her thumb into her mouth, but instead pressed her fist against her lips.

Her muscles jerked at a sound that came from the front of the trailer. A protective stiffness drew her frame into a closer ball.

Through slit eyes, Ava watched Grammie grab at the sides of the opening. The woman rocked back and forth to provide momentum to pull herself up and inside. Ava knew about the pain her great-grandma had in all her bending places. After closing the door, she shuffled to the back of the trailer, leaned on the bed, and stroked Ava's back.

"Ava," she whispered, "your mommy wasn't always like this. It's just that things have gotten so out of control for her."

Ava nodded her head.

Grammie stared hard into Ava's face. "Talking is hard for you, even to me now, isn't it, dear? I'm starting to forget what your voice sounds like, little one."

Silence.

"It's okay, I know you'll talk when you think it's important enough, to *who* you think is important."

Shadows of aspen leaves danced on the canvas sides. With the soft twitter of birds chirping and the gentle backrub, Ava's body relaxed into sleep.

***

As Jonah sucked in more air for another distressed howl, James heard his wife let out a heavy sigh from behind him. He opened the screen door and hoisted Jonah up over his shoulder like a sack of potatoes. He turned to give the mother of his children a self-righteous glare, lips pressed tight and brows furrowed. She shot back an apologetic grin and headed into the house behind them.

She's laughing. Why doesn't she realize my time is important?

As he walked through the living room with his whimpering bundle, he heard her feet make petite thumps up the stairs. He lugged Jonah into the kitchen and set him on a chair stool at the center island.

The room held what he called a chaotic mess, what Nikki called evidence of creative activity. Crayons scattered everywhere. He just missed smashing a blue one into the tile with his shoe. A ball of circled scribbles decorated a sheet of butcher paper that lay on the island. The words "Dinosaur goes into hole, in, and in, and come out far away" appeared in neat print beside the artist's creation.

9

He shoved aside two boxes of cereal and an empty yellow bowl with several bloated Cheerios dotting the bottom. Under a towel, he spotted the cookie plate and handed Jonah a chocolate chip replacement.

The silence was immediate.

"Conner," he called and listened a moment. "Conner!" This shout reflected the frustrations of the entire morning. He heard a small shift of movement below.

He squatted down and opened the cabinet door in the island.

"Hi, Daddy." Conner sat hunched over inside. A riot of soft blonde curls topped his head, and a crumb-sprinkled grin tried to give the appearance of total innocence. "My cabinet."

"Yes, that's yours to play in. Please tell me what you did to Jonah."

Worried blue eyes stared back at James. Here was where Nikki would scoop him up and cuddle him. This was where James should put him in time-out. Instead the boy himself took the lead and crawled out of his sanctuary. He wrapped his arms round Daddy's neck and said, "I sah-wee, Daddy, I sah-wee."

"You need to tell Jonah that."

Conner went to the tall chair that held Jonah. "I sah-wee, Jo-naaah."

Jonah, mesmerized by the cookie in his hand, had obviously forgotten what the offense had been. He gave Conner two play whacks on the head, and they both giggled. A moment later, Conner helped Jonah down from his perch, and they were soon wrestling on the floor like a pair of wild mongooses.

James decided to do a quick pull of email from work before he fussed with the GPS. He could still keep an eye on the boys, and Nikki would be a while getting ready. He made a place for his laptop on the counter and stood as he typed.

After only about fifteen minutes James heard an urgent rush of feet barreling down the stairs. His wife bolted into the room.

"Oh, ma gosh, I'm gonna be late," she blurted out as she grabbed a water bottle from the fridge, twisted the cap off, and took a swig. Her hair hung in damp ringlets, still wet from her shower.

James shook his head in confused frustration at her statement. His next words snapped out his mouth. "Late? What do you mean late?"

***

Ava stirred at the sound of quiet steps on the squeaky floor, and a deep male voice jarred her awake. "Hey, kid, you're sleeping too long. You won't sleep tonight."

She opened her eyes slowly, prepared for anything. Ben stared down at her. She nodded her head and gave him a wary look.

"Come on now, get up. Your Ma wants us to go into the town and get some supplies." He made a quick shift in his stance as if the trailer had tipped.

Why would Ben ask me to go with him, and where's Grandma?

The thought passed through her troubled mind, but she refused to ask.

He explained without her voicing the question as a crooked smile spread across his face.

"Your Ma and Grammie are taking a walk. I probably shouldn't leave you alone, considering what happened this morning." His face beamed friendship. "Besides, I could use your help deciding what we need." He had a magic way about him when he wanted to, like Prince Charming. Ava knew that's why her mom liked him.

But the yucky smell of his breath made her afraid. Grammie had told her never to ride with Ben after he'd been drinking, but this was in the morning. The stink must be from last night.

She nodded, sat up, and straightened her yellow t-shirt over denim shorts. She pulled the barrette from her hair, struggled to replace it, but gave up, allowing the loose strands to fall free.

A few minutes later, Ava buckled herself into the front seat of the jeep. Ava usually sat behind the driver's seat in the back, with Grammie.

Ava peered out the window to search the campground one more time. She hoped to see a glimpse of Mommy, for reassurance. She saw movement through the aspen trees behind the outhouse.

No, not Mom.

11

A man with a long gray ponytail adjusted an overstuffed backpack onto his shoulders. He helped a boy dump trash into the dumpster and headed to a beat-up van. The boy turned in their direction. With sleepy eyes, he looked right past her.

Ben climbed in and flashed her a reassuring smile. She made the corners of her mouth turn up a little bit. He started the motor and steered out of the camping area. He drove for a while without speaking.

Ben broke the silence. "So, Sunshine, this will give us a chance to get to know each other. I know you don't talk much. That's okay. I can talk for the both of us." He gave a nervous chuckle. Her body relaxed slightly, but she didn't take her eyes off of him.

"Of course, I haven't known your mother for that long, but I think our relationship may be going somewhere. Sure we fight now and again, but everyone does, right?" He didn't even stop for her to answer. "I mean, I know she has a drug problem, but I can handle that. I'm going to save her from it. Besides, she can be so beautiful when she fixes herself up. She has one terrific figure. There are some parts of her body that ... well, you know."

She didn't know.

"I 'spose you're too young to understand. No matter. I think you and me will become great friends."

Ava turned her head to gaze out the window. Ben drove past the school she knew to be near the town. She wished they'd hurry and get there. The jeep slowed, and she looked ahead expecting to see a stop sign. But he had pulled over to the side of the road.

He put the car into park, turned off the engine, and stared at her. "Ava, I just want you to know I'm going to try to do right by your mother." His cheery grin froze, and his eyes became glazed. "You know, you're beautiful a lot like your mother." His face turned serious. "That soft, blonde hair. Big brown eyes and long lashes." He unbuckled his seatbelt and slid his hand over to unclick hers as well. Ava could see there was no store nearby.

Why had he stopped?

Chapter 2

James snapped out his words. "Late? What do you mean late?"

Nikki waved a folded paper in the air. "I didn't read last week's church bulletin. They changed the time for the auction fundraiser that begins the retreat. I didn't stay up making twenty-three Christmas ornaments for nothing."

"That's what you were doing last night?" His words came out astonished with a touch of annoyance.

She took another swig of water and tried to nod her head at the same time. Water squirted from the side of her mouth, and she pulled back to avoid the drops.

"Why didn't you know the time had changed?"

"I have two more ornaments to make after I get there. A mom will be able to give her kids one ornament for each day leading up to Christmas. I was just too tired to glue on even one more sequined bangle."

"Okay, right, right, focus here, Nik. Why didn't anyone tell you the time had changed?"

"They don't know I'm coming."

"No one knows you're coming?"

"I'm going to register when I get there. I told the ladies from the church I couldn't come, because I didn't know you'd want to take the day off so I could get ready, and then you did." She shot him a grateful smile. "Thanks, by the way. And I thought maybe if I worked hard to get the ornaments done, I could go, so ..."

"And you didn't tell anyone from church you were going?"

"That lady ... what's her name? Gladys, I think, said if I changed my mind to just come on up and register at the camp. I don't know any of those ladies very well yet, but maybe this weekend will change that."

James whacked his forehead with the palm of his hand. "Stop!" He pointed upstairs. "Finish getting ready. I'll get the GPS set for you. Give me the address." Nikki flung the bulletin at him. He snatched it from the air and bent down to scoop Jonah up into his arms. "You take Conner. Don't forget your charging cable."

James knew he and Nikki argued a lot because they worked from different sides of their brains. But when they worked as a team, things got done.

In a matter of moments, James and Nikki stood outside the car door comforting two distraught little boys. Both boys cried as if they'd never see their mother again.

Nikki talked over the squall. "I put a casserole in the freezer. Jonah's Bear-blanky is under the sofa downstairs, for bedtime. Don't forget their vitamins in the morning and—"

"I can handle it. You need to get going. Do you have your charger?"

Nikki pried her youngest child's arms from around her neck as James pulled the boy into his. Then she slapped her pants pockets and shoved her hands inside them. Her brown eyes widened as her eyebrows went up.

He frowned and sighed. "Oh, Nikki."

She took off towards the house. After she stepped through the screen door, James yelled after her. "Don't forget the cable *and* the plug! Nikki!" He let out a sharp swear word that echoed down the street.

As he reached to take Conner's hand, he noticed Mrs. Farber in bright pink shorts, a blouse with wild red flowers splattered across it, and fluffy blue slippers. She stood in her front yard, holding her tiny white, yippy mop of a dog. Her short gray curls framed a face that stared at him in shocked curiosity.

He kept his head down and muttered, "Good morning, Mrs. Farber," as he towed his little ones into the house. He knew she probably wouldn't hear him, but he said it out of guilt. Mrs. Farber was the person who had invited them to church when they first moved in.

Several minutes later the whole family, again, stood out in the driveway, Mrs. Farber nowhere to be seen.

14

Nikki shoved the charging cable in her suitcase and slammed the trunk door. "I'm sorry. Usually all I need to do is call my phone and hear where it's at," Nikki said.

"If your phone were on and charged, you could." His voice came out rougher than he intended.

"Don't worry, I'm sure it's in the car somewhere. I know I had the thing coming home from the store last night. But with all the groceries and getting two kids out of car seats, the phone vanished." Nikki pulled on the driver's handle and opened the door.

"Well, if you don't find it, borrow a cell from someone when you get there and call me," he said as he bounced Jonah in his arms. Conner clung to his mom's side.

"Again, *if* they have reception up there, I will. Look, if I have any trouble, I'll find a phone, or someone will call you. No news will be good news." She bent down to Conner. "Listen, baby, Mommy will come back. I promise. Daddy is here to take care of you and brother, too." She gave him a squishy hug and stood to give Jonah a kiss. Then she hugged her husband with the baby in between. She kissed James, and said, "Good luck, I love you."

"I'll need it," he said, and Jonah began to whimper.

Chapter 3

As she drove away, Nikki could see the three standing on the sidewalk, framed in her rearview mirror. Her heart did a twist. It always did when she left the house without her babies. Tears streamed down their little faces. James already looked haggard and spent.

It's just for a few days. One weekend, really. Lord, keep them safe.

She hated going to a spiritual renewal straight from being crushed in an emotional cement mixer. Harsh words and the echoing cries of children tumbled fear and worry into her battered heart. Using money to go off, alone, when the family needed the funds made the guilt rise.

But there are times when a mother has to get away. Not just from the children, or the daily grind, but to strengthen her own spiritual heart.

What had happened to that girl with the desperate passion to fight for the hopeless, to change the world for God and country?

The wheels on the bus go round and round, round and round, round and round ... Even the tunes that play in my mind rotate over and over like Mom's ancient round vinyl disks. The proverbial broken record.

She sighed, and realized she also needed a break from James. They quarreled and snapped at each other more often than not.

I need to find out if I measure up to what God wants from me. Have I made a mess of things? I give everything I can, but it's never enough.

"Turn right in point eight miles." The woman's pleasant but authoritative voice made Nikki jump.

"Okay, Sadie, I'll watch for it." Her mom had named the GPS Sadie the Direction Lady. Mom liked Sadie, but she got on Nikki's nerves. Her voice popped out and demanded attention. That thought reminded her of the cell phone issue.

As the car coasted down the hill to a stoplight, Nikki racked her brain as to where that confounded contraption could possibly be. James had a passion for electronic devices. Despite their economic situation, he inundated his wife with gadgets that she was forever losing, forgetting what button to push, or not charging the batteries of.

What Nikki saw as a waste of money, James thought necessary. This latest piece of futuristic wonder had a slim design that fit perfectly in her pocket but allowed it to slip into recliner chairs, under movie theater seats, and onto restroom floors. The mother of all black holes happened to be … the car.

I am always losing things! I've got to try harder.

She really fought to keep all the ribbons of her life tied up in perfect, color-coordinated bows. Each time they dropped into tangled messes, she'd pick up a heavy stone of guilt. Arms would ache and rocks cut flesh, but she couldn't release them. Even small mistakes had begun to dig scratches that bled as she tried to repair things she couldn't control.

"Stay right and turn right in two … hundred … feet."

She obeyed the bodiless voice and let thoughts of lost electronics and impossible standards fade away.

For now.

She reached for the CD player and made a fast switch of songs from a purple dinosaur to an album by The Fray. Leaning back, she continued toward Hwy24.

Nikki glanced up the mountainside and saw a Ferris wheel jutting up above the pine trees. This brought a new wave of guilt at leaving her boys behind. The North Pole Amusement Park nestled on the mountainside. James wanted to take the family there, but they hadn't had the time, or the money, to go.

And here I am, heading off to a retreat. Stuff it down, girl.

Nikki continued to drive along the twisting highway as it wriggled its way up. She sang at the top of her lungs with the CD to drown out the guilt. She rolled into town, everyone slowed as tourists clogged the one main road that led through Woodland Park.

Coming out the other side, the scenery transformed from businesses and cabins to meadows and mountain views. The green tint of new sprouts laced the branches in the stands of aspens.

17

Sadie had stopped her persistent nagging. A long time spread out before the next turn.

With a gradual release, tight cords of stress unbound and fell loose from around her body. She imagined them turning into slithering snakes behind the car and dissolving into smoky wisps.

Until the sign, CONSTRUCTION AHEAD, forced Nikki to switch to the brake. As the cars in front of her flashed turn signals and slowed, she could see a woman wearing an orange vest, standing in the road. She shook a detour sign with authority as Nikki's car approached.

After Nikki made a reluctant turn to the right onto a gravel road, Sadie spoke up. "Recalculating."

"Don't bother, Sadie. It'll only confuse you."

"Recalculating." Again, instructions came as the detour signs told Nikki to take another unauthorized turn.

To Nikki the voice seemed more insistent. "Don't let it upset you, Sadie. It's not your fault."

Great, now I'm trying to calm the fears of a machine. We should never have given her a name.

When Nikki ignored the persistent voice, Sadie eventually stopped announcing her recalculating and preferred route. She said, "Please, return to the highlighted area." Then GPS went into sleep mode.

She slowed over the rough pot holes and let other cars take the lead. Soon traffic had vanished, but Nikki's neck muscles tightened. The car bumped and clunked over the unpaved gravel on a long stretch now void of other cars and detour signs.

Wait a minute, where are the signs?

She hadn't passed one in a while. Had she? How long had it been?

After several panicked moments, she attempted to pull over, but the road had narrowed and all she could do was stop. With no other traffic in sight, only thick trees and brush surrounding the road, fear sliced through her stomach. Think, think.

God, get me out of here. Don't let me be lost!

In an odd flash of nostalgia, she remembered how, in college, she would have ongoing conversations with God. He spoke to her back then. Now her world had become too urgent to waste time in such deep thought.

Maybe she should give Sadie another try. Nikki reached over to reset the device. It popped off the window into her hand. She groaned as she fumbled to reattach it. She heard the solid snap, and entered the correct address.

She hoped.

"Drive three hundred feet and turn left, then turn left."

Knowing this meant Sadie wanted her to turn around, Nikki made a three-point turn and faced the opposite direction.

In Nikki's mind, Sadie's voice reflected a smug, self-satisfied voice. "Continue driving for four point six miles and turn left."

Keeping an anxious eye out for the missed detour sign, Nikki tried breathing in long, deep pulls to redirect her anxiety. A reviving of hope kindled in her heart when she passed a little red cabin nestled in the trees along a mountain slope. At least there were still signs of human population.

A distinct growl rumbled. A reminder that breakfast had been a long time ago. No stopping at a restaurant anywhere near here. An apple would be nice. If the kids had been along, she would have packed a snack. She had a vague hope that a baggie of Cheerios might still be hiding under the seat.

She guided the car in following another of Sadie's commands. This road looked more like two tire tracks in the forest than a public throughway. Another turn and a straight shot led to a grassy hump. With a shocking realization, Nikki let the car crawl near the edge where the ground dropped off into the small creek below.

"This can't be right!" she shouted.

"Drive two hundred feet and turn left."

"I can't! I can't you stupid piece of..." Words failed, but as she realized no children were in the car they came all too readily.

Chapter 4

Ben leaned toward Ava and stroked her cheek. She pulled away and crouched closer to the door.

"What's the matter, kid?" His words held a faint slur, and his tone turned sharp. "Think you're too good for me? I'm gonna be your dad. You'd better shape up."

He waved his arms around like he was talking to a crowd of people. "Everybody knows I would be a great dad. E-ver-ee-bod-dee! Not like my old man, that stupid drunk." Angry, loud, and filled with hate, more words lashed into the air. Ava trembled as fear rose inside her.

With an abrupt change of mood, he turned to Ava and said, "But all that's in the past, isn't it? Come here, baby."

He jabbed his arm out toward her. This time he accidently smacked the top of her head. She ducked lower, and her hand pressed on the handle. The latch clicked, and the door swung open. She fell back but managed to slip her legs around, down, and out. Letting out a growl-like scream, he flung his body across the seat and reached for her just as she pushed on the outside metal with all her strength. The door must have slammed into his hand. He blasted out a storm of words that frightened her even more.

Ava ran. Grass and weeds slapped at her legs. Panic raced in her heart. She sped along the side of the road and then cut into the woods. Ava slid down a hill. At the bottom, as the dirt flew up around her, she glanced back and saw him.

Clutching his hand close to his stomach, he stood to at the edge of the road and bellowed. "Come back here! Right now, you..."

Fear drowned out the rest of his words as she bolted between two trees and dove under a bush. Ava tried to hold her breath, but her trembling pushed out a snort every few seconds. She slapped her hands over her mouth and peered through the branches.

Ben charged down the hill and stopped. He glanced around, and then darted into a stand of trees.

He'd gone off to the right. Ava struck out on a path to the left. She burst through the brush into a small meadow. Stopping to catch her breath, she bent forward and heaved air into her lungs. Trying to think what to do, she made a frantic search around in desperation. Across the meadow, she saw Ben.

Worse yet, he saw her.

This time, his long legs covered the ground faster than her mind could react, but she took off running and stayed just ahead of him. Ava could hear his breath, hard and fast. His feet seemed to smack the earth just behind hers. Coming to a hill of large rocks, a thought flashed into her mind so fast that she moved before a second one formed.

She jumped onto the first rock, and scrambled up the hill of boulders, and slid to the other side. Her skinny legs moved her like a mountain goat. She paused and peered back through a gap in the rocks. She saw Ben skid to a stop just short of the pile.

Curses again filled the air, and her name headed the list. He ran to the right, to get around the boulders, making no effort to follow over the midget mountain.

The girl sucked in a sudden breath. From her height, she could see he only had to detour around to the other side, and he would reach the clearing to cut her off. But if she went back, he would see her. She had to reach the clearing first.

"He's coming. He's coming." Her words, a raspy whisper, spurred her on. She scooted down the rocks, scraping her legs on the rough edges.

"He's coming. He's coming." Jumping from the rocks, she reached the clearing first. She had to do something. She couldn't keep running. He was going to catch her.

Taking a step back, her foot kicked a thick branch. A movie of a cartoon character whacking a coyote over the head with a club played in her mind.

21

But she was too short. A large boulder sat beside the path from where her bad guy would come. The pile of rocks next to that would block him from seeing her when he came barreling around the corner.

Ava clambered up the rugged surface of the rock and stood with club in hand. But instead of holding the stick above her head like in the cartoon, she held it over her shoulder like a bat. Feet spread apart and body turned the way she learned playing T-ball. She shut her eyes.

He's coming. He's coming.

His furious steps hammered down the path. She prayed for help to no god in particular, opened her eyes, and swung with all her might.

A loud crack stung the air. Ben had been running at full speed, and the club smacked right across his face. The branch splintered and shot out of her hand. He collapsed to the ground and cracked his head a second time on a rock. Blood oozed from his hair into his eyes.

Ava barely managed to keep from toppling off the boulder. She slid to the ground and stared at Ben.

He didn't move.

She thought of running again, but Ben lay so still. The wind picked up in the tall pines and made a moaning sound.

Not knowing what to do, she crept up to his side. The blood on his face dripped into his shut eyes. Ava reached out and gave his shoulder a tentative poke with her fingers.

He stayed still.

Like a broken doll.

A rush of thought washed into her mind. All the terrifying movies her mother had allowed her to watch flashed through her. The creature, not really dead, turns at the last minute to devour the hero. The villain grabs the child by the wrist and stabs her to death.

The images appeared so real.

Ben's hand shot up to grab her throat with a strangling grip. His face grim, covered in blood.

She jerked back and screamed. "No! No!"

But as she fell backwards in fear, reason pulled her to reality. There was no hand, no angry face. Ben lay silent and bleeding.

Now she knew. Staring at the blood on his face. She whispered her fear aloud. "He's dead." She pulled in a panicked breath. "And I killed him."

She gave his body one more push with her foot. No response. Tears, held back in the heat of the chase, now streamed down her cheeks. Her nose trickled. Deep sobs filled her. She sat beside Ben and collapsed into total misery, pain, and most of all, terror.

The pines seemed to sing out her sin as the wind swept through them. She cried there for a very long time.

Not knowing what else to do, Ava stood up. Dizzy with fear and sorrow, she walked into the trees, hoping help would somehow swoop down upon her.

She stumbled back to the road, not far from where her crime had taken place. She stepped out onto the shoulder and began to walk, tears still washing down her cheeks.

Caught up in her grief, she barely noticed the few cars that passed. Their breezy wake and crunch of gravel made her body shiver.

Her focus zeroed in on a black Labrador across the road, watching her with empathetic eyes. In her mind, she called out to him for help, but even as the word formed in her thoughts it melted in hopelessness.

A crunching noise made her insides jump.

"Hey!" Strong fingers jerked at her arm and spun her around. "Where do you think you're going, little missy?"

Ava reacted with an explosive, ear-stabbing scream and tried to pull her arm free.

"Whoa, whoa there, hang on. It's alright, I ain't gonna hurt ya."

Ava focused in on the face. Instead of seeing the blood-smeared image of Ben, she saw an old bearded man with crystal blue eyes. The color of sky sparkled with humor under bushy eyebrows, and beneath blond and gray strands of facial hair lay a gentle grin.

He hiked up his overalls and squatted down in front of her. Eye to eye, he studied her face with concern. "Little one, you're looking for your mama, aren't you?"

Ava sniffed and nodded her head in an emphatic yes.

"We can find her, morning glory, don't you worry now." He stood, then reached down and wrapped his large rough hand around her trembling fingers. The two walked together back in the direction Ava had come from. A dark vehicle was parked on the side of the road.

The old man stopped before getting to the van and peered into the forest. Something had caught his eye. He squinted and frowned at a shadowed area near a clump of trees. Then he grinned with a bright friendly smile, held up his hand, and waved.

"Good afternoon, friend," he called and continued to walk toward the van. He pulled the handle on the back-passenger side and slid it open. "Okay, little one, here we go. We'll find your mama, and the whole family will be together again."

Cold iced her hands and feet. She accepted the kindness and with a faint curiosity she leaned into the van before stepping inside. A glance into the back made pulled back in alarm. She tried to yank her hand away from the man, but he held tight.

His tone changed. "What's the matter, Priscilla? I said GET IN!" He picked her up, tossed her into the seat, and slammed the door. Rushing to the driver's side, humming as he went, he climbed up, started the engine and charged off down the road.

Her mother's often said words rushed back to her.

Taken! You'll be taken. Spirited away to ... who knows where?

The fear slammed through her as numbness spilled down to her toes.

Prickles danced over her skin, and lightness filled her head. No tears left. All sobs drained from her broken heart. Her chest hurt from breathing so hard. As the world around her melted into mist, she realized she didn't feel afraid anymore.

She didn't feel worried.

She didn't feel upset.

She didn't feel.

Ava raised herself up enough to look out the cracked side window and placed her tiny hand against the pane. Would anyone know where she was? Even God?

No.

Because I'm invisible.

Chapter 5

Nikki couldn't believe after all the fuss about the GPS, she ended up having to ask for directions. After her slight emotional breakdown, she turned the car around and retraced her route. She got as far as the cabin she had spotted earlier and found the owner along the road fixing his fence. After he explained to her twice how to get to Florissant, she had him draw a map on a scrap of paper.

Her car now sat along the side of a dirt road outside of Woodland Park. She dug inside her purse, looking for the bulletin with the camp's name and address on it. She even pulled out the luggage and checked the pockets of her jacket. She blew the hair off her forehead and with a grunt of defeat went back in the driver's seat.

Of course, naturally, she would forget that important piece of information back at home.

She needed to find a public phone. Did they still have those?

As she started the engine, a movement caught her eye in the trees across the road. Deer had a proprietary air about them in this area. This was their home, and she was the visitor. She kept watch for any sign of deer leaping across the road.

Hand paused on the gear shift, she waited. Not deer but a small child pushed out of the brush. The girl's body seemed to pull her forward in an odd, mechanical way. Nikki straightened and put the car into drive.

But something about the little girl kept her from taking her foot off the brake. Her ash blonde hair swirled about her delicate face. Though the child held her head high, her shoulders heaved and quivered. Nikki could see the girl's wet face pull into a look of unspeakable sorrow. Nikki rolled down her window and could hear sobs blending with the forest birds.

I should help.

Indecision kept her from leaping out of the car.

26

Wait! What if her parents are nearby? No use being accused of accosting a child.

Nikki watched. The waif, oblivious of her surroundings, pushed herself along the dirt shoulder. An occasional car sped past, but no one slowed. A flash of hope crossed the young face as she scanned across the road and up the hill. Nikki turned to see a black dog standing at the top.

Could the girl have lost her dog? Was this why she trembled with such sorrow?

After a slight pause, the girl continued. Nikki turned in her seat and did a visual search of the surroundings. Maybe someone was looking for the child. Nope, no one around.

She allowed her car to coast forward as the little one trudged on. With reason shouting in her brain, which Nikki ignored, she stopped her car and opened the door. She wondered how to approach the youngster so as not to frighten her more.

As she swung her feet out, she heard the crunch of footsteps coming from the girl's side of the street. A man with a stringy beard, wearing denim overalls, strode decisively behind the girl.

Okay, here comes someone.

Nikki closed her door, rolled up her window. She clicked on her seat belt but waited to be sure of the outcome. The man grabbed the girl's arm and pulled her around. A scream of terror bolted out of the child as she pulled away.

Nikki froze. But the next second she had her seatbelt off and reached for the handle. She turned again and saw the man squatting down in front of the girl. Calmer now, the two stared at each other.

Maybe he'd just surprised her.

The man smiled and led her back down the way he had come. Nikki continued to watch. The pair could be out for a Sunday stroll. After stopping at a muddy van pulled off on a side road, the man slid open its side door.

Relief swept over her. He must be a grandpa, or an uncle. She settled back into her car, pulled on the seatbelt, and glanced in the sideview mirror.

The child took a tentative peek into the van, and then jerked back with a look of fear. The man said something with a

27

stern face, scooped her up and tossed her into the van. He hurried to the driver's side and slammed his door. His motor roared.

MOVE!

She put her car into drive, but kept her foot on the brake. Unsure of what she had just seen, she hesitated.

MOVE!

The urgent word shouting in her mind made her step on the gas and spin the wheel.

God, is that you?

Before the van pulled away in a billow of dust, Nikki caught a glimpse of a vulnerable young face peering out the cracked side window. Her small hand pressed against the pane. Nikki pulled onto the road and followed the van.

Chapter 6

Nikki sped up to catch sight of the mud-splattered white van. She'd dropped back too far. Around the next curve, she saw it.

He made a quick turn off the main road. She clutched the car wheel and yanked it.

Really, God? I don't want to argue, but...

She twisted now to the left, fighting to keep the car from fishtailing off the pebbled road. The washboard surface rumbled beneath the tires.

That's right, kiddo, look in the direction you want the car to go.

Risky moves could make him notice her.

How long has it been?

She glanced at the clock on the dash. The twenty minutes seemed like hours. The pursuit now cut onto a backroad heading into the mountains.

Does the man know I'm following him?

As she came around the next curve edged with thick pine, a glare of brake lights shot an orange glow into billowing dust. He'd stopped.

Nikki eased down on the brake to prevent another skid and gave a solid push at the end. She backed up and slipped around the corner she'd just traveled. Hoping he'd not seen her. Through the tree branches, she could see the dirt settling. Several white-tail deer strolled across the road in front of the battered van.

Using this pause, Nikki searched the car for her phone. Her hand shoved between the seat and middle console and pulled out a comb with a crumpled receipt. Putting the car in park, Nikki unbuckled the belt and leaned over to see under the passenger seat.

Nothing.

She ran a hand under the driver's seat.

Where is that stupid thing?

A sharp blast from the man's horn brought her head up with a jerk. The last doe reared up in the air and bounded into the thicket. She hurried to buckle her belt and put the car into gear.

What am I doing? Lord, are you sure about this?

She pushed the shift into drive. Her neck muscles pulled tight, and cold stabs froze in her stomach.

God, give me strength.

Nikki eased around the next turn. The van took the corner like one familiar with switchbacks. The road sent them across a vast yellow and green meadow with views of the rugged mountain ranges. She slowed down, wanting him to get far enough ahead of her to not raise suspicion.

Another forest drew the road in, and his van disappeared from view. She pushed the accelerator harder. Blood pounded in her chest, and a floating dizziness took over. Tensed muscles gave the sensation that her arms had disconnected from her body. She willed both hands to hold onto the wheel.

The image of the frightened child staring out the cracked window kept her going. But at the same time, a vision of wild geese being chased kept flapping in her head.

Driving into the shady green of aspen boughs and tall pine, she searched ahead. She hoped to catch sight of a dust trail or brake lights. Through the trees of the next curve, she saw a flash of red. But after the turn, even the remnants of dirt clouds had disappeared. Many side roads led off to unofficial and privately owned camping sites.

Father, where did he go? Have I lost him?

Her car rolled to a stop at a dead end. Ahead, a sign stood beside an entranceway. A chain stretched across the opening. The attached sign announced that next week opened the camping season. With no one in sight and no activity past the metal links, Nikki sighed and turned the car around.

Stings of cold fear began to subside. She gasped oxygen into starved lungs and closed her eyes.

Okay, God, this is the best I can do. I can't do more than that. If it even was You speaking to me.

Confused, discouraged, but a little less afraid, she punched the gas pedal. She wouldn't get to the church camp now until after dark, if she could even find it.

James is right. I'm not focused enough. How could I let a feeling get me so far off track?

She released her death grip on the wheel. But before calm returned, the explosive roar of a gunned engine came from behind.

Bam!

The SUV jerked forward. Her head snapped back. Someone had crashed into her bumper. She glanced into the rearview mirror.

It's him!

Nikki tromped on the gas pedal. Her car lurched forward. A bolting shock of fear snapped in her heart.

Where had he come from?

The Explorer careened into a serpentine skid. The vehicle slipped across like a drunken snowboarder as Nikki over-corrected the turns.

Jesus ... help!

A warm, peaceful calm flowed out from the center of her body. She relaxed her clenched grip on the wheel.

Able now to straighten the spin, she regained control. That is until her front wheel slipped off the road into a boulder. The impact on the tire angled the top-heavy SUV into a roll.

It's a dream, a movie.

The seatbelt cut into her chest. A wall of plastic pressed her face. The world shattered into a teeth-jarring spin. The roof smashed in, the floor slammed up, gravity slung her in all directions. Intense, vibrating sound exploded inside her ears.

Then everything stopped.

Another wash of shock removed her from the scene. Time slowed in her mind. Details glowed with amazing clarity. Waterfalls of glass and bits of metal rippled to the ground.

The car settled and Nikki inhaled dense, dust filled-air. She choked and gasped.

Liquid warmth spread into her hair. Her quivering hand eased up to her head. Nikki pulled her arm down and saw fingertips smeared red. A metallic taste of blood registered as her tongue touched inside her cheek.

Feeling no panic or fear, Nikki sat like an observer. A dark cloud swarmed inside her head and engulfed conscious thought. Just before the blackness conquered all reason, she heard a deep voice singing with hypnotic beauty,

"Everybody wants to go to heaven, but nobody wants to die."

Chapter 7

Darkness. He could barely see. A faint glow of white seemed to float across the grass and then stopped dead.

"Oh, no. No, no, no, that dog will not pee on my lawn. Not again," James growled. He slapped the blinds back down and ducked out the front of the house. He left the door open. If one of the boys cried out in his sleep, he would hear them.

The little white dog met him with barrage of yipping. High-pitched, fierce and completely fearless. James stooped down to get on the dog's level. Holding his right hand out as if he had a treat, he snatched the dog up with his left.

After clawing several harsh scratches into her captor's arms, the pup quivered and licked James's hand furiously.

"Let go of my Cricket!"

"Mrs. Farber!" James snapped out his words. "I have asked you nicely, several times, not to allow this mop to pee on my lawn."

"Do not shout at me, Mr. Rolen." She grabbed for the animal and held her precious fur ball close to her chest.

He bellowed, "I am not—" then lowered his voice and continued through gritted teeth. "I am not shouting. I just want you to realize that Cricket is ruining my grass. I mean, look at my lawn. It's like a giant green pizza covered with dried out pepperonis. I don't have a dog, Mrs. Farber, and my children certainly didn't do it."

"Oh dear, you are disgusting. My baby doesn't understand the difference between your lawn and mine. She has a free spirit. And –"

"Well, she better learn, and fast, or I'll cut her free spirit short myself." James turned his head to listen. A faint cry could be heard through his open door.

"Are you threatening my dog?" Her eyebrows shot up, and her blue eyes glared at him. She reminded James of the borg queen capturing Captain Picard on Star Trek.

"I just want you to keep track of that dog."

He heard a slightly louder call. "Moooommy!"

"Where is your wife, Mr. Rolen? I have something for her." Her countenance had changed when she mentioned his wife. James couldn't figure out how Nikki could make friends with the most unpleasant people.

"She's on a retreat right now, in the mountains."

"But I saw her jogging this morning, and your child is calling for her," she said.

"She left this morning."

"Moooooommmmmmmyyyy!"

"Listen, I have to go. Please watch that dog? Will ya?"

Mrs. Farber pulled Cricket closer to her in a protective way and flounced back to her home. James hurried into the house and up the stairs.

He stopped for a moment on the landing to orient himself as to which boy called out.

"Mommy!"

Conner, it was Conner. He stepped into the room and knelt by the small bed. A glowing yellow bear lit the way.

"Hey, Buddy, what's wrong?"

"I want Mommy." He sniffed and pulled his bear-blanky up and rubbed his eyes.

"Mommy's on a trip. Remember, son? But I'm here."

"But I want Mommy."

"Yes, I understand, Conner, but Mommy isn't—"

"Moooommmmmyy!"

"Okay, okay. Conner, you're going to wake Jonah." He pulled the covers back and picked up his son. Conner tucked his head onto James' shoulder and draped his arm around his daddy's neck.

After taking Conner downstairs and explaining he wished Mommy was there too, James got him a drink in his sippy cup. On the way back to bed, Conner fell asleep. James tucked him in and stood for a few moments over his bed.

I hope I can sleep like that tonight.

It wasn't until early evening that concern slipped into the back of his mind. Nikki hadn't called. He suspected the reason to be lack of cell phone coverage, but knowing this didn't relieve his worry. And it irked him that she wouldn't ask to use the camp phone.

He quickly got ready for sleep and crawled under the blankets. Though he had the whole bed to spread out on, he stayed in his spot. He stared at the vacant side of the bed and worried.

The day had gone pretty well, all things considered. James had ordered out for pizza despite the casseroles Nikki had made. In the afternoon, he had gotten out the hose and some squirt bottles. He and his boys had a water fight. James had no trouble winning, but he knew the time would soon come when he would face two teens with super soakers.

And for dinner? Leftover pizza.

Nikki should be there. Why doesn't she call?

At last his lids closed, and his body relaxed. Then the dream came.

With a giant super soaker in his hand, he bolted around a lake. He shot a stream into the water as he ran. Then he stopped dead. He saw something floating in the water.

No, not floating, swimming.

Wait, not swimming, drowning.

Someone was splashing and kicking in desperation.

He could see the red hair surrounding a pale face. Carrie! His sister was drowning. He threw down the gun and dove into the water. As soon as he reached her, he put his hands under her arms and lifted her up as he kicked furiously. He raised her head out of the water.

"I can do this. I can save her." His own voice pounded in his dream. She began to slip in his grasp and drifted down into the water.

He woke.

11:31 p.m.

He rolled onto his back and breathed deeply to allow his heart rate to come down, and to catch his breath. It seemed so real. His sister was dead. He knew this part was not a dream. But she'd died of cancer. If he'd been there, he might have been able to make the doctors listen. Forced them to save her.

Then sleep tugged.

Computer screens filled with data that floated in front of his face. The nodes had crashed and he couldn't tell if the systems had monitored the problem. If he didn't work fast, the whole nation would be down.

How could he fix this problem? It made no sense. He couldn't even see the numbers clearly.

He woke.

12:48 a.m.

Then sleep.

He held Nikki in his arms as they danced on the lanai. The Hawaiian beach lay just yards away, but they saw only each other. She looked into his eyes and then placed the side of her face against his. The warmth of her smooth cheek spread a peace throughout his whole body. He knew he must keep her safe. She needed him to. During the next spin, she vanished.

His body jerked and he sat up in bed. He saw her sleeping next to him. Relieved, he rubbed his hands over his eyes.

He woke.

2:00 a.m.

Her side of the bed remained as empty as before. He tried to reason with himself.

It's not like she's never gone on a trip before. Why am I so upset? I guess this is the first time she's been away this long, since the boys were born. If only she had her cell phone. Then I could help her if she needed me.

Well, at least she has the GPS. That would keep her from getting lost.

Chapter 8

Ava took in a long breath of air and let it out in a slow stream. The slight thawing of fear caused her body to melt down into the seat.

Why did he take me? Where are we going?

Slumping down, she clutched the armrest. The old man had sped up, but continued to hum his cheery tune. Eventually, feelings began to return to her legs.

Where's the seatbelt?

Too frightened to search, she stared at the fabric design on the seat in front of her. He stopped in the road. Ava thought about jumping out when she saw the deer crossing in front of the van.

The man didn't seem upset. He was saying something quietly as the animals crossed.

Counting, he's counting the deer. Maybe he's not a kidnapper, just a nice man taking me home.

One last deer started to cross.

Honk!

The man yelled, "No! Too many, that's too many!" He banged on the wheel. The van shot forward as the deer jumped into the bushes.

She'd lost the chance to run. But another thought came, and she twisted and pulled herself up. She wanted to take a good look in the back seat.

"Priscilla!" The man yelled.

She snapped back into her seat.

"This is going to be a game. You need to hang on tight." He sang louder now and tapped the steering wheel as he drove.

Ava clutched the arm rest. The scenery outside her window had turned to a thick forest. With a quick stop that almost tossed her out of her seat, he swung the wheel fast and pulled into the trees. Then he turned around and parked. Ava peered between the front seats through the windshield and saw that the road now crossed in front of them.

The man raised his hand in the air and shouted, "Seatbelts for everyone! Seatbelts now."

Ava turned toward the side and made a frantic search. This time she found the strap. One yank and click, she was secured, but not safe.

Ava watched as a big blue car cruised past them. She checked the man with a glance.

What would he do?

He sat.

The humming stopped but not the drumming on the wheel. With both hands he tapped the top twice, the sides twice, and then the bottom once. He did this again and again, harder and harder, watching the road.

The same blue car drove past, going the other way. The man eased out of the trees onto the road.

"Halleluuuuuuuuuu-yaaah!" he screamed as he gunned the engine. Ava's eyes widened, and a yell blasted out her own throat, her loudest, longest screech ever.

She held it until the van smashed into blue's back bumper. The collision tossed her in her seat. The belt kept her from falling out.

The driver in front didn't stop and neither did the man. The blue car made a roaring noise and shot ahead.

"Yahooooo! Sing it boys." He drove like in a crazy game of Mario Carts. Ava shut her eyes tight. She tried to hold her breath, but the van bounced. She couldn't. Ava lurched forward.

The van stopped dead.

From outside came a crash louder than thunder. Ava saw a tornado of dirt and car filling the forest. Pieces smacking back against the van sounded like hail.

A quiet fell. Ava peered out the window at the wreck. The roof was smashed in. Metal bent, crinkled sides, and dust floating up like smoke from the blown-out candles on a smashed cake.

Now what?

The man got out, singing as he went.

"Everybody wants to go to heaven. But nobody wants to die. Oh, no, no, n-o-o-o-o-o. Sing it, boys!"

Chapter 9

"Help me Rhonda. Help, help me, Rhonda, Help me, Rhonda, yea."

James sat up in bed, reached over and snatched up his phone. "Hello? Hello?" No answer.

The Beach Boys continued to wail out for Rhonda's help. James squinted at the face of the phone and realized his alarm had awakened him. He dropped the phone, slapped the top of his alarm clock, and fell back into bed.

A pang of disappointment rose inside him. Nikki hadn't called.

Moments later he could hear little feet scurrying down the hall. Conner climbed onto the bed, plopped on top of James' stomach, and curled up onto his chest.

"Oof! Watch it, buddy." James wasn't used to getting up early on a Saturday. Nikki usually took morning duty.

"Daddy, I hungwee and I have to go pee."

"Well, good for you, Conner. Let's take care of that last part first."

James was happy to notice the Pull-Ups were dry. He got out another one from the stack on the dresser. "Wash your hands."

Another small voice came from down the hall. "Mo-o-o-mmyyy!"

James scooped Conner up and kissed him on the head. Then he tossed the boy onto the blankets of his bed. "I'll be right back, buddy. I need to get brother."

He shuffled down the hall and took Jonah out of his crib. "Mommy's on a trip. Remember? Do you need a change, son?" After this morning ritual, he carried Jonah back to where Conner waited and plopped him down next to his brother.

"Okay, guys. What shall we do today?"

"I hungwee," Conner said.

"Okay, we start with breakfast."

James knew the lazy calmness of the morning would not last. He had to think of an activity to get them tired enough for a good long nap this afternoon.

The park. That would be perfect.

He'd bring a lunch in the backpack. He could use the two-seater jogging stroller to get them there.

After breakfast, he loaded up the pack with food, water, and sunscreen. He managed to splash red liquid from an open juice box onto his socks before he decided water would be best. Getting hats, shoes and just the right sippy-cups for each child took a bit of time.

When his little brood arrived at the park, James was surprised to see another dad he knew there. The families had met a few times at neighborhood events, like the Fourth of July.

James unloaded the troops, and slathered on the sunscreen before sending them off to the trenches.

James knew that Nikki would have carried on an entire conversation as she readied them for play. James focused on each task like a military mission.

Jonah toddled into the sandbox, plunked down and claimed his territory with the small shovel his dad had given him. Conner ran to the jungle gym.

James left the stroller by a picnic table and stepped over to the other dad.

"Hello, Robert," James said. "Where's Evie? Are you the man in charge today?"

"Hi, James. Yeah, Evie's off shopping this morning. The park seemed like a good idea,"

"I know what you mean. My wife's off doing her own thing, too."

"Shopping as well, I suppose."

"Well, not ... watch out!" James pointed to a small brown-haired boy who had climbed to the top of the jungle gym and was trying to stand.

"Jeffery!" Robert took a step toward the child. "That's too high. I told you to be careful,"

Jeffery smiled at his dad, and without warning launched himself in the air. Robert had a fraction of a second to ready himself for the catch.

"Wow! Now that's what I call trust," James watched as the boy wiggled out of his father's arms and ran to the swings.

"It's scary, isn't it? How much they trust in us. I don't know if there's anyone I have that much faith in."

"Know what you mean." In silence, the men sat at a picnic table.

"Think the Broncos can get to the Super Bowl again?" Robert swigged from his water bottle.

"I sure hope so. The coaches seem to know what they're doing."

James enjoyed the chance to kick back with another dad. Talk of sports, cars, and things that blow up were the topics. The conversation interrupted now and then to keep their charges safe. Sand remained the theme in each reprimand—the throwing of, the rolling in, or the eating of the versatile substance.

After their lunch, they each packed up and got ready to leave.

Robert said, "You know our boys really get along well. Maybe we should have our wives plan a playdate, or something?"

"Sure, I bet Nikki would like that idea."

"How about tomorrow morning? I could buzz Evelyn on her cell right now."

"No, that won't work for us. Anyway, I thought you went to church on Sunday mornings."

James tucked Conner into his side of the stroller. Both boys were happy and tired.

Score!

"Oh. Oh, yeah. Of course, church. How could I forget that tomorrow's Sunday?"

James faced Robert. "What church do you go to? Maybe it's even ours. We don't know everyone yet."

"Uh, no, no, probably not. That is, our kids would have known each other and...um." He met James's eyes, blinked, coughed and then said, "Okay, I can't do this. I don't like to out and out lie."

42

"What do you mean?"

"Well, it's like this. Evelyn and I don't really attend church."

"Then why...?"

"Most of our acquaintances seem to be... I don't know, religious. And Evelyn has noticed that when we tell them we're agnostics, suddenly the playdates are canceled. I know it sounds silly, but we sort of pretend to be Christians so our son has a social life."

James stood a moment. Stunned at the confession. Yet in the back of his mind, he could hear Nikki commenting on how they would need to be sure their children had Christian friends. Ones that wouldn't lead them astray. But now this man stood before him.

What should I do?

He massaged the top of his head. "Well, I mean, I'm truly sorry you feel the need to do that. I hope my wife and I can be the exception. Give me your email address, and I'll get back to you."

Robert paused, sighed, and took out his wallet. "Here's my card. I hope I hear from you," he said. But his voice didn't sound hopeful.

They said their good-byes and each headed down the park path to their homes, in opposite directions.

Chapter 10

"Sing it, boys!" the old man belted out as Ava watched him run to check on the smashed car in the forest. He came back humming and pulled Ava out of the van. He placed a plastic zip-tie around her wrist and with a second tie he attached her to the outside handle of the front door, leaving the sliding backdoor open. Then he hustled back to the wreck with its engine still smoking.

Ava pulled on the tie as hard as she could until she saw the man come back carrying someone. A lady. One arm dangled down, and her head tilted back on his arm. Blonde hair draped loose and swung with each step

She's from the wreck.

The man, now gentle, put the woman into the van.

Adults are crazy. Now he's so careful. Why did he try to hurt her in the first place?

The woman's face appeared so white and the blood so red, Ava turned away.

She's dead. She must be dead.

He reached into the back and yanked out a scratched-up metal box, popped open the lid, and began to root around in it. After pulling out bandages, scissors, medicine, he reached back again for paper towels and a water bottle. The old man moved like her doctor did when she cut her arm once, as if he had done this a million times before.

Ava clung to the door handle of the van. She waited for the old man to finish fixing the injured woman. The pile of bloody towels from cleaning up the lady's wounds made Ava think of Ben. Her legs almost collapsed under her.

This is my punishment. Being taken by this terrible man.

"Okay, Priscilla, I think Mamma is going to be just fine. You get back in and sit by her. Here, I'll move her all the way over first.".

He stepped into the van and scooted the woman over beside the far window. Giving her head a little shove, he attempted to prop it against the back of the seat. Her head fell forward twice, until he adjusted how she sat.

The man pulled the seatbelt across her. It snapped back. Mumbling with angry growls, he pulled again and clicked it into place. He scolded the belt with non-sense words.

Turning to Ava, he cut the zip-tie off the door handle. Ava climbed onto the bench seat beside the woman. As the engine started up Ava did her best not to touch the blood on the woman's shirt.

After a while, Ava gazed into the woman's face. She looked a little like her teacher, Mrs. McAlister. This worried her. It couldn't be. Teacher had to be home safe.

What if she dies right next to me? Like Ben. Was this my fault, too?

A trickle of blood slipped under the bandage on the lady's face. She jerked in her sleep. Her head bobbed against the window and more blood smeared onto the glass.

The memory of Ben's face merged with the woman's. Ava squeezed her eyes shut to block out the sight. But in her mind, Ava's own hands were covered with a sticky, red mess.

Blood!

* * *

Nikki dreamed. She heard a child crying, wet tears on soft baby cheeks. Nikki floated in a wash of memories. Her heart burned with nuclear blasts of love for Conner and Jonah.

Did she hold them? Her empty arms hugged the nothing as she slept.

The scene changed, weaving in and out of the blackness. People streamed down the aisle. Her father stood at the front, tall and imposing, yet his head was bent and tears flowed down both cheeks. His stance held humility and strength. She scrambled down the side aisle, hoping for a better glimpse.

These people, with bright-colored, well-worn clothes, were so affected by the thought of a God that loved them that they cried aloud. They fell to their knees at the front of the church.

Their whole lives would change. She'd seen this in many of the African villages her father preached in. But this time, her heart joined them in their tears.

Mercy. They absorbed God's mercy like a thirsty child. As if the word had never existed before.

She wanted to hold them all. She would never forget what it felt like to help someone know their creator.

A sick turning in her stomach of doubt and guilt caused her to stir.

Have I done enough? Been good enough?

Nikki became aware of a hard object pushing into her side. It blended with the sharp pain in her head. But she didn't open her eyes.

Nikki shifted ever so slightly and could feel that she sat in a car-like seat, the side arm jammed into her ribs. Her eyes still closed.

Where is this again? Home? No. I was being chased. Did I crash? Am I still in the car?

No vibrating movement. This car stood still. She struggled to turn an aching head to one side and slit one eye open. Then both.

There, staring directly into her face, sat a small angel with soft hair and huge brown eyes.

"Hello? Where am I?" Nikki asked.

No answer.

Do angels talk?

No, this couldn't be an angel. Sorrow, fear, and worry fused across the young face. She was up on her knees beside Nikki, nose to nose. This was the little one she'd seen walking on the road.

Nikki must be in the man's vehicle. But how?

Lifting her hand to her sore head, she realized it had been bandaged. He must have stopped to help her.

I'm such an idiot! It was an accident. He stopped to help me.

No one sat in the driver's seat. Nikki wrapped an arm around the quivering child and drew her close. She rested her head on Nikki's shoulder. Nikki leaned down and whispered into her ear.

"It'll be okay. I'm all right. I'll help you."

A muffled snicker floated from the back of the van.

Nikki strained to painfully shift her body and squinted to pierce the shadows of the back area. She perceived a slim figure. Adjusting to the darkness she saw a young teen boy hunched over in his seat, with a weary expression of a secret knowledge.

"He's crazy, you know," he rasped out, with a stone face.

Then she saw the chains around his waist.

Chapter 11

Blood!

Ava kept her eyes squeezed shut. This blocked out the lady's wounded face, but could not wipe away the memory of Ben's bloody body in the dirt. She rubbed her palms together to take away the thought of that red mess on her hands.

She jerked with a hard shiver and opened her eyes. Her hands were not red. The lady slept beside her.

Not dead.

Asleep.

She forced herself to stare into the back seat. In the dim light, she could make out the shadow of the skinny older boy. This was not the sight that had frightened her, when she first peered into the van. The terror in his eyes as he shook his chains at her was why she tried to run.

Now he slouched with his head turned to the window. He seemed uninterested, until she caught his eye in the reflection. Then he gave his head a slight shake in disgust. He had tried to warn her, she knew.

But it hadn't saved her.

The old man finally stopped at a gas station with a small store. He slapped a new zip-tie on her and chained her to a metal bar under the front seat. He closed dark shades that were fixed on all the back windows and went in the store.

After a short time, he brought back snacks, water bottles, and other things. Some he had in plastic bags, but a few he pulled out from the top front of his overalls. He stepped into the doorway of the van, reached to the back, and unchained the boy.

A waft of dirty-boy smell fill Ava's nose as he passed. As he got out he looked down, snarled hair draped across his face. After getting out he snapped his head to one side to fling the strands back. Then he stretched his long arms over his body as he walked to the restroom at the back of the building.

They must have given the man a key. He returned the boy to the van and then escorted Ava.

In the bathroom, Ava tried to think what she should do. Leave a message? How? For who? Not the police, she had murdered someone. Her mom? Her mom could barely take care of herself, much less rescue her. In the end, she washed her face and hands and left.

After downing one of the water bottles and a candy bar, Ava slept the rest of the way. She woke to nighttime darkness. The van had stopped. Through the front window, she could see a small brick building. She turned to the boy in hopes of getting a clue of what to expect. He stared straight ahead with bored eyes.

The man spoke to her. "Settle in there, Priscilla. This may take a while. We need to be sure everyone's gone."

She had almost fallen back to sleep when the man opened his door and came around to hers.

"Okay, the bathrooms are free now. We can get out and stretch our legs. We'll spend the night here."

When she got out, she saw that they were at an empty rest stop. He allowed her and the boy to go in the bathrooms, but he stayed near the entrances until both came out.

"Sit down at the table under the tree," he ordered.

He took one of the bags from the store and tossed it on a picnic table. The bag rattled with a metallic sound when they dropped. After he pulled out a number of dog choke collars, he looped them together to create a chain rope. He used these to attach both children to the picnic table.

The man smiled as he worked. "These are just for here. To keep you both safe. Don't worry. When we get home, you won't need them anymore."

Get home?

He began to sing. "The chains will be broken, by and by, Lord, by and by."

Then he laid out the rest of the snacks in a row on the table. He changed the order several times before he was satisfied.

"Pray!" he commanded.

He closed his eyes and folded his hands. The boy copied him.

Ava sat up straight. She watched with a worried fear.

The man prayed, "Lord, we ask Thee to bless this food. Purify each crumb and morsel. Rebuke Satan and the evil intent that may have been placed on this food by his willing workers and their contaminated hands."

The boy prayed next. "Lord, bless this food. Protect us from all evil."

A silence followed. Ava didn't know what to do. The boy opened one eye and nodded at her.

Do I have to talk? I can't!

Her mind froze at the idea of speaking. The stress of what the consequences might be if she didn't pray made it worse.

The man turned to her with a calm face. "Pray?" he asked.

She couldn't.

Like a snake striking, the man's fist cracked into the side of her head.

She hit the ground hard. Pain took her breath.

The man wasted no time. He unchained and lifted Ava up by pinning her arms at the side with his bear size hands. She faced him as he walked.

He shook her as he yelled. "I told you to pray. You little slut. You piece of garbage. Don't you understand I'm trying to protect you? Keep you from being burned? From the fires, worse than Hell!"

He shoved her into the boy's seat, and shut the door. A metallic clatter followed the slam, and the man left.

What happened?

Confused and shocked with pain, she lay still. But as the moments passed, a small hot coal of anger sparked a thought in her mind. He hadn't chained her. She lifted the shade over one of the windows. The other two ate at the table, not looking at the van.

She crawled into the seat ahead of her. Careful not to touch the sleeping woman, she checked the door.

Locked.

Now she remembered the sleek steel box attached to the outside of the sliding door and one on the front passenger side. *Did every door have that extra lock?*

She leaned forward to reach the sliding door and yanked hard on the handle. Yes. The latch clicked, but the door wouldn't move. She glanced at the woman sleeping on the middle bench. The deadly quiet and the blood soaking her blouse made Ava shiver.

She didn't bother to check the driver's side. With a troubled sigh, she fell back and collapsed onto the seat. She curled up and held her head. The fierce pain now took all her attention. She crawled to the backseat past the woman who didn't move, and lay down.

Hunger growled in her stomach, and thirst made it hard to swallow. Worried with thoughts that a dead person lay nearby, she sang inside her head. She hummed a quiet tune her Grammy had taught her and tried to be invisible.

Sleep finally won out over pain and fear. She woke only once in the night. In a dream, she saw red lights and a heard a strong voice asking questions. She woke to discover the lights real, the voices, too.

She peeked out the side window and saw a police car with lights flashing. It sat near the rest stop entrance with one door open.

She slid over to the other window. The boy slept with his head on the picnic table.

"Thank you for checking on us, officer. We'll be gone in the morning."

"Okay, then, you and your son can stay just tonight. I'll be by in the morning to check. Have a safe trip. Nice to meet you, Elam. Good-bye now."

Ava thought about banging on the window, but what good would that do? Though her stomach gave another loud complaint she drifted back to sleep, and didn't wake until a rough jerking on her arm woke her.

The boy's voice commanded her. "Wake up, kid. Come on, get up. Hurry!"

She opened her eyes to see the boy's frantic face.

51

He pulled her up in the seat. "Elam's gone into the restroom."

She said nothing, but raised her eyebrows.

"You don't understand. You got no chains on. He chained me, but forgot to lock the sliding van door."

Hope flooded into Ava, then fear. She pulled back from the boy and shook her head no. He'd be back too soon for her to get away.

"Dude, he takes a pickin' long time when he washes up. He does everything three or four times. It can take hours. Go! You have to go. Now."

Ava pulled in all of her courage to scramble to the seat in front of her.

"Uh, uuh," the woman groaned.

Ava kneeled on the seat beside her and searched the lady's face with piercing focus.

"No," said the boy, "No, she's too hurt. You can't wait for her to wake up. Leave. Kid, get out while you can."

Ava went from fearful not knowing to strong sureness. She couldn't leave the lady behind. Careful not to touch blood she shook her arm. At first little shakes, then with great urgency.

"It's no use. Go! Get out of here. Now!"

The woman groaned again and moved slightly. Ava stopped shaking her and watched her face for signs of life.

The boy sank back in disgust. "Well, I tried."

Not willing to give up, Ava sat up taller on her knees, leaned in closer, and shook harder. She stopped and watched. The woman turned her head and opened one eye. Then both.
"Hello? Where am I?"

Ava didn't answer.

The woman lifted a hand to her head. Bringing it down, she stared at her fingers. Then, after giving a long slow gaze to the front of the van, she turned to Ava.

Ava sank into the seat and held back her tears.

No. No tears. No time.

The kind woman sat up. She put her arms around Ava and pulled her close. "It'll be okay. I'm all right. I can help you," she whispered into her ear.

Sweet relief flooded Ava's heart.

A soft laugh came from the back seat. The woman twisted around to look behind her.

"He's crazy, you know." The boy whispered.

"What? Who's crazy?" The woman struggled to get the words out.

"You don't have time for me to explain things. You and the kid have to get outta here. Fast."

They didn't move.

The young man leaned forward and put his face into the woman's and screamed.

"Run!"

Chapter 12

Pain throbbed behind Ben's eyes, like someone had used his brain for a bass drum. He rolled to his side and lifted his hand to touch his head. A gritty moistness covered his eyes. He wiped his closed lids and looked at his hand. Blood caked with dirt stained his fingers.

He attempted to sit up, but a sick blackness overwhelmed him. Gingerly rolling onto his back, he tried to force his mind to remember what had happened.

Not the first time I've woken up with blood somewhere. That's what comes with being a falling-down drunk.

Memory of the intense anger and frustration came first. How could one tiny girl bring about so much rage? The exact details of how he came to be there he couldn't reach. He knew it had something to do with that little brat.

He didn't think he'd done anything to her. This thought made him glance around to see if she cowered nearby. He didn't see anything but a large rock formation and trees.

Ben recalled being angrier than he had ever experienced, and racing through the woods. If he ran, he couldn't have been too drunk, right? His brain, though infused with throbbing pain, didn't have that same foggy disorientation of waking from a brain-crushing hangover. He forced himself to think harder. The vision of a bark-covered branch flying toward his face and slamming into his head made his body cringe. This caused an added shock of excruciating pain.

"That little creep hit me." He groaned out the words through gritted teeth. "She must have. She smacked me with something."

With a slow push, he struggled again to sit up and searched the ground. A shattered branch nestled nearby in the grass. He reached down and picked up a broken piece. Blood crusted near the break.

A wave of dizziness combined with nausea caused him to turn over and lean face down. He rested his cheek in the dirt. When his stomach settled, a flash of clarity came.

I left the jeep parked on the road. But where's the road?

He dragged himself up and leaned against one of the rocks. As a hunter, even in this state, he could see the scrapes in the dirt from where he'd charged around the boulders. He heaved oxygen into his lungs to rally enough strength and stumbled back to his vehicle.

He pulled himself into the front seat. He started the motor and released the clutch. The dashboard blurred and swam in dizzy swirls. The light around him dimmed. But before he went completely under the wheels picked up speed and lunged forward. The jeep slipped over the edge of the road and bounced down the incline, smashing into a tree with a violent crack.

Chapter 13

Both boys were asleep by the time James got home from the park. He gently lifted each boy and carried them to their beds.

James walked into the living room and fell into the recliner in front of the TV. Worry for Nikki crept past thoughts of getting overdue work finished on his laptop.

He checked his phone, again. He couldn't stop looking to see if she'd called. His fear of missing the ring bordered on fanatical.

No call. He almost dialed her cell. But if Nikki had found it, she'd have called, unless there was no cell coverage. He made an attempt to remember the name of the camp. But the name wouldn't come.

What am I doing? I'm worrying like she's a little girl. She's just fine. It's like on our honeymoon when I got so worked up that she didn't get back from scuba diving on schedule.

For a moment, he went back in time. The feeling of terror that he'd lost his new wife relived inside his mind. When she walked through the door draped in a towel, two hours late, he full out ran across the room. He wrapped his arms around her and almost knocked over his bride.

He smiled to himself. That was a long time ago. Right about this time of year.

Wait, is it?

He checked the calendar. Their anniversary was coming up.

Oh, great! Now I have to think of something to give her. Nikki went on the retreat, and money is even shorter than usual.

All he wanted right now was his wife back. Not just from the retreat. He'd noticed the drifting apart. He loved his children, but they were ... well ... always there. The bills had been piling up too.

Dear God, help us get more money and time for us to be together.

Okay, God will take care of it. Every time he prayed a prayer like that, he had a vision of a giant vending machine.

56

Oh, and God, we'll go to church tomorrow, and I've been helping the boys to pray before meals, and at night.

There, he almost forgot to put the quarters in. He reclined the chair all the way back and turned on the television.

A lovely, blonde news anchorwoman filled the screen. "We have a report of an Amber alert tonight. A seven-year-old girl was reported missing after a traffic accident in the Woodland Park area. Her mother's boyfriend apparently crashed on the side of the road and was rendered unconscious. The child had been riding in the car. She either wandered off after the crash, or someone might have picked her up. This is a picture of the missing child. Her name is Ava Martin. Also, be aware that the girl is very shy and does not speak. Please notify the Woodland Park police if you have any information."

Chapter 14

"Run!"

The boy screamed into her face. That same urging roared in her mind.

MOVE!

She wasn't sure if she could move. But the girl tugged on her, and she found the strength. With great effort, the child managed to slide the door open. Both stumbled out and squinted at the morning light.

Now what?

"Here! Take this!" The young man shoved her purse out the door as he pointed into the woods. "Stay off the road, but close by it. Elam saw cops last night. If you see em', flag em' down." Her bag seemed heavy, and she fingered the water bottles through the canvas side.

The girl didn't speak, but her expression changed to panic and urgency. Pulling with surprising power, the young one dragged Nikki along. Nikki fell to one knee, and the child made a distraught groan. Nikki pushed up from the ground, and both struggled across the rest area and into the woods.

Where to now, God? Father, tell us what to do.

Pausing in a small clearing, Nikki gasped in air. The girl pointed to an opening in the brush. An animal trail, traveled, but not a real path.

Light-headed and foggy-minded, she struggled to move forward. Her legs wobbled as she leaned more on the child. How far could they go on like this?

Father, help. Help us. I'm scared. I don't know how, but I still trust you.

They stumbled along for another twenty minutes and came to a shallow creek. "If we follow this downstream it'll bring us down the mountain." The child squeezed her hand in response.

It might take us farther from the road, but that would help cover our tracks.

The rocks were slippery. The water cold. Stumbling and falling often, she splashed through the rippling water. The dizzy world blended into one nightmare.

They stopped where the stream widened and rested on a tiny muddy shore. Nikki took out the water bottles. She gave one to the girl and watched her guzzle down the liquid.

"My name is Nikki. What's your name?"

The little one only stared at her with wide, brown eyes. Her forehead creased. She opened her mouth, but no sound came out. Tears tumbled down red cheeks. She collapsed into Nikki's arms and cried.

They stayed there, both crying now. Nikki waited for strength to return.

A blast cut through the trees.

Gunfire!

They froze.

Again, a shot echoed. Then several sharp booms hit the air. The young girl sat up and motioned Nikki to move up over the small hill at their left.

Right, we should move away from the sound.

At the top of the hill, Nikki scanned the clearing. A familiar shape rose over the trees.

Long's Peak? Are we that near the Rocky Mountains?

Small fingers pulled on her hand. The girl motioned to the bottom of the hill, where several bushes grew beside a large boulder.

Nikki took one last glance at the mountain and at the sun's position. Then she and the child half walked, half slid down the slope. They snuggled under the branches of the bush and waited.

The girl motioned with her hands. Palms down, her mouth pursed together making a sh-h-h-h sound.

Invisible.

The word popped into Nikki's mind as clearly as if it had been spoken. They needed to be invisible.

Chapter 15

Chance watched the woman and the little girl head to the woods. The woman tripped. Priscilla, or whatever the girl's real name was, helped to steady her.

They'll never make it.

The two stumbled across the dirt toward the forest. The woman went down to one knee and the little girl cried out. Priscilla pulled on her arm just enough to give the lady the strength to stand again. Both then stepped in among the trees. He caught glimpses of the girl's yellow shirt through the foliage. Soon all he could see was leaves and branches tossing in the wind.

He'd done all he could think of. Yelled at them until he worried they were too stupid to listen. He'd yanked out the woman's purse, and shoved two water bottles in it for them He told them about the cops Elam had seen.

Now he let out a satisfied sigh, and settled back in his seat. He wanted to go with them. But this could be their only chance to escape.

I can't go back anyways. Nobody there for me. I'm not even Chance anymore. Am I? I'm Jake. His Jake.

Must have been 'most an hour before Elam came charging out of the cinderblock building. He had to have seen the van door wide open.

"No!" he shouted as he ran. "Where are they? Jacob! Tell me, right now. Where are they?"

Jake took a deep breath. He would need all his energy and acting skills to deflect the man's insanity. "They took them, Pa. They came and took them."

"Oh no, no. When? I didn't hear anything."

"A huge helicopter came down over there." Jake pointed to a clearing. "They swept them up and snatched them away."

"No, you're lying. I would have heard a chopper. I know a chopper sound. All those years, bloody, wounded young men came in choppers. I'd fixed them up, and they brought them back broken all over again." He stepped in the van, grabbed Jake by the collar and yanked, pulling the boy's face to his own. "What really happened? They carried them off, didn't they? Off into the woods!"

"Yeah, Pa. That's right. They took them into the woods. But it's all right. We don't need em'."

"Need them? Of course not." He pushed the boy back into his seat. "They need us. They're family. God sent them back to me. Not the same, but God knows best. He is all knowing and I know what I'm doing. I mean, He knows."

Elam stepped from the van, pulled his hair back into a ponytail with a rubber band from off his wrist. Then he ran around to the back, opened the door, and rustled around. He came back with something long.

A rifle.

"Pa, you don't need that."

"Jake, you don't understand. I must get them free. There is no place safe. No place. Only danger. We have to save them."

Elam's eyes were filled with tears, and sweat already matted the hair on and around his face.

Elam unlocked Jake's chain tether from its anchor under the seat. A violent yank on the links sent Jake stumbling out of the van. Next, he attached cable ties to wrists already raw and sore. He attached a chain between the ties, giving his hands some freedom of movement. Another dog chain collar looped this to Jake's waist chain. Elam grabbed up the tether links again as he held the rifle. After he slammed the van door shut, Elam took a careful sweep of the ground around the rest stop.

Jake hoped a car would pull in right now. But no. There'd been only a few the whole time they'd been there. Too far from civilization for loads of tourists.

"This way," he said. Jake was shocked to notice Elam entered the forest at the exact place the females had. "Why didn't you call me? I would have kept them free."

61

"I tried, Pa. I tried." He stumbled along behind, bumping into Elam now and then. Elam's pace, though stop and go, had a frantic thrust. He kept his eyes on the ground to track.

"I know you tried. I've tried and tried." His voice raised in pitch. "We all try and try. But it's no good. There!" He pointed to the ground. "See that? They must have carried them. I see only two tracks."

A rush of panic kicked Jake in the stomach. How could Elam have picked up on the trail so fast?

Ingrained talent over-rides insanity, once again.

"No, that can't be them. There's not enough tracks. There was at least five people and—"

The sound of a plane interrupted him. Elam's attention now focused overhead.

Elam whispered, "It's them. On the plane. I hear them talking. They're coming now. We have to hide." Elam dropped the chain and clutched Jake's wrists. He dropped into the bushes, yanking him down. Crouching there, he fiddled with the rifle.

"What are you doing? Pa, answer me."

"We have to be ready, son. I have to load. No use if we shoot with an empty gun, now, is it?"

Jake thought about running. He sat in the dirt, realizing his opportunity had finally arrived. But something kept him glued to the spot.

How can I leave this madman with a rifle? Maybe I can calm him down and then go. But he'll find them and kill them. Like the others.

Elam snatched up the chain again. Taking a carabiner from an inside pocket, he snapped it to the end of the loose links. He clipped this to his belt. Elam stood up and aimed his gun into the air toward the distant plane.

The shot pushed Elam back. Jake bent over and covered his ears. Elam recovered his balance and blasted off two more.

"Pa, Elam, you can't do this. That won't even reach the plane."

"They landed. They'll pick up on our trail. I can hear them. They're coming. We have to find the girls. You know what can happen if they keep them? Trouble, so much trouble. Death and fire. Fires worse than Hell. The world has become evil, Jake. Jesus is coming back again. It's the prophecy." He shot two more rounds into the bushes behind them. "Let's go!"

They plunged into the thickest part of the leaves. The chain cut into Jakes's waist as Elam plowed ahead. He held onto the connecting metal links with his hands to lessen the sharp pain in his back.

Elam turned and fired behind them.

Jake ducked to the ground.

Don't let anyone be back there. Don't let anyone get hurt.

Jake repeated this mantra in his head. Knowing no god heard, but wished that something did.

Maybe the universe heard. Whatever that means.

Now Elam began to run down a faint path. Jake pulled along by the chains, had all he could do to keep from tripping on tree roots.

"Pa! Father! Elam, slow down, I can't keep up. Stop!" The ground seemed to fly up at him when he fell. He couldn't protect his face from smacking into the dirt. Curse words shot through his mind as he landed. His chains yanked him forward until Elam, too, stumbled. The old man hit the ground hard.

Spitting dirt out of his mouth, Jake lifted his head. His arms, tied in the front, allowed him to use his wrists to push himself up. He could hear Elam groan, arms and legs sprawled out flat in the dust.

But before Jake could get his wits about him, Elam had pulled himself to a sit, and then stood up. The chains tightened. He shouldered the rifle again and aimed three more shots into the forest.

Jake heard three bullets fly and one click.

Then several more clicks. Elam threw the rifle toward Jake.

"It's outta ammo. You carry it." He brushed himself off and added, "You okay, son?"

Before He could answer, Elam swung away and stared intently into the woods.

63

Jake grabbed at the rifle and held it close. Then he broke open the gun and gasped a quiet breath. The chamber held more bullets. It must have jammed.

A quick glance showed Elam still staring into the woods at something only he could see. The thought of using the rifle on Elam made a quick pass through his brain. Instead he shook out the three shells into his hand. He dropped them into the abyss of forgotten treasures from life before Elam. The leg pocket of his cargo pants.

They trudged on a way and ran into a small creek.

Elam rubbed his hand over his beard. "Maybe they'd use the water to cover their tracks." He spent a good while inspecting both banks of the water. "Yep, they probably went downstream."

He took three strides into the cold water and stopped. "On the other hand, they may think we would think they would do that."

Jake, still chained to Elam's waist didn't move from the side of the stream. He knew this decision was going to be a while in the making. Elam fussed for hours over what side of the bread to butter, much less what path to take.

Elam muttered as he trucked back and forth. "If the landlords knew which way the porcupines flew, they would have the answer. But the night owls will tell it all. When they see the sky well up with tears, and tears, and tears, and years. I will show thee the way, sayeth the Lord God Almighty." He stopped and gazed downstream.

Chapter 16

Sunday morning, and James struggled to get the stroller out of the car. He hadn't planned on coming to church that day, but he received an urgent call from Riley, the audio-visual man in charge of the sound system. The person scheduled to run sound for the first service had forgotten to let people know he was out of town. Now they needed a fast replacement.

I guess God took me up on my bargain to go this Sunday.

James hated last-minute calls. He had hoped his tribe could sleep in since they stayed up so late the night before. No one had slept well. Conner and Jonah seemed to have conspired to be a tag team of sleep and wakefulness all night long. When one went down, the other took over the crying and bad dreams.

He settled Jonah into his stroller, grabbed Conner's hand, and headed through the parking lot.

The first person they saw was the greeter, Mrs. Farber. She was the one who had convinced Nikki to come to her church. Even though Nikki had taken a year of Bible College before she went to a university, they'd both stopped going to church for a period of time. Then, after the kids were born, they wanted to be sure their children had the benefit of growing up in a church.

James wasn't sure what the benefit was, but it certainly helped with the baby-sitting pool. Several young girls had hit them up right away, offering their services. Nikki was the religious one in the family. Her parents had been missionaries.

James didn't mind all the religious talk. He'd gone to church as a kid. But he often resented how much time it took away from family and other friends. For the most part, they seemed like nice people, but not much better than his acquaintances from work. Except for the no swearing part, of course. How many potlucks can you be expected to go to?

He managed to skirt around Mrs. Farber and headed into the basement where the nursery and toddler rooms were. Turning the corner, he almost rammed the stroller into the pastor.

"Oops! Sorry, Pastor Thomas."

"Oh, don't worry about it. I'm always a little scatter-brained before the service. Um ... James, right? Riley tells me you're helping us out with sound this morning."

James noticed the pastor's face had done a 180 change from frown to smile.

"Yes, Pastor, I'm happy to help out."

"I see you have two young men here ready for our Noah's Baby Boat class and Paul's Toddling Tentmakers class. How is your little family doing?"

"Well, without Nikki it's been—"

"Oh, excuse me, I see Mr. Turkelson is finally here. I need to ask him to set up more chairs in the fellowship room. Hope you enjoy the service."

"Oh. Oh, sure. No problem." James saw that two families had stepped ahead of him into Conner's room. He glanced at his watch. He'd better hurry.

After he had settled the kids in their classes, he made his way to the sound booth. He checked with the worship leader to see if there were any videos or PowerPoints that he needed to be aware of. Being well-versed with computers made him a valuable member of the AV team, but it prevented him from interacting with the other parishioners. That was okay.

The point of today's sermon seemed to be teaching fellow Christians to be aware of a world that would take Christ from them. A great worry of socialism, humanism in the schools, and sex in the media wove a feeling of trepidation. A lady in front of him shook her head with emphatic agreement.

"Within these walls, God offers a place of love and mercy."

I'm so tired. I could use a little mercy. And a drive-thru window for lunch.

The pastor's voice droned on. "...the secular world needs to hear..."

I'd better not forget to locate Jonah's bear-blanky in the nursery. Don't want a repeat of last week's church-wide search.

"Just believe, that is all they need to do, that's all we need to do…"

That's my cue. Get PowerPoint ready.

"Christians need to stick together, keep our minds holy and pure…"

After the sermon, someone announced a rally for Christians against something, something, followed by a potluck.

James enjoyed mixing the sounds for the ensemble. Keeping the levels high enough for each instrument and blending the singer's voices. He upped the sound for the drums on the song "Grace Like Rain." He often broke out into air drums in a low-key sort of way. This church was a bit reserved for too many outward displays, but he did notice some arms would rise during that type of song.

The last prayer came none too soon. During the previous silent prayer, he'd drifted off.

"In closing, dear Lord, we pray for our young homeschooled children and their parents, the Christian schools and their dedicated teachers that hold the future of the next generation. Give them all patience, guidance, and keep them in your protective, watchful eye. Amen.

"Now just a reminder, we do have a coffee time directly after the service in the Fellowship room. Our second service begins in a half an hour. Thank you all for coming and peace be with you."

James briefly wondered why the public-school kids and teachers didn't deserve prayer as he got to work shutting down systems. He reached for the projector remote and caught sight of Mr. Carson coming down the aisle. He watched as the black man with a slight frost in his beard hustled along shaking everyone's hand. Some he paused to give a hug.

He stuck out in the room nearly complete with white faces. A few darker colors blended. James had secretly questioned why some churches were mostly white, others black, Korean, or Spanish. Some had the audacity to have a total mixture of faces.

His thoughts were cut short when he realized Mr. Carson was heading toward him. For an instant, he thought about ducking beneath the console. Not that he didn't like the man, but Carson tended to be overly friendly, and this made James uncomfortable.

"Jimmy!" Carson called out. He raised a hand in greeting long before reaching the sound table.

"Um, it's James."

"James, James, James, how are you this fine Lord's day?"

James shifted the remote to his other hand and held out his right. "I'm doing all right, Mr. Carson."

"Now, now, none of that Mr. Carson stuff. My name is Ray." He slapped James's hand away and gave the younger man a bear hug. James tried to pull himself out of the embrace with dignity as Ray continued to slap him on the back.

"Tell me now. How is that beautiful young wife of yours doing?" Ray asked.

"She's hanging in there. She went off to that women's retreat this weekend."

"Really? Then I'll be in prayer for her." His eyes creased with sincerity. "And for you too, with those two young ones to care for. Keepin' those youngsters in line all on your own can't be easy. I know, oh, I know." He laughed with an easy chuckle that made James smile, despite his strong desire to encourage an end to the conversation. "That's not where you got those nasty scratches, is it?" James looked down at his arm and saw the red marks from his encounter with Cricket.

"No, oh no. That was from someone a lot more devious than two little boys." James pulled his rolled-up sleeves down over his arms.

"Say." Ray patted James on the back. "Have you been able to connect with the other young parents in church? Maybe in a small group or something?"

"No, not yet. I mean Nikki has some but—"

"Oh, I know it must be hard to get involved, being a young professional like yourself. It can be difficult to find a niche."

"Yes, there are a lot of people here. Um, Mr. Carson, I mean Ray, if you don't mind my asking— what brought you to this church? I mean this particular one?"

With an emotionless, blunt, down-to-earth tone, he said, "God."

"Excuse me?"

"God did." His face held a matter-of-fact look that meant it was explanation enough. "Say, would you like to come over for dinner tonight? My wife won't mind. She didn't go on the retreat this year. And now that our children are out of the house, and no grandchildren yet, she craves being around little ones."

"Oh, no. No thank you. I'm sure Nikki will be back this afternoon."

Ray gave a loud guffaw, holding his hand over his stomach as he leaned backwards and continued to laugh. "I don't think so. I've heard the young mothers of our fair women's ministry have a tendency to make sure they get home after bedtime. That way they miss one last night of putting the kids to bed before they are back on duty, so to speak." His smile did not transfer to James this time. "They're a tricky bunch."

James dropped his shoulders, and the exhaustion on his face must have shown, because Ray reached out a hand and grabbed his arm. "Now, now, she'll be back soon enough. No reason to get all queasy about it." Ray chuckled a little under his breath. "Give us a call later, and you can come on over. Really, it's no trouble."

"What's no trouble?" Mrs. Farber had sidled up to Ray and James.

Ray stepped back and raised his eyebrows with surprise. "Oh, good morning, Ruby. James and I were just ... just... talking. Well, I need to get going right now. God bless." He continued to back away, nearly falling over a toddler that held a cup of goldfish crackers. Ray's fast getaway was not lost on James.

Mrs. Farber turned her gaze on James. Her words had a sharp tinge to them. "So, is your wife around ... today?"

How does she make the most innocent question sound like an accusation?

69

"No, Mrs. Farber, she's still out of town. I need to go pick up my children from their classes right now. If you will excuse me?"

"Well, I need to speak to her as soon as possible. You need to tell her that. You won't forget, will you?"

"No, Mrs. Farber, I wouldn't dream of forgetting you." He managed to squeeze between her and the back pew. Deciding to leave the projectors on for the second service sound guy, he made his escape.

Chapter 17

Ava made the sh-h-h sound to signal for quiet. The nice woman understood. She wrapped her arm over Ava's shoulders as they lay under the bush and tried to be still. Ava was good at this. At home, she'd hide in her closet, trying not to be noticed as she listened to the screaming. If one of her mother's boyfriends found her, she would be dragged into the fight. Somehow it always turned out to be her fault.

She didn't know why. Maybe she was bad.

Under the bush she smelled dirt and pine needles. Nearby new buds of green aspen leaves gave off the fragrance of spring. At home, even in the closet, she could smell drink, smoke, and the sweet, odd scent that floated out of the funny pipes.

A sound made them both jump. Footsteps and then voices drifted over the hill.

"They stopped here. Probably tired by now."

Ava and Nikki looked into each other's eyes. Nikki's burned with hope, as if she knew something that would keep them safe. Ava could feel a spark move inside of her, too.

"Come on, Pa, they're long gone. Let's just go back. You and me, we'll go back home and be okay."

"No! This is God's plan. To have my family. It's not safe in that world. Don't you see? We saw Priscilla at that camping site for a reason. You saw how they treated her. Then God gave me your mama back, too."

"Right, because *this* life is so-o-o much better for them."

"You understand, then." A dead pause followed until the same voice said, "There are tracks leading up over that hill."

The trudging sound of them coming up the hill came nearer. Ava closed her eyes. It made her invisible when she did that.

"Shoot! With this slab of rock here, I can't read any signs." Another long pause. Footsteps sounded close to their bush. Ava

71

opened one eye and peered through the leaves. Elam squatted down and stared at the dirt.

He stood. "They must have gone back to the creek. Let's follow that and see if there are any signs farther downstream."

The sound of their footsteps faded away. Soon only the rushing waters and wind in the trees could be heard.

Nikki sat up. "We must go back the way we came. Back to the van and the road. Hurry!"

***

Fighting the terror and a fogged brain, Nikki stumbled through the icy stream with the child. With each step, she sent up a panicked prayer.

God, help. Show me. Guide us. Jesus. Father. Please, Lord. Help, us!

Then as her feet numbed in the cold water, words came to her.

The Lord your God is with you.

A tsunami size tidal wave of peace came with the words. A wash of knowledge that whatever happened, God knew about it. She would make it. That surge of trust she used to feel came flooding in.

Her prayers changed.

Thank you, Jesus. I hear you. Thank you. Bless your name.

***

Ava could tell her new friend had grown weaker. The falling, surging ahead, only to trip again happened so often, Ava worried they'd never make it.

Nikki came to a sudden, full stop. Ava shivered as the water splashed at their legs. She turned back and grabbed Ava's trembling hand. With an energy that seemed supernatural, Nikki pulled Ava out of the stream and slipped into the bushes along the bank.

"They're coming back," Nikki said.

On the other side of the shrubs lay a meadow. With no other choice, they made their way across the open field to the pines beyond.

Ava's neck and back hurt. Not just from being hit earlier, but from trying to help the grown-up woman. Nikki's hand pressed down on her shoulder for balance. Ava had to use more of her strength to hold her.

The wind picked up. Leaves and dust flew into their eyes, but they kept going.

Ava shot a quick glance back. She saw flashes of movement through the trees.

"Stop! Over here, Jake. They came out here."

Nikki and Ava stopped at the sound of the shout. Nikki grabbed Ava's wrist. They took off through the tall grass. The forest was a few yards beyond. Cover and safety.

One moment running fast. The next Nikki's hand let go and in headlong flight she dropped to the ground.

***

Nikki melted into the earth. Her legs disappeared out from under her. Like floating into the air, she fell. The landing gave no crushing blow, as if a great hand had caught her and laid her down.

She heard a rustling sound and a warm pressure leaning against her side. The child's small hands rocked Nikki's shoulder. Hearing a grunting sound and a jerking pulled, her body rolled onto her back.

Nikki saw the girl's frightened face. It faded in front of her.

A foggy cloud spun inside her head. Nikki fluttered her lids down as her eyes rolled back under them.

***

Ava hurried to Nikki. She lay limp, not moving.

She couldn't drag Nikki's body out of sight. Crouching down in the grass could only hide them for so long. The men were coming fast. For a moment, she thought about racing out across the field to keep them from Nikki.

No, running would leave Nikki helpless in the meadow.

Instead, she crawled through the tall grass into the trees. She would watch over her. Maybe she could scare them somehow or get help.

The men seemed drawn to the exact spot where her friend lay. When reaching Nikki's limp body, both stared down at her in shocked silence.

Then a shout rang out.

"Medic! Another man down! He's one of theirs." Elam knelt beside Nikki. "They must have left him behind enemy lines. See if you can get a pulse." He leaned forward. "Yes, it's strong. Thank God. His buddy must be hiding nearby."

"Buddy? What buddy? Elam, I wish you'd stay in one delusion at a time." The boy scanned the meadow as he talked.

One second Elam bent over Nikki with empathy, and the next he held up a huge gleaming knife. To Ava, the blade looked as long as her arm.

"Dude, Elam. I mean, Pa. That's new, where did that come from?"

Elam ignored him. His face turned toward the forest. Toward Ava.

"I don't know if you can understand my language or not. But if you don't come out here with your hands above your head, this man dies." Elam held the knife up and twisted the blade in the air, showing off its power. "You know I'll do it. I can't risk you going back to your troop and telling them where we are." He paused. Waiting.

Chapter 18

Walking through the fellowship room, James encountered a minefield of friendly faces. He had to stop every few feet to shake a hand or answer a loving greeting.

"How are you?" asked a woman with a vaguely familiar face.

"Fine, fine."

A man grabbed his hand and shook it. "How are you doing, really?"

"Well, really I—" Before he finished, the man was shaking another person's hand.

He crossed the room, muttering to each person. "Fine, fine. I'm just fine," until he made it out the other side and down the stairs to the classrooms.

He retrieved both of his kids, stuffed away all their belongings, and hoped nothing would get left behind. He headed out, toward the foyer to the parking lot. On the way, he noticed a cluster of people in some sort of distress. As he walked past he caught some of the conversation.

"It's them durn liberals. Always protesting something. Ought to a be a law against them. What do you think, Grace?" said a stocky man as he turned to the woman next to him.

"Well, we should call the police then. The man is on our property," Grace said in a fearful voice.

"Now, now," Pastor Thomas replied. "Let's not get all worked up. We need to send someone to the end of the driveway and check it out."

James looked out the large windows by the front door. There at the very end of the long road to the parking lot stood a man. He seemed to be holding up a poster.

"It's probably about our changeable sign out front with the pithy sayings."

"Or last week's sermon. I thought you came across a little strong on the giving time and money theme. It makes people uncomfortable."

"It was on the Good Samaritan, for Pete's sake!" grumbled the pastor.

James stopped the stroller, bent down, and pretended to fix Jonah's blanket. He wanted to know the outcome.

"I'd protest against too many of those old-fashioned hymns," offered another voice. "We should sing those contemporary, modern songs, like that one about raging fire. What is it? Oh, yeah, Pass It On."

"Okay, okay. This is getting ridiculous. Let's ask someone who came in recently." Pastor stepped up to some teenagers who had stopped at the drinking fountain. "Excuse me, but did you happen to notice what the sign says that the man out there is holding up?" he asked as he pointed out the window.

"Oh, yeah. It said he needed money. Out of work or luck or something. He was shaking and trembling, though. Could barely stand up."

Everyone paused, and then let out a quiet, simultaneous, "Oh."

"Well, we should still do something," said an indignant Grace. "It looks bad having a homeless man on our doorstep, begging."

"How about helping him?" the youngest of the teens asked.

"No, son. We might get sued for helping him the wrong way," the pastor said. "Besides, all the homeless know if they come back during the middle of the week, we have a benevolent fund."

"But what if he needs it now?"

The stocky man jumped in with his two cents. "I work hard for my money. Why shouldn't he? You know he'll use it on drugs anyway."

"That's just an excuse not to help. Like those men in that story Pastor told last week," said the youngest teen. He turned to Pastor Thomas for support.

Pastor struggled and then said, "Yes, of course, we should help, but there is a right way and a wrong way to go about this.

There's protocol and legal hassles to be aware of. I can't tell you how many times I've been conned by people church-hopping for handouts. I don't have time on a Sunday morning to—"

"That's what one of the men in the story said. No time," offered an older boy.

The pastor gave irritated sigh. "Also, it could be dangerous. He could be high and not aware of what he's doing."

"Ah, like the threat of robbers in the story." Now Grace had chimed in.

"Now listen," the stocky man said. "If we give money to this man, more will come. Before you know it, we'll have a whole stampede of homeless people at our door on Sunday mornings. We need to be prudent in our giving. Wise stewards of Gods—"

"Wait." Grace pointed outside. "Look!"

James offered, "It's Ray Carson. What's he doing?"

They watched in silence as Ray got out of his car. He ambled up to the beggar. They talked for a few moments. Ray had his hand on the man's arm. His grip steadied the wavering stance of the vagrant.

Ray took the sign from him, pulled money out of his own wallet and placed it in the other's shaking hand. Then Ray guided him to his car. They both got in and drove into the church parking lot.

The group watched in stunned silence as Ray helped the man out of the car and brought him into church. He took him past the little assembly into the pastor's office.

Ray stuck his head out the door and called, "Thomas, you coming?"

Pastor Thomas jerked out of his shock. He closed his mouth and straightened his jacket before he strode into his office.

Silence continued for a beat longer until Grace said, "Well, that takes care of that."

Without a word, the original little group walked off in different directions.

The teens looked at James, and he shrugged. As they walked off the youngest said, "What's 'Pass It On?'"

Chapter 19

Ava stood. Her weak, small arms held high and head bent down. She could not let the man hurt her friend.

The rock-hard expression of stern anger and resolve drained from Elam. Confused emotion froze on his face for a moment.

He slid the knife back into his belt sheath, dropped Jakes chain, and ran to Ava's side. He fell to his knees and caught her up in his arms. Ava pulled back but allowed the hug.

"Oh, my dear God. Oh, thank you, God. Priscilla, did they hurt you?" He released the hug to look her over, then pulled in again. "I knew we would find you again. It's us against them, isn't it? You're safe now, little one. Let's go home." He reached into the knapsack that had been slung on his shoulder and brought out the chains.

Ava saw the sad eyes of the boy who had tried to set her free. He frowned as he shook his head in disgust.

Safe? God won't keep me safe. I'll never be safe again. I've done bad things.

Elam secured Ava to a tree, mumbling as he worked. "No one leaves. Every child is safe and tight, every lock will hold the flight." Then he left with the boy.

He came back for Ava. At the van, more chains, doors locked. He left and returned with Nikki.

They were allowed to eat the rest of the food and water. While the two ate, Elam tended to Nikki.

Is he a doctor? How does he know he can help her? She needs a doctor.

Ava's body hurt, and her mind melted into mush. Back on the road, she leaned against Nikki. When sleep came, she dreamed about a hospital, and the doctor was Superman. The one from the old, old cartoons they showed on the TV. Now Nikki stood before her, whole and cleaned up. Then all she could see were her dark-colored eyes, and arched brows. That feeling of peace and strength again flowed from them and filled Ava.

***

Nikki struggled to push through pain and open her eyes. Her brain locked in a dark mist. She fought for consciousness. With a slow awareness, she realized that her body was slumped on a vinyl-covered bench seat. Her cheek pressed against a window, a child asleep beside her.

Back in the van? In anguish, her brain blurted a swear word into her thoughts. It came so hard and fast she physically jerked.

Disappointment weighed like a rock on her chest. Fear welled up, but a familiar soothing rush of peace pushed it back.

Words flowed into her mind.

The Lord your God is with you, He is mighty who saves.

The strength she used to feel from God's presence now hovered close. It had not taken long for her heart to turn to her source of strength. The crisis brought her right back to His side.

She rested her head back and began a praying stream of communion that had no real words. Whole thoughts, feelings, responses sent by the Holy Spirit that allowed God access to her soul.

It used to be like this all the time. Where had it gone? Lost with adulthood? A mother too busy to pause for God. His presence melting fears and shoring up shattered confidence.

She sat in relaxed peace, as the sound of the motor rumbled, and the turning of the wheels rocked the van.

Don't give up. Remember Conner, Jonah, and James. Dear God, get me back to them.

With her clearer mind, she tried to use every opportunity to figure out where they were. Peering under the black shades or ducking her head to see out the front window she searched for clues. The van rolled through small towns, past hills with occasional cabins tucked in the trees. But occasionally she caught glimpses of a sign from a grocer, or a fish and bait store. Not knowing how far they had traveled while she was sleeping made it difficult to place where they were. All she could gather was they were heading north.

Elam's voice cut into Ava's sleep. "Wake up, Priscilla. Lunch." The car had stopped. The smell of hamburgers and fries greeted her as she sat up.

Ava turned to check on Nikki before she even accepted the food being offered to her. Nikki looked down at her with a slight smile.

"Hey, there. I'm feeling better. Still weak, but better."

Nikki took the burger bag from Elam, brought out the food, and handed it to Ava. "Here, we'd better eat."

Elam beamed a huge smile. "That's right, Honey. Listen to your Mama, now." He turned back to the wheel, started the engine, and the van heaved forward onto the road.

Ava settled back in her seat. A vision of her favorite TV family flashed in her mind. The dad getting fast food with the mom telling them to eat. The son is maybe listening to music from his phone in the backseat.

Nikki stared deep into Ava's eyes and whispered. "Priscilla, we'll get another chance. Be strong and courageous for the Lord your God is with you."

What happened? Miss Nikki, how can you be so calm? She must think I'm good enough for God.

Ava tried to see out the window. No, the shades still blocked the view. A stoplight ahead, with cars passing, proved to her they were in a town. But where? What town? Could she see a sign or a road marker?

Peering up, Ava watched her friend eating with calm bites. But her arm shook, and her face winced with each move.

The afternoon passed, dragging like the last lesson before recess. Dinner time came, Ava knew because her stomach told her. But Elam gave no signs of stopping. She had to go to the bathroom but didn't know how to ask. Talking was not an option.

Soon only the lights from the dashboard and the two beams that lit the road gave any brightness.

Relief came after a few miles. Elam stopped in the middle of the dark, empty road. "Bathroom, anyone?" He barked out. "I've gotta go."

Everyone had a turn walking off the side of the road. When it came to Ava, she rushed out as soon as the chains came off. Elam grabbed her arm. "No monkey business. Don't wander off. There are bears out there, you know."

At the thought of bears, she nearly took care of her business on the spot. Instead, she gathered her courage and scrambled into the bushes.

The deed done, the blackness that surrounded her became like a smothering wall. Throwing her hands out in front of her, she crouched, touching the rocks and grasses that covered the ground. She crawled her way until the lights from the car guided her back.

Elam slept for a while, right there in the driver's seat, with the van parked on the road. They all slept.

In the middle of the night, Ava woke when Elam started the engine and drove on. The twisting turns of the road as they traveled higher and higher rocked her back to sleep.

***

Nikki dozed in between fitful waking jolts after Elam drove off again. Finally, after miles of bumping and bouncing, a sudden stop jerked her fully awake.

"Rise and shine, and give God the glory, glory," Elam sang at the top of his lungs. "Hey, everyone, we're home. Rise and shine, and—" he clapped, "—give God the glory, glory, children of the Lord!"

Nikki and Ava made slow moves to sit up and peer out the front windshield. Ahead, Nikki could see a gate with a wall extending from it on both sides. In the early light, the barrier, bumpy and jumbled with stuff, seemed created from another world.

Elam stopped the van and got out to open the gate. It rattled and groaned, sounding alive. He climbed back in his seat, drove ahead, and got out again to close the opening. This took a while for him to relock all the chains that held the gate closed.

Nikki tried to decipher what she was seeing. A long stretch of mish-moshed hodgepodge of junk formed the high wall. Hand painted signs of "Keep Out" with warnings of being "shot first, questioned later" wove into the structure. As if someone had tried

81

to build something sensible from whatever piece of trash they could find.

***

Junk!

Ava gaped at the fence that bulged with old pieces of wood, doors, and rocks. She could even see the shape of a bathtub crammed in on one side, intermingled with barbed wire.

Elam drove on a way, over a twisted and rough driveway. But instead of a house, he stopped at a camp-like area. He got out and went to the back to take off everyone's chains.

Stiff and sore, Ava climbed out of the van. She gazed out at the strange place and rubbed her sleepy eyes.

Canvas tarps, ropes, and blankets stretched above areas giving shelter, over places to sit. Like that game show where people live on an island. But here she saw no palm branches or sandy beaches, only hilly mounds of disgusting garbage.

Ava took a deep breath. Instead of fresh pine, a rotten stink filled her nose. She coughed and rubbed her face. Her stomach turned with the awful, sour smell.

***

Nikki gingerly climbed from the van and put a hand to her head to keep it from swimming.

"Here we are, family! Just like home." Elam smiled as he now hummed his song.

More like a refugee camp with no people. A short rock wall surrounded a large fire pit. Scattered around was a small collection of debris shelters nestled on the ground. Off to one side a shallow runoff stream dribbled through the camp.

She had seen these before in Colorado. People made them by shoving a long log at an angle against a standing tree and arranging sticks along it. Debris of branches, grass and whatever covered the sticks. They looked like little huts, or leafy pup tents.

Giant blue-tinged evergreen trees, stood at attention along the mountainside. The solemn towers swayed in the wind and sent a whispered roar across the camp.

Ava shivered. Tucked against the mountainside she saw one small building. Part built like a house, and part crammed together with a bunch of old stuff.

He must be a junk man. He collects junk. Is that why he took me?

The camp sat beside the shack, and water from a stream could be heard nearby. The pines stretched above them, making Ava feel like a ladybug in a field of buffalo grass. Another chill rippled over Ava's skin. She touched her shorts. Worry must have shown on her face. Jake came by with a blanket and wrapped it around her.

"We'll have to figure out something warmer for you to wear. It's not winter, but nights get cold. Mornings, too. I'll start a fire." He went about doing this with an everyday calmness. He looked at home.

But Ava was not home.

***

Elam helped Nikki across the camp toward the cabin. Even this had been stitched together with random materials.

He unlocked the door. Stepping inside the one room shack, Nikki gasped at the piles of boxes and newspapers that filled every corner. The cramped room held an old metal bed on the left wall, a small wood stove to the right. The farthest wall was the actual mountainside.

A pile of greasy car parts and plastic containers towered along one side. As her eyes adjusted more to the dimness, she saw rope ladders hanging on the back wall. Her eyes followed them up to little cubbies that had been dug into the dirt. Old newspapers were jammed inside some. Others were stuffed with old clothes or garbage. One or two held folded blankets and pillows.

A damp, earthy smell from the dirt wall mixed with a smoky odor. The ever-present stink of rotting garbage hung in the air, so strong it made her tongue twinge. Elam smacked the dust off a dilapidated queen size bed covered in threadbare quilts. The metal springs twanged as he helped her lie down.

Elam yelled out the door, "Jake! Bring in some hot rocks out of the fire after you get it going, and some burning coals for the stove." Then he spoke to Nikki. "There ya go, Mama. You need to rest."

Nikki kicked off her shoes and slipped under the covers. Moments later, the little girl shuffled inside. She had a red and turquoise southwestern blanket wrapped around her. Her wide eyes took in every detail of the darkened room. When she saw Nikki, she scurried over to her, climbed up on the bed and then curled up next to her.

Nikki, glad to be able to comfort the child, wrapped her arm around the little waif, all the while wishing she held her own sons.

Chapter 20

Naptime. Ahhh. Blessed naptime.

James rolled over in bed. A sudden sharp pain stabbed his back. Conner's little foot jabbed his dad in the spine with the force of a pile driver.

I s'pose this is why Nikki makes them take their naps in their own beds.

James still had Conner's high-pitched whine grinding inside his head.

"No nap, Daddy, it's Sunday."

"No nap, Daddy, Mommy's not here."

Conner hit all the usual excuses— scared, thirsty, and the all-inclusive, "I don wanna."

Because James wanted some rest, too, having Conner in bed with him seemed like a good idea at the time. James could hear Jonah snoring with a loud satisfying rumble in the other room.

Well, at least they're asleep.

After supper—delivery of course—the boys wrestled with him on the living room floor. When the tumbling and tiger growls subsided, they lay exhausted and gasping for breath. With the boys still giggling, worry for Nikki crept into his joy.

Ray said the ladies liked to wait until after their children's bedtime to come home. But would Nikki do that too?

She knows I need her to come home as soon as she can. Doesn't she?

The evening stretched on, and the worry slipped into anger, and then to fear. After he put the boys to bed, went back to the living room and stared out the front window.

Come on, Nikki. Come around the turn. Come to me, Babe.

But no. No Nikki came cruising down the street.

What time is it?

He glanced at the clock. Eight. Not really knowing where this camp was located made him wonder how long a drive it should be. If he remembered right when he set the GPS, he'd thought she'd be there in about three hours. But what if this camp kept them long, for a service or something?

He took out his laptop, sat down to pull some work email, and stared at the screen. He clicked on the TV, but didn't hear the words. Memories of his short temper plagued his mind. His impatience. His needing things to line up in a row. The financial burden they were under had made him explode over simple things.

She knows I love her, right? Did I remember to tell her that when she left? Lord, please get her home safe. I need her so much.

Thoughts of "If only..." began to fill his mind.

If only she had her phone. If only I knew where the camp was. If only I hadn't let her go. If only I hadn't caused her to need to go. If only...

Chapter 21

James woke with a jerk of fright. He blinked at the sun coming through the picture window. When his brain kicked in, he ran to his bedroom to see if Nikki had come home.

Empty.

He checked the garage. The sight of the vacant side stabbed at his heart. He searched the entire house. Frantic and desperate, he tried Nikki's cell phone. Even though he knew she'd lost it. It went directly to her recorded message.

After listening to her sweet voice, he cried into the phone. "Where are you, Babe? Please call me. Please, please!"

He resisted the urge to call again just to listen to her recorded voice.

Then he called the pastor of their church. This set off a chain of calls to the homes of the women who had attended the retreat.

Nothing.

No one had heard, or seen, Nikki that weekend.

He took in a huge breath of air, straightened his back, and forced himself to think with a calm mind.

"Okay." He whispered to himself. "Time to call the police."

Nikki's parents were in Indonesia. He'd wait to call them. In case this was all a terrible mistake.

But he contacted his own mom and dad.

They rushed over. His mom got the boys out of bed and dressed. She promised to keep them occupied in their rooms while his dad gave James support when the authorities came.

James opened the door for the men in uniform. He could see Mrs. Farber's peering at them from off her front porch. He didn't care. He could only think about Nikki.

The two officers strode into the house, made a visual sweep of the living room, and sat down on the offered chairs.

The tall man with a mustache did the talking. The other officer seemed like a teenager.

James and his dad sat together on the sofa. Pop held a hand on James back, for support.

Ramrod straight, James forced his mind to concentrate on what was being said.

"These things usually end up as a miscommunication." Officer Matsko voice had a comforting deep, rich tone. "But we'll need some details about her. Do you have a recent picture?"

James thought. Picture? His face must have looked blank.

A picture of Nikki, of course.

"Of course. I mean, sure, I can find one." He pulled himself up.

"You don't have to get it right now. Let's get the details down first."

As he rattled off a list of questions, the rookie, Officer Vale, wrote everything down. Height, weight, hair color and other details.

"When was the last time you saw your wife, Mr. Rolen?"

Before he could answer, the doorbell rang, and James shot up to answer it.

A trim, dark-haired man with a concerned expression peered through the screen door at James.

"Pastor Thomas, thank you for coming." James opened the screen and lowered his voice. "The police are here."

"I was worried about Nikki. Perhaps I could be moral support."

"Yes, yes, come in. Maybe you can help." James brought the pastor into the living room, introduced him, and sat back down. He wanted to get help for Nikki as fast as possible.

"When was the last time you saw her?" asked Officer Matsko.

"Friday morning,"

Officer Vale looked up from his pad.

Matsko lifted an eyebrow and pulled his head back to gaze squarely at James. "You haven't seen her since Friday? Why didn't you call sooner?"

"I didn't know anything was wrong. Nikki left to go on a woman's retreat up at a camp in the mountains. I thought that's where she was. But when she didn't come home Sunday night, I called around and no one had seen her there. They said she never arrived."

"This was last Friday? Didn't anyone at the camp contact you when she didn't arrive safely?"

The pastor spoke up. "No one knew she was coming."

Everyone turned to him, and he spoke again. "No, really, our people had no idea she would be there. We definitely would have let someone know."

Then all eyes turned to James.

"It was a ... a last-minute thing. She didn't think I would ... ah ... could take care of the boys while she was gone. But I could."

Why am I stammering?

"I see." Officer Vale wrote more on the tiny pad. "She didn't let anyone know? Not her friends or the camp?"

James stared ahead, remembering his surprise when Nikki told him her plan the day she left.

Pop spoke up. "My son is fairly new at this church. They don't have many close friends there yet." He gave James a push on his back. "Isn't that right, James?"

"Oh, yes, that's right. Nikki was hoping she could make friends on this trip."

Pastor Thomas jumped in. "We have a very friendly church. Was there really no one you could connect with?"

James turned and stared at him.

Does he think he's helping?

"Does she have a cell phone?" Matsko asked.

"Yes."

"Did you try calling her?"

"I tried this morning, just before I called you."

"You didn't call before that?"

James took in a deep breath. "No, she couldn't find her phone before she left. We looked but..."

"Wouldn't she have called when she arrived at the camp?"

89

"Not Nikki. If there was no cell coverage, she wouldn't think to find a land phone. She said no news would be...you know...good news."

It all sounded so lame, saying it out loud.

"I see." A long pause stretched out as Vale wrote an extensive note. "Did anyone see your wife leave for the camp?"

"Well, the boys were with me, of course."

"How old are your boys?"

"They're two and three years old."

The two officers looked at each other.

"Oh, wait. Mrs. Farber, our neighbor. She probably saw Nikki leave. She lives right next door." He pointed out the window at the blue house.

"Do you have her phone number as well?" said Vale.

"No, I mean, wait, I s'spose Nikki does, in her phone, but..."

"She lost her phone." Matsko finished his sentence. "Funny how dependent we are on those cell phones nowadays. Don't worry, we have ways of tracking phones down. And we'll talk with Mrs. Farber in person."

They seemed to be wrapping things up. James supplied the description of Nikki's car and the license plate before they stood to go. He found a few pictures of her in a scrapbooking mess from an album she'd been putting together.

Photos, stencil letters, and scrapbook paper littered the dining room table. He realized most of the pictures were of him and the boys. Nikki was the photographer in the family. He brought the pictures up on his computer and ripped it onto a flash drive to give to the officers.

"We'll notify hospitals and run down a few things. If nothing turns up quickly, we may need to put this out on the news media. The photos will be important." They stood to go. Pastor Thomas followed their lead. "Call us if you think of anything else, and we'll be in touch with you."

James wanted them to run out to their car, speed off, search the mountain, and bring her back. Right now! "Is there anything I should be doing?"

Matsko shifted his weight to his other leg, cocked his head toward James and spoke with a calming voice. "Stay by your phone. She could just be lost and searching for a way to call you." He smiled under his mustache. "Go ahead and continue to check around. Someone may have seen her. Give me her cell phone number. Like I said, we might be able to track her down through that if she lost it in her car."

James told Officer Vale Nikki's number. He wrote it down. James shook their hands, thanked them, and saw them out.

Pastor Thomas hung back. "Would you like for me to pray with you before I go?" the pastor offered.

James turned to his father. He nodded his agreement. James searched the preacher's eyes for comfort. "Yes."

They stood by the doorway, held hands, and bowed their heads.

"Heavenly Father, please bring Nikki home."

Yes, God, please. Where could she be? Why did I let her go without a cell?

"...because you know what's best, Heavenly Father. Guide her through whatever difficulty is preventing her from getting here. Almighty God..."

What did he say? Oh, yes, bring her back, Almighty God. Home, she needs to be home. I don't even know what to feed everyone tonight. Is there a handbook on what to do next?

"Give someone, anyone, Heavenly Father, even a child, courage to pick up a phone to speak hope and mercy to this loving husband and ..."

The police said I may need to go to the media to ask for help. Would I look like those poor grief-stricken souls I've seen on TV? Or the lying ones?

"Don't allow Satan and the evils in the world to keep her from a safe return. In Jesus' name, amen."

James's dad spoke, "Thank you, Pastor. We'll be in touch with you."

Back in the living room, James collapsed into the recliner. His mom came in with the boys. Conner ran up to his daddy and climbed into his lap.

91

James glanced up at his mom. "Can you and Dad watch the boys for a while?"

"Of course, son. You should try to get some rest. Dad and I will be here." His mother's lip quivered, worry pouring out of her eyes.

"I can't rest."

Conner whispered into James's neck. "Daddy, when is Mommy coming home?"

"Soon, Conner." He gazed down at Jonah leaning at his knee. "Soon, boys. Daddy is going to find Mommy. Right now. You stay here with Grandma and Grandpa." He looked up at his parents.

His mother immediately swooped down to lift Jonah and take Conner's hand. "That's right, boys. You can come bake cookies with Grandma this morning. You can share them with Mommy ... when she comes home."

Chapter 22

Nikki had fallen asleep immediately with Priscilla snuggled beside her on the bed. When she woke up, only Elam loomed above her, rousing her to take some pills.

The child? Gone.

Glancing outside, she noticed the reddish glow of dusk. Had she slept the whole day away? She probably needed the sleep, or was it the pills that put her out?

She touched her head. The bandage had been changed again.

"It's most suppertime, Mama. Don't worry, I won't make you cook tonight." From one of the cubbies in the dirt wall, he took out some cans of Dinty's stew. "Jake can slop this in a pot for us and cook it over the fire. We'll just pray over it extra hard."

Jake walked in, and Elam threw the cans to him. Without a flinch, Jake snatched them from the air.

Elam chirped. "Cook these up, son."

Nikki could almost smell the stew already, she was so hungry. She hoisted herself up to set her feet on the floor. The cold wood made her pull her toes up.

The bed is so warm.

"Where's Priscilla?" she asked.

"By the fire." Jake grabbed an iron pot and a can opener from a wooden crate on the floor and walked back out the door.

She saw two lumps under the covers at the foot of the bed. Pulling the blanket back, she discovered the source of the heat. A towel wrapped around a large heated stone. Jake must have brought them in.

Elam, his back to her, had lost himself in counting the cans. He kept starting over and touching each can as he counted.

Nikki felt an urgent need rise within her.

"Elam? I ... I have to go to the bathroom."

93

"Twenty-nine," touch, "thirty," touch, "thirty-one," touch. "Elam!"

"Thirty-one." He didn't turn to look at her, but stopped to point off to one side. "There are thirty-one stones on the path, at the back, to the place of relief. Begin again." He moved his finger back to the start of the row of cans. "One," touch, "two," touch.

Nikki hoped those were instructions for her need.

She wrapped the blanket around her and slipped on her shoes. At first, she couldn't stand. She sat down again to wait for the dizzy, swirling room to settle. Then stiff with pain and aching muscles, she stepped out of the door.

Standing by the cabin, she could see the child staring into the fire while Jake concentrated on opening cans. Smoke from the campfire caught in the low-hanging branches. The white-gray ash hung in the trees like a hovering ghost. Spots of new green sprinkled in the twigs. Water's rippling sounds intertwined with calls of evening birds and snaps from the fire.

She made her way to the right around to the back of the cabin. Here, where the wall merged with the mountain, a stone path led off to the right. Too sore and too tired to count the flat rocks, she assumed it would, indeed, be thirty-one.

Branches of pine and aspen arched over the path, making it feel like a secret tunnel. At the end, a stone-like throne sat over a small black hole. Low bushes and foliage nestled around the structure's sides and back.

Not happy with how open the facilities were, she laid her blanket across a nearby bush. At first whiff, she held her breath.

Where does the hole lead? How deep is it? No, don't think. Get it done.

After using leaves for cleaning and a hand rinse in the small creek, she moved fast to get back to the fire pit. Priscilla's face beamed when she saw her coming toward them. Nikki settled beside her.

The three sat like stunned refugees after a war, staring into the fire.

Nikki spoke, "Jake? Is he your father?"

94

The boy snorted and laughed. "That bastard? Of course not. My name isn't even Jake."

"What is it?"

"Chance, but you'd better call me Jake. He wouldn't like it if you didn't. Heck, I've started calling myself Jake."

Both sat in silence until Jake peered into the pot and said, "Done."

Elam could be heard shouting even louder in a military cadence. Nikki smelled the hot meat, and vegetables bubbling in the broth. Canned food or not, it made her mouth water.

"I'll break The Count over there out of his number madness," Jake said. "He'll go ballistic if we eat before everyone's blessed the food." He got up to go.

"Jake, wait. We can escape, again, right? Tonight, while he's sleeping."

Jake turned his dead eyes back to Nikki. "No."

"What? Why?"

"Lady, you wouldn't get two feet."

"Okay, maybe not tonight. But when I'm better?"

Priscilla crept her hand into Nikki's and looked at Jake.

He shot back, "Do you know how to get down the mountain? Because I sure don't."

"Why not follow the road? Or a stream?"

With a flat hopeless tone, he said, "Because he would kill us. I don't mean like, my dad will kill me if I get caught. I mean he will murder us."

She saw the fear in his face.

He tried to hide the tremble of his lip with his hand. "He's said he'd chop me into pieces, stuff me in a bag, and toss the bag over a cliff." He leaned toward them. "And I believe him."

Priscilla squeezed Nikki's hand and made a whimper sound.

Fierce emotion strained his expression and he pointed at the gate. "Besides, it's a maze out there. He took me hunting. The road twists and turns." He showed the twists, snaking his arms and hands in the air. "It goes up and down the mountainside, connects with others that vanish. The stream disappears underground. Got separated from him once. I was so lost. Thought I'd never see anyone ever again. I was stinkin' glad he found me."

"But together we can do it. He's just an old man."

"Just a— Look, lady, you *do not* know what you're talking about. I tried to warn you. Why couldn't you have just gotten away?"

Despite this spark of anger, his body language, crumpled and defeated, revealed his complete acceptance of what he could not change. "Get used to it, breezy. This is home now."

The cabin door slammed open. "Need to check the walls. Be back." Elam had an animal skin draped over his shoulders and a long walking stick in one hand.

"But ... supper?" Jake threw his hands up in exasperation.

"Back soon."

At Elam's retreating figure, the boy mumbled, "Right, what does that mean? Could be seconds, could be weeks." He turned back at the girls. "He can't eat until we've blessed it. And now he's going out to find imaginary bad guys that put holes in his blasted walls? Are you kidding me?" He spat on the ground. "Sometimes he takes the van and comes back with more junk. Uses it to make the wall stronger. Bigger. More threatening. He's nuts."

Walking back to the fire, he sat down and picked up a chunk of wood. He held on to one end and bounced the other against the wall that surrounded the fire. He gripped the log with both hands. The wood sprayed out splinters as he smacked on the stones.

"Jake," Nikki said. "How did he get you?"

He continued to whack at the stone. "Stupid, I guess."

Instinct told Nikki to wait for him to form more words. In the silence, Priscilla tugged on her hand and pointed to the boiling stew. Nikki smiled at her and held her finger up as a sign to wait.

Jake stopped pounding the wood and stared into the forest. "How far back should I go? Well, my mom died when I was little. I stayed with my dad for a while. He couldn't handle a kid. Foster homes after that. A lot of them, actually. The last one I ran away from."

"Were they abusive?"

"Yeah, I thought so. I thought *they* were crazy Christians. Always heading up protests about something or other, and making me go to their church. Can you believe I ran from them, because they were too strict? Brother!"

"How long has it been?"

"What month is it?"

"April. Almost May."

"It's been about—" He rubbed his hand over his chin, "—six months, give or take."

"How did Elam find you?"

"Laying on a piece of cardboard in an alley. I'd gotten wasted that night. Woke up with a killer hangover and a side order of puke next to me. So anyway, I just left with him. Stupid! But he isn't always whacked-out mean. He goes in and out. Maybe it's better here in some ways." He cradled the wood in his fingers. "Not having any cigs was the hardest to deal with. Wow, is that ever a cruel way to quit." He turned the log, inspecting the bark. "But, apparently, I won't be going to hell."

"What do you mean?"

"That last family had me pray the ... what was it? Oh, yeah, the sinner's prayer. If you answer these four questions correctly, and pray, God somehow keeps you out of hell. Then they didn't have to care about me anymore. Now I was fixed. I ticked that box off, I guess."

In the same tone, he might use if he'd stepped in mud, he said, "Christians!"

Nikki jumped, startled at the anger in his voice.

"They're all the same. They think they're so smart. So perfect. They want to force everyone else to believe what they do, about everything."

"We're not perfect. Believe me," Nikki said with a soft laugh, almost to herself.

Jake narrowed his eyes and raised his chin as he glared at her with a hard stare. Words blasted out his mouth. "God Bless America! You're one of them, aren't you? You're one of those flippin', Bible-thumping, know-it-all Christians." Anger seethed in his face as he sat up straighter. "Of course! I should have seen it

97

coming. You probably thought Elam was gay, or something, and had to stick your nose into his business. Well now, how'd that work out for you?"

He slammed the piece of wood into the fire and let out a swear word that cracked into the night. The flames billowed up with a heated splash, and Jake stomped off.

Nikki stared after him.

"Okay, then." She sighed, paused, and then gazed down into Priscilla's frightened eyes. "One scared follower of Christ, one angry teen." She leaned in and stroked her hand under the child's chin. "One sweet, silent child ... and one old man, crazy as a June bug. This should be interesting."

The bushes behind them snapped, and Elam came striding out of the forest. His face grim, his arms pumping with movement as he stormed past the fire. He went directly down the path Chance had taken when he left.

Fear made a tight fist in Nikki's chest. Moments later Elam charged back, half-pushing, half-dragging the struggling youth to the campfire. Jake's face was bloody and his shirt torn. He threw the teen at Nikki's feet, knelt, and screamed into the boy's face.

The little girl threw herself into Nikki's lap and clutched her neck.

"Apologize! You apologize right now. You cannot talk to your mother that way! You say you're sorry for raising your voice to this holy woman, or I will tear your smug face off. I'll rip your eyes out and feed them to the rats." He ground the boy's face into the dirt, then pulled his head up by his hair.

Through his bloody mouth, the boy could only whisper. "I'm ... suh ... sorry."

Nikki wanted to pull them apart and protect the hurting boy. But she knew that would only make it worse. "It's okay! Elam, I accept. I'm fine."

Elam looked at Nikki. His eyes always appeared as if they saw something different than what was really there.

Who does he see?

He lessened his grip on Jake and let him fall in the dust. The old man knelt beside him. "God will judge!" he roared.

Then pulling in sobs between phrases he rambled on. His words picked up speed as he spat out his sermon, fist raised. "Honor! Honor mothers and fathers. The world creeps in ... and contaminates the minds of young people ... If I don't keep watch, the corrupt, defiled world will erode and rot God's great goodness. We cannot put them on the frontlines of the battle against Satan's army. Protect the weak and blind and burned and ... dead."

He stopped and sucked in air. Then with quaking hands, the distraught man reached down and wrapped his arm under the teen's chest, and pulled him up until the boy's head rested face down in the crook of his arm. Wet streams of fear washed down the old man's craggy face. Tears of pain smeared with blood moved down Jake's.

Elam patted the teen's head with gentle strokes. His aim slipped to the boy's back, and the strokes came down as blows. He hit harder and harder until his hands closed to fists. The thuds of the beating made Nikki cringe, and the girl hid her face in her hands.

Nikki set Priscilla aside and caught Elam's arm with both hands. "Stop!"

Elam froze and stared at Nikki as if he'd just then noticed her.

She whispered, "Please, stop."

With a slow turn, Elam rested his gaze on the crumpled body in his arms. "What have they done to you? Oh, dear God, what did they do? Did they ambush you in the forest?" He transferred the boy into Nikki's arms, "Please, take him." He swiped a dirty sleeve at his tears, made a long drawn out sniff, and said, "Supper smells done. Let's eat."

***

After dinner, no one but Elam spoke a word. Afraid even to look up, Nikki stared at the ground. Fear trembled like a live current through her body.

Elam began reading aloud, randomly, through the Bible. The words scrambled at times as he added his own thoughts. The three captives forced to kneel in the dirt. Back aching and head swimming, Nikki heard what she needed to hear.

"The Lord your God is with you, He is mighty to save..."
Her mind snatched the phrase. Elam hurried on to another passage, and his voice boomed into the night.

Chapter 23

James gripped the wheel. His eyes ached from searching the sides of the road. Swallowing back burning bile, he continued to pray.

God, I've never come to you with so great a need. Let me see that blue SUV, with the bent antenna. Where could she possibly be? Oh, God. Jesus. The boys need her so. I need her.

Moving at a slow, methodical speed, he made quick stops and swerved at even a glimpse of blue through the trees. Drivers behind him honked with obvious frustration, often giving him the angry finger.

His mind shifted into self-recrimination.

I couldn't protect her, could I? I couldn't even provide for her, not in the way she deserved.

He came to a construction detour past Woodland Park. He followed the detour signs around until he came back to the road. After a moment, he pulled over.

Could she have gotten confused here? Should I go back and look?

He followed the detours. He also went down some of the side roads, just in case.

Nothing.

His phone rang.

"Mr. Rolen? This is Officer Matsko. We think we've found your wife's car."

"Her car? Really? Wonderful. Is she, all right?" James yanked the wheel and pulled to the side of the road.

"Actually, we found her vehicle. Not your wife."

After a pause to let the words sink in, James said, "What?"

"I'm sorry. Your wife wasn't in the car. Where are you? Are you at home? We'll send an officer out to your house."

"No, I'm ... well, I'm just past Woodland Park."

"Woodland Park?" Another pause came before the officer spoke again. "What are you doing there?"

He couldn't help letting his words express his anger and frustration. "Looking for my wife."

"That's ... interesting. You're only a few miles away from us. Take the road back into Woodland Park and then toward Rampart Range until you see us."

Oh, God, God, God.

"Be right there." He threw the phone onto the passenger seat, pressed the gas, and surged forward. Tears dribbled down his tense cheeks.

When he saw the police vehicles, he tightened all his muscles and made his mind focus. He didn't slow, but continued to speed down the gravel road. He slammed on the brakes in front of the activity.

He jumped out and ran to the side of the road. An officer caught his arm.

"Wait. Sir? You can't go down there."

"My wife, that's my wife's car. Please, I need to get to her."

The officer's foot slid down the hill, and James wriggled away.

"Sir, sir! Come back!"

James ran down the slope and hooked an arm around a thin tree trunk to slow his descent. At the sight of the flattened Explorer, the crumpled bent metal, shards of glass everywhere, he stopped dead. A moment later, he ran to the driver's door. Again, arms held him back.

Deep, calming, but with authority, the voice finally reached James's numb brain. "Mr. Rolen, James, you can't touch anything. Stop, talk to me. James!"

Officer Matsko pulled him back. "Is this your wife's? We've already checked it out." He grabbed James's shoulders and turned him around. "Listen to me. She's not there."

"Where is she?"

"We don't know. And unfortunately, the good Samaritans that stopped to help have contaminated the scene. They even drove their cars over the tire tracks. Your wife may have wandered away to try to get help. But there's no luggage or purse in the car."

Wandered away?

"We need to search the woods." James shouted. "Nikki!! Nikki!!"

"Sir, we're getting a search party together right now. The Colorado Search and Rescue Team have been notified. A child has also been missing in this area since Friday night."

"Are they connected?"

"We don't know. I know this is difficult, but I need you to calm down. We'll want you to come over to the station so we can ask you questions."

"Questions?" James shook his head to force himself to think clearly.

Matsko tugged on James to set him in motion back up the slope and followed him. "Be thinking about anyone who may have a grudge against your wife. Also, we'll need a rundown of the people you've seen and things you've done in the past few days."

"Of course, anything. Anything!"

At the top, Matsko helped James to lean on the hood of the car. "I'll have an officer take you home. We can return your car to you later. I don't want you to drive right now." He glanced at the front of the car. "Did you have an accident?"

"Me?"

The officer pointed to the front crumpled bumper.

"Oh, no. That was Nikki."

Matsko paused in thought, then put both of his hands on James's shoulders and squeezed tight. "Listen, you're going to go through hell on earth until she's found. You have to find strength from somewhere. Your kids need you. Your wife needs you to be strong."

More than a pep talk to James, the words burned like a hot brand scorching his heart.

He was her husband.

He'd take the burden.

He must bring her home.

Chapter 24

Nikki's legs throbbed from kneeling so long. Elam's droning of scripture wound down and he abruptly left. She didn't move until she was sure he'd gone.

She limped back to the cabin with Priscilla. Nikki scrounged through her overnight bag before bed to find warm clothes for her and Priscilla. She laid out one of her sweatshirt hoodies. This could make a dress-like top for the girl during the day, and long winter socks would keep her legs warm all the way up under the shorts. She found a Rockies t-shirt for the little one to sleep in.

"Good-night, ladies," Elam called into the room. "I'll lock you both in, tight, to keep you safe. All that praying will keep away evil. You'll never be hurt again." He picked up the chains and locks and carried them to the door. "Jake and I will take the shelters by the fire. Keep the flames at bay, so to speak. Don't fret now, Mama. You and I will be back in the same bed again, when we get back home. Good-night."

A chill ran over Nikki's body. She cringed at the thought of sharing the same bed with this maniac.

Get back home? What did he mean by that?

***

Days passed. The continuous dread of more violence hovered inside Nikki's mind. It astounded her how fast Elam crossed from calm to seeing monsters lurking behind every leaf.

Jake often stepped up to take the brunt of the insanity. He kept the focus off the little girl, who somehow knew how to avoid attention. She scurried under the radar as much as she could.

Aside from the insistence on rapt attention to his rambling prayers, and listening for hours on end to the Bible, Elam did nothing abusive to Nikki.

Today, Elam left early to check the wall for breaks. Jake served lunch from the canned food selection and everyone settled in for the long afternoon.

Boredom ruled inside the unlocked cabin. Unlocked, but no one was free.

Nikki stretched out on the rickety bed. She touched her head and realized the pain had lessened. Her mind was clearer now, but not enough to plan an escape.

Next time, Lord, we need to be ready. If I can get anyone to muster courage to make an escape, that is. If I can figure a safe way out. If I can...

She sighed. Her fellow inmates stared off into space with vacant, discouraged expressions. Jake leaned his chair back on two legs while his feet rested on a stack of papers, His arms crossed over his chest. Priscilla tucked inside a blanket lined cubby, asleep.

A worried chill and a deep darkness fell over her as she closed her eyes and dropped off to sleep.

Nikki woke with a snap and a burst of agitated energy. With a churning unrest, she couldn't lie still. She got up and futzed around at the mess in the cabin. She grabbed a scrunched-up garbage bag and filled it with moldy pieces of food and filth.

Jake watched her as she straightened stacks of books and threw piles of junk out the door. Dust billowed like storm clouds.

Jake coughed with pronounced irritation.

She reached above Jake into a cubby and pulled on a pile of yellowed newspapers. They cascaded onto Jake's head.

He yelled in disgust. "What are you doing? Why are you cleaning?"

"I might as well make things nice. And I can't sit still."

"Really? You think you can make *this* place nice?"

She pulled blankets from one of the storage cubbies, took them outside and smacked out the dust. Bringing them back in, she covered a bulging cardboard box with a tattered yellow blanket. She stacked a wooden box on top of a car battery and covered both with a piece of plywood. Then she spread a bright patched quilt over them to create a table.

"You know, he'll notice that. You can't know how he'll react," Jake said.

105

She hadn't thought of that. "Well, when he left, he said take care of the place."

"That's not what he meant."

She knew that. But she continued to straighten and clean. Something inside drove her to fix the mess. She even found a bucket and some soap to wash the one window in the old shack. At the end, she let out a satisfied sigh.

That's much better. It helps, right? Doesn't it help? At least, it smells better.

She glanced out the open door. Heaps of trash, which Elam refused get rid of, towered like monuments to her hopelessness. Fire still crackled in the pit at the center of the compound.

Have I changed anything? Really?

She pulled in a ragged breath and looked around the cabin.

Jake continued to stare out the window. His lip swollen and cheek bruised purple. Chains and locks lay in a heap on the floor. Ready for Elam to slap back on in a moment's irrational thought.

Reality sunk in as grief and fear cascaded over her.

No, nothing has changed. We're still here. In this wretched place. My children have no mother, and I'm still trapped.

She almost collapsed to the floor under the weight of hopelessness. She dropped the dust cloth on the small table and rallied strength to step outside. Making her way to the water that trickled from off the mountain slope, she slid to the ground against the trunk of a tree. Tears pooled in her eyes.

"Oh God," she confessed, "what can I do? I can't make this better. Lord, I can't fix this."

I take great delight in you.

"But, God, I failed. I came to save the child, and now I'm caught, too. My family stripped of their mother, because I messed up!"

I will quiet you with my love.

She slumped forward, and tense muscles relaxed. The storm of fear began to subside. The memory of a toddler's tight hug and a sweet baby smooch flooded her heart. "Help my family to feel you, too, Father. My children, oh, please, give them calm, peace. Help

James, my dear James. I miss him so much. *He* would know what to do."

She wondered if the words had God flowed into her mind were from the Bible. She forced her legs to push her up to a stand, went into the cabin and found Elam's Bible. Stuffing the worn book under her arm, she stepped back outside.

Jake didn't even look up.

By the fire, she opened the Bible to the back portion and went directly to the concordance. She searched for the words to help find where this verse could have come from.

"*What* are you doing?" Jake's voice made her jump. He stood behind her.

She made a quick swipe at her wet cheeks. "I'm searching for a verse."

"Are you crazier than him? Haven't you heard enough of that crap?"

"Just because Elam uses these words as weapons doesn't mean they aren't worth hearing."

"They *are* weapons, though, aren't they? Sword of the spirit and all that?" Jake swung his arm around as if it held a sword. "Cutting up humans with a crazed, two-edged blade?" He plopped down beside her.

"That's *not* what that means."

"Come on, the family I stayed with quoted Scriptures all the time to prove everyone else was going to hell."

"God's word fights *for* people, not against. He is *for* you."

"Not me. You know why?" He snapped his fingers. "He doesn't exist!"

In the silence that followed, fighting words churned inside Nikki's head.

Then a click switched in her spirit.

Nikki spoke, "I'm sorry."

"Why are *you* sorry?"

Why am I sorry? Why did I say that?

"I'm sorry that ..." she paused, then spoke fast. "That people can be so busy fighting for Christ, they forget to *be* Christ."

"What does that even mean?"

"A lot of us spend so much time telling others what we would never do, we forget the things we should be doing."

Jake glared at her.

She might as well get it all out. "And, I admit, we must seem like know-it-alls. Because we're afraid that people won't believe. So, we pretend to know things that we're not so sure of." This confession sounded a tad like heresy. "Because we ... I ... don't want anyone to miss what I *am* sure of."

Jake picked up a stick and smacked the dirt.

Nikki sighed. "But we don't know everything. Okay? I admit it. We just don't."

"All I know is, if there *is* a god his followers are jerks."

"It looks like that to you, doesn't it?" She pressed her lips together and took a deep breath. "I'll remember that."

He threw a rock into the water.

Chapter 25

"Daddy, can I go outside and play?" Conner asked.

"No, I'm sorry, son. There are too many people out front right now. And I don't trust those reporters to leave you alone even in the backyard."

"What do they want?"

James didn't know how to answer. Ever since he gave a statement to the media, cameras had been camped out on his doorstep.

His mom stepped in the room, scooped Conner up and took Jonah's hand. "Come on, sweethearts. Let's find a video to watch."

Dad looked up from studying a map of Colorado. "James, maybe we should take the boys back to our house. If we can sneak them past the mob outside, that is."

"I'm sure most people just want to help, but others are like sharks." James wiped a hand over his mouth as he thought. "Yeah, that would be a good idea for you to keep them. Maybe when we go to the candlelight vigil tonight, you can take them home with you."

"We can work it out. Did you call Nikki's parents?"

James paused, choking in a breath. "Ya. It was so hard, Pop. They entrusted their daughter to me."

"How did they take it?"

"Scared, worried, but kind. As I expected. They're on their way. Shoot!" He slammed his hand down on the kitchen counter. "I don't want to be here. I want to be out searching. I shouldn't have let the police talk me into going back home."

"You needed the rest. You won't be of any help if you don't eat and rest, son." His dad's eyes welled up with ready tears. "They'll need to quit for the night soon, anyway."

Pastor Thomas had arranged a prayer vigil every night that week. James had been to each one. People from the church, people

109

he had never even spoken to, approached him with promises of support and prayer. His urgent request had flown across prayer chains and over social media in record time.

Please, pray and be on the lookout for 31-year-old Nikki Rolen. This mother of two little boys has been missing since Friday afternoon in the Woodland Park area, in the mountains of Colorado. Her husband and family are desperate to find her.

"We take care of our own, James," Pastor Thomas had said last night after the vigil. "God watches over His people."

"That's right, James," the food committee lady added. "He won't let anything bad happen to Nikki."

But He had. God had let this bad thing happen to his wife. Still, James prayed like he never had before. It changed the way he spoke to God. Emotion drifted in and out of his words. Anger, fear, sorrow, but not joy. No, not joy.

This pushed his faith to the wall. The self-absorbed, petty prayers he had brought to God in the past felt fake. He needed a real God.

He needed one right now.

"James," his mother called from the family room. "There's something about Nikki on the news."

Most likely a replay of his plea to the public, but it could be important. James and his dad hurried into the other room.

He saw a woman standing with a reporter in front of a blue house. James said, "Wait a minute, I know her. That's Mrs. Farber." His mom turned up the sound.

"Yes, I know the Rolens. They're my neighbors, and they go to my church." Mrs. Farber wore a chunky necklace and jangling earrings. Not her usual attire. She must have dressed up for the interview. Cricket cuddled in her arms. "I'm not one to go on about others but yes, I did hear them fighting, often. And Mr. Rolen, James, was very mean to my adorable little dog, Cricket."

The camera zoomed in on the moist eyes and fluffy face of her "adorable" dog.

110

"Oh, brother," James groaned.

"As a matter of fact, they were arguing on the Friday morning she disappeared. Her husband even swore at the children."

"I did not!!"

"Shhhh!" said his dad.

The reporter asked, "Did you see Mrs. Rolen leave that morning?"

"No, I only saw them arguing in front of the children. I came out later, and the car was gone. I've asked James several times where his wife was since then, and all he could answer was 'She's out of town.' I even heard one child calling to his mommy late that Friday night."

"How did you hear that?"

"I was out front talking to James, and his door was open."

"Thank you for speaking with us tonight." The reporter turned to the camera as Mrs. Farber side stepped out of the shot. "Back to you, Rich."

From his seat in the studio, the male anchor faced the camera. "We have also just learned that the husband did not look for his wife for three days from the time he saw her last. He allegedly waited from Friday to the following Monday to inquire about his wife. Three days after she drove off to a women's religious retreat that no one knew she was going to. After recovering the woman's cell phone, it was discovered that he never tried to call her phone until Monday."

"What?" Dad was incredulous. "How do they have all this information?"

"Wait! Did you hear that? They recovered her cell phone. How come I have to learn this on the news?" James snatched up his phone and called the detective assigned to his case. He left a message on the voicemail.

Mom grabbed up James's jacket and said, "You can't think about that. You need to be at the prayer vigil. That's what's important right now. Dad can go with you. I'll leave after you and take the kids. The media will most likely follow you."

The plan worked, as far as James could tell. The mob ran to their vehicles after recording every facial movement and bob of his head.

He knew it must look like a funeral procession as he led the parade to the church a few blocks away. The public had been faithful about coming, but there seemed to be fewer people tonight.

I suppose even something as important as this can get old. That's okay, they can pray at home.

He went directly to the table that held the small candles to be lit for the vigil. As he made his way over, he tried to give these kind people an appreciative smile. But only a few returned it. Most dropped their eyes and didn't respond. A nervous twinge turned in his stomach.

He stared at what the church ladies had placed out in honor of Nikki. It had all been explained to him. A blue tablecloth, Nikki's signature color, spread over the table. Two candles, representing Conner and Jonah, sat on either side of a framed missing person's poster of Nikki. One larger candle sat in front of the picture. Fresh flowers had been placed in a small vase to one side. At the far end was the box of candles.

James closed his eyes and breathed in to steel himself. He opened them and looked into Mrs. Farber's icy stare.

"Mrs. Farber." James tried to keep his voice calm. She turned away and hurried over to the small group of people already holding lit candles.

Anger bit into his throat as a warm hand rested on his back. "Hello, son."

"Pastor, thank you for being here again."

"Of course. Nikki is a blessing to us all. She deserves everything we can do. How have you been holding up?"

"I don't know. I'm so twisted inside. This is a horrible nightmare."

"Of course, it is. Why don't we join the others?"

Pastor Thomas took the lead in prayer and then asked if anyone else would like to say a word. James stared at the ground. He successfully fought back threatening tears. If he let them loose, he worried he'd not be able to get back control. He had to stay strong.

When the leader announced the first hymn, *Amazing Grace,* James almost lost it again. The song was one of Nikki's favorites.

To distract himself, he glanced around at the faithful people. On the other side of the circle, he saw Ray and his wife, Edith. Tears streamed down Edith's face. They saw him and both made a slight nod. After the guitarist's intro cord, all the voices sang out.

"Amazing grace, how sweet the sound, that saved a wretch like me. I once was lost..." James's throat closed tight at the word "lost."

Chapter 26

"This ain't the first time she's run away, ya know?" Ben tried to sit up higher in his hospital bed and pulled on the sheets.

"Is that right, Mr. Knap?" said the officer as he shifted his feet, a clipboard in one hand and the other resting on his belt.

"That's right, officer. She tried to run away that very morning. Right, Cora?"

Cora pulled in a long sniff before she answered. "Well, I think she just got lost in the forest that time. She didn't really run away."

Ben smiled, put a hand on her arm, and looked at the officer. "She's always making excuses for her. You know how it is. But, as I said, all I remember is this deer jumping out in front of us, and I slammed on the brakes."

"You had a blood alcohol level of point nine in your system.

Let's see, do I cop to a drunk driving charge, or risk them digging further and end up being charged with an attempted molestation? Which could lead police to the ones no one knows about?

"I have no good excuse, officer. My father recently passed ou— I mean—away, and I've been in a depression."

Cora yanked her arm away and glared at him. The officer might have noticed. Ben reached for her arm again and gave a seemingly tender and gentle squeeze. Cora winced.

Ben said, "I'm feeling a little dizzy right now. Do you have any information about where she could be? If not, I need to rest."

"No, we don't. I'm sorry. And we haven't received any credible calls from the Amber Alert so far. If I were you, I'd put up more posters with her picture and info about her being nonverbal. Contact the website for missing and exploited children listed on the pamphlet we gave you earlier."

Cora spoke softly, "Isn't she too young to be a runaway?"

The officer gave the couple a solemn look. Ben knew what he was thinking.

The slime ball thinks we weren't good enough for Ava.

With a sad shake of his head the officer said. "You'd be surprised, really, you'd be surprised." He moved his hand off of his belt, turned, and walked out of the room.

"Ben, you shouldn't have said that about your father. They can check that."

"You worry too much."

"And you were drunk. What if, when they find her, they try to take her away from me?" Her eyes were red from crying, but he could tell she was sick. Bad sick. Junkie sick.

"It'll be fine. Where's your grandmother?"

"She's at the motel."

"Motel?"

"A church in town heard about the accident and put us up there."

"Do you have the water bottle?"

Cora reached into her cloth carrying bag and pulled out a blue water bottle. She glanced at the door before she gave it to him. When he opened the lid, the alcohol aroma mixed with the hospital's smell.

Ben swallowed the liquid. The ecstasy of craving fulfilled spread through his body.

"What do you have for me?" Cora asked.

"I got pills. The kind you like, don't worry. I saved some from my meds. When you come back to get me tomorrow, I'll have more."

"Where's the cash?"

"What cash?"

"From Grandma's Social Security checks. The ones I cashed before we left on vacation. It can't be gone already."

A vacation was what Cora called the wandering across the country they'd been doing. Scamming and scheming to keep themselves supplied with dope and drink was what they really did.

115

Ben closed his eyes and sighed dramatically. "I'm taking care of it. You don't need to worry about it."

"Why can't I keep the money?"

"You'll spend it all on dope."

"I need it for food. Grandma and I need to eat. I spent the last I had on that drink for you! We aren't served three meals a day off a hospital tray, like you!"

He gave a quiet but sincere curse under his breath. "Keep your voice down. Like I said, the doc told me I could go home tomorrow. They don't want to keep a charity case in very long. Come back here to get me, and I'll get the money for you. Got that?"

"What do we eat?"

With reluctance, he said, "Okay, get my pants out of the closet there." He pointed to the cabinet. "I have a couple of bucks in my wallet. See what you can do with that."

She gave a sigh of relief and rubbed her hand across her forehead. After retrieving the money, she said, "But what about Ava? Will they find her?"

"Of course, they will. She's not smart enough to go very far. I'll go out myself and look for her when you come back for me." He took her hand when he saw her hesitate. "I'll take care of everything. We'll find her. Trust me, I will find her."

I have to.

Chapter 27

As the dawn shone through the blinds, James reached across the bed to place a hand on his wife's back. The thud of his arm on the empty sheets zapped a shot of fear into his stomach. He stretched across her side of the bed for just a moment more, before the surreal rush of dread hit him.

She's missing. The nightmare I wake into, instead of from.

Now he regretted sending his sons to his parents' house. He needed them. He wished he could hear little feet running into his room to wake him.

"Good, good, good, good morning!" Conner would call as he tumbled into James's bed.

Maybe I should go to my parents? No, then the mob would follow me to there. This was best.

He grabbed the remote by his bed and switched on the TV. Found a news station and listened, hoping to hear news of his wife. He didn't have to wait long.

"Another break in the Nikki Rolen case. A friend of the couple remembers seeing Rolen's husband, James, in the park on the Saturday after his wife was last seen. This person told the reporter, that Mr. Rolen did not seem upset or worried about his missing wife. But the man did notice a splash of red drops on his white socks. Could these have been drops of blood? This man and others from his church, also noticed scratches on Rolen's arms. Could these have been defensive wounds?" The screen cuts to a pre-recorded tape. Ray's befuddled face appeared on the screen.

"Yes, I did notice the scratches on his arms. I thought it was just tussling with his preschool boys."

"Is that what he said they were?" the woman reporter asked.

"Um, well, no."

"What did he say?"

Ray thought a moment. "Oh, yeah. He said someone more devious than two little boys did it." He opened his mouth to speak again, but the camera cut away.

"That's all we have for now. The authorities tell us they they have no comments for us at this time."

"Thank you, Kathy, for keeping us up to date. Sounds like another scenario where the husband could be the prime suspect. Next up, young dolphins have washed up on the shores of the Gulf of Mexico. Right after this."

He snapped off the TV.

James felt like throwing-up. He knew the husband was always the first one blamed, but he'd never expected this. He looked down at the almost healed scratches he had received from the *adorable* dog. Would this mean they might miss evidence because they were stuck on him as a suspect?

He got up and peeked out the bedroom window. Only one news van parked across the street. He grabbed some clothes and headed for the shower.

He stood for quite a while letting steamy water cascade over his back. He forced his mind to go blank, until frantic thoughts wormed into his exhausted brain. His heart beat like he'd had a shot of adrenalin.

How much more can my body take? My arms feel like lead, and yet I feel like slamming my fist through the wall.

Bang!

A loud, explosive pop jerked his entire body. He turned off the water. He heard another. It sounded close by.

He pulled on his pajama pants, stopped in Conner's room to get a bat, and ran to the living room.

As he peered out the living room window onto the porch he saw three more blasts explode. Wood chips hurtled into the air. He caught a glimpse of teens racing away.

He yanked open the front door and flung the bat over his shoulder, ready to take a swing. Flashes popped into his face. In shock, he rubbed his eyes. When his sight came back he saw angry, shouting people rushing into his yard.

"Get off my lawn!" he screamed.

"Murderer!" A woman's voice yelled out.

"I'll call the police if you don't leave right now!" He made a short charge at the crowd with his bat.

The mob surged backwards. Tripping over each other to get back to the sidewalk.

One man yelled, "You can't keep us from being on *public* property!"

Another angry shout blasted. "What did you do with your wife, Mr. Rolen?"

Breathing hard, James turned to inspect the damage. Five splintered dents marked deep gouges in the wood. Burn marks surrounded the spots where the small explosives had been set off.

Cherry bombs. Kids!

He rushed back into the house, slammed the door, and collapsed on the sofa. He'd never had to deal with this kind of hatred before.

I can't stay in this house anymore. I wonder if someone from church could help me.

The doorbell rang.

He jumped up and yanked the door open. "Okay, buster, you can just—"

Police stood on the porch, several of them. Two held black trash bags and had plastic gloves on. One held up some papers.

"Mr. Rolen, we're here to do a search of your home."

"What are you looking for?"

"We can't say. Would you please get dressed and step outside?"

James peered past them and noticed the cameras rolling from news crews.

"We have a warrant, Mr. Rolen."

Embarrassed, violated, and extremely frightened, James sat on the curb between two officers for several hours. They took out stuffed plastic garbage bags, brought in equipment, and carted off filled cardboard boxes.

When the circus ended he was allowed back inside. The house, a rifled mess, made his skin crawl. Creepy to know others had been going through your things.

He went to bed. Exhausted, he slept for a long time. When he woke up and had recovered enough to think with a clear mind, he called Pastor Thomas.

Thomas's tone took James aback. "Don't you have some relatives or something to stay with?"

"No, I really don't. My parents are watching the boys, and I wouldn't want the news media to be drawn to them."

After a few moments of silence, the pastor spoke. "Okay, well then, let me see what I can do. I'll call around and get back to you."

After he hung up, James wondered why Pastor Thomas didn't say come over to his house. He went into his room to pack.

I can come back to check on the house. Nikki and the police have my cell number. They can still contact me.

His phone rang.

"Hello, Mr. Rolen, this is Detective Rice."

As if being swallowed into a wave of ice cold water, his body shivered.

"We'd like you come downtown. We have a few questions we need to ask you."

After a stunned pause, James said, "I'll be right over."

When he got to the station, Detective Rice ushered him into a small white room. Empty, except for one table pushed against the wall, with two chairs flanking it.

Rice settled into his chair. "Have a seat."

James took off his jacket and tossed it on the table before he pulled out the chair.

"No, you'll need to put your coat on the back of your chair, please. Not on the table, there's a microphone there. We want to be certain that the sound is nice and clear."

"Oh, sure." James pulled his jacket off the table.

"As you can see, this room is being videotaped. Have you ever been interviewed by the police before?"

"I was questioned a few times about my wife. But not here."

"Essentially, we need to know the answers to several questions. For instance, Officer Matsko noticed you had scratches on your arms, Jim, the day he went to your house. Others have said they saw them as far back as Saturday. Can you tell me how you got them?"

Silence.

James glanced down at his arms, his hands relaxed in his lap. "Call me James, please."

"What do you have to say, James?"

He sighed and rolled his head back, then looked at the detective. "Those scratches came from a run-in I had with Mrs. Farber's dog. On Friday night."

In a calm friendly voice, the detective said, "The night when you talked with her in the yard? That's not the way she tells it, James. She says you were angry at her dog, but that the dog was friendly and you were even holding him in your arms petting him."

Flabbergasted and totally at a loss for words, James stared at his interrogator.

"She also says she heard your son call out to his mom. Even after you went back into the house. That's after the time you said she'd left, isn't it? Your credibility is getting thin here, James."

Again, James had no way to answer. The words would not come.

"Something else, we also would like to know about the red drops that your friend—" He glanced down at his paper work, "—Robert, saw on your socks that Saturday."

That's what they were searching for. The socks.

James stretched back into his brain to figure what the drops could be. Then a scene appeared in his mind as he remembered squeezing the red juice box before the picnic in the park.

"That was from a juice box. You know the kind kids use, with the little straw and—"

"Do you have those socks?"

He couldn't remember where they were. At the bottom of his closet, or did he throw them in the washer with his sweaty gym clothes? Wait! Oh, no.

"I may have thrown them out," James said.

The officer leaned forward. "Really? Why was that?"

"They were stained. I mean, with the juice. Not anything else." He could feel a drop of sweat roll down his back. "I think I tossed them." James was aware of how nervous his voice sounded.

"Well, either you did or you didn't, James. It would do a lot for you if you helped us out."

With a calm demeanor, Detective Rice continued, "This Robert also reported that when he asked about your wife, you told him she was shopping."

"No, I never got a chance to say where she was. We were interrupted and–"

"Then there's the business of your front bumper being damaged. Someone rammed your wife's car off the road."

"I told you how that happened. Nikki backed into it!"

"The bottom line is as soon as we get the expert's evidence of DNA from the car, or your socks, this will blow wide open. James, you never even called your wife when she went missing. We recovered her phone inside the car. You made only one call to her phone, and that was on Monday morning. I can see you're an intelligent guy, James. Confessing now would look much better than confessing after all the evidence is in."

James tightened his already gritted teeth. "I didn't hurt her."

"Stuff happens in a marriage. Accidents, or in the heat of a moment bad things can erupt out of nowhere."

"No! I would *never* hurt her. She just disappeared."

"Is Nikki somewhere where we can find her easily? That we can call someone to get her? Or will we need you to lead us to her?"

James closed his eyes and tried to demand this moment to not exist.

"James, which direction are we heading here?"

"I didn't do anything to Nikki. I swear. Please, you're wasting time with me. I'll give you all the information I can, but I *don't know* where she is."

The rest of the morning dragged on in the same vein. The detective continued using his calm persuasive voice to lull James into a confession, interspersed by strong denials from James.

Detective Rice's phone rang. "Yeah, okay. Okay." He hung up and said to James, "You're free to go. Please, *do not* leave town."

James was left so drained that he couldn't remember where he'd parked the car. He found his vehicle, but the battle to get past the newshounds in front of his house only added to his exhaustion.

Back inside he collapsed into his recliner. In the quiet of the empty room, he stared at the ceiling.

Late in the afternoon, he got a call from Pastor on his house phone. "James? I'm sorry, but there was no one available to help you out."

"Really? No one? But there must be well over a hundred people in our church."

"Yes, well, I couldn't call all of them, of course. I'll make an announcement on Sunday. Then I'll get back with you."

"You can tell me right then. I'll be there on Sunday."

There was an uncomfortable pause. "Oh, you will? That's wonderful, James. It's my duty to minister to the lost."

"Lost? You mean Nikki?"

"What? Oh, uh, yes. She is lost, isn't she? But actually, I'm wondering if it would be best for you not to come on Sunday. I mean the media and all. I'd be happy to come to your house and pray with you anytime you need it. But all the churches in the Springs, and in the country, have been weathering bad publicity in past years. I just don't want to stir things up any more than necessary, you understand."

This time James paused. He closed his eyes, waiting to gain control of his emotions. "You think I killed Nikki, don't you?"

"Not me, James. I don't have any idea what happened to Nikki. But there are people that have been starting to wonder."

"You're worried about publicity? My wife is *missing*. My children don't have their mother."

"Look. If you had nothing to do with it, that's fine. But if you did, there's the whole abuse thing and—"

"Are you really telling me not to come to church?"

"Certainly not. I would never tell anyone that. But let's let this play out."

Now James lost it. "Play out? Play out! What do you mean? Make sure I'm not guilty first? See if Nikki really does come home? What kind of a pastor are you?" He slammed the phone down.

123

He leaned on the kitchen counter, then collapsed to the floor. Sobs rose from deep inside his chest. He leaned back on the lower cabinets and sat there crying until his eyes burned and his head pounded.

"God, where are You? Am I lost, or are you?" Anger and frustration flared in his chest. With teeth clenched, he pulled himself up to his knees, pointed his finger and yelled at the ceiling. "You listen to me, God. I've obeyed all the rules. I'm a good husband and father. I go to church and donate my ten percent. I've never even gone to an X-rated movie, for Pete's sake. I'm good! Now my Nikki is missing? Maybe even dead? *You* broke the deal, God. *You* did!"

Limp, spent, and broken beyond his comprehension, he dropped back to a sit and cried.

He whispered, "God, I love her so much."

The phone rang. James jerked up and stared at it, but didn't move to get up. He didn't want to answer the call. The ring intruded on his grief. But what if it was Nikki?

He stood and picked it up. "Hello."

"Hello, uh, Jimmy? I mean, James. I ... well, I heard you needed a place to stay. You'd be welcome at our house."

James couldn't speak.

"James, are you there?"

"Ray? I ... I heard you on the news."

"That's right. I just answered as honestly as I could." Pause. "So, would you like to come over?"

The clock ticked in the family room. "Yes, thank you."

An hour later, James was putting his things in their basement spare room. Edith fussed about, showing him the clean towels and where the extra blankets were if he became cold in the night. Ray stood by the door and watched.

Overwhelmed by her kindness, James barely spoke. As they said their good-nights and Edith hustled up the stairs, James caught Ray's arm.

"Ray, what made you decide to let me stay with you?"

"God."

"Really?"

"Listen, if I'm going to be mistaken about you, I'd prefer to err on the side of mercy. God wasn't about to let me get away with sitting back and not stepping into the fray when I could help."

"I guess mercy really is something Christians give to other Christians."

"You guessed wrong, son. Mercy's bigger than that."

Chapter 28

Jake watched Elam as he worried over one wire's position in the wall. He bent it back and forth, making it lean to his exact, insane liking. The repeated motion mesmerized Jake until he had to shake his head and look away to break free.

Elam mended the gaping hole in the fence. His latest panic attack had subsided, and in his obsessive, detailed way, he demanded perfection.

Jake turned to Nikki and Priscilla to give them a small smile and a reassuring nod. Elam's wacked out mood swings had to be scary for them. The two had the wary expression of frightened animals, even as they picked up scraps from around the break.

Who, or what, kept breaking the junk wall?

Jake figured it had taken them five to ten minutes running to reach the break. No wonder they didn't hear anything at camp.

Elam must have spent years erecting this monster. The thing snaked completely around the rugged property. King Elam's realm had to be as big as the farm his second foster family owned, cornfields included.

Around the break they were mending, rubbish had been tossed in a haphazard mess. The barbed wire twirled out like curly strands of hair.

Jake shoved another jagged edged metal scrap into the meshing of junk that patched the wall

Elam exclaimed, "This should keep everyone out."

Right, keep everyone out and everyone in. I've become my own keeper. It doesn't matter, because keeping him happy is the only way to survive.

With a final smack of the hammer and a last examination, Elam grinned at his family. "Great work, everyone! What a team we make, right? Let's go get some supper." He turned and stared into the woods. A sharp "Shush!" came from his lips.

Nikki's hand slipped past him to Priscilla, and she drew the child to her. Jake stepped between them and Elam. This could be the onset of another ranting, or a hallucination fueled by fear.

Elam made a deliberate blink.

Could this mean a rational thought?

His whisper rasped. "The evil has entered the fold. I hear it."

Or not.

Elam's knife came out, and he swung it through the air. Jake stepped back to avoid a slice.

"Run!" Elam snatched Priscilla's hand from Nikki's and dragged the little girl into the brush in the direction of camp.

Jake bolted after them.

I'm really getting tired of racing through the forest.

The snap of branches and the thud of running feet followed behind him. This had to be Nikki.

Glancing back, he did a double take. A flash of something dark moved behind her.

It couldn't be. A mind plays tricks. Fear using its power to make the worst seem real.

He slowed to allow Nikki to come pounding up beside him. He grabbed her hand and they ran together.

With his free arm, Elam hoisted Priscilla over his shoulder and, like a pirate protecting his booty, he swung his knife ahead of him. Jake worried, what if Elam tripped, he'd stab the kid.

Even knowing the madman ran from shadows, a sharp bite of fear dug into Jake. Did he hear a crashing sound following them through the woods?

When they reached the open area of the camp, Elam hustled everyone into the cabin and followed them in. He shut them all inside with a slam and secured the latch. With violent thwacks, he tossed objects against the door. Mumbling to himself, he loaded the rifle.

Elam's eyes, bulging wide, quivered and twitched with fear. Tears and sweat poured down his panicked face.

"I won't let you take them!" he screamed at the window, unaware that his rifle muzzle swung with wide swipes around the room. "Get back, family, all of you. Hide! They may be armed. They steal food from the righteous and make their marks with wicked claws." Trembling violently, he struggled to open the window a slit and shoved the tip of the rifle out.

Priscilla scrambled into one of the dirt cubbies and hid under a musty blanket. Jake and Nikki ducked behind the bed.

Elam cracked gunfire out the window. The explosions stung in Jake's ears. With each shot, the dilapidated cabin rocked.

Elam screamed out his anger in a raspy, strained voice. "I banish you evil spirits, you demons from blackest hell. By the blood of all that is holy, I command you to leave." In between shots he yelled. "Go...to...hell!"

Jake peered over the bed and caught a glimpse of movement outside the wall. Dark shadows blocked the light that seeped through the cracks in the siding. It sent a chill rippled over his body. They slithered across on one side and then the other.

The roof quaked with each blast. When the gun clicked empty, Elam yanked his rifle inside. Then as if being pushed by an angry giant, the walls trembled one more time. A loud, wretched, growling wail split the air as a piece of wood fell from the ceiling.

Then quiet.

Jake gulped a breath, then he sucked in air as fast as he could let it out. He sat back and wiped his forehead. Nikki's eyes were clenched closed and hands clasped together as she whispered words under her breath.

Did she hear the wail? Was that Elam?

The madman threw the rifle onto the floor. One arm leaning against the wall, he let out an exhausted breath that sounded like a whimpered cry. When he lifted his head, sweat poured down his now ecstatic face.

He swung the door open, ran out into the clearing, and howled his victory. Jake stood with Nikki to peek out the door. No sign now of what had rocked the cabin.

Elam twirled and hopped from foot to foot. His wild shouts rang into the forest. "Yeah! Yeah, take that! You hear me? Don't you even *think* of coming back. You can't have my family! I win! I keep them safe. You wicked, slime ball demon!" He pounded on his chest. "Only God can take them from me!"

128

Though trembling, Jake imprisoned the fear inside the tombs buried in the deepest part of his mind. Back where he kept all those bloodied zombies that cursed his young life.

His stomach growled for supper. He wished they had some canned stew left. The last two nights of tuna had made his stomach turn.

Nikki went back to help Priscilla down from her perch and led her outside. Like soldiers after a bloody battle, each one found a place to sit and recover beside the fire. No one spoke.

Jake pushed the ashes around with a stick. Out of the corner of his eye, he caught a change in the camp. The piles of trash closest to the cabin had been spread out and flattened. As if a giant had rifled through them.

Shivers danced down his arms at the oddness of the sight. The same way the shadows on the walls and the ghostly scream had touched off terrors he kept locked away.

The sight of the trash and the freshened smell of moldy food raised a sour belch into his throat.

"Oh, great." He mumbled an unemotional comment of sarcasm to himself. "Awesome. Juuuust awesome."

Chapter 29

Pancakes, bacon, and coffee were three aromas that could always get James out of bed. But it did take a moment to remember where he was. Realizing where and why took all the anticipation of a good meal out of him.

After a quick shower, he dressed and ran up the stairs in his stocking feet. James entered the kitchen. Edith scurried about flipping the pancakes and moving the bacon to a platter.

"Edith, you didn't have to go to any trouble for me."

"Oh, I know. Ray told me. But if one of my sons was going through something as terrible as you, I'd do it for him. Sit down there and let me pour you a cup of coffee. Take milk and sugar?"

"Yes, thanks."

Ray ambled in and sat at the table. "So, what are your plans for today?"

James gave a heavy sigh. "Well, work has given me some leave, so I don't have to worry about that. What day is it?"

"Saturday," Edith said.

"I need to sneak over to my parents' house. I want to see my boys. I bet they're really confused. And scared. At least I've been able to keep the media away from them, so far."

"I know." Edith perked up. "You can ride in the backseat of my car. Then when we get to your parents' house, you duck down and hide. Then you can text your mom a secret code—"

"Secret code?" Ray's eyebrows shot up.

"Well, maybe not a code." She suppressed a quick smile. "Anyway, she has an automatic garage door opener, right?"

"Yes." James wondered where this was going.

"Then she could open the garage door for us from the inside and we'd drive right in. If there are any of those nosey-newshound-noodle-heads about, they'll never know you came and went."

Ray took a long gaze at his wife and said in his graveled voice, "Never knew you were so devious."

Edith beamed at James. "I do love mystery and suspense novels."

"I see," said James. "Sure, we could do that, if you don't mind?"

Ray shook his head. "Well, I don't know if we can—"

"Mind?" Edith jumped in. "Of course not, I'll go change while you eat. Ray, you can clean up after breakfast."

Ray sat up straight. "Now, wait just a minute here. Hold up there, Edith. I don't have time to—" Too late, she was gone. "I don't know how she does that."

James chuckled a little. But he choked back even that slight burst of humor. Grief and fear pushed it down.

Ray shook his head, then changed the subject. "Are you going to church with us tomorrow?"

James didn't answer right away. "Pastor Thomas thought it would be best if I didn't come for a while. Until after Nikki is found."

Ray pushed back his chair and sat up taller. "What? Why?"

"Oh, something about bad publicity. And if I'm an abuser, it would make the church look bad."

"He said what? That's nonsense! You know, he may be my spiritual leader, but sometimes he really gets in my craw. I've known some mighty fine pastors that would've whupped his behind for saying that. Well, maybe not whupped, but chewed him out plenty."

"I don't know, Ray. I've been thinking..."

Ray raised his voice with obvious aggravation. "Does that pastor think only perfect people go to church? All dressed up and spouting verses? Is that the only kind he lets in? But ya know, maybe people should unglue their butts from the pew and go where the people really are. Dad-gummit!" He stood, picked up the empty plate that had held the bacon, shoved it onto the counter, and said, "Excuse my French."

James noticed Ray wasn't exactly defending anyone's innocence. "Is he right, though? Will it hurt the church?"

"Listen, Pastor Thomas isn't a bad guy. He's been stung before. He got fired from a church once for speaking out too strong on a subject. So, now he lets his fearful congregation run over him." Ray sat back down with a heavy plop. "Listen to me, the world is changing. I'm just saying followers of Jesus need to get off the blasted bleachers and get in the game."

"Ray, do you think I hurt Nikki?"

"Well." He sighed, dropped his head, crinkled his brow, and then pulled his gaze back up to James. "It don't look good."

Edith practically bounced into the room. She had on jeans and a green turtleneck sweater. A large drooping hat and dark sunglasses covered half her face. "I'm ready," she announced.

Ray raised his eyebrows but said nothing.

"Um, thank you, Edith." James stood. "I'll just go get my shoes on."

***

Even though they saw no reporters in front of his parent's house when they arrived, Edith insisted James duck down in the backseat. She pulled her hat forward over the sunglasses and hunched down. James had called ahead, and his dad opened the garage door as they drove into the driveway.

When he entered the kitchen, he was attacked at the legs by two anxious little boys. James knelt and held his sons close.

He spent the morning watching them play in the backyard. At the first sign of grandchildren, his mom had made his dad put a sandbox in their backyard. Now the lawn, scattered with play toys, could be mistaken for a daycare center.

As the children dug holes in the sand, he glanced back at the house. Through the window he could see his mom and Edith sitting in the kitchen. They had reached across the table and clasped each other's hands. Their heads bowed.

"Daddy!" Conner ran up. "Where's Mommy?"

"I don't know right now, Conner. But we'll find her."

"Is she lost?"

James didn't know how to answer. He decided in favor of honesty. "Yes, Conner."

"That's okay, then."

132

"Is it, son?"

"Yes, because God knows where lost things are."

"How do you know that, Tiger?"

"Mommy told me. She said if I'm ever lost and don't know what to do, to pray to God, and listen. He will always help."

"Mommy told you that? She's a smart mommy, isn't she?" He cleared his throat and swallowed to loosen the tightness. "So, did you already pray for Mommy?"

With a serious three-year-old face, he answered, "Yes, I prayed."

A strong wave of curiosity flowed over James. "When you listened, what did you hear?"

"God singing."

"You heard singing, Conner?"

"God, Daddy. I heard God singing."

Chapter 30

Ava centered all hope onto Nikki. This woman had to be the one to keep her safe.

She stayed by her friend's side at all times, except for when she sought the dark comfort of her little den. She'd climb the rope ladder on the mountain wall inside the shack, then sweep her hand inside the cubby to check for bugs. She'd curl her small body up on top of the blankets stored there. The tight space and the gray shadows made her think of the closet at home.

Right now, she snuggled up against Nikki's back, in the creaky metal bed they both slept in. The room, gloomy and dim, held only a pale glow from the windows and wall cracks as sunrise peeked in.

The door rattled and slammed shut. "Let's go, Priscilla. After morning prayers, you and I are going to town."

Ava sat up.

Is this a dream? Is it Ben or Elam that called me?

Nikki turned over and wiped the sleep from her eyes. "What are you talking about, Elam?"

"The stash is getting low, and I need to scout out the enemy."

Nikki sat up. "But ... why Priscilla? Take me, or Jake. He's strong and can carry things."

Elam looked down and whispered as if talking to the ground. "It's safer this way. And I can't do it myself. And I must keep the baby safe. Besides, she won't be tempted by the world." He spoke to them with a stern shout. "No! Priscilla and I will go!"

Before he went outside, Elam reached into a high cubby and brought down a dust-covered box. He pulled something from it. "She is to wear this. This is the proper thing for little sister to wear." He held up a dress and rubbed the cloth between his fingers. He lifted the material to his face and smelled. With a hushed, voice he said, "Can you smell blue flowers in the spring? Fresh after the raining tears?"

He broke from his quiet words and, with a sneer, flung the thing onto their bed. Without looking back, he strode out the door.

Ava tried to show her worry and fear to let Nikki know how much she didn't want to be alone with this man.

"Honey, I know you don't want to go, but you may be able to help us. You need to be strong. Try to attract attention. Maybe someone will call the police."

Oh, Nikki, I can't, I can't. This is a bad place, but the police will put me in jail.

Tears slid down her cheeks. Nikki sighed and gave her a hug.

Knowing better than to lie in bed, Ava quickly got her clothes on. The dress had tiny blue flowers, a round collar, and a skirt that went down to her ankles.

Outside, Elam demanded she pull her hair back and had Nikki tie a bandana on her head.

When Elam went out to the stone-throne, Nikki and Jake had a chance to talk.

Ava listened.

Nikki said, "Jake, where does he get the money to buy all these things?"

"Oh, he doesn't buy anything. God *provides* it." He gave her a half smile and put air quotes around "provides." At her blank look, Jake said, "He steals stuff. He tells himself that God placed it there for him. Once he 'found' a gold watch and pawned it. How mighty and generous is our God."

After a rambling prayer and a few handfuls of frosted cereal, Elam loaded Ava into the back of the van and chained her in. Before he closed the door, she watched him go to the cabin. He came out with a length of steel cable. Elam had showed it to her once with pride, saying it could hold five hundred pounds before it would break.

Elam secured the cable to chains around Jake's waist, and another cable to Nikki's. He barked commands. "Bring wood, and follow!"

He took them to the other side of the cabin. Ava lost sight of them.

Elam came back for a bucket and scooped water from the shallow stream. He walked back behind the cabin.

His voice echoed through the pines and carried back to her. "Don't worry. We won't be long. Wait here for us."

Ava worried about her friends.

What if it stormed? What will they eat?

The van lumbered away. A big jeep would have been a better choice for this raggedy road, but Elam never noticed the bouncing. Rattled and jerked by the van's progress, Ava hoped it would not break down. That would leave her stuck in the woods, alone with Elam.

***

Nikki gave the steel cords a mighty yank, grimaced, and fell back on a log. "So, why did he secure us this time? And why here instead of nearer the cabin?" She struggled to sit up. "At least we can walk around a little."

"He's probably worried we'd follow the van back to town." Hopeless surrender had begun to slip from his eyes in recent days. Now Nikki saw a bit of courage burning. "And I would, too." She watched the rickety crate bounce down the dirt trail beyond the locked gate.

"He put us back here to be sure the evil outside world can't see us while he's gone. I mean what if a contaminated ice cream man happened by and saw us tied to this tree?"

In silence, Jake rolled rocks into a circle. He placed some small twigs into the middle, lit the match Elam had provided, and blew puffs onto the tiny flame until the wood caught.

"It may be a long wait." He picked up a blade of grass and put it between his teeth. "Maybe not." He even cracked a small smile. "Time for some chillaxin'."

Nikki turned to Jake. "What do you know about Elam? How did end up here? Like this?"

"Don't know much. He's so paranoid it's hard to tell what might be real. He used to talk about the rest of his family. He said

136

the world had tried to capture them. Take them." He leaned in closer and lowered his voice. "Know what I think?"

Nikki shook her head.

"I think he killed them."

"Killed them?" The first quick shot of unbelief left, when she realized who they were talking about. "Why do you say that?"

"You mean, besides from the huge knife he carries around, his hand-to-hand combat training from Vietnam, and his tendency to shoot at people?"

She blinked and swallowed hard. "Yes, besides the obvious."

"He has terrible dreams at night. Yelling out names, Priscilla, Jake, and others, too. I think one was a wife. Then he'd put the smack down and go non-linear cray-cray. I mean really whack. Scared, too. He used to talk about his wicked family and then his beautiful family. He talked about them in present and then in the past. Now that you two are here, he doesn't mention them at all. It's like you've taken their places. But he started calling me Jake right off, and I had to call him Pa or Papa. So, Jake must have been part of the family, too."

"If you called him Pa, how did you know his name?"

"He talks to himself. And a lot of invisible people."

She pondered the theory. It seemed plausible.

Nikki leaned back. A bored sleepiness drifted over her. Why did Elam want Priscilla to go with him? Was she safe? Nikki could picture Priscilla's strong but worried little face as she allowed her own drowsy eyelids to close.

Chapter 31

James stepped into his home through the garage side door. He'd parked down the street. The house held an ominous aura, empty and foreboding.

After Edith had driven him back to her house, he'd switched to his own car. He then drove to the mountains to help searchers. The sun had just dipped behind Pikes Peak, giving the sky an orange glow.

Now he needed a few things and wanted to check on his house. Not wanting to turn on lights in case a reporter would notice, he bumbled his way through the shadows. In the darkness, he tripped over Jonah's scooter and knocked his knee against the fireplace. He stuffed down the curse that sprang to his mind. He made a quick apology to the God he needed to please.

For Nikki's sake.

As he rubbed his knee, his mind registered a noise. The sound had come at the same moment as the pain. At first, he thought he had made the noise, but no.

The house is settling, that's all. It's those pipes that drive Nikki crazy.

On his way to his bedroom, he stopped in Conner's room. He grabbed a few special books off a nightstand for his son. Then, going down the hall, he saw a faint light under his door.

A shock bolted through him, until he remembered the computer program he'd installed that turned lights off and on at night. Glancing back, he noticed another small lamp burning in the hall.

Inside his room, he checked the laundry holder in the hopes he hadn't thrown out those socks. The basket was empty. The police had taken everything.

He could see Detective Rice's face in his mind. Eyes accusing, that quiet tone asking where the socks were.

From his chest of drawers, he pulled out a Bronco sweatshirt. His eyes fell on his wedding photo next to a lamp. Picking it up, he sat on the bed and stared into Nikki's face. With all his heart, he wished his mind could reach out to hers. Go to where she was, right then, and end the nightmare. He took the picture with him.

He walked back through the hall. In the kitchen, he grabbed a glass, filled it, and downed the water.

A sharp noise from the next room made him choke. Water spit out his mouth. Listening, he grabbed a knife from the butcher block. He ducked down, squatting on the floor.

Idiot! It must be a tree brushing against the house.

The floor creaked in the dining room. He scooted to the opening and peered around the corner. In the dim light, he saw a silhouette of someone standing by the window. He pulled back.

He looked again, and the figure was gone. Only a floor lamp left in its place. Imagination does weird things. He glared at the knife in his hand and slipped it up onto the counter. He stayed down, closed his eyes, and dropped his head into his hands. After a moment, he pushed up with his legs to stand. As he stood, a scream let loose near him and a hard object smashed into his head.

Stunned, but not out, he pushed the person away with a strong shove. Again, the bear statue swung through the air. Its wooden paws still clutched the welcome sign.

The voice screamed out, "Drop the knife!"

"I did!"

"Murderer! What did you do with her? Tell me! Tell me!"

The person hit him over and over again. James turned his back and bent down to shield his face from the beating. Finally, the rain of blows paused, giving James enough time to lash his arm out and restrain the Tasmanian devil. His arms wrapped around the intruder as the person flailed about with wild frantic sweeps.

The bear dropped to the floor with a loud thud. Cups in a standing holder swept off the counter and crashed to the floor. James hit his back on a sharp corner. He let out a pain-filled howl.

Realizing the slightness of his attacker, he took control.

She screamed. "Let me go! Let me go!"

Now he recognized the voice and tried to create calm with his words.

"Mrs. Farber, stop. I'm not going to hurt you! Stop! Stand still. What are you doing?"

The woman pulled in a breath and relaxed into James's constraining hug. She let hands drop to her sides, and sobs convulsed through her body. As she went limp, James pulled her over and set her in a chair. He knelt in front of her.

After the waves of tears subsided, James asked, "What are you doing here, Mrs. Farber? How did you even get in?"

"Did you kill her? Please tell me. Is she still alive?"

"I didn't kill her. I don't know where she is."

"Did you bury her? Maybe you dumped her body up on Gold Camp Road."

James used his commanding dad voice. "What are you doing in here?"

"I brought the photo. Cricket made me think you'd left. So, I came with the picture I took of Nikki and the boys." She drew in a deep but shaky breath, eyes red, puffy, and wet. "I ... I promised her I'd have the snapshot framed and bring it to her. But I can't now. So, I brought it here, to her home. But once inside, I thought about searching for evidence." She let her body slump, hands covering her face. "I couldn't find anything, and being here, in her home, made me so sad. I could feel her presence. I remembered the last time we talked over coffee. Right here in this kitchen." She wept with genuine grief.

It took several minutes for James to calm her enough for her to listen to him. "Mrs. Farber, I didn't kill Nikki. I didn't. She's out there, somewhere. We have to find her. But how did you get into my house?"

She reached into her pocket, and held up a key. "Nikki gave me a key, in case she ever got locked out."

He plucked the key from her hand. "Okay, listen." He reached to the counter for several paper napkins and gave them to the woman to dry her eyes. "I know you and my wife had a strong friendship. I mean, after all, you were the one that invited us to church."

140

"No, I didn't," she said between sniffs.

"But I thought that's what Nikki told me."

"No, she invited me."

"What?"

"When you first moved in, I hadn't been to church in a long while. Not since my husband passed away. When he died, I guess I pulled up into myself. He was the outgoing one. He had the friends and the connections in church. And then when he passed ... well ... I guess sorrow made me a little self-absorbed. I couldn't understand why people gave me such a wide berth. Recently, I've realized that what people saw was the barbed wire I surround myself with. Protection, I guess."

She took a moment to use the wadded napkins to blow her nose. "But Nikki? She went right past that. She'd talk with me over the fence, just chatting with an old woman. Then she asked if I went to church. She wanted to find a good one. I told her about the church I used to go to. She invited me to come with her. *She* invited *me* to church."

Oh, Nikki. My dear, sweet Nikki.

"Mrs. Farber—"

"Call me Ruby." She hiccupped.

"Ruby, let's get you back home. I'll give you my cell number, and I'll take your phone number. I'll keep you in the loop as to what's going on. Okay?"

"What *is* going on?" She sniffed.

"Well, I guess I'm the most obvious suspect. But I didn't hurt her. Trust me, if you can."

She answered him with a head shake and wide eyes that blinked back tears. He laid it all out for her. He dragged up every bit of suspicion that the police had against him. Every piece of information he had about her disappearance. Not even his most profound fears and anguishes were left out.

She listened with deep concern on her face.

After a huge cleansing sigh, she put her hands on his shoulders. "Okay, James. I guess if Nikki trusted you enough to marry you, I'll take a chance on you. But I won't let you bamboozle me, you hear?"

Chapter 32

Hours later, the road smoothed out, and Ava fell asleep. A sharp honk jarred her awake. She sat up and peeked through the windshield.

She saw a gas station, and a few small shops lined both sides of a short, paved street. Past that, the van crunched again onto a gravel road. Here, she caught glimpses of a few houses among the aspens. Elam turned onto a side drive and parked. Ava tensed every muscle.

"Be right back." Elam jumped out of the vehicle and locked his door. He didn't come around to her side but trudged down the road. Ava tried to keep track of where he went until he took a sharp left, directly into someone's yard.

Ava settled into her seat. At first, she worried he wouldn't come back, and then she worried he would.

Later on, someone walked past. The person tried to look inside through the dark windows.

Afraid, she ducked down behind the seat until he walked away. Maybe he wanted to steal the van.

Ava trusted no one.

She let her mind drift. The conversation between Jake and Nikki had caught her attention, the one about God. She didn't know much about this. She realized people believed different things about Him. Elam made God sound mean. Nikki talked about God in a different way, like her Grammie did.

Jake said there's no God at all. She liked the thought that the trees and rabbits could be God. She peeked under the shade covering the windows and stared at the trees.

"Praise the Lord! The Provider has provided!" Elam opened the back and shoved things in. He was singing as he got into the driver's seat. "Bringing in the sheaves, bringing in the sheaves, we

shall come rejoicing bringing in the she-e-e-e-e-eaves!" Whatever
sheaves were. Looked like more junk to Ava.

Elam drove off, and for the rest of the morning, he repeated
this process of bringing in sheaves.

His song droned on as the drive seemed to go forever. Until
he stopped by a large warehouse at the back of a big store.
"Hallelujah! Yes, God is good. This is where you come in, little one.
Do you see that truck behind the grocery store? I want you to go up
to those men unloading. You won't need to say a thing. Just climb
up on the dock, that tall platform, and stand there until I come for
you. Got it?"

She shook her head.

"You'll get it." He unchained her and lifted her out. He
turned her around and shoved her in the direction of the men.
After getting back in the van, he drove around the corner.

She stood there. Would God help her? She shuffled over to
the men, crawled up onto the platform and waited.

"What's the problem, kid? You're in our way." The bearded
man held a crate of canned food. His shoulders heaved and he used
his knee to boost up the box.

"Frank! What's the holdup?" A fat man almost ran into the
first guy. They both concentrated on her.

How can I let them know I need help?

Words of anguish trapped inside her throat.

Help me!

The bearded man had an angry expression, but his words
didn't sound mean. "Look kid, if you're lost, go around to the front
of the store. Go inside and ask one of the cashiers for help."

The second man sounded cross. "But for Pete's sake, get out
of our way. You'll get hurt."

She stood there.

I should tell them I was kidnapped.

"Priscilla! Oh, Priscilla, there you are. Are you bothering
these men?" Elam hustled over to them, reached up to the platform,
and lifted Ava into his arms. "I'm sorry, gentlemen. She just
wandered off. I'll get her out of your way."

He hurried off, carrying Ava. She stared back over his shoulder and prayed.

God, help.

To Ava, the men seemed to get smaller as Elam carried her away. He turned the corner and headed to the van. He sang in a whisper as she bounced along.

"Bringing in the sheaves, bringing in..." He paused his singing to open the sliding door, put her in, and locked her chains. "...the sheaves. We shall come rejoicing bringing in the—" He slammed the door.

The far back bench seat had been folded down to make room for God's provisions. She peeked behind her and saw two new flat crates of food. Reaching her hand over the seat, she took a can out. The label read Spam. A second flat crate held ready-to-eat snack-size applesauce.

Elam started the engine and drove off.

The next stop was at a campsite. A sign bordered by barked logs read "The Pinecone Castle Camp." He rolled into the parking lot. Before he brought Ava into the lobby with him, he warned her. "I guess I don't even have to tell you this, but say nothing."

A woman sat behind a counter in a small office. Ava took in the animal pictures and statues of bears that decorated the office.

"Welcome, my name is Maggie. How can I help you?" Her voice was soft and cheerful, like Ava's Grammie.

"Howdy, Maggie." Elam slapped both hands on the counter. "I think we'll camp here for the night."

She leaned over and looked out the picture window. "Are you camping out of your van?"

"Well, we're on our way back from camping with relatives. A family reunion."

"You must have been camping for a while." She chuckled and made a slight wave in front of her nose. "By the way, we have shower facilities and restrooms."

She brushed back a strand of light red hair and gazed down at Ava. "And who is this sweet thing?" Maggie smiled down at her.

To Ava, it felt like hope.

Chapter 33

Nikki lay still, in a half-awake half-dreaming state. She thought she heard Conner calling her. She flung out her arm to grab at his warm sweet hand. The movement only caused her to jerk awake, and the jolt pinged pain in her stiff neck.

As the sun slid behind the slope, the air became cooler. The mountains brought dusk quickly, and Nikki worried about Priscilla, praying she would get back safe. They'd been gone so long.

Father, what if they never come back?

The wood supply had dwindled to a few sticks. Jake reached up into the tree beside them and yanked down a dead branch. He broke this into pieces and laid them over the fire.

The flames licked up on the dried twigs, and smoke billowed from the wood. This surrounded them and brought a depressing helplessness back into the air.

"Listen!" Jake held up his hand.

Intertwined with the usual evening animal sounds, she heard a low huffing. Peering through the eye-stinging ash, Nikki strained to see.

Over by the trash pile, she saw dark movement. Then two gold orbs glowed like twin candle flames over the heap.

***

Ava flinched when Elam put a hand on her back, grinning with pride. "This is my favorite little gal. Yes, sir. She'd never even seen real mountains before." Elam leaned closer to Maggie. "She's very shy. Do you have grandchildren, Maggie?"

"Oh, yes, I do. Would you like to see the cutest pictures?" She pulled her finger down her tablet, tapped and turned it toward Elam. Ava slid into a chair in the waiting room and faded from sight. She knew they had stopped seeing her. Worry for her friends back at camp played in the back of her mind.

145

We were supposed to be back long ago. What are my friends going to do? Can they reach the cabin for food?

Maggie gave Elam a map of the camp. "You have fun now. If you go down the drive to the left, you'll find plenty of nice private spots. Good night."

Elam maneuvered the van to the left and to the very back of the camp ground, He found a secluded spot next to a stream.

"I feel God speaking to me." His voice had a raspy, serious tone. "We'll stay here for a while, then leave after we've checked out what God is telling me about this place."

He made sure Ava ate some applesauce, then escorted her to the outhouse. Then the two went for a walk around the camp. Elam wore a ratty backpack. After a quick browse at each campsite, Elam explained his plan to Ava. As they approached a tent or camper, the old man would engage the family in conversation. Then with a nod or a discreet hand gesture, Elam would indicate to her what to take.

She slipped a cup in her skirt folds. A bottle of ketchup went behind her back. Once when he talked with a grandma, he had her slip inside the RV to look for medicine. She found several bottles inside a suitcase.

At the end of their "walk," they went back to the van. Inside, Elam took their provisions out of the backpack and checked them over. "Praise God. We've quite a collection. You're a real prize." He patted her arm. "Yes, you are."

A little flush tingled her cheeks. For some reason, she couldn't hold back the bit of pride that grew in her chest. Then they heard a knock on the sliding door.

"Elam, could I talk with you?" Maggie's recognizable voice came through the door.

***

Bear!

Nikki remembered how her father had always said to keep food away from the campsite, in a sealed container, hanging in a tree.

She poked Jake and pointed to the heap. In the dusky light, small twin orbs floated over the trash just a few yards away. The shadowed form of the lumbering bear filled in behind the spots of light.

She scanned the fire for a flaming stick. None big enough. Through gritted teeth, she instructed Jake, "Don't look into his eyes."

"Maybe they'll eat and go," he whispered.

She turned to Jake and questioned. "They?"

"I see more than one, don't you?"

She squinted and discovered a smaller version of the first one sitting on its haunches, sniffing a box.

Her stomach knotted. "Yes, maybe they'll get full and go away. Black bears rarely attack, unless people get in between the mother and her cub." She swallowed hard as the mother growled and gave her youngster a teasing slap on the nose. "On the other hand, they can wake up hungry and cranky after coming out of hibernation in the spring." She lowered her voice. "Like now."

Nikki watched for a long time, trembling, trying not to move or breathe. If she hadn't been so terrified, the bears might have seemed cute batting at the empty cans, and poking their heads into boxes.

Nikki whispered, "I get them being attracted to the food smell. But how did they get past Elam's wall?"

"I don't know, but I don't think this is the first time."

"What do you mean?"

"Remember the night Elam dragged us through the woods? After we fixed the wall? Elam said something was chasing us. Maybe that time it wasn't all in his head."

The larger bear growled at the smaller one over a promising cracker carton. She seemed frustrated that the free meal was running out. Nikki had heard news stories of rare Colorado bear attacks. Most happened because overly sympathetic humans fed the creatures and were attacked when the food ran out.

The mother's interest focused now on a banana peel. She pressed her paws together as she sat back on her haunches and lifted the limp skin up to sniff it. Then she opened her mouth and stretched out her long tongue to capture the dangling end. But with

147

a sudden jerk of her black head, she dropped the peel, and turned toward them.

Her black eyes darted toward Nikki and Jake. She made a low rumble deep in her chest. Nikki turned around and realized the cub had circled behind them and was drinking water from the trickle of a stream.

"We're sitting ducks," Jake whispered. "We're blocking her from her cub!"

Nikki lifted the steel cord, pulled, and said through gritted teeth, "How?" She thought a moment, then whispered, "Okay, listen. Don't make any sudden moves. You should get on my shoulders. We'll look bigger. More threatening."

"What?!" Jake squeaked.

The agitated bear moved toward them. She growled a low, threatening moan. She stopped and lifted her huge body up on her hind legs and sniffed the air. The sheer bulk of the creature made Nikki shiver.

That's when Nikki noticed Elam's rifle. He'd abandoned the empty weapon after hunting the day before. It leaned against a tree. No bullets, but wood and metal make a strong club. Would the steel cords reach?

Jesus, help!

The bear stalked Jake with eyes narrowed and mouth drooling. Nikki crawled to the end of her tether, stretching out her arm as far as she could. Her fingers shifted the rifle's butt and the gun fell beside her. She snatched it closer just as the creature charged at Jake. The mother slashed out knife-like claws, then backed up.

Dust swirled.

Jake wailed. Blood soaked his ripped sleeve. Before a second breath, she yanked the weapon up and held it like a club.

"Here I am! Come get me!" The bear turned toward her.

Can't run, can fight.

The animal lunged at her. Nikki screamed, swung wild and cracked her on the nose. A howl filled the air. She jumped back and stepped into the fire's hot coals. Heat and sparks washed through the trees.

Nikki saw Jake take something from his leg pocket. Something small.

"Give me the gun," he commanded.

"It's empty."

"Give me the gun!"

Anger bellowed from the beast. Jake jumped to Nikki. He snatched the rifle up, opened the chamber, and crammed bullets inside.

Nikki screeched out, "Bullets, where on earth?"

The monster swung her head from side to side, then plopped down and let out a fierce snarl. Claws slashed the air. Black, cold eyes blazed with hate.

Jake aimed the loaded gun down. The muzzle touched the twin steel cords around the log. He blasted, and metal strands flew apart across the dirt. In the same movement, he pulled the rifle up and aimed at the now charging bear.

A bullet ripped into fur. The beast collapsed in the dirt and struggled to get back up. Jake threw the gun down and grabbed Nikki's hand.

Jake screamed, "Run!"

***

Elam shoved the goods back into the pack and popped open the door. Ava's stomach knotted.

"Elam." Maggie had a pile of folded towels with two bars of soap sitting on the top of it. "I wondered if you'd like to use the showers now. I could help your little girl get started in the ladies' shower. I know how difficult it can be for a man traveling alone with a little girl."

Getting washed might feel good. Would Elam let me out of his sight? ... Yes. He knows I'm a chicken.

Maggie was so kind. She showed Ava how to turn the shower on and off. From her pocket, she took out a small pink bottle of shampoo. She explained that when Ava finished she should bring the towels and shower key back to the office.

Could she tell Maggie the truth? Ava opened her mouth and sucked in enough breath to blurt out every fearful detail.

149

"Yes, dear, did you want to tell me something?" Maggie's face was soft and trusting as she waited for Ava to respond.

The words jumbled into Ava's mind and jammed into a clogged-up ball. She tried to practice the words in her head.

I've been kidnapped. My friends are lost in the mountains. I killed my mommy's boyfriend. Call the police. No! Don't. Wait! I–

"Don't worry, honey. Your grandpa is right next door in the men's shower. Just call out loud if you need him." Then she left.

The words still raced through her even as she watched the door close. Every muscle drained of strength, and a cold hopelessness took its place inside her body.

Dumb, worthless Ava. Dumb, disappointed, and ... dirty.

She stepped into the shower. The water was chilly at first but warmed to a delicious, soft spray. She liked the berry smell of the shampoo but washed fast. The small, unfamiliar shower stall made her uncomfortable and nervous.

After she used the clean towels to dry herself, she put the dress back on with the hoodie Nikki had made them take. Then, like a miracle, a tickle of encouragement warmed her. Strength flooded back in. The tired fear that drained her will had washed away in the suds.

She almost skipped back to the office. Well, not skipped, but walked with her head up and her back straight.

Can I do this? Can I tell her?

Chapter 34

CRAZED HUSBAND BEATS OFF ACCUSERS!

The headline splashed across the front page of a gossip magazine. The picture showed a maniacal-looking Gary Busey-type in his pajama bottoms, swinging a bat over his head. James' face appeared almost deformed as it twisted with anger in the photo.

He picked up the rag and turned it around in the rack, with the backside showing. Then he paid the cashier for the trail mix and hurried out the door.

He jumped into the backseat of the car. From the front passenger seat Edith asked, "Are you okay? You're kind of pale."

"No, Edith, I'm not okay. I've just seen something I never in a million years would have thought I would see." He told them about his front page spread in the magazine.

"Oh, my dear, don't worry. No one reads that trash." Edith spoke with confidence, but she sneaked a quick guilty glance at Ray.

They rolled into the church parking lot, and James looked around for reporters. He saw them set up on the lawn by the front door, like big game hunters on a safari.

"Wait," he said. "Go around the block and drop me off at the corner. I don't want the media to connect me with your car."

It didn't take long for the reporters to recognize James as he walked down the long driveway from the street.

Maybe I should've worn a disguise. Has it come to that?

They swarmed around him. At least they didn't shout out questions and accusations. Pastor Thomas came out with some other men to help him get through the commotion.

"Thank you, Pastor," said James.

The Reverend nodded to him and gave him a quick pat on the back. James walked directly into the sanctuary, not wanting to talk with anyone. The room held a few people already seated. James sat down in an empty pew. He didn't know what to expect.

Normally, the hand-shakers and the God-bless-you crowd would have hit him up at the door.

As each row began to fill, he noticed an odd thing. Widow's row filled up first, the place where the widows usually sat together. Then the youth and their counselors joked and jostled their way to their seats. The young families were always last. He understood why, being from one himself. But row by row, the people crowded into place,

Except for his pew.

He surveyed the long empty bench beside him. An invisible wall had gone up. Some sort of bubble surrounded him. He tried to smile at a few familiar faces, and some responded, but others gave him a glare or turned away.

He closed his eyes and bowed his head. Maybe if he pretended he was in prayer, no one would notice how out of place he felt.

A gentle touch on his shoulder made him look up. Edith flapped her hand to shoo him over. Grateful, he scooted down the bench so Ray and Edith could sit beside him. She patted his hand before he bowed his head again.

He listened to the prelude.

The music that comes before the first song, that's before the announcements, before the first song set, before the...

His mind rambled through the whole scheduled service. Hoping it would hurry the process somehow.

He didn't hold out hope for any miracle of peace, but Nikki would have wanted him here. He kept his eyes closed until a warm pressure against his other arm made him open them.

Now, next to him on his right side, back ramrod straight, sat Ruby Farber. She faced forward with an expression that said, "Don't you dare mess with my friend." Some parishioners gave her a suspicious sideways glance and whispered to the person next to them.

James had to smile.

He had a difficult time concentrating on the service. But one part of the sermon stood out in his mind. Pastor Thomas quoted a verse from Zephaniah. James didn't even know there was such a book. It sounded like a name for a backwoods farmhand.

The last part of the verse that talked about God singing caught in his mind. It said, "He rejoices over you with singing." Where had he heard that before? He immediately saw, in his mind, the solemn face of his three-year-old son.

"God, Daddy, I heard God singing."

His eyes pricked with tears.

When the service was over, everyone left the sanctuary and went into the fellowship room. James stayed by the opening, not wanting to go in. Ray stood with him.

Ruby pulled her face into a pleasant smile as she passed by him. "Have a good day." Then her glower returned. She pointed a stern finger at James. "And keep me posted." She marched off.

Edith came up behind Ray and James. "I need to get some toy donations down to the Sunday School rooms. Ray, come and help me."

James said, "I can help."

"No, no, it's just a few things. Besides, the reporters would follow you to our car."

"Oh. Oh, yeah." James scratched his head, worried. "Well ... I know. I'll wait for you by the basement door, out back. Drive around when you're finished. Maybe the reporters won't look for me there."

James made his way through the church kitchen to the back-basement stairs. From around the corner, he heard heated voices. He stopped and listened, not knowing if he should go back. Then he heard his name.

"But what do we know about James Rolen?" said a gruff male voice.

"I don't care. I won't do that." James knew the voice. Pastor Thomas.

"Listen, we can't condone murder. This congregation simply cannot let him continue to be a member of our church. We've got to be wary of the wolves at the door. You know Satan is trying to find any way he can to ruin God's work here. Paul even said to the churches in the New Testament to –"

Pastor interrupted. "We aren't condoning murder, but we can't cut off sinners from being a part of our church, or we won't have one! Besides we don't even know if he's done anything."

"God says to avoid the very appearance of evil." A woman's soft, but stringent, voice spoke.

"I wouldn't be surprised if our numbers have already gone down because of it. You know next week is the push for the new building fund."

"I don't care about that!"

Several voices cried out, "What?"

"I mean, I do care. It's a good thing. But I'm the spiritual leader in this congregation, and I must lead by what God is showing me. God offers forgiveness to everyone!"

With strong emotion the woman screeched out, "Even those accused of murder?"

"Yes."

Chapter 35

Ava gazed up at Maggie and placed the wet towels and soap on the counter.

"Hello, sweetie, you look all cleaned up," Maggie crooned.

No, I still can't. I can't make the words come. But something has changed inside of me. Something good.

"Thanks for bringing in the towels and soap." Maggie reached across the counter to take them. "You sit down right there. Your grandpa isn't finished yet."

Ava settled into one of the chairs next to the door. Her wet hair gave her an all over chill, but hope brought a warmth that made a dent in her fearful heart.

Another customer came in, ready to check out. The woman had a huge purse, stuffed and fat. In search of her wallet, she spread objects out on the counter. A small rubber bear, a brush, makeup, a cell phone, and a Hot Wheels car.

Wait! A cell phone!

Ava's heart beat faster. The woman chatted on about being sure she had her wallet. Somewhere.

Ava got out of her seat and came around the end of the counter. She rested her chin on top. The woman pulled the bag off the ledge, turned, and used her knee to hold up the purse so she could dig down deep. In the same way Ava had done all that day, she reached her hand over and slipped the phone off the counter and into her hoodie pouch. She stood a moment longer and sat back down.

"Oh, here it is!" She waved her wallet in the air. "I knew the thing had to be in this bottomless pit."

Elam came to the door and motioned for Ava to come. She glanced back at Maggie and smiled. Then in her silent way, she followed him out.

Back in the van, Elam went into a running chat with himself. Mumbling and smiling about glories unseen.

Ava sat back and fingered the phone in her pocket. When Elam wasn't looking, she took the phone out and made sure it was turned off. She knew about keeping batteries fresh.

Eventually, she fell asleep. She woke in the night when Elam started up the motor and headed out. A buzz of excitement hummed through her when she thought about the phone. Guilt wove into the joy. The stealing had been all Elam, except for the last.

But this woman seemed nice. Like Maggie. She would have wanted to help her.

If we get rescued, I'll give the phone back.

They rolled into camp as sunlight crept over the mountain. When released from the van, Ava ran through the camp and beyond the cabin. Happy and excited to see her friends, she expected to see them sleeping by a fire, waiting for them.

But Ava froze. In front of her sat a dead fire pit, beside it steel cords tossed like snakes on the scrambled dirt. She saw splashes of dark red cut into the dust. This she recognized. She'd seen it before, mixed with dirt.

Blood!

Ava slumped to the ground beside the bloody dirt. Her mouth gaped open and eyes squeezed shut. Strained sounds slipped out her throat.

Dead, dead. They're dead. Like Grandpa, like Ben, like me.

"No, no!" Elam screamed, "The evil, the burning acid has eaten the holy." Elam held his closed fist up into the air. He ran around the fire pit and back to the cabin. "Attacking, like the vicious and vile." His rifle laid in the dirt. He snatched it up and raced inside the cabin as he mumbled in a raspy voice. "We must hide from the evil world."

Returning, he loaded bullets into the gun as he walked. Ava leaned forward and put her hand in the dirt beside the blood. Sorrow trembled in her heart, cold tears dripped off her hot cheeks.

His voice changed from panicked to calm authority. "No time to grieve, child. We need to move."

Ava wondered if the evil had really come. If she had stayed, could she have helped them, or would she have been eaten, too?

Elam grabbed her arm and pulled her up. He attached the chains to her waist and again to his belt. They walked toward the trees.

His voice changed again. "To live is to die, die is to gain, gain is to live. We die from this world. If we hide from the fearful, the tearful, careful plotting wretches straining to be alive, we have nothing to give. Lost, lost, we are lost, lost in the cost, the cost is a wealth of pain, where there is no gain."

With each phrase, Elam took a step. He went through the gates with Ava trailing behind, clinging to her chains to keep up. With his head down, he tracked the ground.

Elam trudged in random zig-zags inside the large compound. Ava's legs could barely keep moving when he stopped dead. With a quick jerk, he pushed his hand back at Ava, and then froze still. He stared at Ava a moment, as if the wheels were turning in his head. "Priscilla, you go ahead. You were always the best tracker in the family, even though you're so young."

He gave her a shove forward. He even dropped her steel leash and took a stronger hold on his rifle. Ava stepped out, not knowing where to go. She pushed her way through tall grass and bushes.

She headed toward a spot that looked more open. As she got closer the way cleared to a rocky slope. Her legs, weak and trembling, would not quite go where she directed them. Her foot slipped on the smooth pebbles, and she went down.

The air rushed up at her as she went over an edge. The fall hurled her into the gully, sliding her over sandy boulders as she rolled.

No screaming.

Her arms shot out to try and catch herself. Tumbling down, she braced for the bottom.

A thud rippled through the gully when she landed, and a soft "ugh" sound escaped Ava. No pain at first. Her eyes were squeezed shut, but she touched the ground with her hands. This did not feel like dirt.

Soft, furry, and wet?

She slid down the lump she'd landed on and looked up. Staring at her with glazed eyes and open mouth was the largest bear she had ever seen.

"Don't move, Priscilla, I'm coming."

She couldn't move. The terror froze her.

Elam hurried down, but once there, he eased up beside Ava. Then he let out a huge sigh. "It's okay, girl. It won't hurt you." He gave the furry arm a kick. "The critter's dead."

Ava sat back on her haunches and glanced at herself. Red blood covered her hands and smeared down her front. Her eyes became fuzzy, and head spun.

"Stay here," Elam commanded. "I need to mark this spot for later. We'll have meat all winter."

Ava scooted away from the hulk. She settled on a smooth rock that rested against the slope. An odd sound coming from the trees from above made her jump.

A soft whirring, grrring voice. The bushes parted, and a furry ball pushed through the branches. A snout appeared and beady eyes stared down at her.

A tiny bear. A cub. That must be his mom.

Like a dam broken, tears poured from her eyes.

No mom, alone, and helpless. How will this tiny bit of thing survive with no one? He'll be alone.

A snap of warm determined fire sparked in her heart.

Maybe I can help it. I could feed him from the trash at camp. He'll hide behind the cabin. We'll be best friends.

Ava stretched out her hand to him.

Don't worry, little one. You're not invisible to me.

She took a quick glance at Elam. He was pulling branches together and sticking them into the ground. But how could she get food to the bear without Elam knowing? She hung her head. No, it was best to leave him.

Ava hoped he wouldn't see his mother, whose blood drenched the dirt. She watched the cub lick his paws and stroke his head like a gentleman getting ready for a date.

She heard a click sound from above.

A shot thundered. With a jerk, the cub flew back and he dropped from the tree. Blood splashed in droplets into the sunlight. The cub laid flat on the ground. As if a plug had been pulled, he lay broken and still.

Like Ben.

His little eyes still open, he stared into the sky. His pink tongue slipped out of the side of his mouth.

Ava looked up at Elam as he lowered his rifle. His face melted from stony cold to sadness. He whispered, "I think it's better for him this way, Priscilla. Because ... because the tender mercies of the wicked are cruel."

Chapter 36

"You've had bullets all along?" Nikki glared at Jake as they sat high up in a pine tree.

"Hey, I forgot about 'em. They're in my junk-pocket. Besides, Elam never leaves his rifle out. Lucky break."

"Where's the bear?"

Jake checked around under them. "We lost her. I think I got her in the head."

"Maybe she ran away like we did. I don't see her." She searched across from where they had just come. "Praise God!"

"Yeah, praise god. We're in the forest, with a wounded bear stalking us, a crazy man hunting for us, and no food. I suppose god is testing us?"

"No, I personally think God is showing me He's in control."

Jake banged his forehead on the tree trunk.

"No, really, I think at times God allows His people to come to the very edge of disaster, and then He miraculously pulls us back. So, when the unthinkable does happen, we know He had a reason for it, and He is still in control."

"Rrriiight."

Nikki clung to her branch and searched the area. No sign of bears.

Blasts cut into the air. Gunfire. Three shots.

They turned to each other, and both said, "Elam."

Jake stretched his neck, trying to locate where the sound came from. "What should we do?"

"We can't leave without Priscilla." With one hand, she adjusted her jeans. "And there may a wounded and angry bear, somewhere around here." She sighed. "Let's go find Elam."

They climbed down and took off in the direction of the sounds. Soon they saw the old man and his small companion.

160

Priscilla pulled on her chains. Elam detached them from his waist. She ran to Nikki and threw herself at her. She wrapped her skinny arms around her friend's waist and cried.

Nikki whispered, "It's okay, sweetheart. We're okay."

Elam pointed his knife at her and grunted. "So, they tried to get you, did they? Those monsters try to seduce the good. If you don't stare in their eyes, and are not deceived by the way they dance, you can get away." His head bobbed up and down with a knowing smile. "You both seem okay, though. I think?" He lifted Jake's chin with his knife point. "Son, where did you get the bruised face?"

Jake pulled back and looked down at his most recent injury. The gash that had fresh blood smeared down his arm. "Oh, I don't know, Pa. Maybe someone tried to beat the spit out of me earlier this week."

"Okay, then." He put his knife away and shifted his rifle to his other hand. "Let's go back to camp."

161

Chapter 37

Like ordering a dog to sit, Elam commanded, "Jake, make fire."

Nikki worried about the gash on her friend's arm, but said nothing.

I could clean his wound and dress it with the things in the medical kit.

Elam stood back and watched the boy make a teepee of wood with kindling under it. At the first spark Nikki noticed *fear* flick in the old man's blue eyes.

Maybe I can sneak the kit outside now while his mind is on the fire.

As she walked toward the cabin, the smell of smoke drifted over her. With a quick turn to check on their progress, she bumped into Elam's chest.

He had followed her.

Grabbing her arms to steady her, he laughed. "Hey, watch where you're going there, young lady."

She reached up to rub her nose. "Oh, I'm sorry. I didn't know you were there."

"Where're ya going?" Now his voice sounded flat.

"Inside. I was just...um...I guess I can't remember why. I must be getting old. I'll go back to the fire."

"Nonsense! Let's both go in the cabin." He put his arm around her shoulders.

"But I—"

Elam growled out a word. "Now."

Inside the cabin, Elam sniffed through the room like a Doberman. His face gnarled into a frown, and his eyes shifted from one place to the next as he hummed under his breath.

That crazy old man is just now noticing the changes I made in here? He notices everything, or nothing at all.

Nikki stood near the doorway, worried until Elam pronounced, "Nice work, Mama. The place looks pepped up." His face went back to a gentle, happy grin.

But in a flash, his eyes became serious, but not sane.

Who is he really seeing?

He seemed to take her in from top to bottom. Then he dropped his gaze to the floor. In a shy tone, he said, "Jesse, I have a surprise for you. Just for you."

Reaching for her hand, he pulled her over to the bed. "Sit down here."

Nikki had no desire to sit on the bed. But in this world, she had no choices.

He went to the door, closed it, and picked up his backpack. He sat on the bed beside her and put the bag between his feet. Nikki scooted over to make plenty of room, but Elam slid in closer.

She turned her head away from him as acid reflux burned in her throat.

His countenance became tender and hesitant. Nikki stiffened as if a cold chill had swept the room.

"I don't always tell you, but you know how much I love you. Right?"

She gave a quick fearful nod, and the hair on her arms tingled.

"You're the woman of noble character from Proverbs 31. You'll be that for me." He put his hand on her shoulder and stroked her back.

She took in a breath and held it.

As if unable to meet her gaze Elam gazed down.

"I have something for you." He reached inside his ragged pack and pulled out a black pouch with a golden drawstring.

With shaking hands, he placed the bag in her lap. "Open it."

Nikki let out a nervous sigh.

He snapped, "Open it!" Elam shook his head, as if startled at the harshness of his own voice. "I'm sorry. I'm just excited. Please, open it."

She picked up the bag, startled by its weight, and undid the cords. Pulling it open, she peered in. Darkness. She reached inside and scooped out his prize.

Cold metal threads curled in her hands. She held them up to the light. A necklace with sterling silver and copper strands threading turquoise stones shone with life in the drab cabin.

"It's real. The silver and copper are real, and so is the turquoise. I'm sure of it. God told me to take—I mean get it for you. I was certain you'd love it. Remember when we went to the Grand Canyon? We were, were so ... alive and I was ... all the kids were excited to see the mules."

A tear fell as his eyes locked on her face, and he lifted his hand to the side of her neck. "Do you like it?"

Fear made the word choke out her throat. "Yes."

He stood and pulled her to her feet.

Oh, please, God, no.

With both hands on her shoulders, he drew her closer. Nikki shut her eyes and held her breath. He cupped her face in his hand and caressed her cheek. The old man leaned down and kissed her on the top of her head.

A small, gentle, timid kiss.

"I know you'll put this in a safe place." He straightened, took a step back, and said, "I need to pee," and walked out the door.

***

Jake was sitting close to the warmth of the fire when Elam strode out of the cabin unbuckling his belt. A few minutes later Nikki came from the cabin. Her face looked pale.

"You okay?" He asked.

She nodded and sat on the log by the fire. Priscilla shifted closer to her and leaned against Nikki's arm. They both stared into the flames.

The sun now gone behind the mountain. The fire and the moon their only light.

On his way back from the throne, Elam went to the van and pulled out the prizes God had provided. He lugged them to where all three now sat with solemn faces. "See the bounty our great God has lavished on our family. Go ahead. We can have a feast. The Feast of God's Great Goodness."

"Say, um, Pa? What about the, um, enemy? I think I wounded the mother, and what about the cub? Um, I mean, small evil one."

"They're dead."

"What?" Jake turned to Priscilla's sad face, and she nodded.

"But more will come. So, I have a plan. Did I forget to tell you?" He grabbed a crate of Spam and headed back toward the cabin. His voice boomed as he walked. "We're going home. Yes, sir, no one can hurt us ever again."

Jake pushed in close to Nikki and whispered, "What the heck does that mean? I thought this was home."

Priscilla pulled on Nikki's sleeve for attention. With a little smile, she pulled something out of her pocket.

Something small, and black sat in her open palm.

Jake jerked his head up. "Crap! It's a phone."

"Jake, shhhh. Let me see, sweetie. This is just like mine. Like the one I lost."

In the darkness, with trembling hands, Nikki pushed the on button. She held her breath waiting for signs of life.

A white ball, with a black insignia in it, appeared on the screen. A soft tune played and the light flashed into the tree branches above them.

Nikki slammed her hand over the phone and held it down. Everyone looked at the cabin to see if Elam had heard.

The old man belted out, "Swing low, sweet chariot, coming for to carry me ho-o-o-o-ome."

Hands shaking, she lifted the phone again, careful not to let light shine out. She swiped the screen.

Disappointing words appeared. "WARNING: 5% battery left." The screen went black.

Chapter 38

James snatched his cell phone from the dashboard. He swung the car into Ray's driveway as he pushed the garage remote he'd been given.

"Hello?"

A soft female voice responded. "May I speak to Mr. Rolen?"

"Yes, that's me."

"My name is Cora Martin. I think ... well ... that is, we may have something in common. My daughter is missing."

James drove into the garage and shut off his engine. He stared, unseeing, at the steering wheel. Thoughts scrambled through his brain.

A prank?

A lead?

Another dream, perhaps?

"Mr. Rolen, are you there?"

"Yes, yes, I'm here."

"My daughter turned up missing the same weekend as your wife. Both disappeared in the same area. I just wondered if there's a connection."

"Excuse me. What is your name again? And your daughter's?"

"My name is Cora Martin. My daughter's name is Ava Martin."

"Oh, the little girl on the news. The one too shy to speak. How did you get my number?"

"A church in Woodland Park has been helping my... my fiancé and I. We're from out of town, you see." Her voice, quiet and breathy, lowered even more. He pressed the phone harder to his ear.

"One of the members that brought us food used to attend your church. He still had your church's phone directory. He

166

thought the coincidence was strong enough to give me your number."

"I see."

Great, now people are giving out my cell number.

"I wondered if there might be information we could share?"

He sat up taller in his seat. "Maybe we should look into that. What do you know about your daughter's disappearance?"

"Ben was driving to the store with Ava, and he had an accident. He was unconscious when the police found him, and Ava was gone. That's all we know."

"Where did this happen?"

"Just east of Woodland Park."

"Nikki's car had been in a crash, too. What do the police say about Ava?"

The phone stayed silent for a moment or two. "They think she ran away."

"Has she ever done that before?"

"No... well, she's wandered off before. And that morning she did get lost in the forest for a little while, but I don't think she was running away. She's too young for that. She's only seven years old."

James heard a sound in the background, then muffled, angry whispering.

A man's voice spoke from the phone. "I'm sorry, Cora's confused. Ava ran away. That's all."

The phone went dead.

Chapter 39

"Cell's dead. Or almost dead." Jake glanced at Priscilla's shocked face. She shook her head and pointed to the off button.

"You turned it off?" Jake tried to understand her motions. He looked closer. "You only shut down the screen. Not the phone. That means the phone kept on searching for connection, wasting batteries. Then the system went down when the battery got too low."

The girl grabbed the phone and shook it. Tears formed in her dark eyes, her small face twisted with frustration.

"Sweetie, that won't help." Nikki gently took the cell from her hands. "I wonder if there's even reception up here." She sighed and looked around as if she could see connection.

Jake drew in a deep, shaky breath. "Dudes, you still don't get it. We *can't* get away. Listen to me." He stopped and bit his lip, as if getting courage to speak.

"Right after I tried to escape and he found me, Elam trapped a rabbit. He brought it to me." Jake could feel his cheek quivering. "He took out his blade and sliced off ears, poked out eyes, and ... and gutted the body. Right in front of me, man. I mean, the thing was still quivering as he cut into it. I'll never forget the sound that came from the rabbit." He struggled to pull back tears, and then swiped at his wet cheeks. "Like a tortured baby screaming."

Priscilla reached for Nikki's hand. Both stared, riveted to Jake's agonized face.

He pulled his arms over his stomach, hunched his body inward and shifted backwards. "A sacrifice, he said. If I couldn't keep the rules, it would be better to be sacrificed. Then he pointed the knife at me." He shut his eyes as he strained to push back the remembered terror. His bottom lip trembled. "So, it's just as well the cell is dead."

"It's not dead. Maybe there's enough for one emergency call."

"If we had service. Every time we try, we'd waste batteries. There won't be enough charge left for all that."

"But if we had a charger...?"

"Well, we don't, and there's no electricity."

"What about the van?"

Jake was silent for a moment. Then he shook his head. "No, the van is always locked. Don't you think I would have taken it long ago if I could get in it?" He leaned into her face. "So, leave it alone!"

"There's got to be a reason why God helped Priscilla get this phone!"

"Sure, there is. Because God's messing with us." His eyes glinted with anger as his lips quivered. "Just like Elam does!"

***

Three nights later, Nikki sat staring into the campfire with Priscilla. Jake devoured the last piece of skin from the meal of "holy" potatoes Elam had provided. Nikki glanced over at the more diverse food supply Elam hoarded outside the cabin door.

Knowing the marathon Bible reading would come next, Nikki searched around for anything soft she could put under her knees for cushion.

Thanks, Lord. At least last night's reading in Joshua helped encourage me.

Elam came out of the cabin. "Get up! The voice of God has spoken from the rocks of Jabez. Can't you hear them screaming the words?" He covered his ears and yelled, "Carry my rocks from out of the stream to build an altar."

He led them to the chain link gate that guarded the road and opened it. He hadn't bothered to chain his captives. Fear locked them.

They shuffled along the fence to the right until they came to where the shallow creek seeped under the wall structure. Then Elam directed the group to follow the trickle until it merged with a larger creek where the waters crashed over bowling ball-sized rocks.

Elam shouted over the rush of water. "Stop!" He picked up a small rock and held it to his ear. "This is it. We will carry the stones up the river bank and build the altar. God commands us."

The captives, all three, took off shoes and socks and waded into the stream.

He climbed atop a boulder near the stream to call out demands. Freezing water numbed Nikki's feet. The rocks' rough surfaces scraped arms, and their weight strained muscles. As each burden was lifted out of the river, Elam would shout what evil it represented.

"Sin of swallowing the liquid acid. Sin of watching immoral men and women touch as they dance. Sin of the lazy, slothful, and dead. Sin of tasting food from rancid minds. Sin of allowing the words that fly from boxes of fear to enter the heart."

Elam moved to retrieved rocks and hefted them into a tower with brute strength. As the evening wore on, the pile's height rose over their heads. With almost demonic strength and skill, he stacked the stones impossibly tall. He pulled over a dead tree log to reach even higher.

Finally, he shouted, "Stop! Jake, gather wood for a fire. Fire for burning atop the holy tower." He pointed a shaking finger to the rock's highest point.

Nikki took Pricilla's hand and waded from the frigid water to take a seat besides the towering alter. They collapsed onto the rocky shore. With numb fingers, she helped her little friend pull on dry socks and shoes. Nikki took off her own hoodie and draped it over Priscilla's shivering shoulders.

Discouragement seeped into Nikki's tired bones. She couldn't feel her feet as she put her own dry socks on. The evening hours had drained the light and brought a dark fear with it. The stars and moon gave some light, but did not erase the dread.

This is when we die. Chopped to pieces like butchered meat on this altar.

"Now we burn our sins. Burn 'til the land is sacred. Cleanse it from the fearful dread that has crept past the wall." In a frantic cadence Elam mumbled as he bowed before the altar. "The holy fire will clean and renew. We will obey the Father, or the judgment will come on us all."

Nikki imagined slamming a rock over his head as he knelt there. But she made no move or effort to make it happen.

Jake shuffled back with an armful of twigs. He put the sticks down on the old log. With an exhausted sigh, he bent down to stack a few rocks. He stepped onto them and tip toed up. Stretching out his long spindly arms he shoved the bundle on the top. "Can we eat now?"

Nikki tensed, tightening her arm around Priscilla.

"No!" Elam snapped. "First we light the altar. Each of you will climb to the top and add a flame. Then we eat."

Nikki stood and looked to the top. She couldn't believe how tall the altar had gotten. Could it be nine feet?

Reaching out, Elam grabbed Priscilla and stood her up. The hoodie dropped to the ground. "You first."

Her little hands were red with the cold and her small body shivered. Priscilla tilted her head back and gazed up at the forbidding tower.

The thing must have seemed twenty feet to a small child. Fear lit her eyes. She backed up and shook her head. Nikki saw the child sway.

"You do as I say, girl. You don't understand." He knelt and put his face into hers. He clasped her arms to her sides and squeezed.

Ava turned her face away.

Nikki imagined Elam's hot stinky breath.

"If we do it all, all the rules, God will protect us. Poor child, you can't know, can you? Don't spit or chew, and don't go with those who do."

He picked her up and brought her to the altar, then commanded, "Jake, run back to the pit of eternal fire and bring a stick with cleansing flames on its end. A single seed can produce a rotten harvest. We must protect the garden of our children's minds."

Jake hesitated.

Elam pulled a knife from his belt and held the blade to the child's throat. "Do it!"

With a groaned he took off at a stumbling run. In seeming no time, he raced back through the trees with a lit torch and splashed across the stream. As Elam set the knife down and reached toward Jake, Priscilla pulled away.

Elam snatched the glowing wood with one hand and corralled her with the other. She arched her body and threw herself backwards. He caught her and struggled to pull the girl in front of the altar. He shoved the stick into her hands. "Take it!"

She folded her fingers around the bottom end, and Elam grabbed up his knife. Before he could hold it to her neck again, she swung the flame at his eyes.

Elam shrieked and scrambled backwards. Fear, repulsion, terror splayed across his face.

"Fires of hell! God, You are Mighty," he bellowed over the sound of water rushing. "Save us!"

Priscilla dropped the stick and hurled herself toward Nikki. Nikki reached out to embrace the child. Priscilla rushed so fast into her arms they both fell to the ground.

In a flash, Jake reached for the branch. He missed. Elam snapped out of his terror and slashed his knife at Jake. The boy dodged and fell back. The branch lay at Elam's feet. The thick end of the stick still glowed red hot.

Clutching the girl close, Nikki struggled to stand and hoped to run. But Elam reached them. While brandishing the blade in one hand, he used the other to wrench the precious body from her arms.

"Leave her alone!" screamed Nikki.

Elam smacked her with the back of his hand. Nikki's cheek stung, her legs trembled as dizziness overwhelmed her. She dropped to the ground.

He pulled the girl again to the altar, and holstered his knife. The terrorized child, with eyes wide, face wet and smeared with dirt, went limp in his arms. She heaved with sobs.

Jake struggled to stand. Elam, back in control, took up the hot poker once more. He set Priscilla down. She teetered. He shoved the stick in her hands.

Nikki whispered, "Brave girl."

Priscilla took a small step onto one of the rocks, pulled with her arm, and began to climb. After five trembling pulls up, she cast her eyes down.

"Don't look down," Jake yelled.

"The rocks are falling," Nikki called out.

The pile wobbled, stacked like a Jenga game ready for someone to lose. Priscilla dropped the stick and grabbed onto the rocks with both hands.

"No! No, no, no." Elam's voice erupted with anger, then switched to a frightened child. "You dropped the sacred flame. Listen to Elam. The father says there will be no forgiveness." He picked up the stick, and swung at her. Then he held the hot end against her bare leg.

The sizzle and smell of burnt flesh shocked Nikki's senses.

Priscilla stiffened before she collapsed in a faint. Her body fell backwards onto the rocky ground. Her head smacked with a chilling thud.

Elam raged, then switched to a stark terror as he murmured incomprehensible sounds. Until he shouted, "God save us! He is mighty."

Jake lashed out in exhausted anger. "Really! Seriously, Elam?" His eyes snapped with disgust, and he demanded, "If your god is so great, then why are you *always* so *afraid*?"

Elam froze into a statue. As if Jake had flicked a switch and turned him to stone. He stared sightless, over Nikki's shoulder. His lower lip quivered, and a stream of water dripped down his face. He whispered, his mouth barely moving, "I don't know." He shook his head. "I ... I don't know."

***

Jake carried the unconscious girl back to camp. One slight arm dangled down, and her legs bounced at his quick pace. He placed her by the campfire.

While the old man locked the gate, Nikki ran to get Elam's first aid kit from the cabin and knelt beside Priscilla. She poured cool water over the wound, then searched through the first aid supplies. Finding a roll of sterile cloth, she wrapped the burn.

173

Elam strode past them into the cabin and closed the door.

"Mercy, God, give us mercy." Nikki breathed the words out. A soft, compelling voice that, even to her own ears, sounded desperate and frightened.

How severe is this burn? Lord, I don't know what to do.

"Mercy?" Jake sneered. "Right!"

She looked up at him.

The side of his face still dark with bruises, his swollen lips contorted in sarcasm. "Who is going to give us mercy? We've got no hope, lady. That madman will never let us go."

"The cell phone?"

"The phone's dead. We're all dead, waiting to be buried." He sat down on a rock and stared at the dirt. "There's no hope."

A crushing wave of defeat fell over her. The tiny bit of hope she had left blinked out.

"I know." She whispered and dropped her head. Giving up came easily. No struggle, no more pushing her mind to focus. She held the girl's tiny hand in her own, feeling the soft tenderness of the child's fingers.

Words washed into her mind. She spoke them. "'Surely goodness and mercy shall follow me all the days of my life.'"

Jake said, "Who's Shirley?"

Nikki pulled in a quick, shocked breath. Then a snort and a small laugh came. Snickers bounced in her stomach and shook her shoulders. Giggles grew and rushed through her with a slight hysterical ring. The chortles bubbled up her throat and took her along into a rush of surprised, ridiculous, and unfounded joy.

Jake stared. "Nikki. Nikki! Are you okay?" He reached over and shook her arm.

From her knees she fell over, curled up onto the ground beside the slight form of the unconscious child, and trembled with the mirth. Tears rippled from her eyes, and she squished them closed over the wetness.

She couldn't stop laughing. She had lost control. Maybe she'd never *had* control.

Give it up, my child.

Thoughts focused and words formed in her mind as laughter subsided and she said, "Jake, mercy is the only thing that's going to get us through this. Mercy from a madman, and mercy from an all-loving God that you don't believe in."

Even before she turned to him she heard a very quiet voice. "Mercy? What's mercy?"

Nikki used her arms to push herself up to a sit. She gazed into the face of the hurting young man. She saw confusion in his eyes. He shook his head and raised his shoulders in a shrug, as if to say he had not spoken the words.

They both turned to Priscilla.

Her chocolate brown eyes, bright with tears, were open and staring at Nikki.

"Sweetheart," Nikki whispered. "Did you say something?"

Chapter 40

James turned the knob on the garage door and entered Ray's house. He saw Edith bending over the kitchen sink. She rubbed a washcloth across the faucet, flashing a welcoming grin as she polished. "James, glad to see you're back. I was just thinking about what to make for supper." Her expression changed to concern. "Is something wrong?"

"Not really. I just had an interesting call. It was either another prank, or the mother of the girl that went missing when Nikki did."

"What did she want?"

"To share information. But then a man cut us off. Made her sound like she was a loon." He sat down at the kitchen table.

The back door opened, and Ray clomped into the house.

"Ray! Take those dirty things off outside."

With a heavy sigh, he backed out the door, took the muddy work boots off, and re-entered. "James, is there going to be a prayer vigil tonight?"

"I really don't know. Since Sunday, I haven't heard anything from Pastor Thomas." James sighed and ran his hand through his hair. "Maybe he did decide to give up on me. I guess I won't be going to church with you anymore."

"What? Why not?" Ray's deep voice boomed.

"Well, I don't want to be in a church where they think I murdered my wife. It's obvious they don't want me. You should have seen some of the looks I got last Sunday. I don't know if I've even always agreed with everything they do there anyway." Even to his own ears, he sounded pouty.

"Well, of course you don't. Say, you're not one of those people that demands a designer church, are you?"

"What's that?"

"Oh, you know how it is these days. Everybody wants to customize everything. Coffee, shampoo, even milk! Soy, blech!" He stuck out his tongue and made a face. "People get to thinking that about church, too."

Ray straightened in mock importance. "I want a church with a youth ministry that caters to my kids, music that suits my taste, and a budget that I say is right, or I'll leave."

Edith set a coffee cup and a milk carton in front of James. She pushed the sugar bowl that sat on the table toward him.

Ray relaxed his stance and sighed. "There's no commitment anymore. If things aren't a perfect fit, they vacate. It's like they want a meal but won't pick up a spoon. People get bored, or ticked off by one person's thoughtless words, and leave."

"But... um..." James was stumped. He'd heard people say that, but it didn't sound the same when Ray said it.

"What's happened to church family? If someone in my family didn't agree with me, they'd still be family! 'Less that church gives up on the whole Gospel, or God writes on a wall for me to leave, they're stuck with me."

Edith smiled but shook a dishtowel at her husband. "Oh, Ray, settle down. Get off that soapbox."

"Church is a fellowship of believers, son. A community. Following a bunch of do-it-my-way rules is only religion. We're not just a bunch of people conversating about God and then going home." He rubbed a large hand over his face and pointed right at James. "Right there in Romans 2:29 it says you can be circumcised any which way you want, but God requires a circumcised heart." He plopped down on the chair and thumped the table with the palm of his hand. "So, you coming to church with us, or not?"

"S-sure. I don't know if I understood that last part, but if you say I should, I will."

Chapter 41

"Priscilla!" Nikki gulped in shock. "You can talk?"

Jake scooted nearer, searching the girl's face.

Tears welled in the child's eyes, but she nodded and whispered, "Yes." She rubbed her throat. "But what *is* mercy?"

Nikki glanced at Jake's surprised face and back to Priscilla's questioning one.

"Let's see, I had to memorize the definition once. How did that go? Oh, yes." She leaned in closer, stroked her small friend's hair, and with the other hand held on to the gentle fingers. "Mercy implies compassion that forebears punishing even when justice demands it."

Priscilla knotted her brows and gave a crooked, weak smile that showed she didn't understand.

"Okay, suppose I do something to hurt you, or I wronged you. And you have the right, and the power, to punish me. But you forgive me instead. That's mercy. This is what God promises us, mercy. It's the power to forgive our sins, when we don't deserve it."

"*If* there *was* a god," Jake interjected.

"But what if it's very wrong?" Priscilla whispered. "More wrong and bad than you can imagine?"

"The Bible says God forgives all our sins. Big, small, in between. He has it covered. He has given us mercy. Forgiveness."

"*If* the Bible isn't a bunch of fairy tales," said Jake.

Priscilla pulled herself up a little. "For most people, right? Most people God can forgive, but some bad things are—" She swallowed and cleared her throat, "—too bad."

Nikki placed her hand on the child's shoulder and laid her back down. "No, sweetheart, God's love is big enough for anything."

Jake commented again. "But not the church. No mercy coming out of there, unless you're already toeing the line." He rolled over on his back and stared up into the trees. "Nope. No mercy, only rules and lectures."

Priscilla's tears washed down her face. "Nikki." She heaved in air. "My bad thing is too terrible."

"What could you have done that you think is so bad?"

"Murder! Mama—I mean Nikki. I killed someone." Sobs rushed out her throat so fast she struggled to catch her breath.

Though shocked and confused at the confession, Nikki placed her hand on Priscilla's chest and said, "Take a deep breath, honey. Breathe, breathe in slower." She used her own sleeve to wipe the wet sorrow off the tiny face. "It's all right, love. You'll be all right. God's forgiveness doesn't stop just short of your sin. His forgiveness is bigger than the ocean and the sky."

Jake sat back up and leaned into Priscilla, his face filled with compassion. "Listen to me. There is no one for you to have sinned against. Reason and logic show there is no god. I can give you tons of arguments that prove there isn't. Think, Priscilla, think."

She wept more. When she gained control, she twisted her little body toward Jake and spoke. "I think...I think people fight too loud about God." She sniffed in until her nose cleared. "If God is real, there'll always be stuff we don't get."

Her little brow knotted in thought. "Cause He'd be so big. Maybe the only way to know is to stick up our hand" She stretched her arm up as high as she could. "And see if He takes it."

Shutting her eyes tight, she squiggled her fingers as if trying to touch something solid. She let her hand drop onto her chest and turned to Nikki with a deep, exhausted sigh.

With tender gentleness Nikki held her closer. "It'll be okay, sweetheart."

"Oh, and Jake?" Priscilla gave the tiniest of smiles. "My name is Ava."

***

Nikki looked up at the evening sky splashed with stars. Ava had drifted back to sleep, and Jake slipped inside his shelter for the night.

Time to get the child into bed.

Before she reached down to lift the her, shuffling noises came from inside the cabin. Elam came out the door and stumbled his way over to Ava and Nikki. He opened the first aid kit and rummaged through its contents. Nikki watched as he pulled out a tube of gel and set it down. With hands that moved with professional precision, he removed the bandage Nikki had placed on Ava.

"This is a bad burn, son." He turned a delusional gaze from Ava to Nikki. "How long has this boy been wounded in the field, nurse?"

"Oh, um, a few hours."

"Well, this antibiotic cream should help. It has an anesthetic in it as well. Keep the burn clean, nurse. We won't evac unless there's an infection." He pulled out a small bottle of pills. "These should help him with the pain. How's your injury doing?"

He reached up to Nikki's head. He uncovered her wound and inspected the healing gash. "Seems to be doing well. Let me know if the pain worsens. Or if the nausea and dizziness come back." He put on a fresh bandage. "Well, I'd better check on the men in the critical care unit."

Elam packed up the kit and ambled back. He left the door open, and Nikki could see him inside the cabin, talking to the empty bed.

Chapter 42

Jake squirmed inside his shelter, a hut just large enough so his big feet didn't poke out the other end. He'd expected to fall asleep before his head touched the frayed sleeping bag, but no dice.

Words and events splashed through his tired mind over and over, like the log ride at an amusement park. When he did drift into slumber for a moment, he was the log splashing over the rocks and boulders.

He shuddered awake. *Ava.*

She can talk? All this time, and now she talks? And why didn't she talk? Scare? She killed somebody. Who could that tiny thing have possibly murdered?

He rolled over again. A stick dropped out of the branched ceiling just above him, hitting his forehead. He slapped it away.

Stupid shelter.

But at the same time, he liked it far better than being on the streets. He saw Ava's face again in his mind.

It's okay, I guess, about the god thing. She's probably too young to face the truth. When you're little, you trust anything. It takes time to know you can't trust anyone.

Times he'd trusted flashed through his mind. He'd even taken a crack at Nikki's God once. He wanted to see his real dad so much he tried prayer. Weeks passed, and his dad never showed.

What's the use of a god if he doesn't do what you ask him to? Sure, it would be nice to have every bad thing you've done forgiven. Somehow. I guess that's why people make up gods.

His bloated stomach cramped. He winced and stretched his legs out. All those potatoes gave him gas.

He tried to lie very still in hopes that dreams would come. They arrived in the form of potatoes end on end, spilling into the air. Mr. Rent appeared. His science teacher when he lived in Santa

Barbara. A shock pinched his hand, and he sat up, bumping his head on the center log.

What the heck? Why did I dream about him?

He laid back down, letting memories wonder through his mind. Science class was a blast. Literally. He remembered experiments that blew up, smoked, and shocked the spit out of him. That's probably why his hand zapped in the dream. They worked a lot with electricity. Who knew science could be so juiced?

A thrill shot through his chest when he thought about the time they charged an iPod using fruit and...

"Potatoes!"

He bolted up in bed and again whacked his head. He dropped back down, clamping one hand over his mouth and one to his head. He listened for Elam. His shelter hunkered on the other side of the fire pit, Jake relaxed when he heard a ragged snort.

A potato charger! Dang it, maybe we could charge the phone with potatoes. We have potatoes. I could jack a cable to attach the phone next trip to town.

The smell of fresh blood and a chill of fear crept over him as he saw the bludgeoned rabbit in his mind.

Maybe by having the police come to rescue us, Elam won't be able to hurt us. Besides, it's not just about me anymore.

Now there would be no getting back to sleep. He had to tell someone. Listening again for the rumbling noise, he crawled out into the open. His breath made a cloudy puff into the moonlit air. He rubbed his shoulders for warmth and crept over to the path. A spring frost had shilled the air.

At a rustling sound, he froze.

A night animal. That's all.

He moved forward toward the cabin where the girls were locked in. A bat shot from the trees, and his heart almost stopped.

This is ridiculous. I've gotten up at night before and Elam has never—

A sound came from the fire pit area. He squinted to see through the haze made by smoke and glowing flicks of ember. Silhouettes of black trees cast dark shadows in the moonlight. He saw the outline of a large creature slinking around the rocks. It stretched up, growing taller by the second. Lurching as if unsteady, the shadow turned, and Jake could see the profile of Elam's beard and long hair. His foggy breath shot out like dragon fire.

I'll tell him I'm going to the bathroom. That's reasonable. But who knows what kind of mood he's in. Reason may be the last thing he'll listen too.

Jake jumped behind a bush and sat. Heart beating, hands shaking, he tried not make a sound as he breathed. Eternity passed as Elam made his way along the path.

Instead of following the trail to the throne, Elam made a sharp turn to the right.

Can he see me? Why is he coming directly at me?

Jake closed his eyes and almost prayed. The footsteps came closer and stopped. An acrid smell hit his nose, and a sound of water rushing made him flinch.

Hellapuke! He's peeing! Taking a whiz in the bush right in front of me.

Closing his eyes, Jake held his breath as he pinched his nose. Elam finished and mumbled as he walked back to bed. Jake let out a long slow sigh and shivered.

Not until the sound of Elam's heavy snoring reach him did he get up, careful not to step in anything that might be wet. A wave if relief swept over him as he realized that when Elam snored like that, nothing could wake him. The raspy sound drifted across the camp like a fog horn.

The cabin door would be chained and locked, for sure. He crouched as he went over to the window. Luckily, Nikki had washed it. The moonlight filtered through the cracks in the flimsy walls and he could see the form of the rickety bed.

He knocked on the window pane.

Too soft. No one stirred.

He tapped again a bit louder and longer. He saw quick movement over the bed.

He made a frantic waving motion with his hands and knocked a quick three beats.

Then no movement, until Nikki's form popped into the window's light.

"What are you doing?" Her whisper sounded irritated. "It's too cold to get out of bed. Wait, are you sick?" Now her face peered at Jake through the bottom pane with worry.

"No, no." Jake grinned. "I thought of something. Something very important."

"What is it?"

"Potatoes!"

Her face contorted. "Really? Potatoes? You're hungry now?"

"In one of my science classes at school we used a bunch of different things to charge batteries. One time we charged a battery using potatoes." He wished he could shake her into understanding quicker. "We have potatoes! We can charge the phone."

"That's all we need? Potatoes?"

"Well, we'd need wire to conduct the charge. Then we'd need a cable to plug the charger into the phone and, oh yeah, some copper pennies."

"How many potatoes?"

"We used three potatoes for a calculator battery, but I saw them do it on the internet, and they charged a cell phone."

Worry slipped into Nikki's voice. "How many potatoes, Jake?"

"Let me think. They used...eight hundred."

"Jake!"

Jake's shoulders slumped, and his head dropped forward. He knocked his head on the window. "Stupid, stupid, stupid. How could I have forgotten that little detail?"

"Hang on, Jake. Maybe there's something else we can use? What else conducts electricity?"

"A wall socket," he made a disgusted face. "Car cigarette lighters, lightning?"

"Wait, what makes the lighter work?"

"The car battery. Forget it, we can't get in the van, remember? It probably doesn't even have a lighter. One that works anyway."

"Does the battery need the car?"

"What do you mean?"

184

Nikki held up one finger for Jake to wait then disappeared in the shadows. He pressed the side of his face to the cool window glass, trying to see. In the grayness, he made out a cloth being yanked up. Another scramble of movement and he realized the board from her makeshift table was being taken down. Underneath, he made out a dark rectangle

Nikki came back to the window grinning.

Jake scratched his head. "What is it?"

"A car battery." She flashed another wide smile.

"That has got to be older than dirt." He thought a moment. "It's not even in a car." But a quiet surge of hope spread in his chest.

"What else do we need?"

"Wires, a charging cable would sure help. Maybe I can lift one off someone, next time he takes me to town."

Nikki turned and ran to the end of the bed. She bent down and scrounged about inside her luggage. She snapped something up and hurried back to him.

Like a prize fish on a line she held up a black cord. "A cable like this one?" She grinned. "James, my dear James, made me take a car charger cable just in case I found my phone."

Jake stared ahead until he exploded in an animated whisper, "Score!"

"We can work on getting wires in the morning. Get back to bed Jake. Good work!" She flashed him a bright smile and returned to the shadows.

Chapter 43

Jake's head nodded in groggy half-sleep as he leaned back in his chair. Elam crashed open the cabin door, and Jake toppled over.

"The All Mighty Lord has spoken. The future is clear. Praise His name!" Elam's hair plastered his sweaty forehead and cheeks. The rest flew about his face as he poured out God's proclamation. "God will keep the evil world from invading the hearts of his children."

Ava and Nikki sat up. Both had been drowsing on the bed.

Jake blinked at the late afternoon light shining from the window made Elam's flying blonde strands gleamed like angel's glow.

"Priscilla! Your time has come to serve, once again. God will use the purity of your heart to find the tools to bring us home. We go in the morning."

Then he left.

Jake shot out the door after him. Nikki followed. The old man was already halfway to the junk pile. He reached it, snatched up a gas can, and headed to the van.

"Wait, Elam." Jake caught up. "What are you talking about?"

"God has ordained that my youngest child and I are going to take a pilgrimage before we all make our final journey home." He struggled to get the cap off the gas tank. As he poured from the red jug, gas fumes burned Jake's nose. Bile shot up his throat. He swallowed it back.

"But I'm your oldest child. I should go with you. Choose me, Pa."

"No, I'm sorry, son. This is a job for a gentle heart."

"Elam, she's injured." Nikki spoke softly. "Remember? The burn? She shouldn't be walking around."

Nikki's tone projected calm and quietness, no sharp words. Jake hoped her method would sway the deluded mind.

186

"No." Elam barked.

"But, Pa?"

He swung around to face them. "No!" The word growled out his mouth. His blue eyes glittered crystal cold, and his face contorted with a demented expression they knew too well.

Step back. We need to step back.

Without a word between them, both captives stopped and watched Elam march off. With heads down like scolded children, Jake and Nikki hurried back to the cabin.

Ava already had tears in her eyes. "I can't go. I just can't go with him. Please, don't let him take me."

"Listen to me, Ava," Nikki said. "It'll be all right. Remember last night, we prayed together. We prayed God would give us strength. And now you know that you can trust God."

"And besides all that..." Jake rolled his eyes and shook his head. "This will give you a chance to call the police. But we have to work fast to charge the phone."

"Police!" Ava sat up in bed as her voice hit a high pitch. "No-o-o-o! Oh, please, no. I can't talk to the police." She grabbed Nikki's hands and squeezed.

Jake tried again. "Just call 9-1-1 and—"

"Please, I can't talk to them. I can't. I can't talk. I ..." With that, words left her. Her mouth moved, but only guttural gurgles came out.

"Okay, take a breath. Try not to panic, Lovey. Listen, what if you didn't have to call the police?"

"Who's she gonna call? Pat Robertson?"

"No." Nikki shot him a disgusted glare. "Can you call your mom or dad? Someone you know?"

Jake watched Ava's face and knew the answer. She was like him. No family, or none that mattered.

She whispered, "No."

"That's okay. I'll program my husband's cell number in the phone. He's very kind and ... and not the police. His name is James."

Ava squeezed her eyes shut. She cleared her throat and said in a tiny voice, "Okay."

"Nikki, you could use a text for your husband, and maybe 9-1-1. She won't have to talk at all then. Just press send."

Ava's eyes shone with hope. "Yes, yes, please do that."

"I don't think 9-1-1 will take a text." Nikki said. "But we could send one to James."

Jake nodded. "We have to charge the phone now."

"Let's gather what we need and let it charge during the night." Nikki looked grim but determined. "You'll need to show us how to set it up before bed. When we sleep we'll be locked in the cabin, with you outside."

Jake avoided their eyes but his voice sounded confident. "Sure, sure. We can do this."

***

Jake checked to make sure the cabin door was fully closed.

Nikki sat on the floor, and pushed a strand of hair behind her ear, "Do we have everything we need?"

"Yes, I mean, I think so." He stared down at the snarl of metal strands laid out on the bed. They had been stumped for what to use for connecting wires. The answer came from the most obvious. The wall that surrounded the camp held a treasure trove of the precious threads. "Is Elam still meditating?"

Ava hobbled to the window and peeked out. "Yes, he's listening to a rock."

Jake sighed and uncovered the battery. "Ok." He sat down on the floor and then up on his knees to hover over the battery. He glared at the greenish white crust that surrounded the small posts. "We need to scrape off the posts... I guess. See these two places on the top? It's where we'll attach the wires. This one is positive, this one negative."

Jake pulled out a small dull butter knife from his junk pocket and gave it to Nikki. She used it to scratch off the gunk. Jake pulled wires apart, straightened and laid them out on the floor. He found two he thought should be long enough.

Ava wondered over from the window to watch the process. She kept her hurt leg stretched out and settled onto the floor.

Jake inspected the end of the charger that would have been plugged into the cigarette lighter. "The metal tabs here on the sides

188

are negative, and this point is the positive." Then he pointed to the battery. "We hold one wire onto the plus post on the battery, and one to the minus post. If we get this wrong, we'll damage the adapter."

Nikki squinted and shook her head. "Hold them? Can't we attach them and leave them for the night?"

Ava wrinkled up her nose.

A loud crack made them all jump. A voice boomed. "It's time!"

Jake fell back onto his bottom. A giant shadow stood in the open doorway.

Nikki rushed to throw a cloth over the battery. "Time for what, Elam?"

"For eating, of course. Mama, pull together some potatoes. We'll eat in ten minutes."

"Potatoes take an hour to bake in the fire, Elam."

Silence.

"Elam? We need an hour."

The old man stared straight ahead, then said, "I can't go back in the fire."

"Not you, Elam. The potatoes."

Without warning, his eyes filled with tears. "Will you save them if they burn? You won't let them burn, will you?"

"No, Elam, I won't let them burn."

"Good." He left the cabin.

Jake followed him to the door to see where he went. "Man! Elam creeps up like a ghost. Ava, you've gotta keep a better watch."

Elam went down to the trickle of a stream. He picked up a wet rock and leaned against a tree. The old man put the rock to his ear and slid to his knees. Jake could see Elam's shoulders shaking and heard the distant sobs.

Jake closed the door and came back to the wires. "Boy, he's sure a mess today."

Nikki stood up. "I'll get the potatoes in the fire. Be right back."

After few moments of silence, Jake gave a quick glance at Ava and then, went back to untangling wires. Without looking at her, he asked. "You don't have a family?"

"I do. But I can't trust them," Ava whispered.

Jake nodded his head with a knowing expression. "Gotcha. Me too."

Nikki returned and went back to scraping while Jake twisted the wires onto the plug. Eventually, each piece hooked together except for the phone.

Jake nodded to Ava. "Check Elam before I plug in the phone."

Ava hopped up and shuffled to the door. She opened it and peeked out.

"He's walking into the forest."

"Which way?" Jake asked.

"Toward the stone throne."

"Good, he always takes a long dump before supper. You can almost time him."

"Yes, almost," Nikki warned them. "Unless he breaks with his repeating rituals and imagines the enemy flying overhead."

"We don't have another choice, Nik. We've got to risk it right now." Jake turned to Ava. "Watch the trail. We'll need as much warning as we can get."

Ava nodded.

They brought the cell out of its hiding place. Jake began to work the plug into the phone.

"Stop, stop." Ava sent out the alarm with her hands wiggling in the air. "I hear him."

All activity froze. They listened for the sound of Elam's heavy steps and the way he crashed through the shrubs. Instead, off from a distance, the words of the Battle Hymn soared into the air.

Ava sighed with a tiny nervous giggle. "He's singing."

They all listened again with rapt attention.

"I don't think the sound is coming closer," Jake said.

"It's a part of this particular ritual," Nikki commented. "For today, anyway. Good thing. We'll be able to tell when he's done, or getting closer."

190

In the silence, they could hear the voice singing. Elam changed to an old-time love song.

"Le-e-e-t me call you swe-e-etheart, swe-e-e-theart." His voice drifted into the cabin.

Jake pushed the cord in with a click. The screen stayed black as coal. Black as death.

"Wait." Nikki held her finger up. "Maybe the charge is just too low. I've had that happen with mine."

With eyes that demanded results, Jake glared at the phone. The sound of Elam blasting out his song became unbearable.

What if I just throw the phone against the wall?

With no fanfare, a green battery with a tiny red rim at the bottom appeared on the screen. Like a lighthouse beaming out to ships at sea, the pale glimmer shot hope inside Jake.

Chapter 44

"Have you ever needed God before? Do you trust Him?" Ray asked as they ate dinner.

James didn't answer out loud.

God exists, I'm sure of that. But do I only believe He exists? Or do I have confidence that, right now in this crisis, He can help me?

James tried to take in Ray's questions. His mind crashed with doubt and fear, and his brain throbbed with a banging headache.

Ray's mellow voice rumbled into his ears with urgent concern. James couldn't answer the questions he'd been asked. But unlike sermons and lectures, the intimate caring came through and he couldn't tune it out.

Edith guided them into the living room, where Ray turned on the gas fireplace. They each settled into the lodge-style, overstuffed chairs. Edith had gone all out for the Colorado decorating. Pictures, lamps and knick-knacks of moose, bear, and antlers studded the living room. Every now and then, a hint of African art or a slew of family photos interrupted the theme.

The doorbell rang.

Ray shot a look at James. "You'd better scoot into the back. We're not expecting anyone."

James hustled into the kitchen. He stopped just inside and peeked back around the arched opening. He didn't want to pry into Ray's business, but he worried that the visitor had something to do with him.

Ray took his time getting to the door. He glanced back as if to check that James was out of sight and swung open the door.

"Dale! What are you doing out this time of evening? Come on in." Ray swept out his hand to usher him inside. "Is there something wrong?"

"Yes. Well, it's not exactly an emergency, but I thought you'd want to know. I'm headed over there right now." Dale stepped into the hallway. He took off his Rockies baseball cap, revealing thin, graying hair.

Edith stood up and took a step forward. "Heading over where? What is it, Dale?"

"I got wind that some of those rabble rousers on the church leadership committee decided to call a secret meeting." He rubbed his hand across his mouth and sniffed. "I don't think even Pastor Thomas knows about it."

"What secret meeting?" Ray asked.

"At church. They're mad because Pastor didn't tell that Rolen fella to leave the church. They want to do something about it."

Ray grabbed his cap off an antler hook in the hall. "Let's get over there. We can call Pastor on the way."

James peeked out. "Wait, I should go too!"

Dale's jaw dropped, and his eyebrows arched up as James stepped into the living room.

Ray waved his hand. "James, get back ... oh, dang it, it's too late. What are you doing? Don't you know Dale can spread news faster than a talking-dog-flash-mob-cat video on YouTube?" He turned back to Dale. "No 'fense, Dale."

"None taken." He waved it off with his cap.

James straightened with defiance. "But I think since I'm the reason for the trouble, I should be there."

Ray stood a moment as if listening to an inner voice. "Okay, but stay in the car unless we call for you."

"Let me get my shoes on," James said. "I'll be right back."

Ray looked down at his slippers. "Oh, me too."

As the three men went out to load into Dale's car, Edith stayed on the porch. "You be careful, now," she called.

As Dale drove into the church driveway, the building appeared dark. A few trucks and SUVs studded the parking lot.

"Arthur should replace those bulbs to the walkway lights. Three are out *again*," Dale said as he turned the steering wheel, guiding the car into a parking spot.

Only one small window softly glowed from inside the church. James knew it to be the second and third grade Sunday School. Usually business meetings were held in the fellowship room. But this meeting was secret.

The two older men got out. James stayed behind. Under the porch light Dale pulled on the door handle. Locked. He took out his keys and unlocked it. The men disappeared inside.

Now what? Why have I come if all I'm going to do is sit here?

James caught movement along the side of the church. He saw the silhouette of someone peering into a low window. He sat up straight, worried and alert.

More vandalism? Arthur just cleaned up the spray paint and broken glass from the most recent attack. All because of me, I bet. Is this guy another committee member, or the vandal? Why would he peer in the window and not just come to the door? Now what do I do?

He watched until the man hunched down and headed around to the other side of the building.

I should go tell the people inside. But I'm supposed to stay in the car. I don't want to barge in, but what if this guy's dangerous? Great!

James sighed lung deep and opened the car door. Ducking down, he hustled to the front of the church. He felt silly, but fear of being seen by the stranger kept his head down.

He yanked hard on the handle, and pain shot up his arm as the door held tight.

Still locked. Now what?

He moved around to the side of the church where he'd seen the man go. Continuing to the back of the building, he saw a slit of light shine across the lawn. The light came from a back door left open a crack.

James inspected the jamb for signs of a break-in. The old wood made it hard to tell. The splintered frame showed abuse from years of God's little blessings door-slamming into the building.

He stepped inside the hallway. The light ended at the corner turn.

He crept quietly and tried to keep his breathing silent as he searched. His ears strained for any sound that might direct him to the intruder.

Voices, pitched with emotion, drifted in the darkness.

Surely, a vandal would hear that and leave.

James went left at the end of the hall. He didn't want to go right and encounter the people in the meeting until he had a good look around. This turn, and three steps up, brought him to the sanctuary. Through the side wall windows, he could see sparse clouds drifting over a bright moon. When the light hit the stained glass, portions of the glow spread colors throughout the hall. Revealing moments of brilliance and adding a mystical feel, the blues, with bright spots of red and amber, sent a holy chill up his back.

The stark emptiness of the hall, the night shadows and the quietness gave the room a whole new personality. Mesmerized, he walked down to the altar and sat in the front row. Moon light from a window glittered on the silver cross standing on the communion table. A cross-shaped shadow spread across the wall behind it.

"God." His words soft. "Do you live here? God, do you live?"

He always knew his relationship with God was different from Nikki's. He was the man. He wanted to be in charge and take care of everyone. He never had to depend on God. Not really. Not until he had no way to change the horror that each day held for him.

He knew God lived. He didn't know how he knew, or how he could ever explain it to anyone.

No wonder it's so hard to help someone else understand.

A sharp voice cut into his thoughts. "No!"

He jumped at the sound and nearly slipped off the pew.

He turned and saw a shadowed man standing at the end of his row.

Where's Conner's bat now?

The shadow spoke, "Let me rephrase that. He does exist, but this isn't the only place He lives."

"Pastor Thomas?"

"Yes." He stepped forward.

"Did you hear about the secret meeting?"

"Yes, that's why I came. But I forgot my key. Lucky that back door doesn't always close all the way. We need to have Arthur fix that."

"Was that you looking into the window?"

"I wanted to catch a glimpse of who I was up against." Pastor walked over and sat beside James.

James hung his head. "I'm ... I'm so sorry I've caused all this—"

"It wasn't you, James. Actually, I should thank you."

"Wha—?"

"You started me reevaluating. Thinking. Digging into the Bible and researching on the internet."

"What did you find?"

"That there's a lot of misunderstanding about what it means to be a Christian by both the inside and the outside world. And I do mean outside. Many are outcast by us, marginalized and forgotten. I'm afraid that in our effort to stand up for what we believe, we've unknowingly stepped on the people we're trying to reach."

Thomas used his hands to express his thoughts. "From their distance, we must seem like a big glob of people pointing fingers at them and shouting. They'd be mighty surprised if we listened first, and earned the right to speak our minds."

"What does that have to do with me?"

"You reminded me that 'mercy triumphs over judgment.' If we could all lead with mercy and love, instead of fear and anger, more people would be drawn to God through us, and not in spite of us."

The lights snapped on. James squinted his eyes shut.

A voice boomed from the back of the church. "You see! They're already planning against us. Talking here in the darkness."

"Nonsense," Ray said. "They were only chatting. Isn't that right, Pastor?"

Chapter 45

James jumped up and turned around. Seven church leaders strode up the aisle. Ray followed behind.

"Pastor Thomas, we didn't expect *you* to be here." Dave led the troupe.

"Oh, *really*, Chairman Dave?" The force of the pastor's voice made James blink. Thomas stood to his full height, with a scowl on his face. "What is your meeting about, the one without the pastor's knowledge? I didn't see it on the church calendar."

"I guess we might as well get it out in the open." Dave huffed out his chest and straightened his back. "Pastor Thomas, we feel that you haven't been listening to your board members. We are your employers. We pay your salary."

Into the dead quiet of the ensuing pause, James heard the building settling with a crack.

Pastor Thomas let out a deep breath. "No, you are not my employers. God is my boss. I'm your spiritual leader, Dave."

Voices erupted around James in a scramble of emotions.

"No, no, no!"

"Is that scriptural?"

"See here, I never said whose side I'm on."

Sounds of chaos echoed into the heights of the sanctuary's wooden ceiling.

Ray rolled his eyes, stepped in the middle, and shouted, "Settle down. Everyone stop!" As the pack quieted, he gave each person a deliberate glare. "We need to hear all sides. There will be no railroading tonight."

He paused again. "Okay, has everyone met James Rolen, here?" People shuffled their feet, some murmured they had, and others shook their head no.

Ray continued, "This here is James. James this is Dave, Hal, Joan, Grace, and Ed. You know Dale."

197

James nodded in their directions.

With self-confidence in his stance, Dave stepped forward and took back the lead. "Let's go to the fellowship room. Get some chairs and sit down to talk."

The group entered the room, and the men arranged the seats in a circle. Everyone sat in a chair, except Dave. "Okay, as I've said, we held this meeting to discuss if Pastor Thomas Reed is still the man we want to have lead this church. And, yes, it has to do with accepting this man," he pointed to James, "into our church."

He pulled out a Bible from off a shelf and cracked it open. "It says right here, in Second John 1:10-11, 'If anyone comes to you and does not bring this teaching, do not take them into your house or welcome them. Anyone who welcomes them ...'" He paused to squint an accusing eye at Thomas and emphasized each of the last words in the verse. "'... shares in their wicked work.'"

"What teaching, Dave?" Pastor Thomas asked.

"Abuse! Possibly murder!"

"We don't know that he's done anything. Besides, you need to read that whole chapter to understand what they're talking about."

"That doesn't even matter." Grace spoke up, and all turned to her with surprise. Her normal quiet manner now surged with obvious distress. "How does it look to the people outside the church if we allow him to keep coming? Just by association we will seem to be condoning spouse abuse." Pale blue eyes magnified by glasses gave her the appearance of a frightened owl.

Joan placed a calming hand on her back and spoke softly to her. "Grace, I understand what the subject of abuse means to you, but—"

"The church needs to be an example of righteousness," Dave said. "We have to make sure the secular world knows what is right and wrong. It's our job!"

"That's not our job," Ray said. "Jesus is our job."

Hal stood and shook his pointed finger. "We also have to be certain the evil in the world doesn't infect us, or our children. We must defend our faith."

"What is your faith, Hal?" Ray asked.

"Going to church, Sunday School, and paying my tithe. That's it. All of it."

"Really, Hal?" Pastor Thomas shook his head. "I'm sorry, but I have to ask, have you *met* Jesus?"

"Don't patronize me! Me and my family have been members of this church for three generations."

"Let's stay on track," Dave cut in. "The matter here is that as a board we specifically told you that James Rolen was to find another church."

Ed thumped his cane on the floor. "Yes, let some other congregation deal with all the reporters and cameras every Sunday."

"Listen, folks." Pastor tried to reason with them. "I really think we should close this meeting and wait until the conference can send us a representative to help us sort all this out."

Dave's face reddened. "No, no. You think they'll back you, don't you? You should just resign and save the church from being split up."

Hal threatened. "Well, I want to say that if he doesn't leave, I for one will. And you know how much my family contributes to the funding of this church."

James could tell by the immediate silence that they did know. He stood and said, "Please, please, you're all talking like I'm not right here. I—"

"Shut up!" three people shouted at James, and he dropped back into his chair.

"No, I will not resign. If I do you'll steamroll over every future pastor you hire. And it will not be settled in a secret meeting. Dave, schedule a congregational meeting for next week after church. The regional superintendent can come down from Castle Rock to help us out." He stared at Dave. "Do you understand me? Dave?"

The chairman huffed and gave a reluctant nod. "Fine. But you better know this isn't going to go away."

The members of the team filed out, but one lingered. Joan hung back and whispered to James before she left. "Not everyone in the church feels that way about you, James. Trust me." She gave him a slight smile and squeezed his arm.

Chapter 46

Cora longed for her child, even over the sickness that came from her addiction needs.

"I'll be right back." Ben slammed the motel door as he left.

Grandma sat in the chair by the window. "You can't do it, Cora. You can't leave without finding Ava." Her eyes brimmed with tears.

Cora picked up her pack of cigarettes and popped one out. She lit the end before she spoke. "I know, Grandma. Of course, but Ben..."

Grandma squeezed the arm of the chair and leaned forward. "Ben doesn't care about you or Ava. He wants my money and your body. You're both addicts."

"No, he wants to help me. He's the only one who understands."

"This is your daughter!" Grandma coughed as the smoke drifted through the room.

Cora collapsed onto the motel bed. She stared up at the ceiling and puffed again. She struggled to find words, and then in an unsure whisper she said, "Ben loves me."

"I don't know anything about that. But I know you love Ava. Somewhere in all that toxic mess inside your body you love her. If I could just get through to you— Cora! What if she's out there waiting for you to come get her?"

Cora sat up and put out the cigarette. "Would she know I'd come?"

Grandma allowed a large tear to escape and spread down the rivulets of her wrinkled cheek. "I don't know, baby. But she needs you. You'll never get past this if you don't try."

Cora rolled over on the bed and curled up into a ball. "I'm sick, Grandma."

"I know."

The door pushed open. Ben tossed a small paper bag on the bed. "Here, Cora. I had these in the car, from the hospital. They're good ones, too. Sweet. They should block out the shakes until we get to the next town."

Cora sat up, trying to look bold and strong. "Honey, we can't leave without Ava." She clutched her hands around her stomach to hide the trembling and soothe the stomach cramps.

Ben barked out, "Granny, get in your room."

Grandma flinched before she struggled to get out of her chair. She gave granddaughter a meaningful glare as she hobbled into the adjoining room.

Cora noticed Ben's red eyes and the smell of vodka that spread across the room. "I need to know where my daughter is."

"Cora, the cops are asking too many questions. You know how they are." His words were slurred but controlled. "They'll twist this into something about me."

"Ben! This is my daughter."

"This is my life. We've already had to make that church move us to a different motel to trick reporters. Listen, my past won't hold up to any more digging into."

Cora whispered, "What do you mean? What have you done?"

"Oh, come on. You know I'm not perfect. I'm ... I'm a drunk. I don't always remember what I do." He knelt beside the bed, grabbed Cora's forearms and squeezed. "But no one knows about the worst of it. Yet. If they did, I wouldn't be here."

"What did you do?"

"If they connect the dots ... I don't know what I'll do."

Cora raised her voice. "What did you do to Ava?"

"Nothing. I swear it." He pushed up from the floor, grabbed the paper bag, and pulled out some loose pills. "Here, take these. I'll get you water." He shoved them into her trembling hand.

Cora stared at the pills. In her mind she heard a voice, distant, but familiar.

Calling her name.

Calling her home.

Home to sanity. The voice faded and fell silent.

What was it like to have the freedom to say no?

She couldn't remember. Ben handed her the glass of water, and she swallowed the pills.

"Cora, I'm sure Ava ran away. Positive. Someone found her. They're taking care of her, and they don't want to give her up."

The pills were slow in giving her relief. She should have crushed them and snorted. But the thought of the drenching peace to come calmed her.

Ben pulled her up off the bed, wrapped his arms around her and rocked her. Time passed before he whispered, "She's better off, baby. You know that. What kind of life is this?"

Here it comes.

She pulled her head back, breathed in through her nose, and blew a slow stream of air out her mouth. Her arms floated with a fuzzy sensation, while her mind drifted into quiet softness.

"Yes," she murmured. "What kind of life?"

Chapter 47

"Glory! The time is here. For no man can fathom the mind of God." Ava cringed as Elam blasted out his morning proclamation. A sour knot formed in her stomach.

The lock rattled on the door, and steps clomped away. Nikki turned in the bed and gave Ava a hug of comfort. "The time has indeed come, Ava. You must have courage."

Ava nodded. Hope, excitement, and dread raced in her heart like leaves in a storm. Her breath came out choked and uneven.

Nikki smiled. "You can do this, girl." She pulled back the blankets for Ava. "Get dressed in the shift Elam gave you last time, but bring the hoodie, too."

Nikki hurried over to check the phone. "Okay. Okay, there's enough power. I'll type in the text for you to send when you find a time. Let's turn it all the way off for right now." She grabbed up her bag. "We can put the cell in the zippered pocket inside my purse and throw a couple of water bottles in the big part. I'll slip that in the van before you leave."

"Nikki?"

"Yes."

"I won't have to talk, will I?"

She looked hard at Ava and blinked once. "You'll be just fine." She turned away fast and got out her own clothes for the day.

Ava dressed. Her tummy growled as she pulled on her hoodie.

I'll feel better after I eat. Will we eat today? I hope I eat.

Nikki and Ava made their way to the fire pit. Jake, already up and feeding the flames, gave them both a tense glare. Nikki sent him a slight smile and nodded. Jake took in a huge breath and relaxed his shoulders.

"Son, say the blessing," Elam demanded.

Jake bowed his head, and the girls held hands. "Bless this slop of which we are about to shove down our gullets with no regard."

Nikki gasped and turned to Elam. He hadn't noticed the words. Jake grinned at her and whispered, "Just checking to see if he even listens."

Nikki slapped Jake's leg and growled, "You do this now? Really?"

Sitting down beside Ava, Elam handed her an applesauce cup. "Priscilla, remember the day I gave you those jacks? You loved them so much. You played with them all day. Maybe I can find some for you again, and you can play on the front porch."

Ava didn't respond.

"Yes, that's right," Elam continued. "Then we all went down to the swimming hole, didn't we? No one drowned."

After breakfast, Elam put the empty gas cans in the van along with a few other odd things. Ava went to Nikki for a huge hug. Then, after a short hesitation, she went to Jake with a timid squeeze. He gave her a quick pat on the back.

Elam came back holding his knife. "Soldiers, get into the bunker. The enemy will be on the prowl."

Nikki looked to Jake.

Jake said, "No, Papa, we'll be all right. The enemy's gone. Remember? We can stay out here while you're gone."

Elam raised the blade in their direction and twisted it in slow motion. His face pulled in tight with anger until his head began to shake.

"Okay," Nikki said in a hurry. "We're going. Move it, Jake." She pushed the boy ahead of her.

Ava followed them inside the cabin.

Elam went to one of the cubbies and brought out some steel cord. He unwrapped the curled strands. "You broke the other ones, didn't you? But I have more." The locks came out next.

Nikki spoke in a calm voice. "Elam, we really don't need those, do we? We'll be inside the cabin."

His words came out graveled and desperate. "You don't understand, I have to keep you safe. What if the bed gets out in the night?"

"Here we go," Jake muttered under his breath.

"That's why I have to keep Priscilla with me. If the doors are flat, then you must open the balls of glass. The air will scream, and the night will be scathed with melting flesh. Listen to me!" He snatched at Nikki's arm and yanked her close to his face. He put his hands around her chin and squeezed. He formed each word as if his whole life depended on them.

"Don't ... be ... afraid."

Chapter 48

Nikki watched through the cabin window as the van turned the corner and disappeared into the trees. Sandy dust sprayed behind the old heap and left a red cloud swirling in the road.

"He locked the gate. Locked the doors and windows and secured us with the cords?" Jake slapped his forehead. "How strong does he think we are?"

"I'm more worried about water and food."

"There are some cans of peaches stuffed in that top cubby over the bed."

"What's their expiration date?" Nikki stretched her neck up. "Wait a minute, how did you see those way up there?"

"The other day, I got curious about him. You know, Elam. Where's he from? How'd he get here? So, when he was phased out, and you two were talking outside, I started snooping around. In all this junk, there must be clue."

Nikki paused to give the room a good look around. Newspapers scattered in corners, books stuffed in every crevice, and about five old shoe boxes crammed inside one of the cubbies.

"Yes," Nikki murmured. "Definite possibilities."

***

The hours slipped by as the van jogged and rattled over holes and rocky bumps in the road. Ava stared at the back of the seat in front of her and bounced the chain with her fingers in time to Elam's singing. Her mind slipped into nothing thoughts.

The van stopped dead. She pulled her mind into the present when she heard the door slam.

Where did he go? Where are we?

She searched for Nikki's purse. Green color showed from under the passenger's seat. Ava reached down, stretching her chain, and pulled the cloth purse into her lap.

She jumped at a rattling sound and clutched the bag. A gas cap turning and a nozzle being put in place had made the sound. Then the back of the van opened, and Elam took out the empty gas cans.

When he finished, he paid at the pump. Ava peeked under the shade and could see him watching her window. Before she could even unzip the purse, he was putting the gas cans back.

Too late.

As he came around to her side, she stuffed her secret under the seat.

He opened his door and peered into the backseat. "Bathroom?"

Ava nodded.

He unchained her and helped her out. He went with her to stand at the restroom door.

Stupid! I should have grabbed the purse.

Back in the van, he turned the key. "Now, I'm going to need you, little sis. You're the only one that can do this. Did you know you were so talented? I did. I always did."

Driving only a block, he pulled up to a corner building, a little grocery store. An old one, not like a big grocery store. He hurried over to her side, unchained her, and drew her out.

He carried her over to the entrance door and put her down. He peered inside the front window, bobbing his head up and down checking out every corner of the inside.

"Empty." He bent down to Ava. "Okay, now, listen closely. Walk in and stand in front of the cashier person. Just like you did in the other town. Remember? You really are positively, super-sonically spectacular." He grinned and held her hand tight to his chest.

Ava sighed. Her heart beat faster, and she nodded.

"This store has what I need. We have to make sure everything is the same. Like when the sparrows come back to the nest. No human scent. Go ahead, go on in now." He gave her a little shove.

Ava slipped in the door and heard bells jingle as it shut. She walked over to the high wooden counter. The front of it was scraped and worn. On tip-toes, she stretched up taller to peek over the lip of the top and looked at the man.

He leaned forward.

"What would you like, young lady? Do you need something?"

She stared at him.

"You lost? Where's your mommy?"

She didn't blink her eyes, but water began to fill them.

"Oh, great. A lost child. Who won't talk." His arms flopped up in the air and back down to his sides. He came around the counter and squatted in front of her. "Is your mom coming from her car?" He stood. "Let's go see." He took her hand and walked to the front door.

Something creaked from the back. Ava spun around.

Elam!

"Hey, there." The man pulled on her arm. "Don't go running off, now."

The man must not have heard. He took her hand and led her out the front door.

The man looked up and down the street. He leaned down to Ava. "Are you from the neighborhood? I haven't seen you around before." He made an exaggerated sigh and stood up. "Well, let's go call the police and see what we can do."

Ava yanked her hand from him and stepped back.

Should I run? Or ask for help?

"Priscilla! There you are, youngster. Where did you wander off to?" Elam came from the alleyway beside the store. He walked over and slipped his hand into hers. "I'm sorry, sir. We're visiting down the street, and she must have wandered away. Thank you for trying to help." He tugged on her hand, and they headed toward the alley. As he turned the corner, he started giggling like a kid. He did a skip-hop and slapped his knee.

"We did it again. You are special. Just special. So very special. Especially special! God bless you!" The van was parked at the other end of the alley. Elam buckled and chained Ava in her seat. Then he got in and drove off.

But instead of heading farther into town, he traveled back toward the forest. Soon even cabins at the outer edges of the town disappeared. The road became a bumpy, one car path.

Oh, no. He's going home. I mean to camp. I missed my chance. How can I call now?

She pictured herself pulling the cell out and trying to use it as they traveled. Could she do that? She reached under her seat and scooped up the purse. With a quiet pull, she unzipped the top. Each little z-z-z sound of the zipper buzzed in her ears like a thousand bees. She slipped her hand into the purse, opened the pocket, and slipped out the phone.

It sat in her lap. Her fears kept her from doing more.

Why doesn't Elam sing now? Is this the right time to call? How many chances will I have?

Elam blasted on the horn and laughed.

She sucked in a gasp.

"Relax, now, Priscilla. This will take a while. You rest back there. We'll be home soon."

Home? Not my home.

She shook her head, emphatic in her no.

Wait, my child, wait.

The words spoke into her mind, but not as if she heard them. More like they appeared already spoken.

She returned the phone to its hiding place, and waited.

A drowsy peacefulness washed over her. She snuggled her head against the door and closed her eyes.

Chapter 49

Arms reached under Ava's legs and back. They pulled and lifted her. Was it mom taking her to bed? No, not mommy.

Cool, fresh air flowed over her face. She fluttered her eyes open to darkness.

"Just sleep, little sis, you'll be all right."

Long strands of his hair tickled her face. Her arms still held Nikki's green purse cuddled in her lap. She opened her eyes all the way. Elam was carrying her toward to a house. Staring at the home in the moonlight, she noticed the height of the roof line and the old-style porch.

Who lives there? Maybe they'll help me. But what if Elam hurts them?

She tilted her head to see Elam's face. He was grinning, and his blue eyes sparkled like the first time she met him. His feet stomped up the steps, and he brought her over to a broken porch bench and laid her on it.

Elam passed his hand over her hair before he ran to the van. He pulled something out and trotted back up the path, hopped onto the porch, and knelt beside her. Covering her with a blanket, he rolled up a towel and placed that under her head.

He picked up her wrist and held her hand. The jerking pulls of zip cords being tightened told her the chains had returned. She watched him secure the other end to the railing.

"You need to wait here for me. You'll be safe." He whispered into her hair. "Don't be afraid."

Before her next thought could come, he left. She heard the motor start and rumble down the road.

He left.

He left?

She sat up and turned to the house. The peeling paint and dust-covered railing made her think no one lived there. Strange

210

black scars rimmed one window. But inside thick curtains kept her from seeing in. Nothing was boarded up. In front of the door, a welcome mat lay with a moose in a canoe printed on it.

Kneeling on the bench and pulling on the chains, she banged on the dark glass. She took a deep breath and screeched, "Help!" Pulling in another shot of air, she cried again. "Help meeeeee!"

The words melted into the forest. No one came.

Thump!

The sound caused her to pull up, yell, and shake all at the same time.

A bright green bundle sat on the wooden slats of the porch floor. Nikki's purse.

She grabbed it up and ripped open the zipper. With trembling fingers, she pulled out the phone. Ava stared at the cell in her hand as if it were a snake. She carefully pushed the "on" button and waited. To her delight, the black screen came to life.

Nothing, then a tremble in the phone. The tiny picture of the battery was shaded in some. Enough.

Now she looked to see if there was service.

Yes.

She brought up texting as Jake had shown her. The draft already written appeared. Her fingers shook and she had to think very hard to be sure she pressed in the right place to send the text.

James, this is Nikki. I've been kidnapped by a man called Elam. Myself, Chance Ryan 13, and Ava Martin 7, are being held captive in the Colorado Rockies, north of Estes Park. James, please come.

She poked at the word "send" and waited. Words appeared at the top of the screen. *Your message has been sent.*

Sent. It's sent, off to bring help. To take us home. Like magic.

Elam might be gone a very long time. After putting the phone away, she tried to snuggle down on the bench. She clutched the purse in her arms like a teddy bear. Now maybe she could sleep.

Moments later a tingling buzz trembled in her arms. The phone had come to life. She sat up, eyes wide, she stared down at the green bundle. Then with fast fingers, she pulled out the cell and pushed the answer button.

She put the phone to her ear and listened.

"Is anyone there? Hello? Hello?"

Fear clutched at her throat. Years and years spent stopping words now trapped her tongue. She needed to speak. She wanted to, but couldn't.

***

James couldn't get to sleep. He turned over in bed one last time, then tossed the covers off in frustration. Last evening's meeting kept running through his mind. He didn't want to be the cause of a church being in a crisis.

What could *he* do about it?

In between the pangs of guilt for the trouble he'd caused, worry for his wife circled in like a black fog. He got out of bed and grabbed his cell phone to check for messages. He threw on his robe, stuffed the phone his pocket, and went up the stairs for a glass of water. He moved with stealth, so as not to wake Ray or Edith,

As he walked past the window by the back door, the bright full moon hanging over Pikes Peak caught his eye. Silvery gleams washed over the mountainside, throwing the terrain into rugged relief.

After James filled his glass, he went out on the back deck. The city lights washed up to the foothills, and the dark mountain rose above them. Peace drenched over him as he sat down in an Adirondack chair.

Sitting in the quiet of the night, without any of the distractions his mind clung to, he understood. Just like that, he knew what he had to do.

He had to give up.

Even while the fears for Nikki never left him, tense muscles released, and the burden of needing to be the redeemer slipped off his back. He couldn't do it, because it wasn't his to fix.

"God. I give up. I can't do this." After a huge cleansing sigh, he continued, "You're in control now. I ... trust You."

A rumbling vibration buzzed at his thigh. His phone.

Reaching in his pocket, he pulled it out and maneuvered the screen with his thumb. He didn't recognize the caller's number.

When Nikki's name appeared, he almost dropped the phone.

Trying to focus on the small print, he read them aloud. If his ears heard what his eyes saw, maybe he could make sense of this.

Kidnapped? Who is Elam? Isn't Ava the little girl that was missing?

He read it over and over.

More information, I need more.

He looked at the call back number. It had an out-of-state area code. He pushed redial and waited.

Someone picked up but didn't speak.

Finally, he asked, "Is anyone there? Hello? Hello?"

Nothing. He wanted to hang up, but he thought he could hear a quiet, frantic breathing on the other end.

A timid, fragile voice whispered, "Hello?"

A child?

"Did you send a text to this number?"

Silence.

"Hello, did you text me?"

The whispered voice spoke, "I clicked send."

"Who is this?"

Breathing.

"Please, I'm Nikki Rolen's husband, James. If you know anything about where she is I need to know."

Dead air.

An almost inaudible whispered. "Nikki said you're nice." James heard his own heartbeat throb in his head. "Elam took us. He ... took us up the mountain."

"A mountain? Can you name a town close by? A restaurant? Anything we can use to place where you are?"

The sound of the child's puffs blew into the receiver. "Um ... I dunno."

"Think, please."

A strangling sound croaked out and again the breathing.

213

"Are ... are you Ava? I've talked to your mom, Ava. She misses you. Think hard, sweetheart."

"Mommy?"

"Yes, and Ben."

"Huh?"

Was that a gasp of fear, or delight? He couldn't tell.

The child's voice became angry. "You're lying."

"No, honey, please. Just tell me. Before you went into the mountains, did you see a sign, something like that?"

"The camp had a sign."

"Camp?"

"We stayed there once. In a town, before the mountain."

"What did the sign say?"

"Dancing Pinecones, I think. Bears and a moose in the office. Maggie lived there."

"Maggie? Who's Maggie?"

Fear wrenched in her voice. "He's coming back—"

"Who's coming? What does he look like?"

"Elam, he's ... old. Very old. In a white van."

"Elam? What's the last name?"

Nothing.

"Hello? Hello!" Blank, dark, nothing. "No, no. Please, you have to tell me more!"

Chapter 50

"Help!" Jake ducked his head and hung on for dear life.

Newspapers cascaded down from one of the high storage squares cut in the wall. Jake clung with one hand into the edge of a dirt opening. He managed to swing his left leg to another shelf. The steel cable tether hung from his other leg. He flung his free arm out to flail at the falling paper. Dust billowed everywhere as the mess landed on the floor and on the bed under him. Musty smells filled the air.

"You look like a monkey in a tree." Nikki chuckled as she coughed.

He stared down at the chaos. Then he pulled himself up to peer into the now empty niche in the wall.

Wait, not empty.

He shoved his fingers into the shadows. His hand gave a quick quiver as it hit delicate spider threads. He patted around until he hit something solid. Ignoring the sensation of spider legs crawling across his arm, he reached farther into the space.

"What's this?" He touched some sort of case or box. Along the front side, his fingers slipped into the handle. He yanked.

The object, lighter than he expected, flew out of its dark hiding place. The motion of the swing almost took Jake with it. He winced as pain shot through the wound where the bear had clawed his arm. He released his grip and let the case fly.

Nikki ducked.

"Be careful!" she shouted like a mom. "Somebody's going to get hurt."

Memory glowed with warmth inside him. His mom used to say that. He pushed it back. Those moments were dead. Gone when she died.

"That suitcase was buried behind all those newspapers." He jumped to the floor.

She wasn't listening. "We'll need to get this all cleaned up before he gets back."

A distant hum came from outside.

"Good grief, here he comes. Hurry." The motor's sound blended with the birds and wind.

Jake scooped as much paper as he could muscle and tried to toss it into the top hole. Half of it came spilling down again.

"Jake, get back up there. I'll hand it to you." She barked the order, and Jake obeyed.

He stuffed the papers in at first, then tried to make them neater. Nikki grabbed whatever else was out of place around the room.

The squeak of the gate and rattle of the locks came from outside. Jake noted that empty peach cans were piled on the one table. "The peach cans?"

"That's okay. He'd know we'd eat." She scanned around the room and then pointed. "The suitcase!"

Just as the door rattled, Jake leaped off the wall, careful to not tangle in the cord attached to his leg. He grabbed the case and shoved it under the bed.

The clicking and scraping noise of Elam unlocking the cabin door jangled every nerve Jake had. He fell onto the bed in a frantic attempt to appear to be napping. Nikki sat at the table and leaned on an elbow.

Whistling a breathy tune of "Blessed Assurance," Elam came into the room. He said nothing to his captives, picked up a stuffed box from the corner pile, and walked out the door.

Nikki and Jake turned to each other in wonder. Going to the open door, they watched Elam pack the box into the van.

They stepped aside as Elam strode back into the cabin.

Nikki pulled on his shirt sleeve. "Where's Av— Priscilla?" Is she in the van? Is she okay?"

He yanked free of her, grabbed a pile of trash, and trudged back to the van.

Jake went to the window. Unless Ava lay flat in the seat, she wasn't still chained inside. Jake knew Ava would be at the window searching for a glimpse of them. Waving her arms, easing their fears.

216

On Elam's next trip in, Jake stood in his way, nose to nose with the old man.

Elam stopped. Surprise washed over his face when he saw Jake.

"Oh, hello." He turned to Nikki. "Good, you're both here."

"Where the f—," Jake stopped the word. "Where else would we be?"

"Of course." Elam seemed confused. "Where would you be?" He grabbed up more junk and walked out the door.

He returned.

This time, Nikki stepped in his path. "Elam, please, where is Priscilla?"

"On the porch." He pushed her aside and scooped up a pile of empty cereal boxes.

She stopped him from leaving. "What are you doing?"

"Moving. We're going home now. Did you forget?" He smiled like a sweet old grandfather.

Jake threw his arms up. "If we're moving, why aren't you taking food instead of junk?"

"Not junk, Jake. Important—" Elam stopped and looked up at the cubby the newspapers had spilled from. He walked to the bed, under the cubby. The disheveled papers stuck out at odd angles. "Yes, important things. Things to make it all okay again. To start the end. To finish the beginning." He paused. "I have something important there. In that space. But I can't remember..." He took hesitant steps forward.

Jake stopped him. "I'll get it for you. Let me do it."

Elam's face stiffened into a red scowl. His eyes squinted and his nose flared. "How do you know what I need? I don't even know."

"Take it easy, Pa. I can find anything, right?"

Elam relaxed a bit and stared into the young face. Then he stuttered, "Of, o-o-o-f course. That's right." Grinning, he placed his hands on Jake's arms and squeezed. Brief pain stung into Jake until the gnarled hands moved up and rested on his shoulders.

"You're Jake. Of course, you would know. Jake knows all about it." He wrapped his arms around him and gave a bear hug

217

that lifted him off his feet. "That's right, my boy. You get it and bring it to the van. Find a safe place, mind you. No one must know about the danger it holds."

Elam reached around to his back and pulled out his knife.

Jake stepped back. "What's wrong, Pa?"

With intense blue eyes, Elam studied the sharpness of the blade. He stroked the edge with his thumb. Using skilled fingers, he changed position of the weapon in his hand. Raising the steel high over his head, he placed both hands on the hilt, and froze.

From still frame to a chaos of movement, he slashed the blade through the air.

Nikki screamed.

Stabbing with violent cuts, he ripped into the bed mattress, over and over. The bed bounced with each slamming slash.

"Pa! What are you doing?" Jake stretched his arm out to protect Nikki.

Elam crumbled to the floor in exhaustion. He sat up, breathing hard. But with a calm expression, he let his gaze move to the ceiling.

"I'm letting them out."

With a sharp twist of his head, he listened, stood, and replaced his knife. Then he glared at the pile of empty peach cans. He strode to the table, scooped up the cans, and headed outside.

Jake dove under the bed and brought out the tan case. Scuffed and marked up, it must really be old. Old, like Elam old.

"I hope this is what he meant." He looked at Nikki. "It must be. Right? That's all that was in that hole except for newspapers."

"Well, he'll probably forget about it anyway."

"But if he doesn't, at least we'll have it. Besides, I want to see what's inside. Do you believe he's taking us away?"

"I just hope it will be where Ava is."

Their eyes met. Jake knew Nikki held the same thought. The fear they couldn't speak. Would they see Ava again?

Alive?

Chapter 51

Anger burned. James slammed on the gas pedal, and the tires screeched as he left the stop sign.

They didn't listen to me. I could have been talking to the wall.

He spun the wheel and slowed enough to bounce into Ray's driveway. The garage door took an eternity to open. He squeezed the car inside between stacks of papers, garden tools, and Ray's workbench. His door opened against a pile of boxes, leaving just enough space for him to squeeze through.

He tried not to slam the car door, but the sound echoed like a gunshot. His frustration grew when he backed his head into a bicycle hanging from the ceiling precisely as the overhead light shut off, leaving him in shadowy darkness.

He felt his way to the back door, and he took a deep breath before he entered the house. Inside, Ray sat in the tiny family room, newspaper in his lap. "Why are you so hot and bothered, son? You look like you want to punch something. Or someone."

James slumped into the overstuffed chair next to Ray in front of a big picture window. Sunlight, dappled shadows through the aspen trees from outside. "I just got back from the police station. I told them about the phone call."

"And?"

"The detective seemed interested, but they still think I did it. I bet they blew it off."

"Blew it off?"

"Okay, not exactly. I guess the text came from a stolen phone. They'll *try* to get a *fix* on the location. But they made sure to mention how easy it would be to steal a phone and have a friend text me."

"Did you tell them about the call you made? What the little girl said?"

"He said he'd look into it and tossed the phone on his desk. He doesn't believe me. No one does. Even you have your doubts."

Ray opened his mouth, closed it, and stared down at his shoes.

James rubbed his forehead. "Shoot, even I have doubts. Could I have dreamt it?"

"What are they going to do?"

"The police?"

"Yeah."

"They say they have to get a warrant to trace the location. I think they're dragging their feet, hoping I'll confess. They already have more circumstantial evidence on me than Ted Bundy." With his elbow on the arm of the chair, he made a fist and pumped it on his lips. "But I won't stop searching for Nikki, even if no one else believes me."

"Well, actually, there are some people that have a bit of faith in you."

James gave a brave smile. "You mean my kids?" His voice cracked. "You should have seen them this morning. They about knocked me over with hugs. When I picked up Jonah, he wrapped his arms around my neck like a python, and Conner had a death grip on my leg."

"They're not the only ones. Come with me."

James got up off the chair and followed Ray into the kitchen. What he saw made him take a step back. The kitchen counter held a ham, a store-bought rotisserie chicken, and three frozen boxed lasagnas.

Edith stood at the open refrigerator. She smiled and held up a frozen casserole.

"More food?"

"I told you Dale couldn't keep a secret. The whole church knows what happened at the meeting. I guess not everyone agrees with our beloved chairman."

"It looks like the freezer section at the grocery store."

"They don't know how else to show their support. This is how church does it. Food. The problem is, I think some reporters found out, too. I saw three cars out front with strangers in them, watching the house."

"So, they agree with me then? The church? They believe I'm innocent?"

"No."

"Oh."

"I mean, some may. Others just don't agree with the chairmen and his way of doing things. There are those in church that do believe you're guilty. The rest haven't a clue to what's going on."

"Well, if the ones that did this were trying to encourage me, they did."

Ray smiled. "And as far as me believing you're guilty? Well, I'm not sure I do believe you did it."

"You mean you *know* that I couldn't hurt her?"

"No." Ray continued as James's shoulders slumped. "I don't know if I believe that quite yet, either. I mean it could have been an accident, or a fight that went too far, or—"

"Now you sound like the police."

"I'm just saying that I'm not going to decide for sure until I *know* for sure."

Edith picked up one of the lasagnas. "Nonsense."

Opening the freezer, she rearranged the items there and slid the meal inside. "You know this young man didn't hurt his wife. Stop your hemming and hawing about it. We need to do something."

Before Edith put the other two lasagnas in the freezer compartment she wrestled out a package of peas. With precision, she maneuvered the frozen boxes into place and slammed the door shut. "Guess we'll have chicken for lunch." She placed the rotisserie chicken inside the fridge. She looked down at the counter, picked up the peas, and tossed them in beside the chicken, and said, "Chicken and peas."

She hustled over to a small desk near the windows. "But first we get to work." Pulling a pink-lidded laptop out of the desk drawer, she then hustled over to the kitchen table and sat. "Let's write down what the girl said and check out the clues." She over at the two men still standing. "Sit."

They sat.

James took out his phone. "Well, here's the text." He handed it to Edith.

"Okay, they're in Colorado. There's lots of wilderness past Estes and on into Montana. The Rocky Mountain State Park is in that area."

Fascinated, James watched as her long fingernails embellished with purple swirls tapped out the information. Since the boys had been born, Nikki rarely bothered with nail polish. A spasm of longing for her shook him.

Nikki, where are you?

"He's a serial kidnapper, all right," Ray said as he hitched up his pants and nodded his head with importance. They looked at him in surprise. "Well, he kidnapped three people. Right?" He turned to James. "What did the little girl say again?"

"Ava, her name is Ava." James looked at the ceiling. "She said this Elam character was an old man. Oh, and he drove a white van."

"That sounds like something a kid would make up. Why would an old man kidnap three people?" Ray asked.

"Oh, hush." She pressed her lips together and pointed at her husband. "You old goose." She returned her attention to the keyboard. "That's good, James. Think. What else?" Edith's hands hovered over the keyboard.

"Ava said they stayed at a camping site before going up into the mountains."

"The name?" Ray cocked up one eyebrow.

"Dancing Pinecone Camp, but she didn't sound very sure."

"Great," Edith said. "We can look that up online." With a flourish, she began typing and clicking with the curser.

"Hmmmm." Sigh. "Hmmm, hmmm, hmmm."

Edith popped her glasses up, squinted, and flopped them down. She repeated this several times. "Aha! Here, there's one campground in northern Colorado with pinecones in the name. Nothing about dancing, though." She scrolled down and leaned in.

222

"Wait. Here's a Dancing Aspen Leaves Campground." She typed both names. They could hear the printer in the next room come to life.

"We should call the camps." Ray took out his cell phone.

"No! I need to go there," James said. "Calling won't be enough. I need to show them the flyers. Watch their reactions to find out if they know anything."

"I've printed out the maps to both places. I'll put all this information in a file and print it out as well. We can go in the morning."

"Now, just a minute here." Ray sat up in a hurry. "*We* aren't going anywhere, Edith Marie Carson. James and I are going."

"Don't you Edith Marie Carson me! I'm not sitting here alone while you two go off having adventures."

James blinked at the speed of this turn in conversation. "I don't need anyone to come with me. I—"

"What if the police follow us?" Edith asked.

"That will be a good thing. They're probably tracking James by his phone anyway. Making sure he doesn't try to make a getaway. But I'm worried about the reporters."

James jumped in. "Listen, you two, I haven't said I'm taking anyone with me."

"Why the reporters?" asked Edith, ignoring James.

"They'll make a big hullabaloo. We won't be able to sneak up on the kidnapper, and this Elam fella will run off, or kill them all."

"Ray! Watch what you're saying in front of James."

"Oh, sorry."

With a heaving sigh, James gave up trying to get his wishes across to the two bulldozers in front of him. "Edith?"

"Yes, James?"

"Ava also said something about a woman named Maggie. Put that down, too."

She clicked the name in as Ray said, "I'll call Pastor Thomas. He might be able to help us figure a way to get rid of the reporters. He's a pretty smart guy, not just about God."

"I guess I should call Cora and Ben." James caught Edith's puzzled expression. "Ava's mom, and her fiancé. I think Ben will be surprised to learn that Cora might be right about Ava."

Chapter 52

Ben snapped his cell phone shut as he headed out the paint-peeled motel door.

Cora sat in a rusted folding chair on the tiny cement patio. Her head jerked up when the door slammed, and Ben brushed past her. "Where are you going?"

Ben ignored her and headed to the jeep. He rustled behind the farthest back seat a moment and came back with a small cloth-covered object.

He looked at Cora. "I got a call from your friend, James."

"James? Oh, you mean the man with the missing wife?"

"Right." He put one foot onto the step and leaned in. "He thinks he's heard from Ava."

"Ava?" She pushed her hand up to her throat. "How?"

"By phone."

"But Ava can't call anyone. She'd be too scared to speak."

"That's what I told him."

"Why didn't he call *me*? Why didn't *she* call me?"

He turned his gaze away from her. "He did. I have your phone. Mine got turned off."

"And you didn't tell me?"

"It's just temporary."

"Ben, I— oh, never mind. What did James say?"

"He wants to check it out."

"Check what out?" Cora sat up, back straight.

"The girl said she'd been kidnapped, along with his wife and a boy. It's probably just a prank call, but the girl gave him a couple of leads to campgrounds, and he's gonna see what he can find out. He asked if I wanted to come."

Cora looked at his hand. "What's that?"

He pulled the object closer to his chest. The cloth slipped revealing black metal.

225

He sighed and let the cloth slide off the rest of the way.

Cora caught her breath and cried out, "A gun? Why do you need a gun?"

"I'm going to a rescue, Cora, not a play date." He opened the motel door. "But I have to find the bullets first."

***

Cora didn't want him to find the bullets. Fear rolled over her like a spiked boulder. Cutting into and weighing on her, until her breath struggled to come out.

Dizziness flooded into her brain, and her heart beat like a wild animal caught in a trap.

Ava, come home. Please, I love you. Ben will find you. I can trust Ben. Then we'll be a happy family.

But by the shaking of her hands, she knew the lie. She couldn't trust him. Something wasn't right. She forced those thoughts into the back of her mind.

She stood. Pushing her fingers to the bottom of her pocket, she felt along the seam until her nails rubbed against two tiny, hard lumps. Scooping them up with her fingertips, she pulled out two blue tablets.

Before she could get inside to crush the pills to snort them, Ben rushed out the door again. The keys to the pop-up tent trailer dangled in his hand. He went around the corner where the trailer was parked. He'd be there awhile getting the top up so he could search inside.

Her hands trembled as she opened the motel door. Her only thoughts were to crush the pain of fear and be washed in blessed nothingness. To be cradled inside the holy land of numb.

Chapter 53

James squinted, searching the street, as Ray cruised through the intersection and pulled over to the curb. "There's one car at the other end of the block from my house. Could be a reporter."

"Or a cop."

James pointed farther down the street. "Another there by those cottonwood trees. And I bet I have plenty of neighbors that would be happy to let anyone know if they saw signs of life at the house."

Ray nodded toward the first house. "Go through the neighbors' backyards until you get to yours. Take your car out of the garage and drive to church. Hopefully, the reporters will get the idea you're going to the Wednesday prayer meeting."

"Your wife comes up with some interesting ideas. Doesn't she?"

Ray made a sour face and said, "Sometimes I think I married Jane Bond."

"See you at church." James got out and made his way into the McCredies' yard. He opened the side gate and stepped around to the back. Three houses' distance from his own, he mentally checked if any neighbors owned dogs.

As far as he knew, only his next-door neighbor had a pet. That little mop of a dog, Cricket. He'd made friends with Ruby, but that didn't mean Cricket had become less of a nuisance.

All the homes backed up to a large ravine. The yards had open fences made of wooden railroad ties. This made it easy for him to slip between the cross beams into the ravine behind the houses. Ruby's had chicken wire wrapped around to keep the dog in. That is, she tried to keep her in. He'd recently nicknamed the nuisance Houdini.

So far, he didn't hear the barrage of barking that accompanied the little white longhaired rat. She must be inside.

Aspen trees dotted the yard, but he used the scrub oak as cover until he reached his own yard.

This should be easy.

Making a leap over his fence, his left foot barely missed a small prickly-pear cactus as he landed. He'd stepped on one of these spiky plants before. Not fun. Alerted, he scanned the ground for more. They grew like weeds.

A sharp sting scratched at his ankle. He turned carefully to avoid needle-like armor, only to be met with a siren of shrill yipping barks. The mutt had snuck up on him, in James's own backyard.

He looked to Ruby's dining room window and saw the curtain push back, showing a quick glimpse of her cherub face. She saw him. She couldn't miss him in his bright orange shirt.

Should he hide, or wait? He really couldn't hide with Sherlock Cricket facing him down. He checked his ankle. No blood, only an angry red scratch.

With a resigned sigh, he glared down at the miniature guard dog as she blared out excessive yaps.

Ruby opened her back door and hurried across the yard to her fence. "James! Oh, James. I didn't know you were back." She puffed out her words, her face distressed and worried. "Get over here, you stupid dog."

She reached over the fence, and Cricket hopped into her arms. "Oh, James, did she hurt you? Why are you back here? Wait. Is something happening? What's going on? You must tell me." Her expression switched from worry to excitement to demanding so fast, he thought she might be having a seizure.

He stretched out his hand to pat her arm. "I'm okay, Ruby. I'll tell you all about it later. I have to be going. I'm in a hurry right now."

"Oh, no, you don't." She shook her finger at him. "You promised to tell me when something is up. And something is definitely up. Fess up, buster, or I'll let Cricket loose on you again." She raised the dog up as if she were a weapon.

"Okay, okay, you win. I don't want to attract attention." He raised his eyes to the sky as he tried to organize his thoughts. He filled Ruby in, including the plan to check out the camp areas.

Ruby stroked Cricket as she took it all in. "That's wonderful! I'll be right back." She turned to go.

"What do you mean? Just go back inside, I need to go."

"I want to put Cricket in her kennel, call Judith to come take care of her, and get my walking shoes on."

James asked with a slight tremble in his voice, "Why?"

"Because I can't walk in slippers, silly. I'm going with you."

"Oh, no. No, no, no. Ruby, I appreciate your concern, but I'm already taking far too many people with me. I need to be discreet."

"You have to take me."

"Why?"

"James, I grew up in that area. I know it like the back of my hand. I know all the people, the stories and rumors, every nook and cranny." She had an annoyingly smug look on her face as she gave Cricket a kiss on the head.

James surrendered. With teeth gritted, he shot out the word, "Fine." He shook his head. "Make it fast. I'll wait for you in the driveway. If anyone sees you, they'll just think I'm taking you to church."

She hurried off before he'd finished his sentence, and he headed to the garage's side door.

***

James gave a disapproving glare at Ruby as she sat beside him while he drove. She had not just gotten her walking shoes. She wore a Broncos cap, and a fanny pack, and she'd brought a backpack with a large water bottle attached. Now she pulled sunscreen out and began smearing it on her face.

"It's almost sunset, Ruby. You don't need that."

"We're in high altitude, boy. You can get burned way easier up here."

"I know that but— oh, never mind. You know we aren't actually going camping, right?"

"I just packed a few things. Who knows where the leads will take us?" She pulled out a granola bar. "Want one?"

"No." He'd not packed anything. He'd not thought that far ahead.

Ruby glanced at the rearview mirror. "Hum, we've got a following. Looks like two, maybe three vehicles."

He pulled onto the church property. A sprinkle of familiar cars dotted the lot. "We're here."

The reporters that followed them parked on the street.

Ruby stuffed the bar and the sunscreen into the fanny pack. James watched as she whipped off her cap and fluffed her short white curls. She started to get out, but then took off the fanny pack and carried it more like a purse. James came around to her side of the car.

She grinned at him before she struggled to get out, dragging the backpack. "I to need be Wednesday-prayer-meeting acceptable, I s'pose."

James reached in to help. He took her cap, put it on his head, and carried her backpack like a laptop bag.

They both headed to the front door. Thomas greeted them as they came in. "Everyone's in the family room."

As they entered, several people came over to hug James. Surprised by the kindness, James made a quick brush across his eyes and turned toward the circle of chairs in the center of the room.

Thomas took charge, shepherding the small group toward the chairs. As everyone settled, he raised his voice. "As you all know, this meeting has a dual purpose. The first is for prayer, and as such, all that is said here will remain in this room. Please, do not share any information you have heard here. Does everyone understand?"

Solemn nods traveled the room.

"The purpose of these prayers is to send off our brother James on a quest to find his wife. Let us pray."

Without another word, they moved their chairs closer and reached out to the hands beside them. Prayer after prayer filled the room like an orchestrated symphony of emotion. Love and urgency intertwined. Calming sounds of whispered "Yes, Lord" and "Jesus" bonded the requests for safety, wisdom, and spiritual insight.

James had never experienced this before. His mind didn't drift, his focus did not waver. He hung on each word as if it were the last lifeline to Nikki.

As the voices died down and only murmurs could be heard, Thomas closed the prayer time. "Hear now from 1 John 3:18. 'Let us not love with words or tongue, but with action and in truth.' Amen."

Pastor Thomas turned to James. "Are you ready?"

"Yes."

"Everyone please wait for us."

James and Pastor Thomas made their way to the men's bathroom. It took James only a moment to change. He came out at the same time as Thomas.

James took in the people's faces. Many amazed, others trying to hide a smirk. He knew the seriousness of the moment kept them from giving full vent to humor. But the sight of the diehard Kansas City Chiefs fan, dressed in a Broncos hat and orange shirt, made it hard to hold back teasing.

Pastor looked at James. "Really? You had to include a Broncos cap? The orange shirt wasn't bad enough?"

James smiled and tugged on the collar of his new polo shirt. "That touch was Ruby's idea."

Ruby nodded in approval of the transformation. "Well, ya had to cover the face as much as possible. It's a good thing you two are about the same size and coloring. Even your hair is similar. If it weren't for the fact that Pastor is so much older—"

"Hey!"

Ruby finished "—You two could be brothers."

In disgust Pastor Thomas pinched the hem of his orange shirt outward and let it snap back. Then he pulled the cap's bill down over his eyes.

"We *are* brothers. Aren't we?" He relaxed into a grin and spoke to the small group that still lingered. "You can start leaving now. A few at a time first, then I'll get going. James, keys?"

James handed them over. "Where will you go?"

"Don't worry, I'll lead those reporters on a merry chase. My Taurus is parked in back. Here's the keys. Be careful, it sticks a little in third."

"Thanks, Thomas. Thanks for everything." James stuck out his hand to shake Thomas's, but at the last second it turned into a bear hug worthy of Ray Carson.

Pastor and several members of the group left at the same time. James watched through a clear spot in a stained-glass window in the sanctuary. As they all had hoped, the cars parked along the street, five of them now, followed behind Pastor Thomas.

A voice called from the front entrance. "Excuse me? Anyone? I'm looking for James Rolen?"

Worried that a reporter had slipped in, James hurried to the front door. A man, with his hat in one hand and a small duffle bag in the other, stood in the narthex. James had a bad feeling about his rumpled appearance and the slight odor of beer. Then a light popped on in his mind, and he knew who he was.

"I'm James. Can I help you?"

"I'm Ben. I spoke with you on the phone."

"Hello, Ben. Well, we're all here, then. Come with me."

James brought him into the fellowship room and introduced him to the others. "Ben, these are some of my friends that are going with us. This is Ray Carson and his wife, Edith. And this is Ruby Farber."

Ben stared at the group of three, and then nodded. From the expression on his face, James could tell he wasn't impressed with this unlikely band of rescuers.

Before they headed out, Ray checked all the church doors to be sure they were secured.

Arriving at the silver gray Taurus wagon, each one stowed their luggage in the space behind the backseats. Ben sat in the front. Ruby made a sour face but got in the back with Ray and Edith.

"Ruby," Edith said. "You seem to be well prepared for the trip."

"Yep."

"Me too. I brought a small bag, just in case."

As James backed the car out of the slot, he again kicked himself for not bringing a change of clothes.

I don't care. I'll sleep in my clothes. All I care about is Nikki.

232

After a short silence, Edith tried to engage Ruby again. "I like those tennies you have on. Are they those special walking shoes I've heard about?"

James could see the hopeful smile on Edith's face in the rearview mirror. He knew she was trying to break past the wall Ruby unconsciously put around herself.

"They're not tennies. They are Best-Stride Walking Shoes."

"Oh. Do you like them?"

"Yep."

That killed any more conversation. James worried it would be a long, uncomfortable trip.

Into the quiet, Ben spoke up. "So, what are the plans? Are we getting a motel along the way?"

Edith and Ruby spoke in unison. "No!"

They looked at each other, and Ruby said, "We need to drive straight through."

"Yes," Edith added. "We can get a motel when we get there. We don't want to waste time."

"We can take turns driving. I know how to use a clutch," Ruby announced.

"Me, too," said Edith. "I learned on my father's truck when I was a teen."

Ray sat up straight. "Oh, no, you won't. We want to get there in one piece."

"Ray! I'm a perfectly good driver."

"You haven't driven a clutch in forty-seven years."

"Ray!"

"What?"

In an angry whisper, she said, "They'll know my age."

Ray slumped against the window and leaned his head on the glass. "Oh, brother."

"Don't worry, everyone," James said. "I can handle the drive up. I've done it before."

"Oh, no, you can't." Edith pointed a finger at James.

Ruby chimed in, "Driving tired is just as bad as driving drunk."

Edith turned to Ruby, "I've heard that, too. Did you get that from Learn.com?"

"Mythbusters."

"Oh, I watch that show. Did you see the one about how little dogs are good guard dogs?"

"Oh, let me tell you about my dog, Cricket..."

At this point, James tuned out. It would, indeed, be a long trip.

Chapter 54

A scritching sound drifted into Ava's dreams as a brush of air smoothed over her cheek. She opened her eyes to see a chipmunk working his tiny paws at the corner of the porch. The morning breeze picked up and blew strands of hair across her face.

Stiff and sore, she strained to push herself up. "Ugh."

The chipmunk scampered off.

She pulled in a deep breath. The familiar smell of pine and mountain air, along with a new sour stink, filled her nose. She lay back on the splintered bench and rubbed her eyes.

"Home?" That was what Elam called this place. Her throat hurts. "Not home." She stared up at the inside of the dirt-crusted porch overhang and watched a spider play limbo on his web. She wanted to take her time before sitting up again.

A large magpie landed on the railing beside her. He moved his head with bouncing energy. The ranger at the campgrounds had taught her to recognize the black head, white belly, and shiny blue wings. His strut made him look like he owned the place. But when his eye caught hers, he squawked and flitted away.

Loneliness crushed down on her at his leaving. She sat up and heard chains clattered off the bench.

Her wrists ached from pulling on the zip ties. Her throat burned from the screams of yesterday.

No one had come.

The familiar cold tingle of invisibility washed over her.

She reached for a water bottle and sucked out the last few drops. She looked over at the other empty one on the floor.

When will Elam come back with my friends? He promised. He promised!

She shook her head.

I can't trust him. Elam's head is all mixed up.

Mommy's voice played in her mind.

Trust me, I know. Trust me, I'll be right back. Trust me, you'll be all right.

But Mommy didn't know ... didn't come right back ... and things were never right.

Her heart beat fast, and her throat closed up tight.

Maybe it's my fault. I don't trust right.

She scrunched up her face to help her think. Now what? Yesterday, she'd called Nikki's husband. She hung up when she heard Elam coming. The phone dropped, flew off the porch, and crashed hard on some rocks. But the sound wasn't Elam, only the wind roaring through the trees, and now the phone is really dead.

Next, she'd yelled for help, banged on the windows, and used every bit of strength, yanking on her chains.

Inside her, the raging storm of worry made her think she might explode into a big glob. Sharp claws of her own fear cut inside her like cats fighting.

God. I need to pray to God. Does He have a name, or just ... God? Father, Jesus. That white bird, maybe? And what should I ask for?

It had to be right. She didn't want to waste her prayer. Maybe He was like a genie with only a few prayers to grant. She didn't know.

She had shouted to God before, screamed for help. Did that count as a prayer?

Nikki prayed. Even when Elam raged, Nikki trusted God.

I need that stuff that helps even if you're invisible. Mercy, that's it. I'll ask for mercy.

She squeezed her eyes shut and whispered, "God, I need mercy." She sucked in a breath and held it.

She waited.

Birds twittered as the wind swooshed in the trees. Letting out her captured breath in a slow stream, she looked down at her wrists, hoping the tight bands had melted away. She listened for her mom's voice calling. Jake's running steps to save her.

Any sound of hope.

Nothing.

Trembling and alone, she sat in front of God, a god bigger than the Wizard of Oz, probably.

236

Why doesn't He help me? Is He only a story? A fake? Jake said He was. I'm so scared. I don't think I can breathe anymore.

A flap of wings and skitter of bird feet drew her attention to the other side of the porch. She turned to see.

A shock of surprise tingled to her toes. A pile of trash now sat on the other side of the porch.

This is new.

Or had she not noticed before? No, she would have seen it when she screamed for help the day before. In her search for help, she'd been on that side on the porch. The chains had been long enough to reach.

Cardboard boxes, piles of newspapers, and old rotting clothes lay tossed across that end of the porch.

He's been here. Elam came back in the night. Dumped his trashy treasures and didn't wake me.

She tried to think what this meant. Had he put her here with this trash to be thrown out?

Hot tears poured onto cold cheeks. The thought of Elam coming and leaving her was too much.

It's true. I'm invisible. He couldn't see me. No one, not even God, can see me.

All those years of trying to make herself unseen by those who might hurt her had worked. Only now she wanted more than anything for someone to see her. Keep her safe. Make her real.

Slumping back onto the bench, she stared straight ahead, not moving. She drifted into the nothing she was. Tears dropped off her chin.

A breeze brought the musty smell to her nose with new power. With another burst of air, rattling papers jumped onto her bench. One fluttered into her face.

She grabbed at it.

At first, unseeing, she glanced at the print, only a page from one of Elam's Bibles. He'd read them to death, then kept every scrap and ripped page of the broken books.

Something pushed her to spread the paper on her lap. She pressed out the wrinkles with her hand. Lots of words covered the sheet. She looked at the first sentence at the top of the page and

237

read the words out loud. "She gave this name to the LORD who spoke to her: 'You are the God who sees me.'"

Ava blinked hard and repeated the words, then finished the verse.

"'For she said, 'I have now seen the One who sees me.'"

She read the words once more, this time to herself. But like a fully heard voice from out of nowhere, the words trembled in her mind.

A flow of fresh tears fell down her cheeks.

The One who sees ... me?

From the middle of her chest, burning warmth spread to her fingers, pushing out fear.

The black and white bird fluttered back to the pile of rubbish and pulled out a piece of bread, crusted green. Dark beady eyes stared at her.

"Are you God, Mr. Magpie? You see me."

The bird blinked.

Feathers rippled and flapped as he bent his legs to push off the deck. She felt the wash of wind blow her hair as he rose.

"No, you were made by God." She let out a giggle and leaned back on the bench. "I get that confused."

No Prince Charming, no superhero, no ninjas dressed in black had come to save her. But this was enough for now ... enough for hope.

Because deep down in her tiny and easy-to-break heart, she knew.

God sees and hears me. He even told me His name.

She whispered aloud to what her own eyes couldn't make out. "Thanks, God-who-sees-me. Now I know you're there."

Chapter 55

"Amazing Grace, how sweet the sound, that saved a wretch like me-e-e-e-e!" Elam belted the words out the van window with great joy and enthusiasm.

Nikki hoped this would not ruin the song for her. The breeze from the outside air whipped his long hair behind him and across his face. Nikki wondered how he could see the road, much less continue to sing.

Jake had been staring out into the forest, but now he turned and met her eyes. He glanced behind them.

Elam had filled the back part of the van with more useless junk.

She followed the direction of his gaze and saw the small suitcase teetering on top of a pile of clothes.

She nodded, but then gave him a questioning shrug. She knew he wanted to see inside the case. But how could they, with Elam right there? They would have to wait for a better time.

Should they be glad the old man was so much happier now? He acted relaxed, surer of what he was doing. In the rearview mirror, she could see his blue eyes give off an unnatural shine. Instead of the weeping and fear of just hours before, he bellowed out one gospel song after another, completely at peace.

How did he not fall asleep from taking Ava, returning here, going out with junk, coming back to get us and now off again? His manic side must be giving him major adrenaline.

Nikki's stomach gave a whiny growl, reminding her it must be past noon. She strained to see out the front window as Elam made a sharp turn off the road. At first, it seemed they'd cut out into the forest. The van jolted and bounced over rough terrain. But then she realized someone had come this way before, recently. The bushes and small trees in front of them had been mowed over.

Larger trees lined up at the edges. This must be a road or drive from long ago.

Soon the van came alongside a steep slope. Nikki raised herself up to see. The drop-off felt like a cliff to her. Elam didn't even flinch.

After more than a few switchbacks, she saw flashes of a blue structure through the trees. As they drove closer a spindled porch with gabled windows came into view.

She pointed this out to Jake. He did a double take and his mouth formed a silent and incredulous, "What?"

Elam changed his tune to a country song about coming home down a country road. Movement under the left side set of windows caught Nikki's attention. A small head popped up from behind the railing.

Ava!

Elam slammed on the brakes, and a cloud of dust sprayed out around the van. Nikki could hear Ava yelling even from where she sat.

"Nikki! Jake! God sees me!" She moved to the steps. Her arms stretched back toward the bench as she pulled on the chains.

Nikki shot a glance at Elam. He had never heard Ava speak.

Elam got out, slammed his door, and went around the van to let his prisoners out. "That's right, Priscilla," he shouted. "God brought us all back together again. We'll be together. Forever."

Thankfully, Elam was still lost in his madness.

Released, both Jake and Nikki raced to their precious little friend. Nikki dropped onto the porch steps and embraced the child, while Jake threw his long arms around them both.

"Ouch, I'm being squished!" Ava squealed and giggled. Ready to pull back, Nikki felt the pressure of another body crushing from outside the pile. Strong body odor mixed with a rotten garbage smell made her nose sting.

A deep-throated laugh followed as Elam tried to hold them all at once. "Yes, yes. We are all here now. The prophecy races. The clock is flying back from its dark nest. Tonight, we sleep, for tomorrow is the last supper."

He stood from his crouch as he let go, and bodies tumbled.

"Jake!" He undid Ava's chains from the railing and pulled out his knife.

"Yeah, Pa?"

"I hate to do this, but you know that to be rescued we must go through the cleansing darkness. Is a month long enough?"

"What?" Jake croaked out the word.

"It will have to be, for tomorrow is the day of salvation." Elam yanked Ava down the porch stairs and around to the right end of the house.

Nikki followed with anxious concern and pulled Jake behind her.

Elam raised his blade to slash vines and leafy growth off two wooden doors that lay slanted on the side of the porch. He opened the doors. A dank, musty smell swallowed them like an invisible cloud.

He turned to Ava and pulled her close to his face by her chains. "Darkness is the acid that wipes the heart clean. Jake?" He turned to the boy. "You know that the father comes back to give the punishment on time, every week. You know he does not fail."

Jake stared back.

"Jake! You know?"

"Yeah, Pa."

Nikki could see Jake's bottom lip tremble. Elam shoved Ava down the stairs into the dark pit. She screamed, and Nikki could hear her tumble and bump down into the blackness. He looked at the others.

"Go!" He lunged at them with his knife.

Nikki pushed past Jake hurrying down after Ava. She could only make out one step at a time. At the bottom, she groped with frantic hands, trying to find the fragile girl. Her foot nudged something soft. The door slammed shut above them. She knelt on the floor and scooped Ava into her lap. The little girl moaned and snuggled in as Nikki reached out and found Jakes hand.

Something alive scurried in the dusty shadows. Nikki's eyes became accustomed to the darkness and she could make out shelves beside the cement stairs. A gleam of light came through a small rectangle window at the top of the wall. Bottles and jars lined up on the slats. A crumbled pile of dirt and rocks blocked off the rest of the room.

As hinges from above screeched, the door opened. Bright light shot down on them.

"Keep this safe." Elam threw something heavy down the stairs.

The door banged shut.

Chains clattered.

And then nothing.

Chapter 56

James slowed the wagon as he turned into the next camp ground on the list. "I thought for sure that last place from yesterday was going to be the one. It had the bear decorations that Ava talked about."

Ray sighed. "Yeah, I think they all have that. It's Colorado."

"Well, at least the man was very nice." Edith's voice had an encouraging lilt. "And today's another day. You go in this time James. Come back and tell us what you find out."

Inside James saw more moose and bear displayed. A bald man with a short beard sat behind the counter. He grinned at James. "Good morning, sir. What can I do for you?"

"I need some information you might be able to help me with." James pulled out the flyer for Nikki and a photo of Ava. "Have you seen this little girl or this woman, perhaps with an older gentleman, at your camp? They're missing."

The man took the papers and examined them. "That the little girl I heard about on the news? We get a lot of kids here. This is a family campground, you know." He pulled his glasses from his shirt pocket and concentrated on the papers. "Nothing familiar. I'm sorry."

James sighed. "Well, thank you anyway. I'm going to leave a copy of the picture and my card here with you. In case you think of anything."

When he turned to go, he heard a woman's voice call out, "Frank, is that the Millers? Their site is all spit-spot and ready for them."

"No, Maggie, it's a man looking for someone. Come on out here. Maybe you can help."

James spun around. "Did you say Maggie?"

243

A woman walked through the open door. She fluffed her strawberry locks as she approached the desk. "Yes, my name's Maggie. What do you need?"

Frank said, "This guy is searching for that lost little girl from Woodland Park. And this lady. He says they may have been here with an old man."

Maggie took the picture from off the desk, put on glasses, and frowned. "Frank! That's the girl that was with her grandfather, the one who skipped out on us without paying." She slammed her hand on the desk. "Not only that, but we had a rash of complaints right after they left about things being stolen."

A shot of hope ripped through James. "You recognize her? What about the woman?"

"No, just the girl."

"Please, what can you tell me about them? Did they say anything about where they were going?"

"That rotten old man tricked me. He acted all kind and gentle, but he ripped us off."

"What do you remember about the girl?"

"I felt sorry for her. She was so quiet. Oh, wait. The girl that was missing didn't talk, right? Let me think. No, she didn't say a word to me. He called her Priscilla."

James grabbed a pencil and a sticky note off the counter and scratched the name down. "Her real name is Ava. Did they say anything about where they were headed?"

"They left in the middle of the night. So, I don't know where." She shook her reddish curls and put her hands to her head. "Wait. The old man did say something about going into the mountains. He pointed toward Johnny Peak. Yes, he said that the little girl hadn't been in mountains like ours before. They were going up there to camp."

Frank said, "There's only one road that leads into that mountain. Just follow the main street right on through town."

"What did the old man look like?"

"He had long white hair and a beard." She scrunched her eyes closed for a moment as if trying to picture the man. "Part of the time he had it in a ponytail. But after he had his shower, he let it hang. It went halfway down his back. Let's see, what else? He wore overalls and carried a ragged backpack. The little girl had a long blue flowered dress on, and a red hooded sweatshirt over it." Maggie put a hand over her heart. "Oh, that poor kid. I think she tried to tell me something once, but she just couldn't get it out."

"Thank you, thank you so much. Call the police and tell them what you told me." James left and ran to the Taurus.

He got in, shut the door, and said, "We have a lead. The Maggie woman Ava told me about was there. She remembered them."

Cheers erupted within the car. James related all the information he had just gleaned.

With a paled face Ben asked, "What's next?"

"Let's go into town and show her picture around there, too. Someone else might have seen them."

***

James took in the scene of the little tourist village. Quant shops lined the street. They held a variety of mountain crafts, elk and hiking themed t-shirt shops, candy carts, and ice creameries.

Ray took a swig from his water bottle and said, "Let's split up. Ben, you come with me on this side of the street. James, you can go with the ladies down the other."

The morning dragged on with no success for James and his companions. So far, no one had recognized the photos. As lunch time approached the ladies slowed. A stream marked the end of the street beside Pete's Soup and Sandwich Shoppe.

Edith made a beeline for a park bench overlooking the water. "I've got to rest my aching feet." Ruby followed her lead and sat with a groan.

Discouraged and tired, James sat down beside them. He saw Ben and Ray come out of the last establishment and he waved them over.

"Any luck?" Ray called as he walked over with Ben.

James shook his head. "Let's go in the sandwich shop for lunch. I think we're all worn out and hungry."

"Sounds good to me," Ben said.

245

James's head hurt. Was it stress or the altitude affecting him? He glanced at Ruby sucking down water from her flowered bottle. Water was what he really needed.

A bell rang as they entered the shop. Décor of dark wood, blue striped wallpaper, and brass accents combined with a variety of knick-knacks. The walls displayed photos of high school football teams and important buildings in the town.

In the corner, a huddle of laughing teen boys sat. Some on seats tipped back on two legs. Others had long arms draped across the chairs and table. Legs stretched out underneath and into the aisle.

James pointed to the Order Here sign and motioned for the two ladies to go ahead of him. Each sandwich had its own special name and filling. Ruby, ordered first, then waited in line while the sandwich was made. When her order came up, she grabbed her tray and settled at a table by the front window.

After James paid for everyone and waited for his food, he chatted with the cashier. "Have you seen this little girl around town? Possibly with an elderly man? She's missing. He has long blond or white hair, goes by the name of Elam." He handed him the flyer for Nikki. "Or this woman. She's missing as well."

The young man stared at the pictures and shook his head. "Sorry, I see lots of people during the day. But they don't ring a bell."

"Thanks, anyway." James put the papers back in his pocket and took his tray. The aroma from his pastrami and sauerkraut Rueben sandwich distracted his worried mind for a moment. But remembering how Nikki loved Rueben's brought him back to the pain.

He went to his seat and set the tray down. But before he settled down with his sandwich, he walked over to the teens who now sat in quiet concentration as they ate.

"Excuse me, gentlemen. Would you mind looking at this picture? We're searching for this little girl and woman. They're missing."

A boy with dark hair covering one eye took the photo from James. "Yeah, we heard you ask Sam about it. That's rough."

He gave the photo to the friend on his right. "I ain't seen her."

James offered more information as each boy examined the flyer. "You might have seen her with an older man, with long blond or white hair. He wears overalls and may carry a torn backpack. He goes by the name of Elam."

One of the smaller boys with a Rockies baseball cap on sat straight in his seat. "Hey, you know who that sounds like, man? That crazy ol' bugger who has that junk-fort way up in the mountains."

The gang burst out laughing, and a lanky kid spoke up. "Yeah, yeah. He has long hair and always wears those dirty overalls. I've seen him a couple of times wandering around town. But I thought he had a boy, not a girl, with him."

"I thought so, too."

The first boy spoke to James. "He's a, you know, what do you call them? A hermit. His place is stupid hard to find. Me and some dudes I know been there once. We got lost on the way back. Didn't think we'd ever find our way home."

"What's your name, son?"

"Tim"

"Why were you there?"

He ducked his head down to the table and chuckled. "Well, actually, we gave him a hard time. We pulled down the junk he puts up around his place. Thinks it protects him or something. He came charging out with a gun." His brown eyes widened. "If I'm lying I'm dyin'!"

"Right, I hear he has bodies buried there, on his property," said a boy with gold and black ear gauges. "Dozens, probably."

A man's voice cut the air. "But that's not Elam. Elam is the ghost."

Chapter 57

Gray and black splotches swam in front of Ava's eyes. She tried to make herself see the dark blurry objects.

"Ava, have you had any water? Ava?"

Nikki's voice. I'm lying in Nikki's lap.

She rubbed her eyes and blinked hard until things became clearer. A soft beam of light floated down from a small window perched high on the wall. Dirt crusted on the rectangle shape, but enough glowed into the room to see. Now she could make out Nikki's shadowed face. The ceiling, with pipes and beams covered with dusty cobwebs, closed her in. Instead of a back wall, a pile of rocks and rubbish filled the space. A damp, musty smell washed up her nose.

"Not since this morning, but at least then I won't have to pee." Ava would not want to try to pee down here.

"I don't want you to get dehydrated. Are you sure you're all right? You slept right through the night. You didn't even stir when Jake tried to bash out the cellar doors. As old as they appear, they're solid." Nikki looked up to the top of the stairs that led to the outside and back to Ava. "But what happened to you when you were with Elam? What did he do to you?"

Ava gave her eyes another good rubbing. "After we stole some things in town, he brought me here and chained me to the porch. Then he left me. I was so scared I would never see you or Jake." She could make out Jake sitting behind Nikki with his head down. "Or anyone, again."

"We're here now."

Jake cut into the comforting. "Did you use the phone?"

"Oh! Oh, yes. I talked to, you know ... him, um, your husband, Nikki."

Nikki gasped. "You talked to James? Are you sure? I thought you were going to text the message?"

248

"I did, but he called me back."

Jake shot his arm up in the air. "Rockin! It had enough charge to take a call, too? That is so stinkin' awesome." He seemed happier about how the phone worked than sending the message out.

A nearby pile of wood made a small shift. A swirl of dust lifted into the shafts of light. Ava jumped at the innocent sound.

A mouse? Or a rat. Eewh.

She snuggled closer to Nikki. "What did James say to you?"

"He wanted to know who took us, and if I knew how to tell him where we were."

"What did you say?" Nikki asked.

Ava sighed. "I have to think." She closed her eyes and tried to replay the words in her head. "I told him about Elam, and what he looks like. I told him about Maggie and the camp."

"Maggie? Who's Maggie?" Jake demanded.

"Elam took me to a campground when we went to the bottom of the mountain. It's where I borrowed the phone. Maggie was the lady there."

"Could you tell them the name of the camp?" Nikki stroked her back.

"I tried to. I'm not sure if I remembered right. But I heard Elam telling her about us camping in the mountain. She even pointed at the road we took."

"Maybe that will help guide him the right way." Nikki combed back Ava's hair with her fingers.

Jake shook his head. "Even if he figures it out, that might lead them to the old camp."

Ava's eyes grew wide, and she said in her smallest voice, "But we aren't at the old camp."

All was quiet for a moment until Jake shifted forward. He brushed aside cobwebs that fell over his head when he sat up. Through the gloom, Ava watched him reach for the object Elam had thrown down after them.

He snatched and dragged the thing across the dust-covered ground. It was small like a doll case, but old and brown. Not pretty.

"What's that?" Ava asked.

"A suitcase. It's what Elam threw down after us. After all that work I did trying to bash out the door, I was too tired to check it out last night." Jake smiled.

"It's small. Where are the wheels and the long handle?"

Nikki helped Ava sit up. "This is an old kind, Ava. People use to carry these when they would stay somewhere overnight."

"Why is it important?"

Jake's face fairly glowed in the dim light. "We don't know, kiddo, but we're going to find out."

He tried to slide the tabs apart with his thumbs. Nothing. Not a click, or a pling sound, no movement of the double tabs or latches. Jake tried again.

Nope.

He banged on the top with his fist and said, "I won't let you win." He reached behind Nikki and pulled back a long bar.

He tried prying the lid open. But the bar was too thick. He found a sliver of a stick to pick the locks.

Nikki placed a hand on his arm. "Don't damage the case so much that Elam will notice."

Jake nodded his head and kept on working. With a tiny click sound the two latches popped up. Jake stared at the case as he slowly lifted the lid.

"Wait!" Nikki squeezed Jake's arm. "Listen."

Steps. Coming closer.

Chains rattled, and the hinges squeaked above them. Jake shut the lid, pushed the latches back down, and shoved the case away from him.

Light poured in from above. "Hey, family! I know it hasn't been a month yet, but we all have needs. Get on out here."

Ava held her hand up to shield her eyes from the brightness. Nikki put her arms around Ava and helped her to stand. Her legs tingled.

"Rise and shine and give God the glory, glory—. Glory me, you all move slower than a tranquilized rock." Elam held the door open and put a hand out as he ushered each one up the steps.

"Come with me, now." He acted like he was a butler from an old cartoon. Ava stumbled behind Jake as he followed Elam into the woods. A small shack stood by a tall pine.

An outhouse?

She gazed back at the big house.

Isn't there a bathroom in there? Maybe it's locked.

Nikki gave Ava a little nudge. "You go first, sweetheart. Can you handle it alone?"

Ava nodded, stepped into the tiny space, and waited for Elam to close the door. She lifted the seat top covered in dust and cobwebs. Closing her eyes, she sucked in a breath. She held it until all was accomplished, and hurried out the door.

Soon each had finished their business. Elam let them drink from a sliver of a stream that ran down some rocks. The water was cold like snow, but tasted good. Then he guided them back to the hole.

Maybe Jake will hit him now. We'll all run. No. If we do, we die. Like Elam says.

Elam waved his knife at Nikki to hurry her.

Cut to pieces.

Elam grinned at Ava and leaned down to whisper loudly into her ear. "I know what you're thinking. Pa would never do this. But who can stop the winds and overflowing waterfalls? Only Jesus."

He let Ava and Jake take their time stepping down the cement stairs. But not Nikki. He held her back. Before Elam dropped the doors, he jumped down the steps and snatched up the suitcase.

"Without this, how will I know what sacraments are needed and the order of the service? Can Jesus keep his children away from the draft if no one shields them from the wind?"

The door shut, and all that could be heard was Jake's mutter.

"Crap."

Chapter 58

Ben moved his hand to his coat pocket and let his fingers touch the smooth, cold glass. If he could just slip away for a few moments, he could take a swig from the bottle he'd stolen from the liquor store. But he couldn't leave now. He must concentrate on what was being said.

"What ghost?" James turned to see who'd spoken. He saw movement in a shadowed corner, and a middle-aged man leaned into the light.

"Elam is the name of the man that murdered his family." The man looked at each face before he spoke again. "Killed himself, too. They say his spirit wanders the woods on the other side of the mountain pass, nearer Gold Junction than here."

"No, no," insisted Tim. "I saw this guy. I felt the bullets whiz past me. I'm pretty sure he's not dead."

"Wait." Ruby scraped her chair back and stood up. "I know that story. I grew up around here. I heard about it when I was a little kid. He's right. Elam *was* the name. I knew that name sounded familiar. We told his story at sleepovers and scared each other silly."

She raised her hands in front of her chest and did a slow wiggle of her fingers. "First, he's on the porch, then he's in the hall, up the stairs. He's on the first step, on the second, He's outside the door. BOO!" she shouted, throwing out her arms and bouncing a little.

Everyone jumped, then chuckled, but Ruby's face stayed serious.

Ben scratched his head. "Sounds like a kid's story."

Ruby's eyes widened. "I know it does. I'm sure people have added to the story over the years, but what are the odds Ava would know the name Elam? This family had a son and a daughter. They were loyal members of the Methodist church in the town. I'm not sure which town right now."

"Great." James pulled out a nearby chair and sat. He put his elbows on the table and rested his head in his hands. "Are you telling me we now have two places to find?"

Ben couldn't stand it any longer. He slipped down the narrow hallway to the men's room. He locked the door behind him and almost collapsed onto the sink. Taking a deep breath, he dug out the bottle. Trying not to spill on his shirt, he took several fast swigs. His hands had already begun to shake. The faster it got into him, the sooner the trembling would quiet.

Careful there, Ben. Save some for later.

With a death grip on the bottle, he stared into space. The familiar rage bubbled in his chest.

If only that little beast hadn't run. Who does she think she is, smacking me in the head? I wouldn't have hurt her.

A vision of the boy in Dallas flashed into his mind. The little terrified face. Ben jerked when the memory of his violence leaked into his conscious thought. Had he buried the body, or did the boy keep quiet? These memories were always foggy, muddy, like sewage swill.

Blood, there'd been blood.

The red color and warm smell wrapped around him. He bent over and imagined a death shroud draping over him. He took another long swallow of drink, straightened, and replaced the cap.

With a long shaky breath, he shoved the bottle into his coat pocket. When he went back to the dining area, he fished out a few bucks from his wallet and went to order a beer. He not only craved more alcohol, but he figured it would mask the smell of the vodka he'd just had.

Ray's deep voice vibrated in the room. "Listen here, Ruby, if this happened when you were a child, this guy would have to be either a ghost or really, really old."

James's head came up, and he addressed Tim. "What was the guy's name that shot at you?"

"I don't know. Um. Wait, some people call him Moses."

"Why?" asked James.

"He spouts out God stuff, and looks as old as Moses."

"God stuff?"

"You know, vengeance, fire and brimstone, things like that."

Edith raised a timid hand as if she were a child in school. James smiled and nodded to her.

"Thank you." She adjusted her position to sit taller. "I noticed a library across the street. If there was some kind of violent event in the past, wouldn't it have been in the newspapers? No matter which town it was closest to? The library might have it in their archives."

"Good point, Edith. Let's finish our lunches and head over." He turned to the boys. "Do you think you can show us where the hermit lives?"

They looked each another and shifted feet. Tim answered, "Sure. That is, I can take you to the area and point to the general direction. It's hard to find, like its supernatural or something. I kept thinking it must be moving around." He paused, his face relaxing to a child's expression. "Oh, I have to ask my mom first. I got in a lot of trouble that first time."

Everyone nodded in solemn agreement.

"Let me give you my cell phone number, and have your mom call me," James said as he took out a pen and grabbed a napkin.

He went back to his seat and took a huge bite of his warm bread and meat. The tang of sauerkraut mixed in the pastrami flavor like the questions that swirled through the facts they'd just learned.

Chapter 59

Elam stretched out his craggy hand. Nikki let him curl his fingers around her trembling ones. He held them with a strange gentleness.

"Come on, Mama, we need some time to ourselves. Let's take a tour of the house. You always have such pretty things on the walls." He squinted up his face into a smile and with a gentle touched his grinning mouth. "I know, I'm a boy, I'm not supposed to notice that kind of thing, but I do."

He led her up the stairs, onto the porch, and to the door. He dropped her hand, bent down to lift the edge of the welcome mat, and retrieved a small object.

A key.

Elam stared at it. A detached and unfocused look came into his eyes. Then an amazing sharpness flashed into the blue, perhaps a flick of sane thought. He turned to Nikki. "Excuse me, who are you again?"

Nikki didn't know how to answer. Should she respond to his delusions, or tell him her real name? Maybe try to take a chance on reaching his sanity.

Too hungry and exhausted to think straight, she said simply, "I ... I don't know."

He chuckled. "I don't know who I am either." He positioned the key into the lock. "But I do know that this is home, and you are not Jessie."

He swung the door open and swiped at the cobwebs. Acrid, dank smells assaulted Nikki. The state of the room filled her with dread.

Elam's face glowed with joy, like a child at Christmas, but Nikki's stomach turned sour.

"Mama, see how beautiful it all is."

Beautiful?

Her heart beat faster like an animal caught in a trap.

"Remember when you and I painted this room? These watery blue walls and the white trim make me think of the ocean." He pulled her farther inside. "How about that staircase? How many times have children scraped the wood over the years with their dirty feet?"

Nikki did a slow head shake in astonishment at the intensity of his delusions.

Elam put his hand on the stairs' bottom finial. He snatched his hand away and looked at the soot covering his palm. "It's dusty? Mama, you never let it get dusty." A dark cloud moved over his face. "How could you let it get this dirty?"

Nikki pulled in a breath.

Anger flashed in his eyes, but as his gaze rose to Nikki's, the emotion dropped away. "It's gonna be okay," he said. "It will be a new day after the last supper."

Last supper? Why does he keep saying that?

Elam glanced upward. Then he turned and grabbed Nikki's hand again. His eyes sparkled blue, alive with excitement. "Come upstairs with me, Mama."

"No!" Nikki pulled her hand away. "No, Elam."

"I bet the quilt you made is still on the bed. The one with light patches of blues and greens, each with different types of little tiny flowers printed on it." He hunched forward and pinched his fingers together, showing how small the flowers were.

This Elam frightens me most. The sane wedged between insanity.

Then he looked hard into her eyes. As if he could draw the clear thoughts he needed out of them. "Please? Come?" His head jerked to one side and back to her again. "Oh, of course, you want to see the kitchen first. That's your favorite, isn't it? Maybe after the darkness has scoured the children clean and the beatings are over, you can make us a meal. I love pot roast."

He babbled on about each ingredient that went into the meal as he dragged her over to the next room. "Allow me to pull the curtain divide open." He swept out his hand, and led her inside. "Watch your step."

Nikki's stomach swirled with nauseous waves as her head spun, but she stepped forward. She surveyed the devastation that Elam could not see. She looked back at the staircase through the nonexistent wall where Elam had mimed pushing aside the curtains. The staircase's blackened spindles were like broken, spiky witches' teeth. The steps led to a landing that hung onto nothing but air. At the front of the house, a portion of the second floor and attic still existed, but the inside walls were scorched and covered in black soot.

Nikki stepped with great caution over fallen beams and splintered wood half buried in dirt with a charcoal skin. She bent down and pulled a small baby doll out from under a board. Turning her over, she saw that one side of the burned face had melted into a grotesque mask. Her fingers lost strength at the sight, and the doll fell with a thud.

Elam continued his monologue. "The boy used to sit at the top of the back stairs and listen to the mother and father talk. I think the boy loved them, but ... I'm sure the pain of having sinned was very great."

Silent tears welled in his eyes.

"Well, you know." He jerked on Nikki's arm and pulled to force her face closer to his. His spit launched out with his words. "If we let them contaminate our children, how will the children know to follow the rules? They don't know God, or they would follow every rule, dot and tittle, comma and scribble." He sucked in a breath and asked, "Have you ever seen brains?" He dropped her arm and looked away. "I have, when the dog was killed."

A fresh sting of fear rippled up her spine. Nikki took in the sights of the ravaged home. Slats of cindered wood shot up through the rubble like the bones of a gutted fish.

A large portion of the back walls and roof were completely gone. Nikki could see blue sky with tree branches dipping in the wind. The bricks on the far side wall were covered in burned char, windows gone. Steps hung along this wall and ran to the second story at the front of the house. Here, rooms were left in a dollhouse scene. Above that, an attic room had a dark skeleton of a bed and a dresser that faced into the open air.

A hole gaped in the kitchen floor. Rubble of ceiling and floor filled the dent. Could that be the basement below? The cellar prison?

Elam took Nikki's hand again and led her farther toward the back wall. Every step disturbed the dead ash encrusted in the dirt, sending up a faint smoky aroma. Her chest tightened.

Consistent with his inconsistency, he walked through a wall that wasn't there into the yard. Nikki sucked in the fresh air as if she were an addict with her first hit of the day. The old burned-out structure held an aura of death. She could imagine that something more than house had gone up with the flames. Her fists tightened as she tried to block out these thoughts.

He led her farther into the yard, to a grassy place under a tree. "Sit here for a while, Mama. I'll be right back."

Nikki sat like a zombie and stared at the ruins. She could do nothing else with Jake and Ava locked up.

Dear God! Had the real Priscilla, Jake, and their mother been burned up in that house?

The faces of her two little boys rushed into her mind. She ached to see them. She would do anything to protect them. A parent must. How could they not?

Father, in heaven, where are You?

Something made her look into the grass. There in green leaves she saw tiny red spots. Strawberries, early spring berries, dotted the plant. Her head pulled up to see if Elam watched her. He was by the wood pile. Being careful not to move too quickly and thus draw attention to herself, she picked the berries. She shoveled as many as she could into the pouch of her sweat shirt.

She put a few into her mouth. After the shock of Elam's tour, she needed this sweet nourishment.

Thank You, Lord. Thank You.

Chapter 60

James relaxed back in his chair and with a sigh looked around the book filled room. He could see Ben stretched out on one of the library couches.

What's he doing? Sleeping? We're all tired.

Everyone in their group sat at a computer station scrolling through archived newspapers, except for Ben. The first night at the motel, Ben had disappeared for about an hour. James figured he went for a smoke, but he came back with a wobbly step and a terrible stink of booze. Now he was all but passed out on the couch.

A deep sorrow filled James, welled up from a compassion he had never experienced before. What kind of life did this little girl come from?

"Hey, I've got something," Ray called out. Then he glanced around with a guilty expression and whispered, "I mean, I found something."

James went over. Ray pointed to a small back page article. "See here, it talks about animals found in the woods that had been dismembered and tortured. Some were dogs that had gone missing."

James reached down and scrolled through the piece. "They found beer bottles nearby. It could have been kids being stupid."

"I don't know. The descriptions of the animals sound pretty gruesome."

"Where did this happen, again?" James leaned in to study the page.

Ray pointed to the screen. "They only give a general direction."

"Print out a copy of that page." He stepped back to leave.

"Oh, wait. Do you see the date on the newspaper?"

James moved in closer. "Print it anyway."

***

"Jake?" Ava's voice sounded little and quiet to her own ears. She sat leaning against the cold wall of the cellar. The side of her face rested on the stones.

"What?"

"Why didn't you try to escape Elam sooner?"

Jake's hand wrapped around a rock. He scratched in the dust on the cement floor "You know."

"Cause he would kill you?"

Quiet breathing melded with the scraping sound. "That, and I've nowhere to escape to."

"Nothing better than this?"

"No. I didn't think so. I was worthless, like he said. Anyway, I made a deal with him."

"What was that?"

"I wouldn't try to escape, and he wouldn't kill me."

"Oh." Sniffing, she raised her fist and rubbed it under her nose. "You had no hope?"

"No hope."

"And now you do?"

He stopped and gazed up at the light beams filtering through the cracks. "Yes."

"Why?"

"I guess not wanting him to hurt you or Nikki gave me courage I didn't know I had."

"Oh"

He continued to scrape in the dirt.

***

Ben had his eyes closed and his hat over his face.

They must think I'm asleep. Good.

He didn't want them to know how little he knew about computers. Besides he still had a buzz on from his last drink. It calmed him, but made it hard to focus.

"James?" This time Ruby sang out. "Here's another one." "Wow, this one is horrific. Look." She leaned in and pointed to the words as she spoke. "It's short. Listen, 'Tragic loss. Fire blazes through a home in the Golden Meadow area. Home burns with

260

entire family inside. Names are being withheld until next of kin have been notified.'"

"Okay, that's a start. Print it. Check other papers in that time frame."

"What *is* the time frame?" asked Edith.

"These are from the 1960s."

Ben had to speak up. "That's crazy." He yanked off his hat and sat up. "That would make the man in his eighties or nineties."

A librarian shushed him from her desk. Quiet? That librarian must be from the dark ages. Ben glared at her as he stood up and walked closer to the group.

"I know," said James. "But maybe there's a family history, or some connection between then and now."

Ray raised his hand. "Here's something else. The headlines are House of Horrors." He read aloud. "Last week the Hanson home, located in the Golden Meadow area, was engulfed in flames. Evidence shows the fire started in the kitchen area. A deluge of spring rain saved a portion of the home.

However, there is now strong suspicion that the children of this home have endured extreme abuse at the hands of the father, Elam Hanson.'"

A phone rang. James jerked his head and then fumbled in his pocket.

Ruby commanded, "Get that before we get kicked out of here."

James pulled it out and whispered into the phone. "Yes?"

***

Elam smiled at Nikki and led her back around to the cellar doors. "I think we'll have the baptism first, then the last supper. Perhaps we'll skip the beating this time. I never liked that part, anyway."

He undid the locks and pulled open the doors. "You need to sit with the children while I prepare the last supper. Then we'll go to the pond." He gave a placid smile. "Don't worry. No one drowns."

Nikki hurried down the steps so she would be settled before he slammed the doors shut.

Jake touched her arm. "Are you okay?"

261

Nikki wrapped her arms around him and Ava. "Am I okay? Oh, Jake, I'm fine. I was worried about you two."

Ava answered, "We're okay. What did you do up there? We heard your footsteps above us."

Nikki sighed. "Let's not talk about it right now. Here. I have something for you."

In the shadowed light, Nikki took Ava's hand. She helped Ava form her fingers into a cup. Then she pulled strawberries out of her pocket and spilled the little red balls into Ava's hand.

Ava leaned down and sniffed them. "Strawberries!" Nikki smiled, but tears pricked. You would have thought she'd opened her best birthday present ever.

Nikki offered some to Jake as well. "Have you noticed," said Nikki, "that every time we come up against a wall of discouragement, God seems to offer us one more thing to give us hope?"

Jake humphed. "You mean a coincidence happens?"

"Doesn't it seem odd how they're so perfectly timed?" she insisted.

"You mean like how perfectly timed I was kidnapped, then Ava, then you? How you both almost escaped but were captured?" He popped the berries into his mouth. "It goes both ways, lady."

Nikki said in a soft voice, "A matter of perspective."

After finishing the last of the berries, they heard chains rattling once more. Elam had returned.

When all were out in the light again, Elam handed them some ragged clothes. "Here, you must wear these to swim. I won't have any skinny dipping, you know."

The clothes were not bathing suits, but old t-shirts and tattered shorts. They had a moldy smell. After using the outhouse to change in, Nikki helped Ava tie up her t-shirt to keep it from slipping off her slender shoulders. Jake's looked out of the sixties. A faded rainbow tie-dye affair.

Nikki whispered to him, "Groovy."

Chapter 61

"Is this James Rolen?" Holding the cell phone close to his face, James turned away from the librarian's disapproving stare. "Yes."

"This is Timothy's mother. He's explained to me what you need, and why. I can't let him go with you, but I'd be willing to drive him in my car, ahead of yours, and lead you as far as possible."

Moisture tingled at the corner of his eyes. "Thank you so much. You don't know how important this is."

"Well, a child is missing, so ... I'm a mother. I understand."

"Can you meet me in front of the library? As soon as you can?"

"It'll be dark soon."

"I know, but we really don't want to waste any time."

A silent pause came from the other end and then a reluctant sigh. "Okay, Mr. Rolen. We'll be there."

James put the phone away just as Ruby waved her hands in the air. "Listen, listen, here's another one. It's an editorial."

She adjusted her glasses and read aloud. "'Last week our town was shocked at the news of the house fire that killed three, and one near fatal injury.

"'The children and adults of this fair city have asked themselves how this horrible event could happen so close to our charming community. The skeletal, charred remains of what was once a home stand as a fearful memorial to the cruel death of a family.

"'The bodies of 40-year-old Sarah Anne Hanson, 42-year-old Elam J. Hanson, and the youngest daughter, 7-year- old Priscilla Jane, were found in the ashes. Only son, 13-year old Elam Jacob Jr., survived.'"

Ruby gasped in a breath.

"'It's apparent that the mother struggled through the flames to rescue her daughter from an attic bedroom. The woman's body was found on top of the fallen main staircase. The body of the girl was discovered chained to a bed in an attic bedroom.

"'The father, authorities say, was closest to the start of the fire. His body, all but incinerated, discovered by firefighters in the kitchen area.

"'Only one family member was spared to tell the story. The 13year-old boy was found unconscious in the locked cellar, barely hurt by the fire but overcome with smoke.

"'After several days in the hospital, he is still so traumatized he has offered little information. The condition of his emaciated body made him appear years younger than his actual age. Fresh wounds and burns covered his frail back. His hands were bleeding and raw from his obvious attempt to claw his way free.

"'Where was our community, while these children experienced unspeakable torture and trauma in this house of horrors? Where were the teachers, the preachers, the neighbors that must have seen signs of their trauma? These are the questions we must ask ourselves. And open our eyes to see tragic circumstances that others may be suffering through, and have the courage to speak out and stop the terror.'"

***

Water, warm yet refreshing, washed over Nikki's skin. An underground hot spring must be the source of the pond. Her hands stirred the water ahead of her as she walked deeper. She dipped down and ducked under. She came back up, spitting water.

Elam sat on a log at the shore's edge. He almost giggled with pleasure as he dangled his feet in the pond.

He called out to them, "I never did like swimming." He splashed with his feet. "But I still love the feel of all that liquid in one spot."

Nikki stood and the water came up to her chest. Ava had to tread water. She floated closer to her friend. Ava's eyes were wide as she struggled to keep her mouth above the water. Nikki put out her arm to hold her.

Jake dove under and came up smiling. He looked different when he smiled. He rubbed his hair and drops flung off.

None of the three said a word. Nikki allowed the softness of the slight current to ripple over her. The clean water floated dirt and sweat from off her skin.

On the other side of the pond, a thick grove of trees grew down to the water's edge. The last supper was coming. This may be their only chance to get away.

She caught Jake's eye, and they both began to move slowly in that direction. Ava, now clinging to Nikki's side, wrapped her legs around Nikki's waist to be carried.

Boom! Water exploding in front of them stopping them cold. Ava clamped her arms and legs tighter around Nikki.

"Halt!" Elam's voice slashed across the water. "You don't drown, and you don't run away."

Elam pointed the rifle at them, his face deadly serious. "We have to travel a good way yet before all is complete." He cocked his rifle. "Come to this side. Now! We can begin the end." He didn't lower the gun until Nikki's feet touched the stones at the water's edge.

Dripping, cold, and desperate to not lose hope, Nikki set Ava on the ground but held tight to Ava's hand. Jake splashed behind them as he walked onto the land.

Elam lowered the gun. With one hand, he reached for the chains that lay at his feet. "Jake, secure them."

Elam trained the gun on Jake as he took his time cuffing Nikki's hands and then Ava's. He locked the chains to a tree. Elam set the weapon down and wrapped his arms around Jake from behind in a bear hug. He whispered into his ear. But Nikki heard the words that made her skin shiver.

"It's time. This will put things right. God punishes those who fail."

He dragged the teen to the water.

Help him, I must help him.

Nikki and Ava yanked on their chains and struggled with the restraints, trying to get free.

Elam shouted, his words mixed with splashing, screams, and the curses coming from Jake. He shoved Jake further into the water. "Holy water, separate from the ocean of sin, cleanse, redeem. Rewind this child's wicked heart."

He wrapped his arms around Jake's upper body. Elam lunged forward. Both dropped under the water, Jake backwards with Elam on top. Elam's head popped up first, above the splashing. "In the name of the fa—" His head slipped under.

Jake came up for a breath and then down.

Elam surged his body up through the turbulence into the air. His body tipped off balance, and his arms flared out until he stood steady. Jake's nose and mouth cleared the water, but Elam slammed his arms down onto his shoulders and held him under. Jake's legs came up kicking.

"Don't fight it, boy. It's much faster that way."

Ava let out a panicked, high-pitched scream.

Chapter 62

Elam stared into the dark water as air bubbles surged up from the blackness. He continued to push down on the struggling boy.

Wait!

Was he looking into the water?

Or up from under it?

He couldn't tell. His brain had turned him upside down.

Air! I need air!

Elam had changed back to himself, to the Jacob child. He stared up through the swirling liquid and saw his father glaring down at him. Small, weak, and afraid, he fought against the strong arms as Pa held him under.

Jacob's lungs throbbed inside his chest.

This time I die? Is this it?

The next minute, air rushed through his mouth and into his lungs. He gasped and sputtered as he came out of the water.

"Don't fight it, boy. It's much faster that way." His father's voice.

Pa dunked him under again, then up.

It's over.

Jacob's throat burned as he struggled to suck in air.

Pa's face shone like he'd won a trophy. "I baptize thee in the name of Father, Son, and Holy Spirit. Praise God, my son. You are now baptized into the faith. You are now safe!"

Jacob coughed up water.

You said that the last time.

He turned to the shore where his mother and Priscilla stood near the water. Their faces concerned and frightened.

After walking to dry ground, Jacob stood shivering in his underwear. Mama spread a towel over his thin body. Grateful, he hugged the cloth around himself.

267

Priscilla reached up to put her tiny hand into his. He smiled at her.

"I'm okay," he whispered.

With no other words than his mother singing *Amazing Grace*, his family walked back to the house.

***

Nikki screamed, "Elam, no. Elam! Stop!"

The splashing subsided. Elam stood still. His shoulders heaved as he sucked in oxygen, and his soaked hair hung in dripping strands down his face. With a mighty pull, he yanked Jake out of the water. He carried the limp body to the shore.

Ava wept, but Nikki held her breath, watched, and prayed.

Laying Jake down onto the rocks, Elam turned him onto his side, facing them. He gave him a whack on his back. Water gushed from the boy's mouth. His body heaved, and his throat made loud rasping, choking sounds. He opened his eyes and rolled onto his back.

"See." Elam struggled to catch his breath. "No one drowns."

The strange chore complete, Elam picked up his rifle, unchained his captives, and directed them down the path. Jake leaned on Nikki. As Elam led his "family" to the front of the house.

She saw something strange set up on the porch. On the bench where Ava had slept that horrible night alone, a small display had been placed.

Coming up onto the steps, Nikki could see the objects but couldn't figure out what they were for. Two unlit candles sat with the suitcase in between, the top open. Pictures and papers were propped against the slanted lid.

Without a word, Elam chained the three to the porch railing. Still wet and cold, Nikki saw Ava shiver and wished she had something to put on her.

Elam blinked at them. "I know you're cold, children. Mama, where's the towel?" He turned to Nikki. "Never mind, I'll get something from the house."

He opened the front door and went in. Both children looked shocked when they caught a glimpse of the inside of the house before Elam shut the door.

Now Nikki wished she had told them about the burned home when she first got back to them. She'd thought she'd have time to pass on the information in a less dramatic way.

Ava whimpered. "The house ... inside there. It's gone. All black. What happened?"

"This is what happened." Jake had stretched his chain out far enough for him to reach the suitcase. He held up the center picture. The scene was a distant shot of a house blazing with fire, set on a mountainside. He reached back for a newspaper clipping and skimmed the piece. "It says here they suspect the father burned his home with his family inside." He scanned further down. "He abused his children and beat his wife."

"Will he burn us?" Ava asked.

"Wait, it says the father died in the flames." His eyebrows shot up. "Is he a ghost?"

Nikki took the clipping from Jake. "How can that be? Is there another clipping?"

With great care, Jake picked through the case. "Here's one. This has a family picture."

Nikki took it and held it up. "The date on it says 1960."

"He *is* a ghost!" Ava's voice quivered.

"He doesn't hit like a ghost," Jake said.

"Wait. The picture has names under it." Scanning the list, she took in a quick gasp. Before she spoke they heard activity from nearby.

"Nikki!" Ava pointed to the side of the house. Apparently, Elam had walked through the house to the van. He pulled out some blankets and headed back the same way.

Nikki tried to put each piece of paper into the exact place it was taken from. She talked fast as she worked. "Listen to me, our Elam is not the father that abused his family. He was and is Jake, the son who received the abuse."

Ava and Nikki turned to stare at the Jake they knew. Jake stared back with his mouth open.

"Hurry." Nikki could hear Elam returning. The three scrambled back where he had left them.

"Okay, here you go." He shook out the coverings and with gentle but firm movements, he wrapped a smelly blanket around each of them. "Now, it's time to begin the last supper. We'll start with the Lord's Prayer." He knelt beside them and gave a hard stare until they all knelt with backs straight.

With his deep and commanding voice, he began, "Our Father which art in Heaven ..."

***

"No! Do it again, Jacob."

"Pa, my throat hurts."

"Again!"

"Our Father which art in heaven, hallowed be thy name. Thy Kingdom come Thy will be done, as in heaven, so in earth."

"It's not right! Again, make the d's stronger. You must say it correctly. Exact. Precise."

"Our Father—"

"Th! I can't hear the 'th' sound strong enough. Say it perfect, it must be absolutely perfect."

Mama came quietly out the front door, onto the porch. She carried a tray with lemonade and treats. "Elam, it's time now for the celebration. Remember, after the baptism, we celebrate." Priscilla sat on the bench under the window, staring out into the forest.

"We're practicing the Lord's prayer," Pa declared.

"I know that." Ma set the tray down on the side table. "But you've been doing that for hours now. You promised this. Would you break a promise?"

Jacob could see his father was torn between the excessive need to be precise in the prayer, and not leaving a black spot in his heart over a broken promise. "But I can't just simply—oh, fine. We'll take a break."

Jacob eased down from his straight-backed kneeling position.

His mother picked up a small plate with a napkin over it. "I have a surprise for you all." She spoke with kind softness in her voice. She held it up and pulled off the cloth.

"Bonomos!" Priscilla cried out with pleasure.

His mother smiled at her and turned to Jacob. He loved the salty-sweet taste of the Turkish taffy, and seeing Priscilla's face light up made him forget the pain in his back.

"Priscilla, behave yourself," Pa warned. He pulled his arm up in preparation for a back-handed swing.

"Stop! Pa, it's okay." Jacob jumped in front of his sister. "She'll behave. Here." He grabbed a glass and handed it to his father. "Lemonade."

The older man took it, and Jacob sat back down with relief. He smiled at his ma. She nodded and with her hand offered the treats to her children.

Jacob noticed that her hair didn't shine in the sunlight like it used to when he was little. Dull strands with gray snarls curled up on her head. Her face seemed flat, tired, with no sparkle in her blue eyes.

He knew being so afraid all the time had worn her down.

She tries to protect us from Pa. But why doesn't she take us away? Leave him?

It was an illness, Ma said. Pa used to be fun and kind. But the illness made him afraid of evil. And everything was evil.

Pa drank his last sip of lemonade and announced, "It's time for Priscilla to go to bed."

Priscilla turned her wide, pleading eyes to Jacob. He spoke for her. "Pa, does she have to wear the chains tonight?"

Pa slammed the glass down on the table. "Yes, Jacob, she does. It will keep her safe in bed. With her door locked. She needs to be safe. You know this."

"But Pa, she's older now and—"

"No! Enough whining. Take her to bed, Ma. Kiss your brother good-night, Priscilla."

Jacob went to her and knelt to whisper in her ear. "Don't worry. I'll take care of you. Tonight, I'll sneak in and free you. Then I'll come later to put the chains on again, before anyone gets up in the morning."

A slight curl of her mouth began a sweet smile that changed her face from worry to trust.

Chapter 63

Ben watched James turn up the radio before he made a bumpy swerve on the gravel road. Their car followed Tim and his mom up the mountain through a dense forest.

"Thank you for joining us on WBJT 103.5 FM. Here is that news alert I promised you last hour, on the Nicole Rolen case. Be on the lookout for James Rolen, suspect in the disappearance of his wife. Rolen has been missing since yesterday evening. It appears he has made a deliberate attempt to evade reporters and police. His whereabouts are unknown."

The announcer continued his description of James. Ray's deep voice rumbled out over the sound of the motor struggling up a hill, and the squeaks of the rocking chassis. "Let's hope Tim's mom didn't hear that."

Ben shifted in his seat and touched the object in his jacket pocket. He'd finished off his bottle and tossed it at the last gas station. With the excuse of needing an aspirin from his bag he grabbed his jacket and moved his gun to the pocket.

"Right," James said. "When she drops us off, we can tell her to call the police as soon as she has cell coverage. I'm glad we didn't contact them before we left the last town. They would have just hauled me back to Colorado Springs."

Ben laid his head against the cool window and closed his eyes. The shaking of the car kept him awake, but his mind drifted. The alcohol spun random, violent thoughts into his mind. His anger toward the little demon grew into red hot coals of hate.

I wouldn't be here if Ava hadn't tried to run. Somehow, she knows what I've done. She's going to tell. I must stop her.

***

Ben woke. The car ahead of them slowed, then parked. Dirt billow out like an Arizona dust devil.

James sighed as he shifted the Taurus and pulled over. He stopped far enough back to miss the dust cloud. "Wait here, I'll see what's up." He took off his seatbelt, got out and walked ahead.

Ben shook his head to clear his thoughts and rubbed his fingers over his eyes. Groans and yawns came from the backseat. While the rest took their time to wake, he got out to join James.

Tim's mom opened her door but shut it again. Tim got out and walked to meet James. Ben could see the mom watching them in her rearview mirror.

With one hand shoved in his pocket, Tim stopped midway between the cars. "Um, my mom says we can't go any farther." He pointed over his shoulder. "That turn-off up there? That left turn? That's in the general direction of the hermit's camp. If you go that way, try not to get tricked by dirt side roads."

He turned to point farther down the way. "My mom says the other turn-off going right, goes toward the ghost house. The burned one, ya know? I ain't never been there, but Mom remembers the story."

Tim cocked his head toward the car. "She says the home is really isolated, but it had a driveway coming off the main route. If the hermit guy drove in there, you might be able to tell by run-down bushes." He touched his hand to his cap. "Yeah, well, anyway ... um, good luck then. Bye."

"Thanks, Tim. Tell your mom, too."

He nodded and walked back, opened his door, and got in. The car turned around and drove away.

Back at the car the others got out and stretched as James gave them the new info. He finished with, "So, I guess we have a decision to make."

Ray gave a mixed groan slash yawn and ambled to a shady spot down from the road. He leaned against a tree and stared at the ground. Edith followed and grunted as she plopped down on a rock. James kicked at a stone and joined them.

Ruby hustled over and with an anxious voice said, "What should we do? Go to the camp, or the house?"

Ben came closer but stayed at the edge.

James scratched his head. "I don't know. He could be keeping them at his camp. That makes sense. Why be at the house if it's burned down?"

Ben said, "Right, but if we go to the camp and they're not there, we'll be wasting time."

Ray ran his hand over his mouth and down his chin. "This guy seems pretty messed up. If he's trying to create a new family, like Ava said, wouldn't he take them back to his house?"

"That's true." Ben said. "Trying to make the right decision seems pretty hopeless to me."

Edith stood and walked to Ben. She put her hand on his arm. "Don't get discouraged there, son. God will help us."

"Oh, yeah. Right. God."

Ruby strode over to Ben's other side and grabbed his hand. "I think we should pray about this."

Ben gave a startled jump and pulled away. "Oh, uh, sure. You folks go ahead and do that." Ben walked backwards as he talked. "I need to take a whiz ... oh, I mean I need to, um, relieve myself." He turned to hustle away.

When he reached the trees, he glanced behind to see the others holding hands, heads bowed. "Well, kum-by-ya," he whispered. "That's right. I need to relieve myself, and get a smoke, and maybe a little something else."

He circled around to the car and quietly opened into the back. Reaching inside, he found his duffle bag. He hadn't wanted to dip into his reserve, but he needed it. He unzipped a side pocket and fished out a flask he'd stashed there.

Glancing back to be sure all heads were still bowed, he took off into the woods.

Finding a secluded, bushy area, he took care of his business and found a log to sit on. He needed to think.

He lit his cigarette and fumbled at opening the small flask. Swearing through the cigarette in his mouth, he struggled to twist it open.

Success.

He smiled and tipped the bottle up to receive the sweet elixir. He closed his eyes knowing what the burn going down his throat would bring. Soon another burst of courage rushed over him and fueled his rage toward the girl. The stirrings of violent thoughts burned brighter with each sip.

It doesn't matter to me which way they go, really. If it's the wrong way, I won't have to worry about them finding her. What will I do if they find her? I can't let her tell them about me.

I'll just have to get to her first.

***

James watched Ben emerge from the forest. As the man came closer, a strong smell of smoke and liquor preceded him.

Ben raised one hand up and spoke with a slight slur. "So, what are we waiting for? Let's get going. We've got important things to do!" He headed to the car and opened the front door.

Ray stepped up and put his hand on Ben's arm. "My turn for shotgun."

Ben's eyes hardened, but he gave him the space. He settled in by the back window. But Edith shooed him into the middle seat.

Ruby whispered to James, "I don't think Ben is going to be much help to us when the time comes. He didn't even ask where we decided to go."

James nodded but kept his eyes on Ben. Not only would he be of no help, but he could possibly be a huge hindrance.

Chapter 64

Ava's head nodded forward, and she whipped it back up. She repeated Elam's meaningless prayer even as her eyes tried to close. The nightmare she lived made sleep seem like a faraway heaven she could never reach.

"Back straight!" Elam growled. "Let me see the words form on your lips." He smacked the floor planks with his knife. It cut into the wood. "No! Let me hear the 'th' sound. Louder, clearer."

His head made a quick turn to the right. He listened to the air.

"They're coming," he grunted in a graveled whisper. He stared up into the sky. "Closer." With the rifle in in his hand, he stood and stepped into the yard. He dropped the gun in the dirt and twirled with arms out and head back. "Closer. Closer. Closer."

His long hair flung out like a rippling fan. Moonlight caught in the strands, giving them a silver glow.

Ava crumpled down from her ramrod-straight kneeling posture. Nikki and Jake eased down as well, while Elam spun in his crazy dance of fear.

Ava stared through the porch spindles as the ghostly figure now swayed and then fell to the ground. He covered his head as he scrambled under the porch, screaming.

"Incoming!"

***

The roar of the planes grew louder. Jacob couldn't stand the sound, but he welcomed death.

No, not true. I must get back home. Alive.

He dived into a foxhole. Movement beside him caused him to jump back.

"It's okay, Jake, it's me. Tommy." He slapped Jacob on the leg. "I don't mind sharing with you."

Jacob settled back down into the mud with his friend. Hard to believe he and Tommy had played a game of chess together just last night. He never thought he would ever have a friend. Even knowing someone could be waiting for him back in the States seemed unfathomable.

Shots whipped above their heads. Blasts from exploding grenades shook the ground. Reaching for his medic bag, he hugged it close.

The sound died. The quiet almost hurt Jacob's ears.

A wide grin spread across Tommy's features and lit up his face. "We made it through. Again."

Jacob poked his head up past a ridge of mud and surveyed the area. He released a nervous sigh. Before he eased back into the foxhole, a screaming sound pierced the air, followed by a huge blast.

He dropped to the ground. "Tommy, stay down!"

Jacob slung his arms over his head and crouched in the dirt. Clots of falling mud and sharp pieces of metal peppered his back and helmet.

The barrage ended. In the quiet, he turned to his friend.

"Tommy—" He froze at the sight of the blood-splattered face. His buddy lay on his back, staring at the sky. A rasping gargle came from his throat, and a jagged piece of shrapnel stuck out from his chest.

A voice screamed. "Medic! Man down! Medic!" Jacob's own voice had yelled the words.

I'm the medic.

Tears blinded him. He ripped open his bag. Feeling around inside, he hunted for something.

Think!

He needed ... magic, something to heal.

Stop! Take a deep breath.

Allowing his training to take over, he reached past the wound and placed two fingers on Tommy's neck.

No pulse.

No! This can't be! We were just talking!

He made a slight move of his fingers and found a weak thread of life.

277

I've saved other wounded soldiers. I can do this.

He checked the pulse again and then shot his flashlight into the wounded man's glazed eyes. "Come on, Tommy. You can do it."

His desperate attempts at resuscitation only made his friend bleed more. In a last-ditch effort, he pulled the metal from his chest, and the blood poured out like from a broken dam.

He knew better, but the evil had to be gotten rid of. It was the only way to save him. His hands drenched in blood as he tried to stay the flood by pressing on the wound.

Jacob shut his eyes. He closed them so tight his head hurt. A hot searing blast of air washed over his face. He looked back at Tommy, but he wasn't there.

Wooden planks hung over Elam's head, and gritty dirt dug into his knees.

Where am I? Oh, God, Father in heaven. Where am I?

The confusion stung like fear. The same gut-twisting, heart-stopping terror that made him so sick his hands shook.

He heard movement above him.

Am I in the cellar? No, under the porch. I must prepare for the last supper.

He crawled out and ran to the cellar. Opening the wood doors, he paused before going down the stairs into the shadows. His legs tingled with numbness, and his vision began to narrow.

If the last supper was to be given, he had to force himself to go into the tight cave. He could see what he needed from where he stood.

He sucked in a huge breath, shut his eyes, and stumbled down the steps. At the bottom, he let out the air, opened one lid, and grabbed four dusty mason jars off a shelf.

As he turned to run, one slipped from his arms, and tumbled to the ground. It rolled further into the shadows. Elam raced up the steps. At the top, he turned to stare into the cellar.

He could see the jar's bottom jutting into the moonlight, taunting him. He considered leaving it.

But the number won't be right. And it must be right.

He set the jars down. Spying a long straight stick, he snatched it up and stepped down three of the steps. He stretched his

278

arm out as far as he could reach. After many tries, he finally managed to turn the jar and hook the branch into the opening.

New sweat beaded on his forehead as he wiggled the stick to move the jar closer to the bottom step. Dropping his tool, he sucked in another breath and took the next few steps while bent over and snagged the jar. He rushed up the stairs, rolled onto the grass, and huffed out air as if he'd finished a marathon.

Fear that had surged subsided, and he collected his prizes. He set them upright on a board. Using this as a tray, he walked to the outdoor water pump in the corner of the front yard. Indoor plumbing had not often been a part of his life.

He rolled up his sleeves and began to pull and push on the metal handle. The motion calmed him. He closed his eyes and waited for the whoosh he knew would come.

The water cascaded from the spout like liquefied crystal glass. Clear, sparkling jewels washed into the jars. Elam smiled.

Mama will love this.

Chapter 65

James slowed the vehicle to a crawl. In the back Ruby hung out the window and scanned the woods. As the wagon jerked and swayed over the rough road, he worried she would bounce out.

He slowed more. "We don't want to miss that turnout. Keep watching." When the road smoothed, he lit the flashlight on his phone and shot a beam into the dark woods.

He heard a determined sigh. The sound of rummaging came next. Soon a second light beam joined his.

When he looked over at Ray in the front seat, all he saw was his backside. Ray had hefted his body out the window to shine his light on the thicket along the right side of the road.

Ben, now slouched in the middle back seat, had been mumbling for the last mile or so. He raised his voice. "That's right!" Slurred. His hand shot up. "We'll find them. And when we do, we'll horsewhip that low-life slug. We'll slash that punk until he's bleeding like a stuck pig." Random swear words hit the air.

Ruby settled back into her seat as Ben's words became more abusive. Ray came in from his window and glanced back at her.

She jabbed Ben in the ribs. "Ben, settle down there. We don't want to hear all that."

"Oh, really? Well, you've never had your baby stolen from you, have you? You never had your heart ripped out of your chest. That little girl was like my own flesh and blood. My darling, sweet, beautiful little girl! Whoever did this is just a big fat—"

Ray shouted. "Ben! Shut! Up!"

Silence, for one tick, then...

"I am the victim here and that was very rude. I—"

James slammed on the brakes, and everyone in the car turned to glare at Ben. He shrunk into his seat but continued to mumble softly.

James rolled the car forward.

Nikki pulled Ava closer, allowing the girl to rest her head in her lap. Elam had disappeared under the porch. His weeping and garbled words didn't concern her. Her ravaged heart, numb to the madman's rantings, did not even quicken it's beat.

Grateful for the time to rest, she gazed up at the sky. This night simply did not end. The bright, full moon bathed the yard with light.

A scrambling noise made her turn to the side of the porch. Elam ran to the cellar doors. He acted out the fears that dictated his every move.

Nikki's mind drifted into half-aware dreams of her two little boys playing. The intermittent nods of her head kept jarring her to half-awake until she floated into foggy swirls of unconsciousness. First, her sweet ones laughed and giggled, chasing a butterfly. Then in a blink, they squirted a garden hose, spraying water at each other in hilarious gushes of playful fun.

Another nod of her head brought her upright. Her boys vanished.

Elam stood in the yard. He was at a metal water pump, filling glass jars. Though the water spilled out brown from the rusty pump, it made her aware that her mouth was dirt dry.

In the moonlight, Elam grinned and laughed with abandoned joy. Her mind drifted.

The next moment, Elam's voice was waking her. His rough hand shook her, and he shouted, "Get up! Everyone! The Last Supper is upon us. Now is the time for us to remember to not forget that we must remember."

Ava shot up. Fear covered her small face, waking her like a shot of caffeine. Nikki had to nudge Jake. He struggled to open his eyes and pulled himself up.

Elam had set a tray of mason jars filled with dark murky water on the floor and his rifle lay beyond reach on the steps. He ran into the house and Nikki knew he sailed out the open back. She saw him come around to the front and hurry to the van parked on the side of the yard.

He sang at the top of his lungs. "Washed away, washed away, washed away, every burden of my heart washed away." He pulled out a brown box, and carried it behind the house front. On his return, he reached farther inside the van and hauled out two gas cans. These he took with him and disappeared again.

The singing became muffled and then grew louder as he opened the front door He held only the box.

Ava reached for Nikki's arm, pulled her closer, and whispered, "Nikki, Elam stole that from an old kind of store, before he took me here. He made it seem like it held a treasure of gold."

Nikki nodded to let Ava know she heard. Stealing something did not seem out of the ordinary for Elam. But what did it have to do with this Last Supper he kept talking about?

Elam bent down to Jake. He handed him a single match. With great decorum, he said, "Now is the time to light the way. Jake, ignite the candles."

Jake rolled his eyes. He must be tired of playing the charades Elam insisted on. He took the match and struck it on the porch deck. He scooted closer, and lit both candles. With no other light but the moon, they glowed with a brilliance that brightened the whole porch.

Elam knelt beside the bench like a priest, staring into the flames. The light played shadows on his emotionless, well lined face. After a long pause, he placed the mystery package on the floor and turned to his congregation.

Bowing his head for a silent moment, he took out his knife. The blade picked up flickering shots of light as he raised it above his head. Slashing down, he tore into the box.

Laying the knife behind him, he opened the shredded lid. Smaller display cartons lined the box, holding bright red and yellow candy bars. Elam reached in, and tore open the plastic wrap around one carton. With reverent motions, he lifted out one bar. He unwrapped the treat and placed it on the floor.

"Those who are many eat of the same candy and become one." Using the butt of his knife, he slammed into the sweet. With a cracking sound, he shattered the bar into many pieces. Placing the knife out of reach, he then picked up one shard of candy and held the element to the light.

"On the night that she was betrayed, the mother came, and after thanking all who were there, she gave each one a Bonomos." He gave the first piece to Ava. He picked up three more. Keeping one for himself, he gave Nikki and Jake the other two.

Nikki stared at Elam. No one wanted to step ahead of his directions. With tenderness, he placed one yellow piece on his tongue and closed his mouth. After a moment of savoring the treat, he glared at Jake. "Eat!"

Jake popped the candy into his mouth. Nikki and Ava followed suit.

Nikki rolled the candy in her mouth.

Sweet and salty, hard then soft, chewy. Taffy? And a sweet banana flavor. Elam's surprises were not all bad.

With measured words Elam continued his ceremony, speaking around the taffy in his mouth. "This, now, is the end. The beginning begins, and all will be made right. Because of the great fall, we had no choice ... the fall fell, fire, hell, there is only one smell more putrid than the flames of hell."

He swallowed and took up one of the jars of nasty water. "After the Bonomos, she gave the cup, saying, don't hurt the child while you can smile, and then beguile to prevent the pain of the slain, the living dead." Beaming, he peered beyond their heads as if a crowd were before him. "Drink now, all of it, all of you."

He lowered the jar. His smile faded and he stared off to one side.

Chapter 66

Jacob watched his beloved sister take his mother's hand and head into the house. He sat down on the bench and turned to Pa.

A change had taken place in his father. Dark, cold, angry shadows on his face revealed a storm about to break. "Jacob."

"Yes, Pa?"

"How dare you question a decision that I have made? You know we must keep Priscilla safe. She doesn't stay in bed during the night. She could climb out her window or fall down the stairs." His glare made Jacob's hands quiver. "Come with me."

"Pa, I'm sorry. I didn't mean to." His last word squeaked out with panicked fear. "Pa?"

His father grabbed his arm and dragged him to the back yard. He shoved him down to sit on a log beside the cold fire pit along the side of the yard. With long even strides, he headed to the ragged tool shed.

When he came out, he held a bundle of long sticks under his arm and a red spouted can.

Jacob closed his eyes.

Please, no, God. Please?

Anger distorted his father's reddened face. Veins on his forehead pulsed, his nostrils flared, and eyes bulged.

"Son, you know that I love you." Pa swallowed. Through gritted his teeth, he growled the rest of his words. "Because I love you, I can't let you become contaminated by a world that has no rules. You've come in contact with a liar, a truth killer, a demon of the flesh."

He slammed the bundle of twigs into the fire pit and pointed the spout of the red can at the pile. Fume smell rushed out first then the contents splashed onto the wood and splattered the surrounding area.

He struck a match and tossed it in. Flames flared like a rocket's tail.

***

Jake tried to choke down the putrid water. He spilled more than he got into his mouth. He hoped to distract the crazy old man from the helpless little girl. Elam continued to stare as if in a trance.

Ava cried. Her silent tears and wet nose drenched her face.

Nikki held the jar up and sniffed at the rim.

In a quick spit, Elam's expression changed. "No! No, no!" He grabbed up the rifle off the steps and ran into the yard.

Boom! He shot into the sky. *Boom!* Another at the house. Then more into the sky.

The water flew as Jake, Nikki, and Ava fell flat to the floor. A jar exploded, and glass shattered. Each bullet strike made Jake's whole body jerked with fear.

Oh crap! We're gonna die.

***

James slammed on the brakes and cut the engine. "Shhhh, everyone. Listen."

In the distance, explosions echoed into the night.

"Did you hear that? What was it?"

"Sounded like gunfire," Ray answered. "Hunters maybe?"

James shook his head. "At three in the morning? Surely they would wait for dawn to hunt." He looked down the road, his heart beating fast. "Maybe we're close. Ray you drive. I'm going to walk ahead of the car to make sure we don't miss the turn." He didn't want to voice what the shots could mean for his wife.

***

Elam shot again at the approaching helicopter and turned back to the porch. He tossed the rifle on the ground and walked with confident, purposeful strides toward his family.

He stopped on the first porch step. Confused.

What was I doing? Oh, yes, the last of the Last Supper. The sacraments have been consumed. Now to our places.

He jumped up on the wood planks. Grabbing Ma's arm, he pulled his knife from its sheath, and cut the plastic straps around her wrists.

285

Gripping Mama tight, he pulled her to a stand. He searched the woman's face with sudden confusion. "Where is the Mama? I don't know where she's at." He allowed the fear to change his stern expression.

She stammered, "I ... I don't know, Elam. What are you talking about?"

"Where does the mother go? Never mind. I'll put her where it's safe." He dragged her off the porch and over to the cellar. He pushed her through the opening into the dark. She screamed as she tumbled down. Slamming the doors with a hurried bang, he secured the handles.

He rushed back, released Priscilla, and took her hand and led her inside the house. The boy yelled for Pa to bring her back.

He should, Jake must be her protector.

With a quick pull and a tug, he lifted the little sister into his arms. Going up the steps on the main staircase didn't seem right. He carried her through the house to the ones at the back.

Priscilla threw her arms around his neck and squeezed as he proceeded up. She yelled, "No, no. The stairs aren't safe. They're burned and broken. Stop!"

It can't be her voice. This child doesn't speak.

Somewhere in the lost part of his mind, he noticed the right wall was gone. He leaned away, his shoulder rubbing against the remaining one as he climbed. Part-way, he had a vision of being high up with nothing but blackness below.

A wall. Shouldn't there be a wall on both sides?

The wood beneath his feet quivered and groaned. A background noise of whimpering, sniffling, and small frightened moans floated into his ear.

Despite his swimming, light-headed state, he continued up the steps. The real person that lurked inside his soul trembled with fear at falling. He clung to the child.

At the top, he made his way down a hall. Putting the child over his shoulder he reached to the ceiling. He opened the hatch and pulled down a ladder.

"Wait! Elam, is the ladder even still attached? Look over, please. You must see the walls are gone. You can see the ground below. Elam!"

Up the steps. Now down the dark hall to the smallest room.

"Priscilla, hold tight while I unlock your door." After he opened the door he shifted his sister back into his arms.

Priscilla clung tighter. "There is no door. Only the frame in a broken wall." She jerked up. "Ah! Be careful. The broken floor's edge is right there!"

He walked to the back of the room and placed Priscilla beside the pink frilled bed that sat under the window. A loop of metal was bolted to the floor.

He reattached the chain to this loop.

"Elam ... Jacob ... whoever you are. Please, don't leave me here. Oh, please. The floor is weak, and hanging out into nothing."

"Don't you want to sit on the pretty bed, Priscilla?"

"It's all burnt up. Look, you must see! It's only black metal and the curly-springy things."

He wrapped his arms around her. In a voice filled with choking tears, he said, "Don't worry, this time Jacob will save you. He will protect you. I promise."

Chapter 67

Heavy footfalls came closer. Jake braced himself.

Crack!

The front door flung open and hit the wall. Elam towered above him. Jake sucked in a gasp. He scooted away until the porch railing pressed against his back.

Elam blinked rapidly, then rubbed tears away with his sleeve. Even as anger burned bright in his eyes.

He caught Jake's t-shirt at the neck and slung him to the floor. Leaning in, he put one knee on his chest.

Jake pushed on the leg with both cuffed hands, trying to catch a breath. A vise-like grip caught one wrist. Jake froze as the cool of the blade slid across his skin. One strap tie fell. Then the other wrist was freed.

Elam kicked the chains aside, then dragged, pulled, and wrestled Jake behind the house. Beside the yard at the farthest point lay the ruined remains of a burning place. Jack guessed to burn leaves and trash.

His tormentor tied him to a tree beside the fire-pit. Cheek pressed into the rough bark. His arms wrapped around the trunk, legs hobbled.

A chill rippled up Jake's back at the sound of a gut-wrenching moan.

Then the sobbing came.

***

The flickering light dappled Pa's face as he spoke. "You think these flames are hot? There is nothing worse than the flames of hell. Do you understand me, Jacob? Nothing! I'm trying to save you." He stared into the burning glow as words poured from the madman's mouth like a sci-fi robot. "Then one of the seraphim flew to me with a live coal in his hand, which he had taken with tongs from the altar. With it he touched my mouth and said, 'See, this has touched your lips; your guilt is taken away and your sin atoned for.'"

Moving as if in a trance, Pa walked over to Jacob. He gently wrapped his hands around him and guided him over to a tree.

Jacob didn't resist or try to run. He cried. Great sobs of anguish at knowing what was to come. After Pa ripped off Jacob's shirt, he tied his helpless hands to a low tree branch.

Turning his head, Jacob tried to see when the pain would come. His father knelt by the fire and used barbeque tongs to pull out an orange glowing ball.

It's coming.

He squeezed his eyes shut and held his breath.

Pain. Searing pain that engulfed every thought radiated from the middle of his back. He thrashed and screamed, pulling on the ropes. The devil coal fell off his back, but the residual pain continued to rip through his body.

Despite the trembling, Jacob tried to suck in air as Pa began to sing. Another was coming, he knew. Listening for the quiet crunch of footsteps mingled with the singing, he shut his eyes again, bracing for the agony.

The stunning shock of the coal washed a wave of disconnecting blackness over him. Pa used the tongs to press harder into his flesh.

Too . . . much. Too . . . much!

With a wild shriek, he twisted his whole body back. He collided into Pa, and the tongs clattered to the ground.

He gave one mighty yank with his arms, and the branch cracked off. Jacob turned and slammed into Pa.

Regret and fear crashed together at the same moment.

Jacob tried to catch his father teetering near the fire. He missed. Instead, he saw the price of his rebellion.

He saw the fall.

Fell. Hell. Fell. Fire. Father. Fire. Shaming, flaming.

Orange-yellow sparks splashed in the air. Fires, worse than hell, ignited Pa's pant leg and surged up his body. Pa's face writhed with terror.

The fast blaze swallowed his body. Drenched in swirling tongues of light, the creature ran up the back steps and into the house.

***

Jake twisted his head to watch Elam. The sobbing had stopped, and he sat frozen, staring at the cold fire pit.

How long will he stare? Could this episode be over?

With a convulsive jerk, Elam turned his head to the house. He began to shake and wipe at his eyes. Bolting with an abrupt charge of energy, he ran to the house ruins and fell to his knees before the back stoop.

Jake's neck and shoulders burned. His muscles had stretched for too long. So tight, they quivered. Pain stabbed like knife cuts.

Stay strong. That little girl is depending on me. She trusts me.

***

"Ma! Maaamaaa!" Jacob screamed as the dark clouds rumbled above him.

Where was she?

Ridding himself of the ropes, he ran into the house after his father. Heat smacked his face as he stepped into the kitchen. The blast made him gasp.

Pa's hands stretched out, reaching for help. Flames traveled up his back to his arms. In his panic, he swiped dishes off the counter to the right of the door. Eyes wide with terror he stumbled and careened to the other side of the room. He smacked into the kitchen table, yanking the table cloth to the floor. Lighting everything he touched. Then with both legs engulfed he fell to his knees and crawled toward the living room. Collapsing in a heap, his screams barely pierced the growl of the now roaring blaze.

Heat, pain, fear. Jacob swallowed back vomit. Sight and smell of burning flesh bombarded Jacob's senses all at once.

Smother the flames.

Jacob searched for a blanket to throw over him. He ended up in the room's far side, behind the kitchen table. Ripping a tapestry of the Last Supper off the wall, he dragged it with him and heaved it over Pa. The material blacked out part of the pulsing light before it too ignited.

290

"Worse!" Jacob realized fire had cut him off from the back door. He looked toward the opening to the living room. Hungry flames were devouring the curtains that had divided the rooms. Fiery bits peeled down from the ceiling and onto the floor.

Pa had stopped his guttural wail. Another cry. Had he heard a distant, high pitched scream for help?

Priscilla! She won't be able to get out. She's locked in and chained! I gotta get to her. Where is Ma? Is she safe?

"Help! Ma!"

Heat unbearable. How could he get to his sister?

The backstairs!

They opened to the kitchen at the far corner and led to the second floor. Then a ladder pulled down from the ceiling and continued to the attic rooms. That way was clear. He covered his face with his arms to block the heat. Almost to the opening, a groaning blasted overhead, and a beam crashed down in front of him.

Now we're all trapped. Where's Ma?

He thought of his sister.

"Jacob! Jacob!" A child's voice screamed above the roar.

How can I hear her?

"Priscilla!"

His mind pictured her tugging on the chains, terrified. Had the fire reached her yet? Or was she choking on the smoke?

Eyes burned and throat ached as he rasped out coughs. He hunched down and backed up as he strained to breathe. His hand touched a hot metal knob.

The cellar! I can go down in the cellar, to the doors that go outside. Then come in the house, up the front stairs, and save Sister.

He grabbed a small towel to shield his hand and opened the door. Stumbling down the stairs to the first landing, he made the turned twisting to the back of the house.

He welcomed the cooler air. It gave him strength.

Feeling in the dark, tripping over junk, he found his way to the steps leading to the sloping wooden doors. Pushing up with the

291

palms of his hands he shoved. But the rough heavy planks didn't give.

Locked!

Could Priscilla be calling for him? Or did she look like Pa?

Ramming with his back, he banged into the evil that blocked his way. The damnable doors that kept him from rescuing her.

He turned to retreat out the way he came, but part of the burning floor from above collapsed in front of him. The cellar filled with a rush of dust and smoke.

Crawling back to the locked cellar door, he put his face up to the cracks where air flowed. A wallop of thunder accompanied a rattling wash of sound. Rain and hail.

God, oh, God put out the fire. Jesus. Jesus help

Screams he couldn't really hear, cut through him. His sister's torture ripped into his soul. His eyes burned and his head throbbed with pain as he coughed with a gritty rasp. Smoke tightened his chest as his lungs filled. A soft darkness drifted over his thoughts until he ...

Chapter 68

James aimed his light into the grasses and stepped further off the road. "Stop!" He held up his hand to Ray in the driver's seat, and then pointed to the side of the road. "The weeds are smashed down. All along here."

Ray called out the window. "Should I follow you off-road?"

"No. Park and wait here. I'll hike up a way and check it out."

A car door slammed. Ben walked with a slight stagger to the front of the car. "I'll go with ya."

James sighed. "No, Ben. I can do this. I won't be long."

"Nope, nope. I am going." He swung his arms as he headed into the brush.

James rolled his eyes at Ray and turned to follow. He stepped over crunched bushes and flattened buffalo grass. James came up on Ben and took the lead.

Thick forest lined either side, making the path more defined. But the flashlight created shadows making each step a dangerous guessing game.

James waited for Ben to catch up. "Are you okay?"

"I'm fine." He grunted as he stumbled and then caught himself. "Is this the right way? It's overgrown so much. Hard to tell."

"The brush is definitely flatter here."

"Man," Ben muttered. "Long driveway."

"Yeah, somebody didn't like visitors."

The road ran along a steep slope. The edge felted unstable and soft. He'd wondered if Pastor's car would be able to make it over this growth, and now the way seemed treacherous.

He realized they were walking on a downward slant. Looking over the ledge he could make out at least two switch-backs. A spot of moonlit blue flashed up through the trees.

"What's that?" He stopped, grabbed Ben's arm, and pointed over the rim. "Do you see that?"

293

Ben bent over and squinted. "I don't see anything."

James stepped closer, latched a hand on a tree and leaned out. "It's a house! I can only see bits of it, but it has a front porch just like Ava said."

"How can you know it's the right place?"

"Who else would have a house way out here? This must be the one."

Ben inched closer to the berm. In one of his over-the-top attempts to appear competent, he threw out both arms in a sweeping gesture. "I don't see any—" His legs shot out as the ground crumbled out from under him. He landed on his seat and slid partway down the slope.

"Ben! Ben, are you okay?" James squatted down. "Are you okay?"

The quiet of the night brought out every cricket and tree rustle. James waited until he heard a groan. "Can you hear me?"

"Yeah, yeah. I'm okay. My ... uh ... leg hurts though. I'll try to climb back up."

Oh, Lord, give me grace.

"Okay, well, see if you can crawl up a little, and I'll try to pull you up." He knelt and reached out his arm.

Ben struggled up and grabbed the hand. At the top, he stood. "Oh, ow, ow! My foot!"

"I thought it was your leg." James frowned and reached out to steady him.

"It's both. I'll be okay. Really, just get me back to the car."

With an occasional over-dramatic whimper, Ben clung to James, and they stumbled their way back to the car.

As they approached, James could see Ray leaning against the hood with his head down. Edith and Ruby rested in the backseat.

James said, "We found the house."

Edith got out of the car and hurried over. "Ben, what happened to your foot?"

"It's nothing. I tripped and fell."

James led Ben to the front seat and helped him sit down. "We need to walk in. The road is rough and besides we don't want to announce our presence."

"Okay, then." Ray called through the open car window. "Let's go, Ruby."

Ben got back up. "Right, I'm ready."

"No." James hardened his expression. "You'll only slow us down."

"I'll be fine. I—"

James moved in nose to nose, placed his hand on Ben's chest, and firmly pushed him back into the car. "No. I can't risk it. I'm sorry."

He reached past Ben, got out a bottle of water, and hitched up his pants. "Let's go!"

***

Ben waited until the sound of rustling branches faded away. He let his mind slip back to moments before, just after he'd fallen down the slope. He hadn't gone down far, but just enough to give him a new perspective. While James called from above, Ben could see a path that cut straight down the hill. Though tall grass disguised its presence, once you realized its place in the maze of green, you could trace it all the way down.

This was his chance. If he could separate from the rest, he could use it to speed ahead. He could get to Ava first. He'd make sure she wouldn't betray him.

He grinned as he bent his leg and bounced on it. Satisfaction with his ability to deceive made him almost chuckle.

Hmm, I'm not a bad actor. Maybe I should look into that.

He pulled the Walther pistol out of his right coat pocket. He'd been smart enough to keep the loaded magazine in his left. In his present condition, he couldn't be sure he could have loaded it.

With his finger off the trigger, he snapped the magazine into the bottom of the gun handle. He pulled on the top of the semi-automatic and chambered a round.

Thoughts of Ava and how she would betray him churned inside his chest as if it had already happened. His anger burned with irrational heat. The familiar mist of reality and dreams twisted in a pattern of hate and rage.

He took his flask out for one last swig, tossed it to the ground, and charged into the bushes.

Chapter 69

Elam pressed his face against the tree as he leaned in nose to nose with Jake. The bark bit into his cheek as he forced out a heavy breath with each word. "You must save her. You understand, don't you? *That* is what you were meant to do."

Elam pulled up from the tree. Shoulders slumped, chin on his chest, he held a blazing torch in one hand. He kept the fire off to one side, at arm's length. Even so the heat drenched his face in sweat. A burst of wind made the light spark and twist.

He lifted his head and tried to think. "To save the brave, the child must be wild. Free, to flee, to be, to see ... the darkness in the light."

With his other hand, he pulled the knife from his belt sheath. This made the torch sway and dip toward the tall grass. Somewhere in the uncluttered part of his brain, he felt a flicker of worry.

Did sparks touch? Did flurries ignite?

The blade shone like a saber.

He put the sharp point to Jake's neck. "You are the savior. Your blood sacrifice will save us all." With practiced skill, he leaned in, twisted the knife, and slashed down the tree.

Ropes dropped to the ground.

Jake eased himself upright from the tree, pulled the ropes from his wrists before he untied the ones from his legs. Odd glimmered flashes of light rippled over his trembling hands.

He stood.

Elam pointed to the house with the knife but kept his eyes on the boy. "The attic." He added in a graveled whisper, "Jacob saves."

This boy, this Jacob, looked frozen like a statue in the park.

Jake's eyes wide, stared at the ground behind Elam. The boy pointed with a shaking hand.

Elam spoke, "Take the knife." He raised his torch above his head, and held out the weapon. When the boy took the knife, he shouted, "Go!"

Jacob ran. But he ran the wrong way. He took off into the trees. Away from the house. Away from Priscilla.

Elam shook in frustration at the sight. But an unexpected calm swept over him.

Jacob will figure it out. He's a smart boy.

He gazed at the torch, mesmerized by its blaze. Turning his gaze down, he fixed his eyes on the hem of his pants. With a slow and deliberate motion, he lowered the torch.

***

Ava sat very still. The floorboards creaked and shifted with every little gust of wind. If she rose up and stretched her neck, she could see Elam and Jake in the moonlight on the side of the backyard. But she didn't watch. Elam played hard games that made no sense.

Laying her head down on the rough charred planks, she curled into a ball and waited.

When will this game end? Will the sun ever come up?

***

Jake ran to the trees. He stopped and looked back. Between Elam and the house, a grass fire crackled. Even the tree he'd been tied to flittered with bright spots of light.

Skittering sparks igniting the grass jumped like grasshoppers. The low flames ran toward the house and to the far side of the yard. Eating up the growth that covered the old burn scar.

Like a ghostly statue, Elam stood alone with the torch now pointing down. His stance showed determination. But when smoke drifted away from his face, the moonlight revealed a lost and fearful soul.

Then the earth and trees swirled in front of Jake in a dreamlike scene. His vision became blurred and his legs gave out under him. Blackness wrapped over him and he dropped to the ground.

297

Worry for Jake and Ava had kept Nikki awake and anxious in the darkness of the cellar. Now she noticed a terrifying new smell sifting through the damp, musty smell. Alarms shot through her.

Smoke!

Fire. Was Elam burning his imaginary pot roast?

A strong stinging odor burned her eyes and nose. This was no barbecue. She felt her way to the doors and pushed up with all she had.

Defeat crushed hope. Jake couldn't get them open. How could she? But before even a prayer crossed her mind, a new thought rushed in. She turned and faced the blackness behind her.

Coughing as she crawled, she felt her way to the back of the cellar. The one small rectangle window near the ceiling gave her a ray of moonlight. Her hands came to a barrier of stones, dirt, and wood. But she remembered the scene from the kitchen above. The floor had dropped down. If she dug up, through the rubble, maybe she could get out.

Stones and wood planks pulled out easily at first. Soon her scraped fingers stung as she dug into the soil surrounding the bigger items. Years of dirt had piled onto the wreckage.

Her hand hit on something. Feeling the cupped form, she realized it was a broken bowl. This could help to carve out the chunks. She sucked in her courage and frantically continued to dig.

***

Jake pulled himself up to a sit.

How long have I been out?

Afraid to look, he made himself turn his head to the pulsing heat. The place where he'd been tied now radiated with consuming fire. No sign of Elam. The fire's glow so strong even the tree was hard to make out.

Jake had to get to Ava. The top of her little head was all he'd been able to see from the back of the yard. Elam must have chained her, or she would run. He tightened his grip harder on the knife.

What about Nikki? If the fire spread to the house, would it reach the cellar?

The main staircase was useless. He had to get around to the other side of the house. Where the backstairs hung on the only sidewall fully standing. The fire in the yard moved as if alive with a blind rage, catching leaves and grass. The breezes snatched wriggling tongues of light and sprayed sparks into the dark.

If he circled behind the yard, into the forest, he could reach Nikki and then climb the stairs to the attic. Or should he save Ava first?

He'd decide when he got there. He pulled the top of his t-shirt over his mouth to block the smoke and charged into the trees.

***

Waking and sleeping mixed in Ava's mind. She couldn't tell what was real. A hint of a campfire smell confused her. Her mind had become a blur of half dreams. She saw her mother sitting on the burnt wire bed. Her Grammy reading in the corner. When the visions became dark and fearful, she whimpered. Every sound made her jump.

She sat up and looked around. The long side of the burned bed was pushed up against the front wall, centered under the window. She was chained beside it on the floor.

The door frame to her right, held only part of the side wall. The ghostly structure rose near the far corner that would have connected to the missing wall.

The room spread open to the night. She sat like an actor on a stage for everyone to see.

Then the floor quivered. Short, repeated shakes.

Another dream? No.

The sound brought a cold dread. Quiet thuds came louder. Closer. Leaning forward, she tried to see into the yard, beyond the ruins of the house below. The ground appeared to move and waver in a filmy gray cloud. A bright fire burned in the back corner. The night air was hazy with a smoky smell.

A dark shadowy form appeared in the stark doorway.

Elam?

In silence, the figure lumbered across the room, edging along where the floor dropped off to the ground.

Not Elam. Bear!

299

A scream shot out from her throat and she scooted against the bed.

Moving a step closer to where the haze cleared and the moonlight glowed, the beast stopped and swayed.

Through a surge of tears and freezing fear, she saw worse than a bear, and whispered, "Ben."

Chapter 70

Feeling with her hands, Nikki dug with frantic energy. Until she picked up something crunchy, with fur.

She shrieked with horror.

Her own scream cut into her nerves like a machete. She flung the body of the petrified animal into the darkness, and shivered in revulsion.

No hysterics. Not now.

Reaching farther into the hole, she scraped into the dirt and heaved out a chunk of wood.

Air flooded into the space with a smoky surge as a waterfall of small rocks tumbled down.

Almost there. A little more, and I'll be free. I must get to Ava and Jake.

***

Jake pushed past undergrowth and around trees. Bits of lit embers floated around the trees like lightning bugs. As he came around closer to the house, loud cracking and pops from the fire brought zombie war movies to mind.

Intent on rescuing Nikki, he burst out of the bushes and headed toward the front of the house. He slid to a stop when he heard Ava's scream and changed his course. The back staircase was the only way to Ava.

***

Enraged at the sight of the girl, Ben lifted his gun. He tried to steady his shaking arm by gripping with both hands. Not daring to step closer for fear of toppling on his unsteady legs, he stayed put. "So, you found your voice, have you? Just in time to tell everyone what a swell guy I am."

"You can't be here. Nikki says there are no ghosts. Only heaven."

He strained to keep the barrel of his gun from wavering in tight circles. One hand came off briefly to wipe his blurry eyes, then back to steady his aim.

"That's right, Baby. Heaven or hell, and that's where I'm going to send you. You won't be able to snitch to anyone. You're the only one who knows, aren't you?"

"Knows what?"

Stiffening with anger, he raised the gun higher. He tried to pull his body up taller. Then smiled, like a cat might after cornering his mouse. "Don't play with me. You know what I mean, the dead ones. The others that died. I know you know."

"You killed them?"

"I didn't mean to. I never mean to. But children break so easy. You get it, don't you, Baby?"

His finger slipped down to the trigger.

***

Ava ducked her face to the floor and braced for a bang. A ferocious howl filled the night, trapping her mind in terror. The room trembled, bouncing her body as it shook.

A loud, shocking boom stopped sound. She jerked, waiting for pain. The noises returned one by one. The crackle of fire. Wind snapping at branches. The gasping of her own lungs. When she looked up, no one was there.

Ben and his gun had vanished.

***

Nikki broke through the last bit of the rubble. Like a prairie dog, she popped her head up from the dirt into the kitchen ruins. Movement from the top floor of the house caught her eye. She could see the partial silhouette of a person standing along the edge of the attic floor where the interior wall had burned away.

It must be Elam.

A loud shriek bellowed. A flash of movement from the left raced towards the man. A gunshot blasted. Two bodies fell.

Nikki ducked into her hole.

When she eased back up two men lay side-by-side just a few feet from her. Though they fell back as one, arms clutched in a bear hug, the one on top rolled off to one side.

"No! Jake?"

The shock held her. Her heart pulsed through her whole body. With a burst of God-given courage, she crawled out of the hole.

Short flames snatched at the outside of the foundation. Before she could sort out her confusion she heard a call.

"Nikki!"

With her hands cupped around her eyes, she squinted through hazy plumes of smoke.

Jake!

"Nikki, what happened?"

"I'll find out. Where's Ava?"

"She's up here in the attic. I'll get her."

Stepping over spots of glowing ash and low filmy smoke, she made her way around to the first of the two bodies. She'd never seen him before.

Who is he? What was he doing up there? Did he come to save us?

She checked for a pulse. The man was alive but not conscious. Turning to the other form, she recognized the beard and the long hair fanned out in the dirt. A pool of red oozed from his chest.

"Elam!"

Hurrying around to his side, she knelt beside him. His eyes were open, with a chilling stare. Then with a very slight turn of his head, he focused on her.

The corners of his mouth lifted briefly. His eyes searched her face with frantic effort as he raised his head up higher. He struggled to take in air and form words.

Leaning closer, she could hear his whisper. "Did I save her? Did I save Priscilla?"

Nikki looked up. Ava's eyes and nose peeked over the edge of the attic floor. She could hear Jake's voice echo down. "Ava, come away from the edge."

"I'm not scared anymore." Ava's thin voice drifted in the air. "Except for going down the stairs, Jake. I'm scared of that." Their voices became bits of sound as the little girl moved farther back into the room.

"Yes. Yes, Elam. You saved her." She maneuvered his head onto her lap.

He relaxed into Nikki's arms, and spoke again. "My name is Jacob." His lips barely moved when he spoke. Blood trickled from his nose. "What happened? I don't know what happened. I meant to set the record straight."

He pulled in a raspy breath. His words shot out in hurried blasts. "I meant to die instead of the ones that died. In the cleansing fire. I turned the torch to my leg, but then I saw Papa. Papa had a gun. He went up the stairs, up to Priscilla. I couldn't let him hurt her. Not ever again. I dropped the flame of redemption, and I rushed to follow him." He coughed and struggled. "I saw him lift his gun. I rushed him before he shot. Did we fall? Did I save her?"

"Yes, you saved her."

He tugged on a strand of her hair and pulled her closer. "Please ... please tell Jessie ... I love her."

"Who is Jessie, Jacob?"

"And tell God ... I'm sorry." His watery eyes blazed with urgency as his nose gushed blood, and his mouth oozed red.

"You need to tell God yourself, Jacob."

He choked and strained to clear his throat.

She tightened her grip and could feel the retching in his gut.

Gazing into the sky beyond Nikki's face, he formed silent words. "I'm sorry."

He sucked in a rattled breath, and a soft whoosh of air escaped. His eyes clouded and went from crystal blue to cobalt. And Jacob was gone.

Chapter 71

A shot rang out. James ran faster. Not caring how much sound he made. Ray ran beside him.

It seemed forever until they broke through the trees. James stopped and looked at Ray. "Where now?" Bright moonlight revealed an empty front yard.

Ray pointed to the back of the house. Black smoke plumed from behind the building.

As they rounded the corner, James saw a woman sitting in the middle of the ruins. Fire snapped and sparked around the foundation where the charred half-walls kept back the hungry flames. Smoke curled and danced like a prowling cat.

He rushed to her, leaving Ray behind.

An old man lay beside her. As if in a trance, Nikki stared at the lifeless face. Beside her, Ben stretched out in the dirt, a pistol near his hand. He moaned and stirred, but James knelt beside his wife.

Her beautiful, grimy face turned to him. She froze. With a slow and trembling hand, she reached up to touch his cheek. A primal cry of joy burst out, and she flung herself into his arms.

He held her tight, tears streaming, until the nudge of urgency broke him from the iron grip. He whispered into her hair, "Sweetheart, the fire. We have to go. Now!"

She pulled back and placed her hand on his face. "Yes, but what about the children?"

"Our children are safe, honey."

"No, Ava and Jake." She pointed up to the attic as she stood, but no one was there.

James heard a shout. "Nikki! Let's go." He swung around to see a boy and a young girl stepped off the bottom step of the stairs.

"We're coming, Jake." She looked down at the two bodies sprawled across the ground. "James, what about them?"

305

James leaned down to Ben. He shook his shoulder. "Ben, get up! We have to go. Now! Move!"

Ben moaned and sat up. His eyes widened at the sight of smoke and flames. "What the—" He pushed up and struggled to stand.

James checked the old man. "He's dead. We have to leave him here. Can you walk?"

Nodding, she leaned into him. James grabbed her arm and pulled her with him back the way he'd come. The heat pressed in like hot hands fighting them at every step.

Ahead of them, outside the crumbled foundation, Ray held Ava in one arm and the other around the thin shoulders of the boy. He was leading them away from the fire.

Edith and Ruby just now came around the corner of the house. They both rushed to Ray and the children. He stopped as they reached him. He looked back for Nikki and James.

Ben stumbled ahead of James. Just before he reached Ray, he made a sharp turn and darted into the woods.

James stopped and called, "Ben, where are you going? Don't go that way!"

Through the smoke he saw Ben scurrying away from them. Burning fingers of light darted up tree trunks. Ben glanced back, and James caught his expression. The fire reflected light and shadows on his scowling face. A chill of evil washed over James. Ben ran into thick smoke and disappeared.

"Who is that?" Nikki had to raise her voice to be heard over the crackling flames.

The little girl had her head snuggled against Ray's neck. She lifted her head to answer Nikki. "That's Ben. He was gonna kill me." She scrubbed at her sooty wet face and sucked in another breath. "Nikki, he told me he killed other children. He's a bad man. A very bad man."

A moment of shock stunned James, but he realized he wasn't surprised.

He's getting away. Lord, what should I do?

Ben appeared again in the haze. This time he came to a brief stop and turned to look back.

He must be wondering if we'll follow him.

He whipped around to run again, but instead smacked right into a tree. He dropped to the ground.

James heard the women gasp. He waited for Ben to get back up. Flames flashed across the dry grass and lit a dead tree near where Ben lay.

"Ben!" James screamed as smoke sucked into his lungs. He coughed until he could scream again. "Ben, get up!"

No answer.

Is this it then, Lord? Is this your answer?

James echoed his thoughts aloud. "We have to leave him. We must get these kids out of here. The fire is building fast."

"No," Ray shouted. "I called for help. Firemen will be here soon."

"Ray, the fire is surging. They won't get here in time. We have no choice."

Ray handed Ava's limp body to his wife. The child melted into her arms. Tears and soot streamed down Edith's face. He kissed her.

Ray stepped closer to where James stood. He spoke directly into his face, nose to nose. In a deep-throated voice, he said, "I know what you're thinking, James. But no man is beyond redemption. Take them to the truck. If I'm not back in five, leave without me."

He faced the fire, and with determination, ran into the forest's blaze.

Chapter 72

"I thought it always rained for funerals." James took in the deep blue skies and green rolling hills that swept up to the mountain slopes.

"That's only in the movies, sweetheart." Nikki tugged on Jonah's little hand. This kept him from racing off to the pond that sat beside the square box of a funeral chapel. "I hope we did the right thing, bringing the children."

"Well, it shouldn't be a long service. And there is no, um, deceased to see." As they entered the sanctuary, the solemn atmosphere gave the room a stark, impersonal feeling. The smell of wood polish and a distant aroma of flowers hung in the air. James guided his family to the front row.

Edith sat alone. She rose to give Nikki and James a hug. Then she settled back and dug in her purse to give each child a mint.

James picked up Jonah and placed him in the pew, where he immediately snuggled into his mom's lap. Conner climbed up on his own with a little help from Ava. With Ava on Nikki's right side, and Conner between Nikki and James, the children expressed their need to be close.

The room held a sprinkling of people. More than he would ever have expected to come. He recognized almost everyone as friends from church. He scanned each face and realized these were the faithful people who had been at the prayer meeting, the night he left to rescue his wife.

He smiled again at Edith when Ruby bustled into the room and sat next to her. An uncomfortable lump pushed in his throat. Not because Ben was in prison, but because he knew Ray lay helpless in a hospital room, in an induced coma. Burned skin laced across his body and up his neck.

The imbalance of justice made his jaw muscles tighten. But he knew what Ray would say. "Life is not fair, but God is good."

A white cloth draped a table up front. A gold-colored tin box filled with Elam's ashes sat flanked by two candles. No flowers surrounded the tin. No framed photo displayed the deceased. The container sat alone in humble starkness

Nikki handed James a necklace for him to place beside the box. She had insisted that the copper and turquoise necklace be rescued from the site where she and the others had been held captive.

James opened the folded sheet that held the order of service. It was a sparse list of two songs, a eulogy from Pastor Thomas, a closing hymn, and a prayer.

The left side held one verse. Zephaniah 3:17. "The Lord your God is with you. He is mighty to save, He takes great delight in you. He will quiet you with His love. He rejoices over you with singing." (NIV)

Since there were no relatives to ask, Pastor Thomas had asked James and Nikki what verse to place there. When James showed the verse to Nikki and explained how Conner had heard God singing, she cried. She told him that this was the same verse God had used to get her through the ordeal.

James noticed the boy Nikki knew as Jake, but whose true name was Chance, sat across the aisle with a young couple. The boy glanced at Nikki and gave her a small smile and wave.

Pastor Thomas moved down from the pulpit to the bottom step of the stage to begin the eulogy. The mood became closer, more intimate.

"Elam Jacob Hanson, Junior. Those of us here are aware only of the man tormented with delusions. We know a fraction of the horrific tortures he endured as a child."

James hugged Conner closer to him. His little mischief maker twisted around and shot daddy a silly grin. James matched the happy face in return. He let the expression drop to somber when Conner went back to flipping through a hymnal.

"Sadly, Jacob grew up to carry on his father's distorted passion. He assumed his Heavenly Father was like the earthly one, demanding, distant, and hurtful."

Jonah reached over and grabbed at Conner's pages. Nikki caught the hymnal before it spilled to the floor. Giving a headshake, she set it on the other end of the pew.

Conner leaned back into his daddy's lap. James tried to tune in again to the sermon. Pastor Thomas had set his notes aside and leaned forward.

"The question is, are we any different? The body of Christ? Do we run from those in the world, or embrace them with love?"

Pastor gave a long silent pause. Even the kids looked up.

"I saw a video once about children with learning disabilities. They asked one child to sit at a desk and draw a line on the paper."

His voice filled with sincerity and emotion. The kids stayed transfixed.

"He concentrated so hard on drawing the line that he kept going right off the edge of the page to the desk, and then down onto the floor and across the room. Forgetting the purpose of the line."

Conner lost interest and snatched up James's tie.

Pastor continued. "Have we done that? Me included?"

When James gently tried to save the silk cloth from becoming a wrinkled mess, Conner slipped off his lap. James reached out to haul him back, but missed. With a triumphant smile, Conner scooted to the side of the stage. He crawled up the steps as the Pastor talked.

"Have we been so worried about following rules and making sure others do, too, that we forgot our purpose? Do we look up from having our nose glued to the righteous road and notice we've drifted from the path?"

Too late now to scoop up his son to save disrupting the service. James held his breath.

"Let's step across the church threshold into the world. Bringing with us understanding, compassion, and hope."

Conner toddled along the back wall. With a fast detour, he made a beeline to the table with the candles and Elam's ashes. James slapped his hand over his eyes when Conner reached up to the table cloth.

Nikki let out a suppressed squeak.

But no crash followed.

James slowly lowered his hand, afraid to look.

Pastor Thomas stood next to the table, holding Conner in his arms. "What would happen if instead of being desperate to be right, we were desperate to love?"

He kissed Conner on the head and laughed.

Chapter 73

A young man stepped up to lead a chorus of "Swing Low, Sweet Chariot." In her mind Nikki could hear her captor's voice again trumpeting over the mountainside.

Following the service James took the children outside to play. Nikki gathered up her purse and moved back a few rows. She scanned the room looking for familiar faces.

She noticed a woman come to the front and place her hand on Jacob's ashes. She bowed her head for a moment. Her gray hair lay in soft curls. Nikki caught sight of a tear glisten down her cheek.

The woman turned away and her gaze caught Nikki's. The woman hesitated, then approached. Her eyes gleamed a deep brown with golden flecks.

She touched Nikki's sleeve and spoke shyly. "Excuse me, Nikki Rolen? I just wanted to say ... well, I guess I'm not sure what to say. I know who you are from the papers. I'm actually surprised to see you here."

Nikki said, "I understand how you feel. Believe me, I'm surprised to be here. You know my name. What's yours? Did you know Elam? I mean Jacob?"

The woman pulled a tissue from her purse. Dabbing at her eyes, she swallowed and spoke. "Yes. I knew Jacob. A long time ago. My name is Jessica Kane. Well, he knew me as Jessie Norman."

Nikki pulled in a breath. "Did you say Jessie? How did you know him? If I may ask?"

"I was his fiancée, before he went to Viet Nam. We were going to be married when he came home."

Nikki couldn't imagine the Elam she knew having someone who loved him. "What happened?"

"Before he left for war, he told me some of what he'd been through as a child. I thought maybe he'd made parts of it up. They were so horrible. But now I know they were true." She stopped to blow her petite nose. "At that time, he had made great strides to overcome his past. We met in church, and he loved God. But when he came back home from overseas, I knew I'd lost him. His mind would drift, and he'd ramble on and on about nothing. We'd be making plans for the wedding, and he would go into a rage. Then the weekend before the wedding, he disappeared. I never saw him again. I guess that's when he became the hermit we now know he was."

She grasped Nikki's hand and held it tight, letting the tears flow freely down her cheeks. "You must understand, truthfully, if he had been in his right mind, he wouldn't hurt a fly. I am so sorry you had to go through what you did." Authentic empathy pulled her face into an expression of deep sorrow.

Nikki squeezed back. "Would you come with me?" Nikki led her up to the front of the chapel. She picked up the copper and turquoise necklace.

"Jessie, I know Jacob loved you. He spoke about you. I think he meant this for you." She held out the jewelry. "He said this necklace came from the Grand Canyon. That he had visited it when he was a child."

When the older woman took the turquoise strands, Nikki cupped her hands around hers.

"Oh." The one word squeaked out, and Jessie pressed her lips tight. She took in a big breath. "Oh, Jacob. We were going to go to the Grand Canyon for our honeymoon. He loved it there because his father took the family once, before he became sick with delusions." Eyes glistening, the woman smiled at Nikki. "Thank you. Thank you, so much." She left the chapel holding the necklace to her chest.

Nikki went over to Jake and reached out to hug him. He gave a quick pat on her back and pulled away.

"How are you doing, Jake?" She smiled. "I mean Chance."

"Fair, I guess." He shot a glance at the couple with him. They had stepped away to speak to Pastor Thomas. "I don't think

313

I'm a very good fit with these new people. They're kind of clueless. Ya know what I mean?"

"Yes, I heard you've had some ... conflict."

"So, where's Ava's family?"

"Her mother agreed to go to rehab, and her grandmother was placed in the county senior home. James and I had always thought about being foster parents. We even started the paperwork at one time. So, we went ahead and finished up. Even though all the paper work isn't completed, the courts gave us custody of Ava."

"Wow, so you're foster parents. Real ones?" He shifted his weight from foot to foot and rubbed a hand on the side of his jeans.

"Well, almost official, but yes." She nodded. "As a matter of fact, we've had a conversation with your current foster parents and the judge. We wondered if you'd like to be a part of our family."

Chance froze. He put his head down. No one spoke. A nervous burn radiated inside her chest. She tried to think of what to say to give him an easy way to refuse.

Chance sighed, straightened his shoulders and looked her in the eyes. He spoke, words blunt and resigned. "I won't go to church with you."

"I won't stop talking about God."

The boy heaved his shoulders and sighed.

"Okay, deal." He reached out his hand, and she slapped hers against it.

"Deal!"

Epilogue

"Jacob."

"Yes, Jesus?"

"You're safe now."

"I know. I'm thinking much clearer."

"You were sick."

"I had it wrong, Lord."

"Yes."

"I was afraid. I thought ... *I* had to keep them safe."

"I know."

"I wanted to protect them from the evil in the world."

"That's my job, Jacob."

"What should I have done?"

"Given love. Revealed mine."

"I'm sorry. What happens now?"

"Don't worry, Jacob. I'll work it all out for the good."

Books to Come

Anchored Hope

Tony and Rose plan a cruise in hopes of healing their marriage. A missing daughter and a devastated mother fill their travels with mystery and danger. Making their trip a cruise of drugs, deception, and murder.

House of Faith

A young couple decide to renovate an old stone church marked for demolition. This would be their new home. But the church holds many mysteries of its former congregation. Including a secret hidden deep under the stones. What connections does it hold to sins of the past and for reconciliation in the present?

About the Author

Faye Spieker lives in Colorado with her husband and three dogs. She's a former elementary school teacher, an artist, actress, and avid suspense reader. She is blessed with two grown sons, a daughter-in-law, and a fun-loving grandchild. She has written children's ministry books, devotions, dramas, and children's programs.

67921412R00198

Made in the USA
Lexington, KY
26 September 2017